LOVE AND HATE
WILL BRING YOU
TO YOUR KNEES

LOVE AND HATE WILL BRING YOU TO YOUR KNEES

LYRIC NOLAN

ARCHWAY PUBLISHING

Archway Publishing books may be ordered through booksellers or by contacting:

Archway Publishing
1663 Liberty Drive
Bloomington, IN 47403
www.archwaypublishing.com
1 (888) 242-5904

ISBN: 978-1-4808-5467-3 (sc)
ISBN: 978-1-4808-5468-0 (e)

Library of Congress Control Number: 2017918895

Print information available on the last page.

Archway Publishing rev. date: 1/9/2018

I want you to close your eyes and think outside the box, way beyond the windows of your mind. Now, imagine the styles of love that have come to you throughout your life. The relationships may have been in all shapes, sizes, and colors of people.

I've come to the conclusion that no one is perfect, and perfection only exists in your mind, even though in your heart, you may feel that they are the perfect one for you. I know better; I've been there. When I look back over my life, I can count the number of love and hate situations that I've experienced.

There's one thing I know for sure: You should not judge my emotions because this could be you too. *Love and Hate Will Bring You to Your Knees.*

CONTENTS

CHAPTER 1
TINA
MONDAY, MARCH 31, 2008

I speed off while listening to Boney James on my way to work, bobbing my head and singing, "I don't wanna be lonely tonight." Damn, I remember that song. That's an old song by the Isley Brothers, but this version is cool. Sounds good.

Got damnit, I hate this light. This damn thing must let only two cars through at a time. By time you get to the light, you could've run into a store and come back. This must be the longest light ever in LA. It's ridiculous. I'm calling this into the city. This is crazy. I got things to do today. I don't have time to just sit here and people-watch on Main Street, looking at these folks in their cars with fake-ass smiles on their faces.

I sigh as I turn down the volume and lay my head back on the headrest. Living out here ain't cool no more. I need to make a move like soon, but in the meantime, I'll just wait to see if I've been nominated for this judge position. Then I'll make a decision. But for right now, I've got a cool sex life with Tina Black, but I'm fooling myself, cause my heart isn't in this relationship, and it's crazy as hell. Why? I've got to be crazy if I'm asking myself why.

I shake my head and smile to myself. I honestly don't know, but I get damn near live-in pussy any time I want it. And she gives it however I want it.

Come on, light. Damn. Change. It'll be Christmas soon. Finally!

I hit third gear and skid off down the road, turning onto Spring

Street and eventually into the parking garage at my office. I pull into my assigned parking space, threw the car in park, grab my briefcase from the passenger seat, and hop out, rushing to the elevator. I push the button for the seventh floor and stood there, thinking, *I hope they're ready for this case because I don't have time to wait for them today.*

After I arrive outside my office, my receptionist says, "Good morning, Mr. Tyler."

"Good morning, Ms. Beck. How are you today?"

"I'm well. And yourself? Oh, Mr. Tyler, Sabrina and your other assistants are waiting in your office."

"Yeah, I know. I told her to get everyone together and start without me."

I walk inside my office and said, "Good morning, team. How's everyone?"

"Good morning, Mr. Tyler," Sabrina replied. You're looking awfully sharp this morning. Nice suit."

"Yeah, thanks. Just a little something I threw on."

"Mr. Tyler, I think we have everything in place," Taylor said.

"Really, Taylor? You're sure? Because I've never lost a trial. I didn't make it this far on a 'think.' It was a 'for sure.' If we lose this case, you all will be fired. So let's see what you got. Let's get started. If it means we're here all night, then so be it."

We worked hard all day, finally knocking off at nine o'clock.

"Now we're ready," I said.

"We got this," Taylor said, throwing his fist in the air.

"You sure?"

"Yeah," he replied.

"Okay, Mr. Taylor, since you got all the confidence, you'd better shine when you get in that courtroom tomorrow. Now, it's getting late. You all did good work today. Everything is strong, but remember to always think outside the box and stay positive. Let's reconvene tomorrow to prep. Be here at eight o'clock sharp."

They all walked out of my office, leaving me sitting at my desk. I'm was trying to decide if I really wanted to bother with Tina tonight.

Finally, I thought, *Shit. I can always get a good fuck from her. She's always ready. I don't give a damn what time I call; she never says no.*

I slide down in my chair and put my feet up on my desk, shaking my head and smiling as I reminisced about the night I met her at the law library.

She was an interesting woman, very attractive. I guess I can say I really did want to get to know her that night. When she realized I was watching her, she sashayed over to my table and began talking to me.

Her voice was soft and sexy. "I noticed you keep staring at me," she said. "I felt you undressing me, with that smirk on your face. Don't you at least want to know my name?"

"Damn, I didn't think I was that obvious. But I don't want your name. It's not important to me. My work is done with you."

"Uh-huh. So what's your name, freak?"

I laughed. "Now why I got to be a freak? Did I make you feel uncomfortable?"

"No, no, you did not. I'm used to men looking at me like that. I thought that was a little funny."

"So you're like that, uh? You get all the attention?"

"I know I got yours."

After we introduced ourselves, she flopped down in a chair across from me and folded her arms on the table; I could see her breasts shining right in my face.

"What brings you to this library so late at night?" I asked, leaning on the table and looking in her eyes, then at her breasts.

"Probably the same reason you're here," she replied. "Considering it's a law library, it might just be that I'm an attorney."

"Oh," I said, "so am I. I'm a criminal lawyer at Patterson Law Office."

"So why haven't I seen you around in the courthouse?"

"Oh, I have my share of the courthouse. I visit them quite often, and who I work for doesn't matter. What matters is you."

We talked there in the library for more than two hours. At the end of the night, I walked her to her car; when I opened the door, she immediately dropped to her knees and began sucking my dick. That took me by surprise.

"Shit," I said, laughing. "Hold up. Damn. You go like that, I may need to take you home tonight."

But there was one condition for Ms. Tina Black: "I ain't fucking you naked, and you got to go home after."

"What you mean by that? And why you want to put a condom on now? You've already mentally fucked me. We already know each other."

"No, we don't know each other. But you're right. I did mentally fuck you, but I haven't physically touched you yet. I don't do no free-style fucking. If you don't want any, then that's cool. We can stop it right here and now."

That night, we fucked like wild animals. I figured she'd want to dive onto the chocolate pop with no coating—not.

After that crazy night, we continued to talk some more. I guess I couldn't get enough.

"So when am I going to see you again?" she asked.

Shit. I smiled at her, showing my pearly white teeth and thinking, *Anytime, if you get down and go like that.*

I said, "Maybe we can go out for dinner one night if you promise to be good to me later."

We went out a few times before I realized her defensive behavior was more than I bargained for. I had to tell her to bring down the feisty attitude.

"Look," I said, "I'm not after you, nor am I trying to fight you. Shit, all I want to do is have some fun from time to time. All that drama shit, I don't do. If you can't reel it in, I better keep you in the house."

"Then how about I cook dinner for you at my house?"

That was a nope, because eating her food didn't work for me. First, she can't cook. And second, I was feeling a little leery of her behavior sometimes. I would sit back and look at her. I swear she was out of her mind, especially when she bragged about the guy she sent to jail and told him he was her example. She got furious when I asked why she would tell him that.

She burst out screaming, "He needed to know, and that bastard won't be out here in these streets fucking up other people lives."

And why do I continue to see her? All I can say is the sex is good. No love. Just a fuck thing. Hum. Oh well. I'm horny as hell now. I knew she was up and called her.

"Tina, what's going on?"

"Nothing much. Just watching a little news."

"Yeah, okay. You feel like some company tonight?"

"Sure, why not? Are you coming over?"

"Yeah, but I can't stay all night. I got to be in the office early in the morning."

"Aw, I was hoping we could cuddle. Maybe next time, you can stay longer."

"Okay. I'm on my way and will be there shortly."

I hung up and grabbed my keys and briefcase. "Whoa! Slow down, dick. Check for your coats, or you're not going anywhere."

I switched off the light to my office and closed the door. With a brisk but cool step, I walked to the elevator. I reached the garage, jumped into my car, and drove off like a madman, exceeding the speed limit all the way to her house.

I knocked several times on the front door. She opened it with a white towel half-draped across her body.

"Hey, babe," she said. "You got here pretty fast."

I smiled and pulled her towel off as I walked past her, leading her straight upstairs to the bedroom.

"First things first," I said. "I need to take a quick shower, so lie right there. I'll be right back."

When I stepped out of the shower, she was lying on the bed, spread-eagle like a *Playboy* centerfold.

"Since you need to be in the office so early," she said, "why waste any time?"

"I agree," I said, without any emotion.

I fucked her like a lion attacking an antelope.

"You're killing me."

"Nah, I'm not killing you," I replied. "I need you around for a while."

She smiled as if I had just asked her to marry me. I continued to fuck her until I finally collapsed on the bed, breathing hard.

"Rick, I want to ask you something," she said after we caught our breath. "I saw some pictures and trophies in your place the other day; what were they for?"

"Look, I didn't come here to be questioned," I said. "I came here for something else."

She gripped my dick and stroked it up and down with her hands, kissing my cheek softly.

"Rick, don't act like that," she said. "Come on, answer my question: Did you play ball? What did you play?"

"Yes, Tina, what gave it away? You don't know who I am after all these months? It never crossed your mind?"

"No. I don't watch sports," she explained. "Am I supposed to know?"

"Are you serious?"

"Yes."

I removed her hand and shook my head.

"I'm Erick Tyler. I played in the NFL for a while. Does that explain the trophies and pictures?"

"I guess it does."

She rolled on her stomach with her face down in the pillow, thinking, *Hmmm, did I just hit the jackpot?* Then she looked up at him with a smirk on her face and said, "So is there anything else I need to know about you?"

"What else do you want to know about me? I'm not offering any information about myself. I answered your question; if you want to know anything else, then ask. If I choose to tell you, I will; if not, then I won't."

"You sound pretty confident of yourself."

"Yup, and why shouldn't I be? I don't just volunteer my information; if you want to know, then you need to ask. Who just volunteers their personal information?"

"Okay, mister," she replied. "Are you married?"

"If I was married, I wouldn't be here with you, sweetheart."

"Are you divorced? Do you have children?"

"No, I'm not divorced, and I have one son."

"Okay, now we're getting somewhere; how old is he?" Tina asked.

"He's twenty-four."

"Rick, why the hell you keep giving me these one-line answers?"

"You ask me one-line questions, so I gave you one-line answers. Look, I got to go now; it's getting late, and I got to get up early."

"Wait, I'll walk you downstairs."

"No, I can see myself out. I ain't going to touch nothing in here. I'm walking straight out that door."

She caught me by the arm, just before I hit the steps, and kissed me on the lips.

"Bye, babe; I'll call you tomorrow."

"Make it later in the day. I'm busy all morning."

Still naked, she strolled back into the room, lay across her bed, and lit a cigarette, taking in a long drag.

Hmmm, she thought. *This one requires some research; he might be a keeper.*

She jumped up off the bed, ran in the other room, and hopped on the Internet.

Oh my, she thought. *I see you're very well off; you got your own business. Oh yeah, you're marrying me and taking me away from all this here. I ain't never working again. I'm going to be your future boo. I gotcha now, big daddy. I got to call my mama about this one.*

She swirled around in her chair with the cigarette hanging from her mouth, grinning so hard she choked on the smoke.

I sat in the car in front of her house for a few minutes, laughing to myself.

Why she acting like she doesn't know who I am? I thought. *She knows me. I'm too well known in this area; who she fooling?*

I sped away, racing down the street until I reached my condo in about forty-five minutes flat.

I'm going straight to bed, I thought. *I ain't washing shit; fucking her all night drained me. Damn, there was a time that I could fuck all night, get up, and go to practice; I must be losing my touch or something.*

I put the car in park, got out, and walked up to the condo building's concierge desk.

I know I smell like I've been fuckin' all night, but I don't even care.

"Early morning, Mr. Tyler?" the valet asked.

"Yeah, Carlos, it is; can you park it? I'll call you when I'm ready for it."

I tipped him a few dollars and then strolled over to the elevator with my suit coat thrown across my shoulder and my briefcase in my other hand.

"Good night, Mr. Tyler; sleep well," said Carlos.

I waved my free hand in the air. "Yeah, yeah."

I stuck the key in the door and dropped everything in the middle of the floor, hitting the steps two at a time. I dropped my clothes on the floor and dove straight into bed.

Damn, I swear I just went to sleep, he thought; *it's 5:30 in the morning already. My ass must be getting old. I can't lose my touch just yet; maybe my workout needs to be a little harder. I'm not ready to give up yet. I got forty-five minutes for a quick workout, then to the shower, get dressed, and out of here, before that damn light on Main Street catches me again.*

"Good morning, Maria."

"Well, good morning to you," my housekeeper said. "Look what the angels done dragged downstairs; your breakfast is ready."

"Thanks, I got just enough time to sit down to eat a little something."

"Well, good, because that's what I made you: a little something, so here's your breakfast sandwich and juice. You can eat in your car; bye, see you this evening."

"Why am I being rushed out my own place?"

"Because I got things to do, and I don't want to hear your mouth."

"I haven't even called for my car."

"Oh well, they know you and your car; have a good day. Bye."

She shoved him out and closed the door behind him. *She lucky I have to be out early,* he thought, *and I love her lil' short ass, throwing me out my own damn place.*

He made it to the office on time, without the light catching him. *Good, but I still think that light is too long. I'm still calling into the city as soon as I get a free minute, got damn city of LA.*

"Good morning, Mr. Tyler; you're a little early today, aren't you?" Ms. Beck asked.

"Yeah, I am. When Sabrina and the others get in, have everyone come to my office."

"Yes, sir, will do," she said.

"It's such a beautiful morning, sunny and smoggy."

"What's up, Whitey?"

"Ain't shit, man," Whitey said. "I see you here early. What's up with that?"

"Yeah, wrapping up this case."

"Cool. I just stopped by to holla at a brotha."

"Man, a vacation is much needed, along with a new woman would be great," said Rick.

"Why? what's going on with you? That one you got ain't enough?"

"Man, this one here is something else."

"Wow, you know how to pick 'em; let's talk about it this weekend. We can hit the golf course and play a few holes; bring your money."

"That's cool; where we playing, at the country club?"

"At the country club, man. I don't gamble with the broke fools at the local course; I gamble with the rich fools. I want their money."

"All right, fine with me; I'll see you this weekend."

Whitey walked out of his office, throwing his two fingers in the air.

"Deuce's. I'm out."

"It's 7:55," Rick snapped. "Where is everybody?"

"Good morning, Mr. Tyler."

"Well, good morning, lady and gentlemen; hope everyone had a well-rested night. Did you all get some breakfast, coffee, or whatever you need to get started?"

"No, I haven't," said Taylor.

"What you mean, you haven't?" Rick replied. "Look here, man: From now on, you make sure you have you some breakfast, or coffee, or whatever you need before stepping in here when we need to prepare for court. You got that?"

"Yes, sir."

"Sabrina, get Ms. Beck in here."

"Ms. Beck, Mr. Tyler would like to see you."

"Ms. Beck, would you please take their breakfast order? We're going to be here for a while."

"Mr. Tyler," Sabrina said, "I don't eat breakfast."

"Sabrina, not today; you need to eat something, so give Ms. Beck your order. We don't have time for you falling out because you didn't eat."

"Now let's get started. Let me put this out now before we get started: We are not taking a hundred breaks; just one in the morning and that's to the restroom, and one other during the day, so make personal phone calls then, and that's only if you need to check on a sick baby, a pregnant wife, a sick husband; all other girlfriends and boyfriends have to wait. Are we clear on that, Sabrina?"

They worked on their strategy all morning long, through lunch and up to the dinner hour, making sure their case was complete and ready for the win.

"Okay team," Rick finally said, "this was a long day, but we've accomplished our mission. You can go for the night, have a safe drive home, and I'll see you in the morning, regular time."

They packed their briefcases and bags and left his office.

It's so late, Rick thought as he drove home. *I ain't fooling with Tina tonight and I see she didn't call either. Good; I've fucked enough to last me for a few days.* Just then, his cellphone rang. *I'll be damned. I spoke too soon.*

"Hey Mr. Tyler," Tina said. "How are you this evening?"

"I'm good, and you?"

"I'm fine," Tina replied, "but I'm missing you. I was calling to see what your plans are for tonight and this weekend."

"Well, let's see. I'm on my way home tonight, and this weekend, I have plans with a friend."

"Uh-huh," she replied. "Well, you need to cancel those plans for this weekend. My mother is having a cookout on Saturday, and I want you to come with me."

"Didn't I just say I have plans?"

"Well, if they don't include me, you need to cancel them."

"No way."

"Whatever; anyway, when you finish with your friend, my mother wants to meet you. I told her about you and me, that we're a couple."

"Oh, yeah? When did we become a couple?"

"So now you're in denial?"

"No, but I think you are; we're not a couple."

"You need some loving, don't you, babe?"

"No, I don't. I'm tired and am heading home."

"Maybe I should come over and rub you down, give you a good massage."

"Not tonight. I got to call my son back and then I'm going to bed."

"Aw, that's so nice," she purred. "Are you two close? I hope I can meet him one day."

"I doubt that will happen."

"Why you say it like that? He might want to meet me if he's close to you; he needs to meet his new mommy."

"Tina, he's twenty-four; I doubt he needs another mother, and like I said, you won't be meeting him. Look, I'm home, and I'm going inside. I won't be calling you back, so I'll talk with you later. Good night."

I can't wait to get in here, he thought as he got out of the car, *and take a shower and lay across my own bed, watch a little TV, relax the mind, but first ...*

"Hey son, what's going on with you? How are you?"

"I'm good, Dad, what about yourself?"

"I can't complain, son; just checking on you."

"You do know the draft starts soon, like in two weeks, so when you flying out?"

"I got time," Rick said. "Today is just Tuesday. I'm not going to let you take the ride by yourself. I'll be there before the draft so we can spend some time together. I got court starting tomorrow, and I don't know how long this trial is going to last, but no matter what, I'll be there."

"Dad, I'm a little nervous. I don't know which way I'm going."

"I understand, son, but you have to make that choice. But look, have you talked with your grandparents?"

"Yeah, they good, and I talked with Karla last night."

"Oh really? How is she?"

"She's good. I talked with Kareem to see if he wanted to come out to the draft pick; he said yeah, but he had to ask Ma to get his ticket. I told him to call you, to see when you're flying out."

"That's not a problem. I got him."

"Okay, cool; anything else you want to talk about? I got to make a quick run."

"Nope, son, I'm good. I love you; talk with you later."

"Love you too, Dad; bye."

Every time I talk with him about anything, it's always about Karla, Rick thought. *He involves her in everything, before me. Damn, what is she, his mother? Not that I'm mad, but why am I second to know shit when it comes to him? Fuck it! That's between him and her, let me take my ass to bed.*

"Um, Mr. Erick Tyler," Tina said aloud, "you played long enough to get paid, and I see you got your own construction business, and it's profitable too. I see you one of those Omega Psi Phi brothers; well, good for you. Damn, I think I love him; psych! Not. I'm just tryin' to get paid, get out this hell of a lifestyle, and from the looks of things, he even got outstanding credit; if you can drive around in an Aston Martin and live in that expensive condo downtown LA, you got it made. I got to give it up to the brotha; he's fine as hell, built for sure, nice tall glass of chocolate milk. Now all I need him to do is go downtown; he need to shop for better treasures. Once he gets a taste, he'll be hooked. My mommy will be so proud of me, and all my haters will be so jealous. Genette won't get her hands on this one. Isn't the mind something? I knew that night I was getting that; he looked too damn delicious to pass up, but I didn't know he had all of this going on. Damn, how lucky can a girl be? I better go to sleep before I have an orgasm, just thinking about my new life. If I don't, I might have to go to his house tonight for another round. But one more thing before I lay down: I need to make some calls to the streets, to see what they know on him."

"Well, that was a good night's sleep," Rick said. "I got just enough time for an hour workout, then hit the shower, get dressed, grab some food, and get outta here."

"Good morning, Mr. Tyler," said Ms. Beck. "You're here early again."

"Yes, I seem to beat the light; it's becoming more and more of a challenge. Today is my court day. Have you seen my team?"

"Two of them are sitting outside your door, and Ms. Wilson called; she's running a little late."

"Okay. Well, good to see you two could join me this morning; please, come on in, gentlemen."

"So, Mr. Tyler, did you get some breakfast?" Taylor asked.

"Yeah, I ate before I left."

"Dang, you must have a good wife; she gets up and cooks your breakfast?"

"I see I got a smart ass trying to dig into my personal life."

"No, Mr. Tyler, I was just saying …"

"Well, I'm just saying mind your own business and eat your breakfast, man. We got a few minutes; if Sabrina doesn't make it in the next twenty minutes, she's left out, and I'm going to be pissed, because I have to wait for her to find parking, which is going to be a disaster, then she got to get screened in at the courthouse. So I suggest one of you get her on the phone and find out where she is and tell her she got twenty minutes to get here. Hopefully we can wrap this case up within a week. I need to get out of town."

Ms. Beck nervously stuck her head in Rick's office.

"Mr. Tyler, Sabrina just called; she's sitting at that light you always get stuck at."

"Tell Sabrina to make a U-turn and meet us at the courthouse. Let's go, fellas; it's time."

"Mr. Tyler," Tyrone said, "how come you're so darn direct and demanding and so perfect?"

"Tyrone I am far from perfect, but I am demanding and direct when I need to be, especially when it deals with my cases, so you need to come correct with what you got and don't take it personal. It's just business. You'll learn that in your career, if you drag your feet, you'll become a lazy lawyer, but if you want to be successful, you become demanding and direct in how you handle your business, and you'll receive the same in return. But now, if you feel I'm being too hard on you, then you may not want to work here with me. I can assign you to someone else, but trust me, you'll be begging to come back to me."

"Naw, I'm good," Tyrone replied. "I'll stay with you; your boy and the other ones is worse than you."

"Have either one of you heard from Sabrina yet?"

Sabrina was running across the courthouse yard, like she was a superhero, with her briefcase flying across her back and jacket swinging in the air like a cape. "Excuse me, excuse me!" she called as she pushed through the line of people waiting to go through security.

"Ma'am, excuse you, but you can't bust the line," the guard said.

"I'm sorry," she panted, "but I have a hearing that's getting ready to take place; actually, it's going on now, and I need to be in there."

"I'm sorry, ma'am, but you have to wait your turn," the guard said. "You knew what time you needed to be here for your hearing; these other people in line also have to get somewhere."

"But I'm Mr. Tyler's assistant."

"Who?" the guard replied.

"Erick Tyler."

"Oh, yeah, he just came in," the guard said, more sympathetically. "So you're Sabrina Wilson?"

"Yes."

"Come on through this time; you lucky he told me to look out for you."

"Thank you, sir, thank you."

"Yeah, yeah; don't thank me," he snapped. "You better thank your boss; if it wasn't for him, you'd be at the end of the line, pretty mama."

Sabrina looked at him and rolled her eyes hard.

I wish I was a genie, she thought. *I'd blink his fat ass onto a flagpole and watch him swing in the air ... fat fucka.*

"Mr. Tyler, I'm here."

"Okay, are you ready, Sabrina, Taylor, and Tyrone?"

"Yes," they all replied.

They were in the courtroom all day, finally leaving at five o'clock.

"This court will resume tomorrow morning, at nine o'clock," the judge said.

Rick and his team packed their files, grabbed their briefcases, and headed for the door.

One of the prosecutor lawyers called over to Rick, "We got this one."

Rick laughed but did not respond as they walked out the door.

"All right, team, we're done for the day," he said when they were all out in the hall. "Get some rest; we'll meet here tomorrow morning at 7:30 sharp. Sabrina, don't be late 'cause you're up first."

As his team departed, Rick thought, *Let me hang around for a minute. I need to find out something about this woman; I bet Judge Zebian knows her.*

He caught the elevator down to Judge Zebian's chambers and knocked on the door.

"Rick Tyler," he said, smiling, "come in and take a seat; what brings you to my chambers? Let me guess: You need some information."

"Yeah, I do, on an attorney I met awhile back in the law library."

"What for?"

"I just have some doubts about their status."

"What's the name?

"Tina Black."

"Let's see what I can find out," Judge Zebian said, turning to his computer

He scrolled through his database, looking over his glasses.

"Got it: Tina Black; she's had a few cases here. Doesn't look like she's had too many trials here; what else you need?"

"That's it for now. I just wanted to know if she was a lawyer."

"Okay. Other than that, what's going on with you? How's life treating you?"

"I've been good, sir; no complaints here."

"So Ric Junior is getting ready for the draft; do we know where he's going?"

"I just spoke with him last night," Rick said. "Whoever picks him, that's who we're going with for now. I'm flying out soon to be with him."

"That young man is a damn good football player, like his dad."

Judge Zebian pushed his glasses up on his forehead, leaned back in his chair, and put his arms around his head.

"So, Rick do you think he'll follow in your footsteps?"

"Maybe, but not all of them," he said. "Some would be nice," thinking to himself with a soft smirk, *I hope he won't be a whore in that NFL world like I was; that lifestyle can be dangerous.* "All right,

Your Honor, thanks for the info. I got to go; we'll talk a little longer next time."

"Not a problem, my friend; anytime. Keep me posted, even though I'll be watching it on the tube with my family. We're rooting for him to go to the Minnesota Vikings as the first draft pick."

They shook hands, and Rick walked out of his chambers.

Since it's a nice day, he thought, *I'll take my time and walk instead of damn near running; that way, I can call Kareem to see if he can go to the pick with me, but I guess I should run it across his mother first. Shit, wait a minute; hold up. I'm not running nothing past her. I'm telling her; he's coming with me, and he can fly by himself, and if she wants to come too, they can all fly out. She's Ric's mother, after all.*

"Hey babe."

"Hey Rick."

"What's wrong, babe? Why you sound so down?"

"Nothing. I'm not feeling well; just a little under the weather, that's all."

"Oh, I thought it was something I said, or did somebody do something to you?"

"Rick, ain't nobody do nothing to me. What's up that you're calling me?"

"What, I can't call you now? Never mind; don't answer that. I'm getting airline tickets for Kareem to fly up to Minnesota for the draft pick. I'm flying out before next Friday; he can fly straight there, and I'll meet him."

"Well, Mr. Tyler, it seems to me you already got it planned out, so my words don't mean nothing, huh?"

Rick looked at his phone in his hand, smiling and shaking his head.

"Yeah babe, your words mean everything; can he go?"

"Maybe Alicia and I want to come too," said Karla.

"Babe, that's great," Rick said. "I'll get everybody airline tickets and a suite for all of us."

"That sounds good, Rick, but I can't come anyway. I have to work."

"Babe, can't you take a couple of days off? I'll pay you for the time off."

"I'm not worried about that," she replied. "You don't have to pay me; it's okay. If you buy their airline tickets and pay for the hotel, that's enough; just take care of them two."

He burst out laughing.

"So babe, it's safe to say I have two other children."

"What? Why you say that?" Karla asked.

"You said take care of them two, and that's what mothers say to the fathers."

"Oh sorry, I didn't mean it like that."

"That's not a problem at all; I'd be honored to be their father. I can take care of them and you, anytime."

"Oh, how sweet of you, Rick Tyler; you say that now, but once you get married, then it will be a different story."

"The only one I'll marry is you."

"What did you say?" said Karla.

"Nothing, babe; how about you all fly out that Thursday evening and go straight to the hotel, and I'll meet you there on Friday afternoon."

"That all sounds good," she said. "I'll let you know about me, but Kareem can go. I'll ask Alicia and see if she wants to go."

"Now why wouldn't Alicia want to come to see her big brother get drafted into the NFL?"

"Rick, I didn't say that. I'm not answering for her."

"Well, I answered yes for her," Rick said. "But I can't answer for you, huh?"

"Nope."

"Okay, so when you going to let me know if you can come?"

"If I change my mind, I guess in a couple of days."

"You guess? Wait, babe; a guess is not good. I need an answer like yes or no. I got to buy tickets."

"Look, I don't feel well, so don't make me cut you with your bullying. I said in a couple days."

"All right, babe; where's Kareem? Call him to the phone."

"You want me to get out my bed and I'm sick, to call him to the phone?"

"Babe, if I was there, I would nurse you back to health, but yeah, I do."

"Yeah, right, Rick; hold on. Kareem, pick up the phone; it's the boss of everybody."

"Who?"

"Rick is on the phone, boy!" said Karla.

"And don't go to sleep, Karla. I want to talk back with you."

"Man, I'm going to sleep; we finished talking. I said I'll call you in a couple days."

"Karla, call me with an answer and don't wait too long."

"Yeah, okay; bye."

"Kareem; what's up, big pippin?"

"Go head, young blood," Kareem replied.

"Draft pick is what's up; you going or not?"

"Yeah, I want to come out, but Mom said she don't have money for tickets and hotel for all of us. I don't know why, 'cause Grandma Effie and Granddad Troy or Georgie would have given her the money if she had asked."

"Yeah, well, Kareem, your mother can be stubborn; she needs her butt beat."

"I think so too, but what did she say?"

"Don't worry about it, Kareem. I got y'all, man, I'm buying the tickets in a couple of days, if you want to fly out that Friday morning, we can meet at the airport, once your mother calls me back with an answer I'll make flight reservations and hotel arrangements."

"All right, that works for me; do you want to speak back with my mom?"

"Nope."

"All right, later then."

After he hit the End button, a voice came across on the other line: "Hi babe, it's me, Tina."

"Hey Tina, what's up?"

"Calling to see if you want company tonight."

"No, I can't have company tonight. I got court at 7:30 in the morning, and I can't roll around in bed with you all night."

"Aw, babe, you too funny; we don't have to make love. We can just cuddle, plus I got something special for you."

"Uh-huh, like what?"

"You'll see when I get there."

"All right, maybe for a little while; meet me at my house. I'm on my way home."

"Ok, babe, be there shortly."

When he pulled up, Tina was sitting on the hood of her car. She jumped down, switched over to him, and pressed her breast into his chest as she kissed his lips.

"Hi babe, how was your day?" she cooed.

"It was good."

"How did your hearing go?"

"Tina, I don't talk about my cases to another attorney unless they're on the case, and I definitely don't talk about it after work."

"Dang, okay, but babe, I'm not just another attorney. I'm your woman, and I was just asking how did everything turn out?"

"All was good; let's just go inside and do this thang; I'm a little tired, but I got a few hours for you."

She adjusted her tight black dress, fluffed up her breasts, and then wrapped her arm under his arm and switched in like she was a million-dollar babe on a millionaire's arm.

He looked her up and down and shook his head. They walked in the front door, and all eyes were on her. She was smiling hard.

"Evening, Mr. Harold."

"Evening, Mr. Tyler."

"Mr. Harold, this a friend of mine, Tina Black; can you please have our cars parked, but park hers up front. She won't be staying long."

"Sure, I got you."

He gave the doorman their keys, and they headed for the elevator.

"Tina, what time is this so-called cookout?"

"It's not a so-called cookout, and it's Saturday at four o'clock."

"Yeah well, that's what it sounds like, so what's the address? I'll just meet you there."

"Why can't you pick me up? There's no need to take two cars. Parking can be a problem; a lot of people are coming."

"Whatever, Tina. That's fine, but I'm telling you now, I'm not staying long."

They stepped off the elevator and walked down the hall; Rick opened the door to his place.

"Oh, sweet. I didn't realize how nice your place was the last time I was here."

She dashed in, looking around, smiling.

"Wow, babe, do you want me to cook some dinner for us? I'm in a cooking mood."

"Nope, I'm good. Maria already cooked. I'm eating her food."

"Who's Maria? I thought you said you weren't married."

"Come on, now; if I was married, would I bring you home? She's my maid."

"Oh, you got a maid; is she here all day?

"Sometimes, why? You plan on breaking into my place?"

"No, silly; just asking."

"'Cause if you do, she do know how to fight; she'll hurt you if you try anything."

"She'll get hurt if she comes after me."

"I'm just kidding, Tina; don't be so serious. She's harmless."

"Maria?" Rick said, noticing his housekeeper, who just walked in.

"Damn, she the maid, and she comes in here acting like that? Bitch would be fired on the spot if I was your wife."

Maria stood there with her arms folded, staring at her, looking her up and down, shaking her head.

"Tina, calm down, and don't you ever call her a bitch again, or your ass will be leaving sooner than you think."

"Well, she acting like she got attitude."

"Girl, sit down mind your business and don't touch nothing or go through nothing that don't have your name on it."

"Damn, can I breathe?"

"Softly. I'll be back shortly."

"Where you going?" she asked.

"To shower."

"Okay, well, I'll take one with you," Tina replied; "some water would be refreshing."

"You know what? That's a good idea; that way, I can watch you in more ways than one. A good fuck would be great right about now."

Rick grabbed her by her arm and led her upstairs to his room.

"Damn," she said, "you're so sexy and fine as hell."

She dropped to her knees and went into another world, licking every inch of him like a kitten, purring like a cat. She licked his inner thighs and down his broad back.

"Hmmm, thank you," said Rick.

"No, thank you," Tina mumbled, adding under her breath, "my rich soon-to-be husband."

"Let's get in the shower, wash, and get out of here."

He turned up the hot water; she blurted out, "Ouch! Too hot."

"No more than you. I'll turn it down a little, but you stay up, keep doing what you do."

She swayed her body under the running water and bounced up and down until she had an orgasm, while licking him like a cat bathing her kittens.

"We got to get out of here," Rick finally said. "It's getting too damn steamy in here, and I'm hungry. I need to eat."

"You can always eat me."

"Uh-huh. I'll keep that in mind, but in the meantime, I want some food. I want what Maria cooked."

He threw on his sweats and gave her his robe, and they went downstairs to the eat-in kitchen.

"Hey, Maria," he said pleasantly.

She had her back turned away from him, fussing at him in Spanish, and he sat down, with no idea of what she said.

"Rick, what is she saying?"

"I don't know."

"I'll tell you what I said," Maria said, placing the plates in front of them. "The next time she calls me a bitch, I'm going to show her how alley bitches fight. And don't you smile at me, Erick. I'm trying to keep your food hot, and you up there playing around with her."

"Ugh, what's this? Jamaican food?"

"Yeah, what's wrong with it?"

"I really don't like that Jamaican food. Are you Jamaican or do you just like the food?"

"Do you want it? If not, then just leave it."

"Do I get something else to eat?"

"Nope, not from Maria you won't."

"She might, babe; you never formally introduced us. We got off on the wrong foot."

"You right, I didn't. Maria, can you come back in here please."

"Why you say 'please' to her? She was acting all funky earlier."

"Shut up, Tina, damn. Maria, this is my friend, Tina Black, and Tina, this is Maria."

Tina snarled at him, "Maria what? What's her last name? You told her mine."

"Her last name is not important to you."

"Then why does she get to know my last name?"

"Because anybody that comes in here, she knows their full name; you're in her home, she's not in yours."

Tina slid the plate to the end of the table.

"You can take this, Maria; I don't want it."

Maria stood in the middle of the kitchen floor with her hand on her hip, tapping her foot and staring hard at her.

"Leave it, Tina," Rick said. "I'll get it when I'm finished."

"Why not her? She's the maid."

"Tina, stop; that's enough. You're crossing the line; don't come in my home being disrespectful. Okay, so you don't want the damn food; leave the got damn plate. I said I will move it. And don't speak to her like that ever again in my home, do you understand?"

"Not a fuckin' problem, and you're not going to talk to me like I'm a damn child. I better leave now before this gets real ugly."

He pushed his plate back and leaned back in his chair, ready to defend himself.

"What you mean, gets ugly? You plan on taking some action in here? You started the whole thing with her as soon as we walked through the door. But that's fine if you want to leave. Go ahead, leave now."

Tina was so pissed, she jumped up from the table and knocked the plate of food onto the floor, then took off running so fast that she stumbled all the way up the steps to his bedroom.

"Where did you get that alley cat from, Rick?"

"It was one of those nights, Maria."

"Yeah, well, you could have left that one in the alley by the trash can. That one is sure enough trash and crazy like a schizophrenic person. Listen to me: I know you're not my son, but I'm going to give you this ear full now. If you're drawn to a pretty face and body, all for some sex, then you need to get a blow-up doll or seek some professional help. That bitch is sure enough crazy right there. Erick, I'm telling you, she's most definitely strange; you need to leave her alone. I don't want to get no calls that you're in the hospital or dead over her, do you understand me?"

He was leaning on the table, rubbing his face.

"Yes, Maria."

"If you don't like what I said, then fire me now, because if she comes over here again, I'm not going to be so kind."

"Dang, what do you plan on doing, 'cause you sounding crazy too."

"I'm going to get that little old bitch," Tina mumbled to herself in the elevator. "I should turn her ass into Immigration. I bet her ass is illegal. That'll fix her; who the hell she think she's talking to? She don't know I'm the future Mrs. Erick Tyler. Watch, the day we say I do, I'm firing her ass; she has no idea who she's playing with. I'll cut her ass into pieces or find something on her and send her to jail. Got damn it. Every time I try to stay on track, somebody make me snap. I can't keep slipping like this. Shit, it's medicine time. I need some smoke and a drink to calm down. That Mr. Goody Two Shoes don't smoke or drink, but he loves to fuck, and he's going to pay for this ass next time. It ain't free no more. Where's my man Benny?"

She called Benny on her cellphone just as she hit the lobby.

"Benny, where the hell are you? Bring me some more of my medicine now."

Carlos saw her coming and began heading toward the door to get her car, but she stopped him in his tracks.

"Hey bellboy, give me my damn keys," she snapped. "I don't need you to get my car. I can get it on my own."

She snatched the keys out of his hand and walked out the front door, straight to her car, which was parked in front of his building. She got into her car, flopped down in the seat, and fired up a joint that was heavily dipped in some chemicals; she took a long drag and sped off, drowning in her own smoke.

"Aw, that's so good. Rick Tyler, you won't play right. I fuck you well and give you all the pleasures; what else is there to do with you? Damn, you making this hard for me. I ain't worked no streets in a while, but I still got skills. I'll break you down, soon. I can be a good wife and mother, if you just follow the game rules."

She burst out laughing and start banging on the steering wheel.

"Okay, maybe not a good mother, 'cause I sent them …"

She was so high; she started laughing so hard that she couldn't stop.

"Okay, I didn't send them away; the fuckin' state took their asses. I almost killed them little monsters, my Suga's babies. I just want to get paid. I don't give a damn about no family or kids; the hell with all that."

She made it home in one piece, floating out the car and into the house. She poured herself a shot and lit another joint. She guzzled that drink, slammed the glass on the table, and then took another long drag.

"Shit, this ain't enough. I know you're in here; where you at, my pretty white horse? Come out, come out, wherever you are. I need to ride. I want my hair in the wind tonight.

"I should break that motherfucka down, maybe I'll expose his ass to the public, if he don't give in the next time. Yeah, that's exactly what I'm going to do; this his last time."

What the hell happen here tonight? Rick thought. *That was some real crazy shit; why the hell did Maria come out acting like that? Do she know her? Maybe I need to question her. Damn, do they know each other? Shit gets crazier by the day. I'm going to bed. I got to get up extra early. I can't think about this now.*

"Maria, I already cleaned up the kitchen; you can rest yourself. Everything is done, but I do have a question before you go to bed. Do you know Tina?"

"No, I never seen her a day in my life. Why you ask?"

"'Cause you two acted as if you ran across each other's path before."

"I don't know her; it was her vibe the moment I laid eyes on her. I got a really bad feeling about her. I tell you, her spirit is evil. You need to let that one go and get away fast."

"Okay, Maria, I hear you."

"I was in my room earlier praying for your soul. I lit my candles and prayed to God. I was almost begging him."

He turned and walked away, heading for the stairs, and she flung some of her holy water on him.

"Okay, Maria. Good night."

"Good night to you too, and may God bless your soul."

"The hell with these sheets," he said to himself after returning to the bedroom. "And knowing Maria, she's going to burn them anyway."

He turned the light off, pulled the sheets over his head, and went to sleep.

CHAPTER 2

THURSDAY, APRIL 3, 2008

"Shit! This better not be Tina calling me at 4:45 in the damn morning; hello?"

"Hey, Rick Tyler."

"Hey, babe; what's wrong?"

"Nothing, just calling you back with an answer, since I felt threatened."

"Babe, I'll never threaten you. I just want an answer, so what is it: yes or no? What's so funny?"

"You still think you're going to chump me, and you're half asleep." said Karla.

He laughed too.

"Babe, you know I wouldn't do that to you."

"Well, my answer is yes. And don't pay me for my missed days at work; I'm good. I'm sorry to wake you. I just wanted to give you my answer before my day got started."

"No, you're fine; it's good to hear your voice first thing in my morning. So you feeling better today? What was wrong with you?"

"I'm good," she replied. "I don't know, must have been a virus."

"How are my children? Are they good?"

"Yeah, I'm on my way to work; they stayed at Mama's house last night."

"Karla, who the hell is Mama?" Rick replied, laughing.

"Boy, you know who that is."

"I know, but it sounds so funny that you still call her that."

"That's my Mama Effie, and I'm going to tell her what you said."

"Then what you going to tell her what you call me?"

"Man, you don't want to know what I still call you."

"What, that you love me? 'Cause you're going to tell me one day."

"No, I'm not, and I'm not going to hold you up, so go back to sleep or get ready for your work day."

"Nope, keep talking to me; you can hold me anytime and anyplace you want. I'm good."

"I know you're a busy man over there; just call me later."

"Wait, so babe, if I call you early in the morning, are you going to talk to me?"

"No way."

"All right, babe, I'll call you later on after I make the flight arrangements and give you the itinerary, okay?"

"Okay, and I'm sure Mr. Tyler got it all planned out."

"Babe, come on, don't say it like that. I just want to make sure we're straight."

"I know you, Rick; relax and calm your ass down. You do too much."

"Yeah that's what Maria keeps telling me."

"Who's Maria?"

"She's my maid, probably more like the damn grandmother I never had. You'll meet her soon; she's hilarious. I love her to death."

"Hum, then you should listen to her," said Karla.

"Well, since you agree with her, Karla, will you marry me?"

She fell out laughing.

"Man, you don't want to marry me; it's been years, and we're different people now. I love you as a friend, and I appreciate the things you do for us, but …"

"But what, Karla?"

"Rick, I'm not the one you really want to marry; we will always be friends. Once you get married, I can't allow you …"

"You can't allow me to what? Look here: I do whatever I want for you all; you don't tell me what to do and when to do. If I feel I want to, then I will."

"Okay, Rick, let's stop this conversation; sounds like you about to blow a gasket. Go ahead get ready for work or go back to sleep; send me the information later. You have a good day; bye."

How the hell she going tell me what I can do for her and then tell me she's not the one for me? he thought.

"Karla, girl, don't make me shake you."

He sat up on the side of the bed with a hard-on, smiling.

"That was a good wake-up call," he said aloud, "but this conversation ain't over, Karla Owens. Soon as I get myself together and to my car, we are talking about this again."

"Benny I know you got my message," Tina said into her phone. "Give me a call; what's in your medicine cabinet? I need more like now."

Time flies when you having fun, she thought. *Better get up and make my day. Damn, Diane, you look bad; pull it together. It's all going to work out. Thanks, little horsey, for the ride last night. I missed you and I love you. I know it's been awhile since I've rode you, but I'll be back for you soon. Rest until Mommy gets home. I got to get outta here now.*

She was twirling around in front of the mirror, looking at herself, smiling and fluffing her hair.

Damn, girl, you look hot as usual; this one of my sexiest dresses. If I should die tomorrow, I want to be buried in this. Yeah, this shows all of me: breasts still full and fluffy, ass still tight and firm, along with everything else. I can still pull them in, and they can't resist; once they get this, it's always hard as hell for them to step away.

She headed down the steps and out the door.

"Oh shit, I forgot to call my mama, I mean Margret; it's a good thing that bitch ain't my mama. I would hate to kick her old fat ass, but I need her now."

"Hi, Margret; we having a cook-out on Saturday. I know it's short notice, but we need to have this thing."

"What?"

"Girl, I'm getting married, and I want him to meet the family."

"When, Diane, and to who?"

"Listen, Margret, just do what I say, and I'll tell you later; damn, just listen."

"Is this the guy you claim to be dating?"

"Yup, and he got money too, honey."

"What? Oh, yeah girl; we getting ready to get paid."

"Where the hell you get 'we' from? I said I'm getting paid. Margret, you get some food together today. I told him we having a big cook-out and lots of people coming, so make some phone calls make this shit happen, okay?"

"Diane, why you wait until the last minute? Today is Thursday."

"So what? Who gives a damn what day it is? Just do it. I already told him I was helping you yesterday to prepare for Saturday."

"Whatever, Diane; I'm not in your mess. Since you're the one getting paid, then you do it yourself."

Tina scurried to the car door, fumbling to get in, and hollered at the top of her lungs.

"Bitch, you get to stay in that house rent free, and your life has been spared, so don't tell me what you ain't going to do."

"Hold up, Diane; if it wasn't for me, your ass would still be in them streets, all fucked up on that dope, strung out, so don't forget, honey: you was getting that ass beat on a regular basis. You thought you was so grand, not bringing the money in here where it belongs, so Suga had to do what's right."

"I tell you what, Mama, he's in jail now, thanks to me, and he'll be in there for some time. Your ass is too old to take them streets no more, cause don't nobody want your old pussy, so my suggestion to you is go along with my program, or your ass will be in jail along with Suga. Now follow the program, and I might break you off something; you might be living a little better, and I might get you a job as the maid to stay at the house all day to keep me updated on everything."

"Well, what about your sistas and brothas?"

"Margret, you all fucked up in the head. I don't have no sistas and brothas; that heroin ate your mind up, crazy old woman."

"Since when, Diane? Suga is their father too."

"He's not my father."

"Yes, he is, and I'm your damn mother, you crazy bitch."

"Y'all ain't nothing to me, but some old dope-headed fools."

"Well, I tell you what, missy: If you want this thing to fly off right, you better go with my damn program, 'cause I'm sure he's going to ask some questions about you."

"Okay, Margret, for now, only until I say otherwise; this time only."

"Okay, then, your father is in jail on ticket violations and a bench warrant on back child support."

"Okay, that's cool, Margret, since he hasn't been sentenced yet, but you do know he's going away for a long time, I promise you that. In the meantime, you round up the food and drinks, and I'll get him to bring the good liquor. Oh, and make sure somebody make that nasty-ass Jamaican food; he loves that slop. I got to go. I'm on my way to the office now. I'll talk with you later."

Let me call this bastard, she thought, *and give a fake apology; a little whining should do it. Give him some good sex tonight; he'll forget all about last night. I know he's up; why ain't he answering his phone? He claimed he needed to be at the courthouse so early, then he should be answering.*

She was banging the phone on the steering wheel, hollering.

I need to talk to you, answer this damn phone. Okay, calm down, Diane; just leave a message.

"Hey babe, this Tina; give me a call. I'm so sorry for last night, but Maria judged me wrong. I'm so sorry; what can I do to make it up to you? Babe, please call me; please, I really need to talk to you. You make my day. I need to hear your voice."

She hung up and threw the phone over on the other seat.

Fucka, he better call me back too, it's six in the morning.

"Maria!"

She came out of the kitchen, looking at him with one eye open.

"Good morning to you, and why you so extra happy this morning?"

"I had a good night's sleep."

"Uh good, that holy water really worked." She looked up to the ceiling and said, "Thank you, Lord."

"Whatever. Maria, I got to go. I need to be at the courthouse early, so I don't have time for breakfast."

"So you called me in here to tell me you had a good night's sleep? Maybe that holy water didn't work after all; you may need some other help."

"No, sorry for calling you like that. I just wanted you to know I'm leaving now, and I'll grab some breakfast when I get to work."

"Hmm; well, I'm up, like always, and I made you a sandwich, wrapped and ready to go."

"Damn, you're good; you get better and better. Can you divorce your husband and marry me?"

"If I divorce my sweet Jose for you, hell will know about it."

He hugged her tight and kissed her on the top of her head.

"Aw, come on, Maria. I love you."

"Yeah, I love you too, but not for my husband. You need Christ in your life, so take your stuff and go. I got something to do, like move some spirits out of here today."

She pushed him out the door; he grabbed his briefcase and keys and closed the door behind him.

"Good morning," Rick said, giving Carlos some hand dab.

"Good morning, Mr. Tyler; your car is right out front."

"Thanks, Carlos, I really appreciate that, man."

He hopped in his car, started it up and pulled off.

"Call Karla's cell," he said, speaking into the hands-free mic. "Hey babe, you busy?"

"Just a little; what's up?"

"I'm calling you back."

"Erick Tyler, I hope you're not calling me back about that conversation from earlier."

"Yes, I am."

"Rick, no; we're not talking about that anymore."

"Yes, we are."

"No, we are not, Rick. No!"

"Karla, you're going to stop fighting me."

"Man, I'm not fighting you. I haven't hit you yet; talk about something else."

"All right; damn, but you're not the boss of me. You always want it your way, bossy! Felipo should have spanked your butt a long time ago."

"Well, he didn't then, and he's not now; it's a little too late. Just what is it that you're calling me at work about now?"

"Nothing really, babe. I just wanted to hear your voice again. Karla, I felt like I pressed you; do you really want to go to the draft?"

"I said yes, we're coming. I got a phone call from your son, fussing at me about why he needs me there."

"Oh, really? He didn't tell me he talked with you."

"Oh, don't cry, babe; what you going to do, beat the boy?"

"Funny, Karla; shit, he's about as big as me. That would be a hell of a beating."

"Yeah, and I would love to see that one; I might give out a lick myself."

"On who, babe?" Rick asked.

"You."

That made him smile hard.

"For what, babe? What did I do?"

But that smile quickly went to a frown when he saw another call come up on his phone.

"Aw, damn, why is she calling me first thing this morning? Leave a message."

"So who's that, your woman?"

Rick ignored her question and asked, "Did you tell your friend or boyfriend, whatever he is, that you coming with me to Minnesota?"

"No, does it matter?"

"Well, do you plan on telling him? I'm just curious to know what his response is going to be."

She ignored that herself and asked, "Did you make the arrangements yet?"

"I'll do them this evening. I got court this morning, so I'm a little busy."

"Fine, I have to go anyway. Call me back later with the information. Bye, get off my phone with your foolishness."

"Okay, babe; have a good day, and thanks for talking to me this morning."

"Yeah, no problem, and good luck on your trial."

He was still smiling, but blurted out, "Now, see, that's a lady! What is it, Tina? I just talked with the love of my life. I'm in a good mood; what can you possibly have to say this time? I got just enough time to listen to this bullshit voicemail."

"Hey, babe, this Tina; give me a call. I'm so sorry for last night, but Maria judged me wrong. I'm so sorry; what can I do to make it up to you? I really need to talk with you. Babe, please call me; please, you know you make my day."

This woman is unbelievable, he thought. *Who in their right mind do the shit she does and come back like it never happened? I don't have time to talk to her. I'll just leave her a message.*

"Tina, hey!"

"Hello."

"Oh, I thought I was leaving a message. I don't have time to talk."

"Babe, I'm so sorry for last night, like I said on my message; do you forgive me?"

"No."

"Why not, babe?"

"Tina, what's wrong with you? Why you keep flying off the handle for no reason at all, just out of control? Your shit is crazy."

"What you mean, babe?"

"Tina, I don't have time to get into it with you; we can talk later. I got to go. I'm hanging up, bye."

"Wait, don't hang up."

Okay, she thought after the line went dead, *he's making this harder on himself; all he has to do is play right and do what I want and then marry me and make me rich. Damn, he's making me work hard for those dollars.*

It's too damn early in the morning, Rick thought. *It's 6:50, and she's coming with that shit already. But Karla, babe, I got to put you out my head for a few hours. I need to focus. We need money; if you keep flashing me your beautiful eyes and smile and that humorous personality, I'll be thrown off track all day, thinking about you. I'll pick you back up later on.*

Good, he said to himself as he pulled into the office lot, *they're here and on time; this is going to be a good but a long day.*

"Hey, Mr. Tyler," said Sabrina.

"Good morning Sabrina; how are you first thing this morning?"

"I'm good. But I need your advice, off the record. I got this weird phone call from a friend of mine back home last night; she said her cousin is missing, and they haven't heard from her in years. Last they heard, she was practicing law in LA. Their grandmother is dying and is calling for her to come home."

"Well, Sabrina, if they haven't heard from her in years, maybe she just doesn't want to talk to them anymore; doesn't mean she's missing."

"No," she said, "they were close to their grandmother, then they had an argument and stopped speaking to each other at one time, but she didn't think it would last this long."

"So what are you supposed to do?"

"I really don't know."

"Well, I'm an attorney, and you're a lawyer in training; we are not private investigators. The only thing I can tell you is to first get some more information from your friend and maybe if you feel up to it, do some research on your own; see what you come up with."

"Yeah, you right; you got a point there. I'll consider it; after this is over, I'll ask around."

"Good, now that we are all here on time, let's make this happen. We need to wrap this up. I got to get out of here next week."

"You going out of town, Mr. Tyler?" Taylor asked, walking behind him like little Opie Taylor, swinging his briefcase.

"Yeah, my son is up for the draft pick, and I need to be there with him."

"Your son? I didn't know you had a son; what's his name? Wait, would your son happen to be Eric Tyler?"

Rick stopped in his tracks and looked back at him.

"Yes."

"Aw, man, he's the shit. Oops, sorry, Mr. Tyler; I didn't put two and two together."

"Taylor, calm down. It's okay; he's not a junior, so I probably would not have put it together, either."

They all continued to walk down the hall toward the courtroom.

"This boy …"

"Taylor, we can talk about that later," Tyrone said. "Let's focus on this first, okay? Sabrina, there's your boyfriend, Mr. T."

"Wow, Sabrina, I didn't know you liked him," Rick replied. "The next time, I'll hook you up."

"Uh, Mr. Tyler, if you do, I'm never going to speak to you again."

"Aw, come on, Sabrina," Taylor said, laughing and poking her on the shoulder. "We can't come to the wedding?"

"Okay, stop teasing Sabrina," Rick said. "Let's put on our game face and roll with these punches in here."

"Sabrina, you keep yourself up front so I can keep an eye on you," Tyrone said. "Make sure you don't slip out for a quick rendezvous."

She was still frowning as if she stepped in something that was sticky to her feet.

"Tyrone, you're not funny."

They entered the courtroom and laid out their materials on the long conference table, waiting for the judge to come in to start the trial. He finally entered the courtroom at ten o'clock, and the war started: Both sides went toe to toe, throwing punches, fighting for their client. The battle went on all that day and all day Friday. Rick finally wrapped it up in the end, and he knew they had the upper hand. Now it was up to the jury.

"Okay, gang," he said, "we're back here on Monday. Hopefully we can get a final verdict from the jury; we did our part of convincing them, and there's no doubt now that they got enough evidence, so let it ride until Monday. You all have a good weekend, and I'll see you back here, same place and time."

They all walked out the courthouse, feeling great about being close to victory.

"Mr. Tyler, you think I can get your son's autograph one day soon?" Taylor asked.

"Sure," Rick said. "When he comes out to LA, I'll make sure I bring him to you."

"Well, what about your autograph?"

"You can get mine anytime, but you don't need it; you see me every day, and you know me somewhat personally, at least you think."

"Yeah, but it's not the same."

"All right, Taylor, I'll even throw in a picture of us; how about that?"

"Cool; then I'll see you on Monday."

That boy is too damn funny, Rick thought, *but he's a good young man. Okay, time to make these flight arrangements and call Karla back, but shit, I can't do it walking. I got too much stuff in my hands. I'll call Maria and ask her to make the flights and hotel arrangements. I know she won't mind; she's my confidant and personal secretary anyway. Plus, she'd be a little pissed if she didn't know of my whereabouts. I thank God for her, cause if she wasn't around in my life, I would have to hire a personal assistant, and it definitely would have to be a dude, 'cause a woman would not work.*

"Hi Maria, I need your help please; could you make some flight and hotel arrangements for me?"

"Okay," she said. "Where are you going and with who?"

"To Minnesota, for the draft pick. Karla, Alicia, and Kareem are flying out too, but I want you to make their flight for Wednesday morning to LA first. They are going to stay overnight at the house; that way, we'll all be on the same flight to Minnesota."

"Oh, how nice. I'll get to meet this Karla person."

"Calm down, Maria, you're not listening; you'll get to meet them soon. You know what? Never mind. I'll make the arrangements."

"Go ahead and talk; I'm listening. I'm just glad you not taking that crazy woman that was here the other night."

"Maria, now why would I take her with me? She don't know him. So let's try this again: I need them to fly out next Wednesday morning and get here by noon. I'll have a car to pick them up."

"This is great," she said. "I need to get started on some things."

"That's fine, but Maria, it's just Friday, and we're not leaving until next Friday. We can all go out to eat, including you and your Jose."

"But we can go to the grocery store later."

"We? Since when you start going to the grocery store with me? I don't need your help. I know what to buy."

"But there is one question."

"What, Maria?"

"Does she eat Jamaican food?"

"Yes, they all do."

"One other thing: Do I need to know anything off the bat, so I don't get in any trouble?"

"Like what? What kind of trouble are you speaking of?"

"I don't know; is she strange, blind, no legs, kids not well behaved, whatever."

He fell out laughing. "Maria, no, she's not blind, and she has her legs, and the kids are well behaved; they're young adults. She's cool; you'll like her. Trust me."

"Son, right about now, your track record with women is not good."

"Whatever, Maria; bye. I'm on my way home. I'm relaxing tonight. I need to get caught up on some things and watch a little TV. I'm in for the night."

Shit, he thought after waking up the next morning, *what time is it? I forgot all about Whitey; damn, I needed that sleep.*

"Whitey, man, what time we meeting up at the clubhouse? I just woke up; give me an hour or so."

"I'm already here," Whitey said. "It's eleven o'clock. Get dressed and come on down."

"All right, I'll be there."

After they played a round of golf, they headed back into the clubhouse to change clothes.

"Chocolate Man, you need some practice," Whitey joked. "I'm sorry I beat the shit out of you; when was the last time you were out here? You suck."

"Man, I got things to do today. I told Tina I was coming over to some damn cookout today, and I need you to bring your ass too, because I don't plan on being there no more than two hours. I need you as a reason to leave."

"All right, man, I'll be there. Text me the address and the time; let's see what you working with. Maybe she got a sista for a vanilla brother."

"Okay, Whitey, just be there. I'm going to Tina's place now to get this over with."

Whitey burst out laughing as they walked off to their cars.

"I'm coming; I'll call you when I'm en route."

Rick made it to Tina's place in thirty minutes; he pulled up to her house and hit the horn.

"This is the first and last time I'm coming to anything she's having," he said aloud.

She came out smiling and switching so hard; she threw her hair back as if the wind was really blowing. She flopped down in the car and leaned over to kiss him on his lips; he turned his head, and she caught him on his cheek. They drove from Los Angeles to South Compton, without him saying a word. She was doing all the yapping on about her family and who was going to be there.

"Babe, turn here at this exit, this street is a shortcut to my mother's house."

He cut his eye at her as they pulled up and he immediately was pissed.

"What the fuck? Am I in hell? Tina, why didn't you tell me we were going to Compton? I would have rented a damn car."

She totally ignored what he said, waving her hand in his face.

"Babe, don't worry about it; just park here in front of the house. You be all right."

Margret was already waiting out front, with her hands on her hips in her too-small, tight maxi dress and her long blonde wig, smoking a joint. Tina jumped out and ran up to her mother, as if she hadn't seen her in years, and whispered in her ear:

"You better play this cool; if you fuck this up, your ass is mine."

Rick got out the car and walked slowly, looking around at his surroundings.

"Oh, Tina, this must be your boyfriend," Margret said. "How are you, good-looking? I'm Mrs. Cock."

She extends her arms out as if she were the queen, for him to give her a hug and kiss.

"Welcome to my home; it's nice to meet you."

He stood there in front of her without a smile on his face.

"Uh-huh, I'm fine."

Tina pulled him by his arm and dragged him through the house to the backyard. He felt out of place, as if he was in another time zone. There was no grass in the backyard; tables were lined up around the fence with red-and-white checked tablecloth, and several types of chairs up against the fence, and some just sitting around in the yard. The more he looked around, the angrier he got, especially when he saw the kids playing in the dirt, while the grown folks were standing around, drinking and smoking weed. The music was blaring so loud, you could hear it a mile away, but he figured he better play it cool, considering he was by himself. Margret walked up behind him, smiling, and began rubbing his shoulder.

"Hey y'all; here's your new brother-in-law."

Tina's brothers rushed up to him as if they were getting ready to jump on him. He braced himself, ready to fight, but instead, they extended their hands out for a shake. Rick nodded his head and gracefully walked away from them, searching for his car and an exit.

"Diane, come here," one of her brothers said. "I need to talk to you; come in the kitchen now. Do you know who he is?"

Her eyes scolded her brother with anger.

"Yeah, and don't call me Diane; my name is Tina, and his name is Erick Tyler. Why?"

He pulled her close into him, slapped her on her ass, and squeezed it.

"Baby girl, you hit the jackpot; you better marry that one. We need some got damn money, and that nigga is loaded."

"We? What the hell are you talking about, we? I'm going to be rich; he's my ticket out of here, not yours."

He squeezed her ass again, laughed even harder, and pushed her away from him as he walked out the door.

"I'm going to be rich too, so if you play your cards right, Tina or whatever your damn name is, we can have it all too, Mrs. Tyler."

What the hell is this damn chick thinking, Rick thought. *I don't live like this, in no damn hell hole. I don't give a damn if this where she grew up; back in the day, hanging out in the projects was cool, but damn, I'm beyond this shit here. I don't do this. I look like a got damn fool down here. I'm a got damn attorney working for one of the top law firms in LA, and I'm hanging out down in this world. I must be fuckin' crazy! I gotta get the fuck out of here.*

Someone crept up on him and wrapped her arms around his arm.

"How you doing, sweet thing? I'm Genette, Tina's best friend. So I guess I'll be seeing a lot of you, huh?"

He peeled her arm from his and walked away.

"I doubt that."

She smiled and brushed herself against him; then she blew him a kiss, motioning with her lips.

"I know you want this. I heard all about you."

"Wow, let me get the fuck out of here. Tina."

"Yes, honey? You need something, or you want to sit in the house? Is it too hot out here for you? What you need?"

"No, none of that; we need to go. I got things to do tonight."

"We just got here, and you haven't eaten anything."

He looked over at the grill and around at the crowd.

"Uh, no, I'm good; if you want to stay, then that's fine with me. I got to go."

"Well, do you at least want a beer before we go?"

"You know I don't drink, nor do I want anything to eat. I only came out because you asked me. I don't do cookouts. I don't know when the last time I was at one."

She popped off on him before she even realized it.

"You should have said that when I invited you. If you're ready, then go; I'll get a ride back to your place afterward."

He popped off at her before she could get another word out.

"No, you won't. You don't have no fuckin' body drop you off at my place; if I don't invite you, don't you have nobody drop you off there. Are we clear on that?"

She felt Diane coming out quickly.

"You know what, Rick? This might not be a good idea right now, so you go ahead, but this cookout was for us. At least let my mother know you're leaving; you can at least say goodbye to her."

He looked at her with the eyes of death.

"No, I'm not," he growled. "You can tell her yourself. I'm gone, and this was for you. There is no 'us.' I'm out of here."

Tina saw Genette eyeing her man as they were arguing; she grabbed him so tight by his arm and held on for dear life. As she walked him to his car, she whispered to Genette, "No, babe, I got this one, not you."

"You know what?" she said aloud. "I think I better leave too. I'll let my mother know we're leaving. I'll meet you at the car."

The ride back to Tina's house was endless. He leaned his head against the headrest as he drove; all he heard was her voice talking his ear off about the brothers that don't keep a job, the sister who keeps having babies by the boyfriend who was in and out of jail, and her father who had been in jail all her life. She talked so much that she finally became a blank to him, and he let his mind drift off onto something else.

"Tina, did I tell you that I am Jamaican?"

Her head snapped around at him, like that kid in *The Exorcist*; she immediately went in a panic.

"What?" she said. "You never said you were Jamaican. You got no accent, nor do you act like them people."

"Yeah, I am."

"Is that why you eat that food?"

He sat up in his seat and leaned toward her.

"No, I eat all types of food. I just so happened to eat it that night when you were over there, acting like an ass. And what do you mean, act like what people? What do we act like?"

"I don't believe you," she said. "Why you telling me this now? I just thought that you loved that slop."

He smirked and leaned against the door while driving. He looked at her fumbling with her clothes and twitting her hands, as if she wanted to slap him, then she realized what she had said and tried to adjust her attitude quickly, trying to recapture her words and thoughts.

"Uh, well, that's okay with me, but I just don't like the food."

"Whatever, Tina. Look, I'm dropping you off. I got to prepare for court on Monday, and I'm flying out of town on Friday, so I won't have time for you this week."

"What you mean? Flying to where? Why can't I go?"

"Because you can't. I'll hit you up when I get back."

She cut her eye at him.

"Yeah, okay. I tell you what: You better not be going to see no other woman."

He never said a word; he just looked at her and shook his head.

"Um."

"I'm not playing," she added. "You better not cheat on me or your ass is going to be sorry."

"Girl, cheat on you? We're not even a couple, so where the hell you get cheat on you? I'm giving you the respect of telling you that I'm going out of town. I don't have to do that. If you're around when I come back, that's cool, and if not, that's cool too. I ain't lost shit; don't think your ass is all that."

Tina felt Diane coming out quickly.

"Rick, you better step on fast, 'cause I'm getting ready to slap the shit out of you; you're pissing me off, and I don't want you to see my other side."

"Tina, that won't be happening ever, and trust me, I'm stepping on it to get your ass home quickly."

He sped right through some red lights, ignoring the traffic cameras. He pulled up to her door and jammed his foot on the brake. She jumped out of his car and slammed his door so hard, she nearly broke the window.

"Tina, if you broke my window, your ass would have been grass."

She threw her middle finger up at him.

"Fuck you, Rick Tyler."

He pulled off, shaking his head.

"Fuckin' couple; what the fuck? Where the hell did she get that from? Next Friday can't get here fast enough."

He pressed down on the accelerator, picking up speeds of 80 MPH, making his way across town; he reached his building in no time flat.

"This is a damn nightmare with her," he said aloud. "She thinks I'm going to marry her? That's bullshit."

He strolled across the parking lot, went through the entrance door, and headed up to his place.

As soon as he walked through his door, he heard Maria call out, "Erick, did you call Karla with the flight information yet?"

"No," he said. "When I got home last night, I went straight to bed. I didn't have time to call her yet. I'm calling her now."

"Um, yeah; now would be great instead of later."

"I'm calling now," he snapped. "Do you have to keep going on and on?"

"Don't get mad with me because you were out with that crazy woman, and now you're uptight 'cause I said something. I told you about fooling with that woman; she's not right for you anyway."

He flopped down on the couch, put his feet up on the table, and starting dialing.

"Hey, Karla," he began. "Sorry for calling so late."

"That's okay; what's up?"

"I got the airline e-tickets; you'll fly out Wednesday morning to LA, and then we'll all fly to Minnesota Friday morning. I'll text you the flight information; a car will be there to pick you all up from the airport, so I'll see you late Wednesday evening."

"Okay, that's good, but let me ask you about the sleeping quarters. I'm sure I already know how you planned that out, but where am I sleeping? In my own room or am I sleeping with you?"

He laughed.

"So what, you don't want to stay with me?"

"I didn't say stay, I said sleep," Karla replied.

"Well, it depends on how you define sleep with me. Do you want to sleep in the same bed with me or sleep with me in the same house and hotel room? There's enough room for everybody to have their own room, except for you, so I guess you do have to sleep with me. I promise I won't bite; just a few nibbles here and there, if that's okay with you."

"Uh-huh. I'll think about that during my flight. That depends on how I feel. I might let you nibble a little here and there."

"Okay, I can take that. I'll make sure I'm on very good behavior so I can have some treats from you."

"Bye, Rick; we'll see you when we get there."

CHAPTER 3
REMINISCING
WEDNESDAY, JUNE 25, 2008

"Ugh, today is just Wednesday; what am I going to do? I need a break from this West Coast."

"What's wrong with you, babe?" Tina asked. "And what you need a break from who and what? Since you came back from Minnesota, you've been acting crazy."

"Nothing is wrong. I'm just thinking out loud."

"What you mean, nothing? I heard you talking out loud, then you jumped up like something was wrong; you scared the shit out of me."

"Really, Tina, I scared the shit out of you? Well, good then."

"Come on, tell me what's wrong, babe. I know it's something; you're acting strange. Are you okay?"

"Nothing is wrong Tina. I'm just getting up earlier. I got some personal things to do today."

"So you're not going in the office at all today?"

"No, damn it. I just said that."

"Then what is it? I know it's something; you've been acting strange lately. Is something wrong with your parents, or is it you got some bitch pregnant and she wants money."

He stood in the middle of the floor, frowning at her as she was screaming at the top of her lungs: "Why can't you tell me?"

"I don't want to tell you," he snapped. "And do I ask you questions when you say that you have some personal things to do? Hell no. I just keep it moving, so just let it go."

"Babe, if we're a couple and plan on getting married, I should know what's wrong with you."

"Excuse me, if? And we ain't a couple with no plans on getting married."

"So what, I'm not good enough to marry? Is that what you're saying, Rick?"

"You may be good enough to marry, but just not for me. Was I talking in my sleep? I don't recall saying anything about marriage to you."

She screamed at the top of her lungs, "You fuckin' dog! You did too say it."

"No, I didn't, and I know I didn't, so stop trying to make me say I said it, and I know I didn't. Ruff ruff, like the dog that I am."

"You think you so damn smart, that you can say what you want to people, and they supposed settle for your answer; well, I'm not!"

She rolled over on the side of the bed, picked up her shoe, and threw it at him as he was walking out the bedroom.

He turned around and walked slowly back in the room; he stood over her, pointing his finger at her like she was a child, and growled, "If you throw another got damn shoe or any fuckin' thing at me in my house again, I'm going to throw your ass out along with the fucking trash."

"I throw whatever I want," she spat. "I'm not scared of you."

"Okay, and that's fine; you're not scared of me, but do it again, and I promise you, I'll do it."

"Fuck you, Rick. You won't be getting no more ass from me again."

"Yeah, right; why? Because I won't tell you what I have to do today? Then fuck it. I don't give a damn about getting no more ass from you; yours ain't the only ass out here."

"I'm leaving."

"Okay, that's fine; you always leave when shit don't go your way. I hope you're going to wash your skanky ass before you go flying out of here."

"No, I'm not," she cried. "Leave me the fuck alone, you bastard."

"Cool then, don't forget your shoes; there's one in the doorway that you threw, and the other is here by the chair, along with the rest of your clothes."

He walked back in the other room, thinking hard to himself just as she walked passed the door.

I know damn well I never asked her to marry me, he thought. *That shit never came out my mouth, not even on a good fuck day.* "Fuck her," he mumbled aloud. "I don't have time for her bullshit today."

"I heard that, you fucka!"

She slammed her clutch bag down on his back and ran out the bedroom door.

"Tina, not today. I told you before, don't put your hands on me, unless you're fuckin' me. Otherwise, keep your damn hands to yourself. I don't put my hands on you unless I'm fuckin' you; that's it."

"What? So now you're only fuckin' me; since when don't we make love?"

"Yeah, we only fuck, and we never made love, or at least I never did."

"Okay, Mr. Erick Tyler, you so smart. I know for sure you won't get any more of this ass, and if you do, you will most definitely pay for this. Watch what I tell you."

She ran down the spiral steps so fast, by the time she hit the bottom step, she slipped on the marble floor and slid into the door.

"If you put your shoes on," Rick said, laughing, "you wouldn't have slipped."

"Fuck you, Rick Tyler," she growled. "You're going to wish you never said that to me. You're going to pray to God you never fucked with me."

She slammed his front door and rushed over to the elevator.

"Come on, elevator," she said. "I need to get the hell out of here."

Each time she pressed the down button, it was as if she were stabbing him in the eye. By the time the elevator got to the lobby, she was screaming and crying so loud that she brought attention to herself.

"This is not going to happen," she cried. "He's not going to treat me like this, I'm good to him."

"Ma'am, are you okay?" said Harold asked, coming over to help.

"Hell, no," she snapped. "Do I look okay?"

"Ma'am, calm down!"

"Ma'am, my ass; leave me the fuck alone. All you need to do is your fucking job, which is to be a sorry-ass doorman."

"Excuse me, ma'am. Okay, let's try this one more time: Now, are you okay? And can I get someone to bring your car around to you?"

"And I told you to leave me the hell alone."

He leaned into her and whispered in her ear, "Bitch, I'm trying to help your crazy ass. I really don't give a damn about you at all, and I hope your day was even more fucked up than it is now. I don't know why Mr. Tyler even fucks with your crazy fat ass. See, you forgot: I know all about you and your family."

She looked at him, trying to figure out if she knew him, but nothing was coming to her mind.

"You don't know anything about me."

"Oh, yes, I do and a lot."

She stared at him as if she were Satan's child. "I should slice your ass up right now," she said.

"Go ahead," he said, "and I will sue the shit out of you for harassment and expose your ass to Mr. Tyler. I would love to tell him who you really are, Diane."

Rick finally made his way downstairs, to be greeted by Mr. and Mrs. Hill from the ninth floor, who were still standing in the lobby.

Damn Mr. and Mrs. Nosey Ass Hill, he thought; *they know everybody's got damn business. I hate to get caught on the elevator with them; fuckin' nosey as shit.*

He put on his fake smile and headed straight to the front door.

"Good morning, Erick," Mr. Hill said.

"Good morning," he replied and kept walking.

"What's up, Mr. Harold?" Rick asked at the desk. "You look like you're having a bad day."

"Naw, all is good," Harold said. "Just a little misunderstanding with someone; nothing I couldn't handle myself."

"All right, cool. I'll be back shortly. I'm taking an early run. I'll grab my paper later."

Shit, he thought, *I better stay on the sidewalk; she just might be hiding out here waiting to run my ass over. She takes shit to the extreme That's one reason why I ain't settled down with her. Good, I don't see her ass out here; let me get my run in, but now if she's out here, she better get me good while I'm running. Otherwise, she's short.*

He put in his earplugs and started jumping in place to get his adrenaline up, turned up the music, and took off running.

Harold looks mad as hell, he thought as he ran. *I bet it was Tina; she took it to the lobby, got damn. Harold must think I'm crazy, but I ain't do shit to this woman. I know I got some shit with me, but damn, do they all get dick happy and turn foolish? Then their true shit comes out. All of them had some shit with them: the drama queen, the needy as hell, the crybabies, and the ones that just want to be in control of everything. All of them the same: black, white, Asian, and Hispanic; it's one in each race. No one is any crazier than the other; at the end, they all wanted the same thing: money. None of them wanted real love.*

Shit, a couple of them had the nerve to take me to court for child support, and I had to do a paternity test to find out neither child was mine. Damn, when you young and think your ass is untouchable, these women show you each time that you're not; they will slash your tires, make threatening phone calls, along with the pretend to be pregnant. All of the games that could have been played, whether it was a success or failure, I've heard it and had them all; been there, done that. Shit is over; I'm not doing it again.

He snickered, still running. *Damn, what kind of life did I have,* he thought. *I guess drama too. But now, as an adult, I've learned from all the bullshit. I definitely make sure I use condoms more than ever, two if possible, and I take the shit with me, ain't leaving nothing behind. I'm now in my forties; it's time to make some real changes in my life. Maybe I'll just take that job after all, find a new woman, fall in love, get married and have children, at least one more, so I can actually see him every day and watch him grow up; something really to think about.*

He turned around and headed back to his building. After cooling down outside, he went in to find Harold.

"Harold, can we chat a minute?"

"Sure, but first let me ask you about that lady that came down here hollering, screaming, and crying louder than a baby; did she come from your place?"

"Yeah, and you know she did. Is that why you were looking so pissed off earlier? Something happened, didn't it? What?"

"Man, I asked her if she was okay; she was crying so hysterically when she came off the elevator. I asked could I get her car, and the next thing I know, she started cursing me out, calling me names."

"Like what?"

"She said, 'You need to do your fucking job as a doorman, you broke-ass doorman.'"

"What? I'm sorry for that, Harold. I'll handle it."

"Look, man, I was just trying to help. Mr. and Mrs. Hill were standing there, and I figured I could calm her down, before they started questioning her."

"I'll take care of her, and I'll make sure she apologizes to you. I'm sorry for all that. Man, you always look out for me, and you're good to me; she's not going to disrespect you like that again."

Oh, this is not going to fly with me.

After showering, he sat on the side of his bed, replaying his messages on the answering machine.

Okay, let's see who called. "You know you were wrong this morning for acting the way you did," Tina's message started. "Why were you being so damn secretive? Was it going to kill you to tell me what you had to do? It really didn't matter, but you made it so damn suspicious that I had to keep asking."

"Hey Rick Tyler, Judge Browe, give me a call, let's talk, my man."

"Dad, call me."

Whatever, Tina. I'm calling my son first, see what's up with my main man, and after I eat, then Judge Browe, cause he's going to talk my head off.

"Hey son. What's up?"

"Nothing," said Ric. "I haven't talked to you since the draft. I'm good; what about you?"

"I'm okay."

"Really? You don't sound like yourself; you sound pissed off. What's wrong? Talk to me, Dad."

"I'm good. I'm good, son; what's going on with you?"

"Just got a little a problem, and I can't talk to Ma about it!"

"Why? You talk to her about everything," said Rick.

"Oh, I'm not talking about Grandma."

"Then who you talking about? Your mother, Angela?" "No, Karla. You met my girlfriend, Shawn?"

"Yeah, what about her?"

"Dad, she's pregnant, and I'm not sure if I'm ready for a baby now. I'm just really starting my career, and I know I'm going to be on the road a lot. I don't want that baby to grow up like me, with no father around."

"Son, I truly understand; if I could turn back the hands of time, things would have been different. You would have been with me everywhere I went and every day, but I was much younger than you. I guess you can say I was selfish in my own way. Don't make the same mistake I did and leave that baby with someone else to raise it, but Ma and Pops did a good job raising you, and I appreciate that."

"I don't know if I'm ready for a steady family yet," Ric said. "If I tell Karla, she's going to hit the roof; she told me to keep myself on track and be careful of having a baby, especially if I don't love her."

"Well, do you love her?" Rick replied.

"Yeah, I do, but I'm not ready to have kids; whatever her decision is, I guess I have to deal with it. I can hear Karla now: 'I told you to use them damn condoms, didn't I? what is wrong with you? Don't you listen?'

"Dad, I'm twenty-four, but I know I'm going to feel like a teenager when I talk to her. I feel bad, like I let her down on that note."

"Yeah, well, I know that feeling, son."

"From who, Ma?" Ric replied.

"Nope, from your grandparents, but with Karla, it was something totally different; it wasn't good when she found out about you."

"Why? What happened?" Ric replied.

He chuckled and said, "Another time, son; let's talk about you."

"Dad, come on, man; this is serious."

"I know," Rick replied. "So is she really pregnant?"

"Yeah; at least that's what she said."

"Listen, son: Just make sure she takes a pregnancy test, and you take a paternity test once the baby gets here, especially if you have any doubts. Having a baby with your girl can be tricky; it may or may not be your baby, even if you did use a condom."

"Yeah, I know, but I don't have any doubts. But if the result comes out positive, I'm more worried of what Ma is going to say than anybody else."

"Well, son, whatever you choose to do, I got your back. I'm here for you. Ric, let me ask you something, though: How long have you been calling Karla 'Ma'?"

"Wow, I started calling her Ma when I was in the second grade; she used to come up to the school, and the kids would ask me if she was my mother, and I said yeah. I never stopped, and she never said I couldn't; actually, she acted more like my mother than Angela. She's always been there for me, on my birthdays, Christmas, and just any other time that I needed her. Dad, you probably don't know this, but when I was in elementary school, I got sick at school; Grandma was at work, and they couldn't reach Granddad, so they called her. She came and got me, took me to her house, and from that point on, I stayed at her house all the time, even when I wasn't sick. She dropped all of us off at school; she did all the mother things with us three."

"Oh, yeah? That's good. I just never heard you call her that."

"I never said it around you; I didn't know how you were going to react to it. Does it bother you?"

"Nope, I'm good with that."

"I thought you knew all that," said Ric.

"I knew she went to your games, but I didn't know about the other stuff. I'm fine with that."

"So Dad, do you still love her?"

"Why you ask?" Rick replied.

"I just figured you still do."

"Yeah, I do, but who did you call about, me or you?" said Rick.

"Well, I called about me, but now we're talking about you. So when you going back to DC?"

"It might be soon. I got to make this call to Judge Browe, about this position. Don't share this with nobody, at least not yet, and don't tell Karla either. I understand you tell her everything."

"All right, I won't. Before you go, how's Ms. Maria doing?"

He heard her coming through the door, snatched the towel off the bed, and wrapped it around his naked body just before she walked in.

"She's just fine," he said. "She just walked in the room, staring in my face."

"You must be talking to my grandson Ric," she said. "I sure hope his mouth isn't smart like yours."

"Love you too, Maria."

"Whatever, bamma," she replied.

"Dad, did she just call you a bamma?"

"Yeah, I taught her that; now she's running it into the ground."

"Let me speak to him," Maria ordered. "Hi babe! How are you?"

"I'm fine, Ms. Maria; good to hear your voice."

"So when you coming out to see me?" said Maria.

"Soon, before the season starts up, I promise."

"Okay; it's good to hear your voice. I'm giving you back to your crazy father. Love you," she said.

"Love you too, Ms. Maria."

"So how many weeks along is she, anyway?" Rick asked.

"She said two months, but I'm not really sure."

"What did you just say?" Maria snapped, overhearing their conversation. "Did I just hear what I think I heard you say? Oh my God, Ric, what did I tell you? You don't listen, just like your father; you make sure you bring yourself out here as soon as possible. I'm not playing with you; do you hear me?"

"Uh, wait a minute," Rick said. "I'm his father. I thought you was gone out the door."

Maria twisted her lips and cut her eyes at him.

"You be silent for a minute. I'll deal with you shortly."

"Okay. Son, I think mother Maria just checked me and handled that on this end," said Rick.

"Yeah, I heard. Wow, next time, just go into another room."

"Like that's going to stop her; she ear hustles very well."

They both fell out laughing.

"Son, let me make this other call, and I'll call you back later tonight. I'll let you know when I'm going to DC, so you can meet me there."

"All right, love you."

"I love you too, son."

"Okay, who's next on the list? If I call Crazy, it's going to be another argument, and if I call Browe, he's going to talk forever; shit, I'm going to eat first."

Maria stood in the doorway with her arms folded, tapping her foot, until he stood up and started walking downstairs to the kitchen.

"Mr. Tyler," she said, very sarcastically, "your brunch is ready."

"All right, lady, let's go eat. Maria, did you hear Tina go out the door this morning?"

"Yes, I did, and I told you that girl is crazy. Where did you get her from again?"

"The library," said Rick.

"Well, you should have left that empty little book on the shelf; she doesn't have no words left, let alone any pictures."

"Maria, calm down, don't start that Spanish, okay? You taught me the language and I know what you're saying."

"Rick, you know, after all these years, you're like a son to me. I don't want to see you get hurt. You had some strange women in your life, but she is the worst; she's very possessive, and it's coming out more and more. It's not good, I'm telling you. You need to cut her loose in a nice way. She's trouble. I've been with you a long time; you've seen my girls grow up and now my grandbabies."

"Yeah, and where you going with this, Maria?"

"When are you going to settle down and get married so I can see my other grandbabies before I leave this earth? All this foolishness you doing is too much; that's where I'm going."

"Maria, you're not going anywhere; what would I do without you? God is not ready for you yet, so you stuck with me."

"Well, since I'm stuck with you, could you do something for me?"

"What's that, Maria?"

"Promise me you give me some grandbabies and get married. You're a good man, but you keep getting these crazy women. I don't know who was the worst, but this craziness has got to stop. I know I'm just your maid ..."

"Excuse me, since when have you been just the maid? If I can remember, you've been more like a mother to me."

"Maybe more like a big sister," she replied. "I'm too young to be your mother."

They both laughed.

"Seriously, Maria, you've taken good care of me, and I love and respect you for all of that; you know I'll hurt somebody over you. I really don't know what I would do without you."

"Well, I really wish you would settle down and find that right woman," she said. "What about Karla? You always daydreaming about her."

"How you know I'm daydreaming about her? There you go again, in my business."

"Your business somehow always turns out to be my business because all we do is talk about Karla. "

"Old lady, I love you do death. I swear you're a mess; you think you know me, don't you?"

"Yeah, I do, and you're the mess; now don't play with me. Listen to what I say and eat your food, so you can make that call. Why don't you take a trip back East and find out what is going on with her? You haven't seen her since the draft; see if she still loves you and if she's in love with you. If she says yes, then it's meant to be."

"But what if she says no?" Rick asked.

"Then move on, but at least go find out before you kill me with this nonsense. I don't like that Tina girl; she's not good for you. She's trouble and could ruin you and your career."

"All right, Maria. Okay, okay."

"Then go make your call to that man, and call Karla while you're at it. I'll clean this up in a few, so take your time."

"No, I'll be back to help you with the dishes."

"Why? I'm not paying you to help me, so don't hurry back."

He walked into his den, turned on some music, and opened the balcony doors. He flipped opened his laptop and sat down at his mahogany desk in his black high-back chair.

"Okay, let me call this chick. Oh, no answer; maybe she's working on something. I'll call her back. I'll just finish up my business."

He read his personal emails, reviewed his bank accounts, and looked over his business records. He stayed in his office for more than two hours, working on his personal business and paying bills.

"Okay, still no answer; I see she's not answering my call. Not a problem." He made another call: "Ms. Barbara, Rick Tyler; is Tina available?"

"I'm sorry, she asked me to hold her calls, including yours."

"Oh really? Okay, thanks." He hung up and walked out of the den. "Maria, I'll be back shortly. I got to handle something first before I make my phone call."

"Okay, you better have a decision when you come back here; you don't need any other distractions. That man is not going to wait for you; he's given you enough time."

Let me end this game today with her, he thought as he drove off. *Fuck a dinner, I'm not playing this with her no more. Damn, of all days, why today? Everybody wants to leave their home, damn traffic.*

He headed toward Tina's office in downtown LA. *Ain't no way I'm taking her to DC to live with me; it would be a living hell, and I'd be in the* Washington Post *fooling with her and her shit. Maria is right: She's too possessive, and it's getting worse. God knows if Karla comes around the family and she see her, it will be hell to pay.*

He threw his truck in park in front of her office building.

He snatched the front door open and took the steps two at a time to the third floor and went down the hall to her office.

"Hi, Ms. Barbara; is Tina in her office?"

"Yes, but she asked not to be disturbed."

"Yeah? Okay, I'll just surprise her."

He walked straight into her office and stood in front of her desk.

"So you are here, just not taking my calls, huh?"

"So what?" Tina asked. "And no, I'm not taking your calls."

"That's all right; you don't have to take them. I'm here now."

"And you're here, why?" Tina replied. "Don't you have some personal business to take care of?"

"Yeah, I do, but first all, that damn commotion you had going on this morning in the lobby, screaming, crying, and cursing like you're crazy: What the fuck is wrong with you? I told you, don't bring that mess to my home, and you did it anyway with total disrespect. You just keep showing your ass."

"Wait," she said, "don't come in here accusing me of something. You don't even know what happen; let me explain."

"Explain what? You had all the time to explain your nonsense when you left those five messages, but you didn't."

"Nonsense? Don't come in here like you're so righteous."

"And you are? You dramatized the whole thing all the way to the lobby, then you took it out on someone who had nothing to do with it; he was doing his job."

"His job? He was in my damn business; that was his job?" she asked.

"Then your business should have stayed upstairs and not in the lobby," Rick replied, "and then you cussed him out in front of other tenants."

"So? Why in the hell you so concerned about him? He ain't nothing but a sorry broke-ass doorman."

"If you didn't want him to ask you nothing, before you hit the bottom of those steps, you should have brought your ass back upstairs, but you didn't."

"So what, you embarrassed?"

"Yeah, I am," he answered. "That was totally uncalled for; you should be embarrassed too."

"Well, too damn bad, 'cause I'm not."

"I called you back, but you not accepting phone calls," Rick said. "Why not?"

"Fuck you, Rick. I'm working, and that was earlier; you should have taken my call earlier."

"Really? It looks like you just sitting there, looking at a magazine, and that's work? Let me sit my ass down; I really feel like snatching your ass out that chair."

Tina jumped up and swung her hand toward his face.

"If you put your hands on me," she growled, "my brothers will kick your black ass."

"What? Girl, sit your ass down; your brothers ain't going to do shit to me. You must think I'm a sucka or one of them fools that you know and try to run; don't let this calm attitude fool you.

"You know me? You think you do; don't underestimate me. I will fuck you up, lady, woman, or whatever you call yourself. You come after me like that again, go ahead and call your brothas. It won't be nice for any of them. Trust me, it won't. Your ass has been totally out of control for a long time, and I put up with your bullshit, all for some ass."

"You got snappy with me because I asked you a question."

"I didn't get snappy. I calmly told you nothing was wrong. I had to take care of some personal things today. That's it."

"And again, I'm asking you, Rick: What's so damn personal that you couldn't tell me this morning? Are you seeing someone else and the bitch pregnant?"

"And I told you this morning, the answer is still no. Look here, I had enough of your drama shit; you just won't let it go. It's personal, and that's all there is to it. I don't want to share it with you, okay?"

"So you don't think you were wrong this morning for what you said to me?" Tina asked.

"You took it too far," he said. "All you had to do was drop it; there was no need for all of the extras, with the throwing and hitting."

"I don't know what you talking about," she said. "There wasn't any extras, as you say."

"Let me just play back to you what was said, missy: First, you called me a fuckin' dog, screaming at the top of your lungs. Then you picked up your shoe and threw it at the door while I was walking out.

I told you not to throw nothing in here; do you remember now? Then I left the room, and as you walked past the door, you hit me in the back with your purse. I told you before, don't put your hands on me unless you're fucking me; otherwise, keep your damn hands to yourself. Do I need to go on, because I can play it back to you. So yes, I was wrong to say that about you putting your hands on me only when we are fucking. Yes, that was wrong, so I apologize for that statement."

"And then you said you don't want to marry me," said Tina.

"No, I don't want to marry you."

"What you mean? I'm good to you."

"Look here, Tina, for the last time: I never said we were getting married, nor did we ever talk about it; you put that marriage shit in your own head. Girl, you're not in love with me; nothing about you says you love me."

"I do love you, and I'm in love with you. I fell in love with you a long time ago."

He shook his head and snickered. "No, you didn't, and no, you're not in love with me. What is it that you want from me? It damn sure ain't my hand in marriage."

"How can you tell me how I feel about you? You don't know."

"Tina, when you love somebody, you don't act like you do. I listen to how you talk to people; your actions show me you don't give a damn about nobody but yourself. It's about what you want, and I've been down this road before. Do I look like your personal bank? Hell no. Do you think I'm stupid, that I'm just going to turn my finances and my life over to you, to ruin me? Uh, hell no again."

"Man, don't get it twisted. I don't need your fuckin' money, or your ass; you always think somebody want your damn money. If you feel like that, then you should have chosen another career in life, like maybe you should have been the doorman. You think the things you do and buy, all those fancy things, and live in that expensive place and always got to have the best, that you're all that. Let me tell you something, Mr. Tyler: You ain't shit and never will be shit, just a lonely ass with money. I got my own."

"Okay, and what I got is mine and not yours or anybody else's, unless I want to give it to them. I worked hard and earned what I have, and if I choose to buy expensive things, I can. I chose my career and my lifestyle to please me. You think because you sucked my motherfuckin' dick and turned a couple of tricks, I'm supposed to be hooked? Girl, I had a lot of pussy, and yours is nothing special. Trust me, I'm not pussy-whipped at all; you're just another piece of ass that was here and gone. See, I can love and give love, but I am not a fool, nor a sucka that's up for a game."

"And just what makes you think you're so damn special, Rick Tyler? God blessed you?"

"Yep, he sure did; he blessed me with a heart and a soul to love. See, when I say I love a person, I really do, not for what they got or what somebody can do for me, because I can do for myself. Money don't make me. I make myself."

"Oh, so everybody loves Erick Tyler."

"There's quite a few that do love me, and some that hate me, and that's cool too. The ones that love me, I care about them people, unlike you. You don't give a damn about love. Do you even know what love is?"

"Yes, I do."

"Just in case you have a different definition from what I know, it's a strong feeling from the heart and soul."

"I know, but nobody is perfect, and neither are you; some people show love in different ways."

He fell out laughing. "Tina, you don't know how to love a dog, let alone a human being."

"Then if that's true, why did you stay with me for so long?" she asked.

"I guess for the company," Rick replied.

"Oh no, Mr. Got It Going On needs company? You couldn't buy any?"

He snickered to himself on that one.

"Yeah, I do from time to time," he said, "but I got you for free. In the beginning, you were fun, but as time went on, I guess I was just settling with no plans."

"Settling? Get your ass out my office, you bastard! You bring your ass in here and talk to me like I'm a fuckin' tramp on the street, and I'm supposed to be okay with that? Motherfucka, you must be real fucked up in the mind. Get out of my damn office."

"I'm leaving anyway. I just came to tell you that this thing or relationship, as you call it, is over. I'm done. And that shit you pulled with Mr. Harold: You owe him an apology, and you should compensate him for the verbal harassment you gave him this morning."

"You don't have no proof of what was said," she replied.

"Yes, I do."

"You're a lonely bastard, Rick Tyler, and you got me confused. I'm not one of your clients."

"I know you're not one of my clients; you couldn't afford me. But there's video cameras at my building; they tell it all."

She yelled so loud that her co-workers heard her. She looked as if she was about to bust the stitching off her too-small skirt; her face was fiery red, and she looked like she could have spit bullets at him.

"You don't know the things he said to me."

"Yes, I do."

"You think you're so much better than the others? Then you compensate him," Tina replied.

She caught herself going into Diane.

Ooh, calm down before you lose your job and expose yourself with this fool; he's not worth it, at least not yet.

"He's not there tonight," Rick said, "so when do you plan on doing it?"

"Damn, you know his schedule like that?"

"I should, considering I've lived there for many years."

"Oh, you fuckin' him too? Aw, you must be gay; that explains why you don't want to marry me. You're confused."

"Now where did that come from? See, that's what I'm talking about: always taking it an extra mile."

"Why you so defensive with him? Is it because I said his schedule?"

"Girl, you're really crazy."

"Now I know why you don't eat pussy: You and your doorman are getting it on. Who's fuckin' who in the ass? So I guess when he's not working his night shift and I'm not there, he's up there fucking you, and that's why you don't want to get married to nobody, you fucking faggot. You bitch."

"Tina, you're really fuckin' crazy. I'm going to stop it here. Just do what I told you to do."

"Who the fuck do you think you're talking to, telling me what to do? I'm not doing nothing."

"I'm Erick Tyler, that's who the fuck I am."

He stood up, leaned across her desk, and kissed her on the lips.

"Bye, and thanks for the ass."

"Wait," she cried. "I'm sorry, I shouldn't have said that. Please forgive me; I was acting out of anger. Why you make me say those things?"

"And you say you love me? Damn, I knew our definition of love was different, girl; you fight dirty. I sure hate to see your ass in a street fight, let alone in the courtroom. "As a matter of fact, I hope I never see you in a courtroom representing anyone. I know how that's going to go down."

"Babe, wait, I'll go there after I get off tonight; we can have makeup sex."

"Naw, I'm good; thanks for last night, though. Remember I'm gay, so why in the hell do you still want to fuck me? What you got from me last night should hold you over until the next man comes along; maybe he'll eat your pussy. But remember, babe: I fucked the shit out of you, and it was good to you."

He smiled and walked out the door.

"Ms. Barbara, you have a good evening."

He saw her holding her head down, trying not to let him see her laughing.

"You too, Mr. Tyler; you too."

I'm so glad he ended that relationship with that crazy bitch, Barbara thought. *I should go catch him and hug him myself.* She rolled away from her desk so quickly that she hit her knee on the desk drawer.

"Mr. Tyler, wait," she called. "Can I speak with you for a minute please? I hope I don't get fired for this, and Lord knows I hope you don't get mad at me for what I'm about to say, but I got to say this: I'm so glad you ended that relationship with her. Lord knows ain't nobody perfect, but damn, I have never seen anybody like her. Thank God you dumped her."

"Uh, Ms. Barbara, how much did you hear?"

"I heard enough, and I think half the office did too."

"Ms. Barbara, were you standing at the door the whole time?"

"No, I was walking past and heard you, plus the door wasn't closed all the way."

"Ms. Barbara, you better be careful doing that; the next person is not going to be as kind."

He turned and hit the steps back to the lobby and out the door, heading back to his truck.

My time is running short down here with this dumb shit, he thought as he drove back home. *I got to make this call at noon his time; I'm taking that job. A change is good. I'll take it for a while; if I don't like it, then I'll relocate to somewhere else. I'll cross that bridge later. Damn, I can't be the only black man going through this dumb-ass drama. I can't even think straight sometimes. I feel like I'm torn between two women. One that want me bad, and the other one I want her bad, but I'm not sure if she wants me as much as I want her.*

He shouted out loud, "Why am I having these most difficult issues? Tina, why are you so damn crazy? We could have done this for a while. Sexually, you're good to me, but you're unstable. Sometimes, I think you need to be placed in a mental institution, and I need the couch for dealing with you and still thinking about her. This is not making any sense at all; if my mama knew this nonsense, she would beat me upside my head.

He shook his head and snickered to himself, reminiscing back to his younger days.

Damn, he thought, *I remember when I was much younger, and she damn near took my whole head off. Pops was standing in the door, watching her knock the mess out of me and Tony, shaking his head, laughing and saying, "I tried to tell them, babe, but they don't listen to me; they all dummies. One follows the other." Until finally, one time, she must have had enough of him saying that and told him, "And I wonder where they got it from. The apple don't fall far from the tree, now does it?" After that, he didn't say another word; from that point on, he told us, if you have a stupid ass problem, come see him and talk it out, so point taken. I'll call him later on.*

He hit the gas pedal a little harder, flying in and out of traffic until he made it home.

"Hey Harold, Tina is supposed to come here to apologize to you for her harassment this morning; let me know if she doesn't show up. I'll rap with you later."

He headed over to the elevator and went up to his condo.

"Maria, I'm back!"

"Okay, well, make your call," she said. "Time is against you; that man won't wait on you all day."

"I can do it now, if you just stop talking to me."

"I'm not stopping you; you called me, remember?"

He laughed and walked into his den.

"Hello, this is Erick Tyler; is His Honor available?"

"Hold on," the receptionist said. "He's been waiting on your call."

"Rick Tyler," said Judge Browe. "How you doing, young man?"

"I'm good, sir; I got no complaints. What about yourself?"

"Oh, I'm good for an old man, no complaints; I was finishing up some things while I was waiting on your call. Before we get to business, I need a few things from you."

"Yes, sir."

"One: Stop saying 'yes sir' to me; I know I'm old. We already established that years ago. I know you respect and honor me and my position, so stop with the 'sir' crap."

"All right, JB; what else?"

"When I get to them, I'll stop you; now let's talk about some things. Rick, I've known you for many years, and your track record has proven that you're a damn good attorney. Your reputation travels well, and it has shown from the West Coast to the East Coast. You are a very well-known man. I'm saying all of this because as you know, I'm retiring, and you've been selected to fill my slot; so what are you going to do? I'm waiting on your decision. I can't hold them off but for so long; otherwise, the board needs to move with another selection. I know you'll do well as a judge on this bench. But man, my biggest concern is I know you're still woman crazy. I know you sitting on that other end with that expression you always gave me, like, 'Mr. Browe, get to the damn point.'"

"JB, you don't know me like that."

"You know I do, and for many years, I've endured that look many evenings; in case you forgot, I knew you when you were a young law student, working hard to become the attorney you are today."

Rick burst out laughing.

"Okay, JB, you got me there."

"We had many discussions and debates on many different topics."

"JB, stay with me now; what are we talking about?"

"We're talking about you. I feel like your father now. You too smart; as I was saying, have you made your decision yet?"

"Uh no, not yet; actually, I was making flight arrangements to come to town to talk with you personally."

"Well, that's even better; how long do you plan on staying in town? My schedule is tight for the next few weeks, but I can move things around."

"Well, I figure about two weeks or so. I need to wrap up some things here before I fly out."

"Good, then we can have dinner and catch up on some things. My second question is, who you seeing now? Is she coming with you?"

"No, there's nobody."

"What? Look here, young man, you need to get a family; you're too well rounded of a man to be alone. Nobody was put on this earth to be alone. Why do you think God created Adam and Eve? If you come to DC, you better not be single. These women will eat you alive here, and you know it. What you waiting for? Ms. Perfect?"

"I don't know, JB. I haven't found the right one, I guess."

"That's what you say, Rick Tyler."

"JB, as soon as I get in town, I'll send you a text, and we can set a date, place, and time."

"All right, young man; you better have an answer for me before you leave LA. I'm not going to hold this offer for you much longer."

"It will be good to see you," Rick said. "Matter of fact, when was the last time we talked about this?"

"What, two years ago," said Judge Browe.

"Was it that long ago?"

"Before we end this call, how's your parents and that growing boy of yours?"

"They're fine. I just spoke with Ric earlier today. How's your family?"

"Everybody is good; those great-grandkids are driving me crazy, but I love it. Now that I'll be retiring, I get to deal with them all the time. Every Sunday, everybody comes over for dinner; at first I used to say, 'Darn, here they come again,' but I tell you, young man, that's a great feeling to see your family and watch those youngsters grow, especially when you growing old like me. Man, if I could find a charge on you for not being married by now, I would. Nobody should grow old by themselves. Like I said, God didn't intend for us to be alone. You had your share of women, and you had the taste of the good life and the finer things in life as a single man; now it's time for you to settle down and enjoy life with someone special and give her the finer things in life."

"You're right, JB, I been pondering on those exact same thoughts."

"Mr. Tyler, what are you going to do? I'm not trying to push you into anything. I just don't want to see a fine specimen of a man go to waste and live out his life alone. Erick, I've watched you grow up from a young student to a very smart, educated man, and I know you have a good heart; I just don't understand how come you are not taken yet."

"JB, I'm going to work on that sooner than you think."

"All right; I'm not going talk your ear off any more, until later."

"JB, you're all right with me. I'll talk with you as soon as I get to DC. You take care."

"You too, my friend," JB replied.

Rick slumped down in the chair, thinking hard on what the judge said.

Damn, him and Maria keep saying the same damn thing, he thought. *I know I don't want to be alone for the rest of my life, so I better make the move first and reach out to Karla. But shit, what if she don't want to be with me? Then I have to start the dating scene all over again, with a different approach. But I'm too set in my ways; who in the hell is going to put up with me and my shit? Well, if I don't want to be alone, I guess I'll have to change some of my ways.*

Maria knocked on the door and peeped in.

"So, Rick, what did he say?"

"I haven't given him an answer yet," he said. "I'm going to fly back to DC for about two weeks or so, and we're going to talk then."

"You act as if you really not sure you want to take this job."

"I'm not; one part of me wants to, and the other doesn't."

"Well, what else did he say?"

"The same things you said, Maria: Get married, yadda, yadda, yah; same thing."

"Okay, yadda yadda yah; so what you going to do?"

"I know, Maria. I need to make a decision quickly."

"Yeah, but I'm not talking about that, smarty pants. I'm talking about you seeking that woman that you're so crazy about."

"I need to make a decision about the job first."

"Okay, so while you sitting there thinking about that job, you need to be thinking about Karla; if you say you love her, then act on it now before it's too late."

"Oh boy, if I didn't love her, I would …"

"I heard that; you would what?"

"Nothing. Let me call her now before time gets away. I need to catch up with her anyway; we haven't talk since back in April."

He sat in his den for the next few hours, thinking about his decision and moving to DC and how he could get Karla back into his life. As he was leaving the den, the doorbell rang.

"Who the hell is that?" he asked as he went over to the door.

"Hey babe," Tina said, pushing her way past him with a bottle of wine in her hand. "I thought I'd come to apologize to your doorman and to you personally; we can toast to a start over."

Maria walked in the living room and saw it was Tina; she turned around and went back in her room, slamming the door.

"Why is she so nasty?" Tina asked. "I swear I would fire her."

"Tina, what the hell are you doing here? I told you earlier it's over."

"Aw, come on, babe; this was just a little fight. We're going to have these disagreements from time to time; that's what couples do. We both said some things to each other that weren't nice, but …"

"Tina, there are no apologies needed. I'm done with you, and we are done talking."

"Look, babe, I'm sorry, but you …"

"Tina, stop, and there's no but. What happened this morning was building up from long ago. I'm mad at myself for letting it go this far, so just stop it."

"This have anything to do with your family?" she asked. "I know you're not still mad about that; I tried to pretend to like them."

"You didn't have to pretend to like my family. I damn sure didn't pretend to like yours. And like you pretended you wanted to go with me to DC to meet them, but you cringed. I saw your face, and then you flew off the handle about some stupid shit when I said we should take a trip to Jamaica. You had a long story about why you don't like Jamaica: It's dirty, the people are poor, you went on and on and how you would never mess with a Jamaican. You only fuck the men there and how they can only wait on you hand and foot, be a servant to you. I thought that was just low. Damn, is that how you feel about people you think are beneath you?"

"Babe, look, I came to apologize, but you won't let me. No, I don't like Jamaicans, and no, I don't like your family either; why can't it be just us? I never seen nobody like you who's that damn close to his family. Why they have to be involved in our lives?"

"See, this is what I'm talking about right here, but let me let you off the hook again, Tina."

"About what? That you're really gay?"

He shook his head and chuckled.

"You too damn funny, girl. In case you failed to hear me before, I am a Jamaican."

"What? You don't look like them."

"What the hell am I supposed to look like, then?"

"You don't have the awful dreadlocks, and you don't talk like them."

He rolled his eyes and shook his head.

"Um, my dad is Jamaican, that one you hate so dearly, and my mother is American. So what does that make me, 'cause I'm far from dumb and dirty, and I am a good fuck, even when you ain't visiting Jamaica. Let's see, my family is very well educated and financially well-to-do, and they all have good jobs, holding it down very well, and we all pay taxes, and we all go back and forth to Jamaica on a regular basis. As I stated before, we got two definitions of love; my love is, no matter how many times we may have our difference, we still respect each other. See, when I love a person, they got my all, and when it comes to my family, a woman that don't love me can't come between me and my family, nor will I let you disrespect them."

"Wait one minute, Rick. You never told me you're Jamaican."

"I did, but you didn't listen."

"I must have misunderstood what you were saying."

"Wow, and just think: You want to marry me but don't know the most important thing about me. And for the record, Tina, you don't have grounds to speak on anybody's family. If you knew your own family like what I saw, you would never judge anybody."

"Rick, don't you judge me."

"Oh, I'm not judging you at all, babe, but it's okay for you to judge others."

"Before you throw rocks," Marie added, "you should check yourself and your own family."

"Why she keep coming out here?" Tina growled. "She always

seems to appear every time I'm over here. What is it you want, old lady?"

"Tina, enough, girl; get out my house, and don't bring your ass back here no more."

He opened the door and escorted her out.

"Oh, so you're fucking the old maid too; fuck you, you bisexual-ass bastard."

He gave her a push out the door, walked her down the hall, and rode the elevator down with her.

"Rick, babe, she started it."

He gripped her arm tightly and whispered in her ear, "Now hear this very clearly, babe: I promise you, if you come here again, I will have your ass locked up for trespassing, and to make sure you understand, I'll be reporting you to the bar. Now I'm going walk you to your car; don't make no scene. Just go ahead and drive the fuck off."

"Let go of me, you fuckin' bastard."

"Tina, go ahead and do it; this is it. LAPD will be here before you get to the street; don't do it to yourself. Let's just end this peacefully; you go yours, and I'm damn sure going mine.

Carlos, that car right there, here's the tag number; if she comes up here again, you call me and the police right away."

"Yes, sir," said Carlos.

Got damn, he thought. *Shit, she's furious with Maria; she just might try to hurt her for real. I better get a restraining order and some police protection. Lord, what are you telling me? My mother told me never to question you, but I just got to ask. Is this a payback? I know I did some dog stuff. Is this punishment? I know I brought some of it on myself, but dang, can you lighten up a little? Please don't give it to me all at one time.*

He went back into his condo.

"Rick! Rick!"

"Maria, not now, not tonight; talk to me tomorrow sometime, later in the evening. Good night."

Gee, single life is rough, he thought. *I'm out of the game. I don't get paid for this shit; it ain't enough money on the table for this bullshit.*

Fuck it! I'm staying single. I don't give a damn if I don't get no more pussy for the next few years. I had enough to last me for a while. I can't do it; maybe I really do need to relocate, but maybe not back to DC. Shit, maybe I'll just become a monk. Move to Egypt somewhere for about a year or two, to save my soul. Okay, that one was a bit extreme, I'm talking crazy now; just watch TV, Rick.

These nights are getting shorter or something, he thought after waking the next morning. *I feel like I just went to sleep. This's going be a long day, but a good day; maybe I should go in late. Naw, better not. I need to move some cases around, update a few partners and Ms. Beck, and go to the courthouse to file for that restraining order. I had enough of her shit, just popping up.*

"Good morning to you, Maria." She did not answer. "Oh, so you're not talking this morning?"

"You told me not to talk to you, remember?"

"I told you don't talk to me until much later. I didn't feel like a discussion last night. Okay, but that's not a problem. I'll take that. I'll see you later; thanks for the food. Bye."

Maria didn't say a word; she remained leaning against the sink, sipping on her coffee, looking at him walk out the door.

"My man. Morning, Mr. Tyler!"

"Good morning, Mr. Harold. I'll talk with you later." "Okay, sir. Have a great day."

Aw, what the fuck is this on my car window? he thought to himself when he saw a note stuck under his windshield wiper.

He snatched the paper off his windshield without reading it, threw on the front seat, and drove off.

"Mr. Tyler, you're looking sharp today," Ms. Beck said when he entered the office. "Something special going on?"

"Nope, just a good night's sleep. Would you come see me in fifteen minutes? But before you go, see if I can get on Mr. Schmidt's calendar for today; any time is good."

"Yes, sir."

He opened his office door and flicked the light on.

"Ms. Beck, where did these come from?"

"Some lady had them delivered early this morning."

He took the flowers off his desk and set them on the floor in the corner.

"Ms. Beck, do you have vacation time coming up?" "Yes."

"Good, take it. I'll be out of the office for two or three weeks; you can take your vacation while I'm gone."

"Okay, great, I think I will, and Mr. Schmidt is available. He said he's waiting on you to come in and talk with him anyway."

"Cool; as soon as I meet with my team, I'll go right in."

"Mr. Tyler, do you need me to make your flight arrangements?" she asked.

"No, it's personal. I'll handle it, but thank you. While you're on vacation, just check your emails periodically and let me know what comes up. I'll be doing the same. Oh, one other thing: Before you leave for the day, stop back in here."

"Good morning, team, come on in and take a seat. I'll be gone for the next three weeks; Ms. Beck and I will be communicating with you via email, so stay tuned into your Blackberries. That's all I have."

"Mr. Tyler, where're you going?" Sabrina asked. "I hope everything is okay."

"Yes, thanks for your concern, and thanks for coming in; I'll see you all before I leave for the day."

He looked at the flowers.

I should throw this shit in the trash, he thought, *but if I do it now, then questions will come. Tina, it's over; stop with this shit.* But when he read the card, he saw the flowers were from Karla.

Hey Mr. Tyler. I haven't heard from you in a while; is this how you do all your women friends? You get their attention at hello, their love, and then leave without any goodbyes. Anyway; I just wanted to say thank you again for the vacation. I really needed that break. Kisses; have a good day! Love, Karla.

Wow, Karla, he thought, *that was so sweet of you; anytime and anything for you.*

He kept reading the card over and over.

How sweet of her; another good thing about her. Thank you, babe.

He twirled around in his chair like a child, smiling.

I'm not leaving you, babe. I'm en route to you real soon. I'll be there by the time you get home from work tomorrow, that's a promise.

He snatched the phone off the receiver.

"Rick Tyler, I thought you were coming to see me," Mr. Schmidt, the senior partner at the firm, said.

"I'm on my way."

"Don't worry, I'm coming down there; stay where you are."

After a few minutes, Rick's boss came into his office.

"So what is it you need to see me about?" he asked.

"I need to go back East to meet with Honorable Browe," Rick said. "He's asking me to take his place after he retires, and he wants a decision on whether I want the job."

"Well, do you?"

Mr. Schmidt cut him off before he could say anything.

"Listen, Erick, you've been with us a long time, and I value your work here; you're an outstanding partner, and anyone would be pleased to have you on their team. I'm going to let you off the hook. I know JB; we go a long way back, along with Zebian. Whatever you decide, I wish you the very best. You just keep representing us very well, young man. I know you will do great on that bench. Take all the time you need, and I'll await your decision. Oh, and by the way, I agree with JB: You need to settle down. I'll be waiting on my wedding invitation soon; we all are."

He smiled, and they both walked out the door.

Rick stopped at Ms. Beck's desk.

"Where are you?" he asked. "Forget it. I'll just leave it in her chair and call her later. I need to make a move, but first let me hit Whitey up on my way out."

I hate to be so direct with this young girl, he thought when he approached Whitey's office, *but why does she always think the men in here want her, flaunting herself? She all right, young black chick, not too cute though, great body, maybe in her late twenties or mid-thirties, but I wouldn't dare fuck her, and I sure hope like hell Whitey isn't fucking her. She doesn't look like trouble, but I don't fuck around with anyone where I work. I don't give a damn how good you look.*

He pointed at Whitey's office door, looking directly in her face.

"Is he in?"

"No, he's in court today."

"Okay, have him call me as soon as possible, when he gets a break."

"Mr. Tyler, you're sure looking and smelling good, not that you don't always look and smell good."

"Thank you."

Without a smile, he quickly walked away.

I got some flowers and a card from my babe, he thought. *I'm not messing that up fooling with you, little girl.*

Good, he thought when he arrived at the courthouse, *it's not too crowded in here.*

"Bernard, I need to get an emergency protective order right away."

"Damn, what you got, man, a stalker?"

"Something like that."

Bernard's laugh was heavy and loud, the few people that was in there and turned around and looked at him.

"Okay, you got it, man." After a few minutes, the clerk came out with an official document. "All right, man, she's not to come within five hundred feet of your building; if she does, she'll be arrested on the spot for violation of this order. What's her name?"

"Tina Black."

"How come I know her? I'll find out from where and get back with you."

"That's cool. No biggie right now; just give me the order. I'll hit you up later."

As he walked back to his office garage, he read Karla's card over again.

Damn, he thought, I can't believe she sent me something. That's a good sign, she needs something extra special.

Not thinking twice about it, he stopped at one of those high-end boutiques in downtown LA, dropping a few grand on her.

"Wow, you must really love this woman," the saleslady said. "I don't know too many men that come in here and know the size of their woman. I hope she loves it as much as you do."

"She will."

"You're home early," Mr. Harold said after Rick drove back to the condo.

"Yeah, need to make a move right quick to the East Coast. Did Tina come back through here?"

"She's actually upstairs; she went to your place."

He took off running to the elevator.

I'll be damned, he thought, *this chick don't stop. Shit, I got all these bags in my hands from the boutique; she'll probably think it's for her, and it's not. Fuck, I ain't explaining shit to her.*

He opened the door and saw Tina, sitting on his couch.

"Hey babe, I was waiting for you," she said.

"Tina, what the hell are you doing here?" he snapped. "I told you last night: it's over. What part are you not getting?"

"None of it, babe."

"How in the hell did you get in here?"

"Maria let me in."

"You telling me Maria let you in here? Where is she?"

The housekeeper came out of the kitchen.

"Maria, did you let her in here?"

"Yes, she said you were expecting her."

"No, I wasn't," he said, turning back to Tina, "but since you're here, here's a copy of the order. Now get the fuck out my house."

"What is this? Oh, okay. You put an order out on me?"

He picked up the phone and start dialing the police.

"I'm leaving this time," she said, strolling and swinging her finger at the both of them. "But next time, I won't." She slammed the door behind her.

"Maria, I got you an emergency protective order; she cannot come within five hundred feet of here; if you see her, I don't give a fuck if it's 499 feet or you're not sure how many feet, call the cops. This hussy is going to make me fuck her up, but I'm trying not to. This woman is crazy as hell; if someone calls it quits, let the shit go. Damn, if Karla told me she didn't want see me, I would be hurt, but I'm not going to stalk her.

"Mr. Tyler, aren't you going somewhere?"

"When was the last time you call me 'Mr. Tyler'? Maria, I'm sorry for hollering at you last night. I was pissed at you for coming out of the room; it seemed like you were itching for something, and you know she's crazy. You need to stay far from her. I don't know what I would do if anything happened to you."

"Did you make your flight arrangements?" Maria asked. "Or do you want me to call?"

"Yeah please, see if you can get me on the next flight out to DC; don't do that again, please. I still love you."

"Okay, yes, sir."

"Maria, stop saying 'sir' and 'Mr. Tyler.'"

"Okay, sir."

"Got damn it if she ain't a smart ass herself," he mumbled.

"I heard you, sir."

"Good, old lady."

"Are you coming back?" she asked.

"Yeah, why?" Rick replied.

"'Cause you packing like you'll be gone for a while."

"If I don't come back, I'll send for you; no worries, old lady. I'll still keep you around."

"Oh, I'm not worried about that. So are you going to see Karla?"

"Yeah, I plan to stop by her house. Maria, she sent me some flowers and a card today; see?"

"So where's the flowers?"

"I left them at work."

"So now that you have her attention, what are you going to do with it?"

"What? I'm going full force after her."

"Okay, you better give me some results."

"Okay, hold up," he said, throwing his hands in the air. "Why's everyone so worried about me being married? Did I miss something?"

"Yes. You missed a whole lot, my son. Now finish getting ready to go; your flight leaves at five o'clock."

"Cool, that's great. One other thing I need is a rental."

"Pick it up at Hertz."

"Damn, you're good. And while I'm gone, you and your husband better not have no damn parties or old folks sleeping over, either."

"Hush up, crazy man."

"And don't make any babies in here, either. I don't want to be the one to stand before reporters, explaining how an old woman and her man had a baby."

"You know what, smarty pants? If I do, it's no more than what you do; hurry up so you can get your flight out of here."

CHAPTER 4
THE BREAKUP
FRIDAY, JUNE 27, 2008

"All right, Maria," Rick said, "the protective order is on the table. I hate to leave you during this time, but you know I have to meet with JB."

"Don't worry about me," she replied. "Take care of your business and work on getting that woman."

"Okay, but if Tina comes here, just call the police, like I said."

"Why? She's going to call you anyway."

"Maria, I told you: Our relationship is over."

"You finally came to your senses; what, she try to kill you?"

"Yeah and no, but she probably thought about it."

"Now do you seriously think she's going to let you go that easily?"

"She needs to. I'm done with her, but as sure as my name is Erick T. Tyler, she'll be calling me soon. Look, I got to go, but you know how to reach me if something comes up."

Maria put her hands on her hips and tilted her head to the side, looking over glasses at him.

"So are you really going to be in DC or somewhere else? I know you."

"I'll be between my place in Virginia and DC. Did you call for me to get a car?"

"I was texting the company while you were talking about nothing; a car will be here in fifteen minutes."

He laughed as he ran down the steps with his carry-on in one hands and a suitcase in the other.

"Dang, you're good," he said, "but I need to make this flight, so I don't have time to listen to you ramble on."

Maria giggled.

"Hmm, you look like … what's that man's name that did the commercial, running through the airport long time ago?"

"Who? There's been so many men running through the airport…"

"The black guy."

"Which one, Maria? There were many black guys running through the airport."

"I don't know his name; you said he played football too."

"Oh, yeah, would you be talking about the Juice? I knew who you meant; I just wanted to hear you go on with the description."

"Funny, you are; well if that's his name, Juice or Liquid or whatever his name is, don't fall, Juice. I can't pick you up."

"Well, I won't fall if you take this carry-on."

"I'll take it, but it better not be heavy."

"It's not. You can make it. Come on, lady, let's go; get a move on. I got somewhere to be."

When they got to the lobby, Rick took the carry-on bag from Maria and said, "All right, I'm out. Keep your eyes open and be careful; she may be lurking around here. She's still pissed. If she comes anywhere near you, call the police. The restraining order is on the table; put it in your room or take it with you."

"Okay, you told me; how many times you going to keep saying it? I will. Call me when you get to your destination."

"Why? You know where I'm going; are you worried about me?"

"No, I just want to make sure I get my last paycheck, crazy man. Get out of here and have a safe flight, and tell your parents hello."

"Good, the car is here," he said when they got to the lobby. "Good timing. Mr. Harold, I'm out of here for a few weeks; would you watch over Maria for me, please? If Tina comes anywhere near here, call this number; he's a good friend of mine from the LAPD. Even if she's not in her own car, get the tag, make, and model and call them, then call me."

"Will do, got yah. Have a good trip, sir."

Mr. Harold hit the roof of the car three times for the driver, giving him the okay to leave.

"Good evening, sir," Rick said to the driver after he put the bags in the trunk. "Thanks for coming on short notice."

"Good evening to you, Mr. Tyler. Donald Smith is the name."

"Good to meet you, Mr. Smith."

"So your flight is at five o'clock; no worry. You'll be there in plenty of time; just sit back and relax. So where you headed to?"

"To the East Coast."

"Oh, yeah? Where at on the East Coast?"

"Washington DC."

"Oh, I got some friends back in DC."

He started rambling on about his visits to Washington. Rick looked up at him through the mirror, trying to hold his face expression.

"Mr. Smith, I don't mean to be rude, but I have to check some messages while you're driving, if you don't mind."

"Sorry about that, Mr. Tyler. I know I can get carried away sometimes. My wife tells me all the time about how I just keep talking when others don't want to talk."

Rick smiled, bobbing his head in agreement as he listened to his messages.

"Hi, Rick, this Tina's mother, Mrs. Cock. Tina told me y'all broke up; is there any way I can convince you to please give her another chance? She's such a good girl, and you two deserve each other. You're good for her, and we're so proud that you found her."

What the hell is she talking about, found her, he thought angrily. *I wasn't looking for her, she just happened to be at the same place and time; we just started talking. It wasn't no damn chemistry. Delete this shit.*

"Bro-in-law, this Tina's brother; what's up, man? What happened? Tina is really upset, man. I hope you didn't do nuthin' bad to hurt my sista. You all right with me, but I hate to fuck you up. You hurt my sista; man, she really loves you."

What the hell is this fool, really crazy? he thought. *He must think I'm a sucka; he don't have a damn clue of who I am. I will fuck his ass up, and who the fuck told her to give them my damn work number?*

He pulled out his personal phone. *It has got to be some better messages on this one.*

"Hello Rick, it's Genette."

Now what the fuck this witch got to say?

"I got your number from Tina this morning; she was crying. Is everything okay? Do I need to come over to your place and check on her?"

What? he thought, even angrier. *I don't give a damn where you go check on her, as long as it's not at my house.* He called his condo.

"Maria, listen, these people are crazy; the nights your husband can't pick you for church, catch a cab home or call Mr. Harold to send you a car. Are we clear?"

"Yes, and stop calling me," she said. "Goodbye, go take care of your business."

What would I do without that foolish un-biological child of mine? she thought after hanging up. *He's such a sweetheart, worrisome as heck, a good man. Lord knows I'll be glad when he finds some happiness and true love one day before it's too late; he needs some more prayers.*

She rolled her Rosary beads in the palms of her hands, hovering over her spiritual candles and praying in her native language. She prayed for his soul to be protected by the angels and for true love to be bestowed upon him soon.

I guess I need to call Cheryl Tyler, Rick thought, *and let her know I'm coming in town tonight. Um, this unusual; why aren't they answering the phone? I know somebody is there.* Someone finally picked up.

"Hey Ma, what took you so long to answer the phone? You had me worried."

"I didn't hear it at first, and your father's got the TV up so darn loud, listening to the news. What's going on, son?"

"I'm en route home and I might need Pops to pick me up from the airport; but only if my rental car is not available when I get there. I should land around ten o'clock tonight, but by time I get my baggage, it may be 10:30 or so. But Ma, listen: I'll text Pops to let him know; tell him don't leave until he gets my text or call, okay? If I can get the rental car, I'm going to my place; if none is available, then I need Pops to pick me up."

"Rick, let us pick you up, and you can get the car tomorrow. it'll be late."

"Okay, Ma, that's cool, but I don't want you all out too late."

"It won't be late, and anyway we're grown; you don't tell us what time we can come and go."

"Okay, Ma, you right."

"I'll let your father know."

"Thanks, Ma; love you and see you soon."

"Bye, babe."

Oh my goodness, he thought. *Sometimes she's not worth the fight. Just let her have it. Geeze.*

"Mr. Tyler, we're reaching the airport now; traffic was light today. Will I be picking you up, sir?"

"Mr. Smith, I'll be gone for a while," Rick said. "How 'bout I call the company and request you upon my return and then we can talk."

Rick shook his hand, placing a hundred-dollar bill in his palm.

"Thank you for coming on such short notice. I really appreciate it."

Mr. Smith opened his hand, and his mouth flew wide open.

"Mr. Tyler, I can't accept this. I already get paid by the company."

"Now you got paid twice," Rick said. "So keep it; buy your wife some flowers or something special. She'll love it."

He made it to check-in with just enough time to board the plane. He threw his carry-on in the overhead and flopped down in his seat, leaning it as far back as it goes.

I got a few hours to rest my mind, he thought, *and I don't want to think about anything or anybody. I need my time.*

He closed his eyes and dozed off.

Damn, that was quick, he thought when he woke from his nap. *I just got comfortable and into a deep sleep.*

"We are now approaching the Ronald Reagan Washington National airport," the flight attendant announce. "We'll be arriving within thirty minutes; please start packing up your belongings, fasten your seat belts, and turn off all cellphones."

Oh well, he thought, *no need in calling them. I know Ethel and Fred are out there waiting, so no need of me going over to the rental car station. I'll get that later.*

He exited the plane and pulled out his cellphone, checking his messages as he headed toward the baggage claim. There was a message from his father:

"Rick, your mother and I are at the airport, hurry up and get your ass out here."

"That man can never leave a nice message," he mumbled, "but I guess that wouldn't be Derrick Tyler, now, would it?"

"Aw, man! Erick Tyler! The all-time best linebacker, can we have your autograph please?" asked a couple of little boys at the baggage claim.

They pulled out everything and anything they had in their backpacks for him to autograph and then took out their cellphones to take pictures.

"What's up, little fellas?" Rick asked. "What's going on?"

"We good, man," said the first little boy.

"Me too," said the littlest one. "Can you take a picture with me?"

"Are you back in the area to stay?" the first boy's father asked.

"No, I'm just visiting."

"Well, if you're here next Saturday, could you come by the boy's practice? That would really pump them up for their game the following week."

"Sure, I can do that, not a problem." He handed him his business card. "Call me with the location and time. I got to go now; my Pops is outside waiting for me."

"Your dad still picks you up?" the littlest one asked.

"Yeah," Rick said, shaking his head and laughing. "I'll see y'all at your practice next Saturday."

Just as he walked out the door, he spotted his father's black-on-black Escalade truck. He opened the back door on the passenger side, threw his luggage and carry-on on the back seat, and jumped in.

"Hey Ma and Pop," he said. "How are you?"

"Hey, son. We're fine."

"Sorry, I would have been here a little early, but some kids caught me coming through the airport."

"Yeah, whatever," Derickie said. "So what's going on that you're back in the area?"

"Can I get in the truck before you start with the interrogations? And why does it have to be that something is going on? Why can't I just come home?"

"You know exactly what I mean, smart ass; every time something is wrong or don't set right with you, you make your way back here."

"Whatever, Pops."

"Whatever, my ass."

"Derrick, if he wants to come home for whatever reason, it's not your business."

"Oh, so you on his side, woman? You lucky I love you and need you for my benefits; otherwise, you and your son would be walking home, hand in hand."

"Whatever, Derrick; just keep driving. So, Erick, why are you here?" *Aw, shit,* he thought, *when she goes from Rick or son to Erick, I know I better come up with a damn good answer.*

"First of all, Inspector Gadget, I got to meet with the Honorable Judge Browe to discuss a position as a judge with the DC courts."

"So did they select you for the job or what, man?"

"Yeah, I need to make a quick decision on that."

"Well, thank God to hear that and it's not anything else; it's something worthwhile, which means you'll be coming back to the area?"

"Maybe, Pops."

"You mean to tell me you flew your black ass all the way back here for a quick decision and a maybe; shit, you could have told him that on the phone."

"Ma, is Tony home?"

"He was when I talked with him earlier."

"Pops, drop me at Tony's. I'm staying there tonight."

"Say what? So what the hell you call me for? Why the hell didn't you call your own damn brother? What the hell do I look like to you, a damn cab driver?"

"You know, I don't know why I didn't call him, but since you're here, can you just drop me off there, please, old man?"

"See Cheryl, that's your smart-ass mama's baby boy. I should have taken his ass back to that damn hospital long time ago when I had the chance; he still got to get damn smart."

"Derickie, leave that man alone; either you going to take him or not."

He laughed and hit his father on the shoulder.

"Well, it takes one to know one, now, doesn't it?"

"See, babe, see what I mean?"

"Just drive, Derickie," Cheryl said. "You love it. So be quiet and leave my baby boy alone. So, Rick, how's Maria?"

"She's fine now," he said. "Kept saying she had a cold, but I know it wasn't a cold."

"Is she still working?"

"Yeah, I tried to tell her, in a nice way, that she doesn't have to work for me anymore and that I'll still pay her, but she wasn't buying it. I was doing all of my own cleaning and washing, all she had to do is cook. She got mad 'cause she thought I had hired someone else to come in. She wouldn't speak to me for a few days, until I left everything for her."

"Rick, that wasn't nice."

"I know, Ma, but what else was I supposed to do? She's no worse than you."

"What do you mean by that, Erick?"

"Ma, you know exactly what I mean; not a piece of harm is meant by that. I love you both."

"Son, if you move back home, is she coming with you?"

"I'm not sure, Pops. I think Maria is really sick. I wouldn't want her to travel just to take care of me. I can do it myself."

"Or your mother can do your place too."

"What you mean, 'my place too'? Whose place does she clean?"

"Your brother's, the other mama's boy."

"Ma, you clean Tony's house?"

"Yes, I have a few times, when Marisa was sick."

"Pops, sounds like to me you're a little jealous."

"You damn right I am," he said. "She's my woman; she ain't y'all's, and she ain't doing it no more, either. If you bring your ass home, you better hire a damn maid; she's not coming out to your place to clean."

"Well, how about I hire you, Inspector Gadget? That gives you all the time in the world to go through my stuff without any questions; you get to see firsthand what's up with me."

"You know, son, I might just take you up on that offer; how much you paying?"

"Nothing; you getting all my information for free. You think I'm paying you to go through my stuff?"

"Well, I ain't doing it."

"Okay, your loss," Rick replied.

Derickie pulled up to the house and parked; he and Cheryl hopped out and headed for the front door.

"Pops, I thought I asked you to take me to Tony's."

"And I thought I told you, you should have called him your damn self if you wanted to go over there, so get out my truck."

Rick rolled his eyes and shook his head. "Please don't let me be like this old man."

"Sorry," Cheryl said. "You will be old, crazy, and mean but still lovable."

"Ma, are you sure he's my father?"

"No," she said, laughing.

"We never got a blood test," Derickie said. "All I know, she went to the hospital for cramps and came home with you."

Rick laughed so hard, walking up the steps behind his father, still shaking his head.

"And you got to love him; Lord knows I do."

"Honey, what are you doing, warming up food for him?"

"Derickie, sit down; I got you some snacks. The man is probably hungry from his flight."

Derickie stood in the middle of the kitchen floor like a spoiled child who can't have his way.

"Well, he should have eaten on the plane."

She put arms around his waist. "Babe, you are still the love of my life; you will always be the first, and God knows my last and everything, so stop acting like a spoiled child and sit down."

She pushed him down in the chair, giving him a big kiss on the lips.

"Love you," she said.

Derickie sat in the chair, looking like Cheryl took his candy. Rick walked in the kitchen and saw his father sitting in the chair like a spoiled child with his arms folded.

"Oh, Ma, what did he do?"

She turned around and looked directly in his face. "And you better not pick with him, either; leave him alone."

"I didn't do anything to him," Rick objected. "I just walked in here. I was just wondering why he's sitting there with his arms folded and his lips poked out. So, Pops, what you do?"

"Erick, didn't I tell you to leave him alone?"

"Yeah, but I'm getting him before he gets me. So what did you do, Pops?"

Derickie swung a punch toward Rick's arm; he jumped back, smirking at his father.

"We had you, that's what I did, crumb snatcher."

Rick laughed even harder and asked, "Aren't you glad?"

Derickie laughed too. "Whatever, man," he said.

"Pops, can you take me tomorrow to pick up a car?"

"What time?"

"Whenever you ready, but don't take all day."

"Okay, boys," Cheryl said, "I'm going upstairs; can I leave you two alone for the night?"

"Yeah, I'm not going do nothing to him," they each said.

"When you two finish, clean up your mess," she added. "I'm not coming back down here to clean nothing up behind you two. My kitchen better be clean, meaning Derickie, wash the dishes."

"Wait," he said, pointing to his son, "what about him?"

"Good night, honey; you heard what I said."

"I'm not cleaning no dishes," he said. "You going to clean this kitchen like your mother told you."

"She said you, Pops; you did not hear her call my name."

Derickie hit him in the arm. "So why you really here, son; what's going on?"

"I told you, Pops."

"So you're not sure if you're going to take that job?"

"I don't know; from what JB says, it sounds good. It would be a new adventure in my life, and the pay is great, but I'm still deciding."

"You do know, son, that you still owe me; I want my money back from them school days. Sending you money every time I turned around. You needed new shoes, new this and that; damn, you were a begging ass."

"Pop, I give you enough money; you keep it up, and I'll reduce your allowance."

"Whatever, son; so who the hell is JB?"

"You know, he used to be my professor at Florida A&M."

"Oh yeah; I guess I have to confess: You been out in LA a long time. I guess I really did miss you, and I'm very proud of you too. I'm proud of all of you."

"Thanks, Pops, I appreciate you and Ma, and I'm proud of you two for doing an outstanding job with us. I couldn't ask for a better set of parents, even though you're not my father."

"Boy, if y'all wasn't my kids, I would've kicked her fat little ass, well, it was a skinny ass back then."

"Pops, you know I love you, man."

"I know, son; I love you too; you did well in your career, and it would be nice to have you back home, but if this is not where you really want to be, then don't do it. I'll just keep beating on Tony, but it would be nice if Niki came home more often. Sometimes, I think that boy hates me."

"Why you say that, Dad? He doesn't hate you; he may want to beat you sometimes, but hell, we all do. Maybe you should try stepping back and stop criticizing him."

"You haven't called me Dad in a long time," Derickie said; "that sounds so good to hear. So you think I need to step back?"

"Yes, just stop challenging him," he said. "Stop giving him orders as if he's a little boy again. Look, we all love you, and we will always be your children; you did your job and raised us to be upstanding citizens and to handle our business in life. Niki is not a child; he's a grown man. It's time you gave him that much more respect. He's my big brother, and I look up to him and Tony, but we are now grown men. He's doing his thing and is damn good at it, Pops. The man is a music producer; what's so wrong with that?"

"Yeah, I respect his career, and I know he's grown, but why we ain't as close, like me, you, and Tony?"

"We're not close to you; we just tolerate you. Remember, you're not our father."

"Whatever, boy; wash them dishes and clean this kitchen like your mother said."

Rick cleaned the kitchen as they continued to talk about some of his old cases, sports updates, people from the old neighborhood, and family members.

"Man, your grandmother is coming in town soon."

"Are you going see her?"

"I have no plans to; what would I say to her?"

"Come on, Pops, she's your mother."

"Okay, and she's your grandmother; what has she ever done for me or you all?"

"Pops, she gave us you."

"Okay, but she should have just killed me, considering the things she did to me and my brother. I can never forgive her; she let her boyfriends beat us, and she left us in places no children should have ever been. I would have rather died. I never shared this with any of you, but my life with her was hell."

The anger and pain in his eyes was very clear. "When we came here to the US, me and Ricky lived with Malory; we must have been about ten years old. Malory was maybe nineteen. She came back home and saw the bad things our mother had done to us, so she brought us back to the States with her. We couldn't get in school, so she home-schooled us. At the time, she didn't have papers on us, and we were not US citizens."

"Did you ever get citizenship, Pops?"

"Nope," he replied. "I'm not a citizen."

Rick looked astonished.

"Don't look at me like I'm crazy," he said. "I'm still here."

"But Pops, do you know you could be deported back to Jamaica, even though you been here all these years? You may not get to come back."

"I know, son, but we had to stay; we got educated. We weren't no dummies. We just couldn't get legitimate jobs and vote, which was fine with me, considering some of the presidents y'all had. But hell, I guess I can't really talk about them too much; the Jamaica's prime ministers were no saints. I worked odd jobs and hustled a lot in the streets, and I was good at what I did. We lived in the Jamaican community, so they looked out for one another. It was somewhat like being home, but in a safer environment with Malory.

"When I was sixteen, I met your mother and fell in love with her. Now don't get me wrong: I had other women, but none like her; your mother was special to me and for me only. I was mad crazy for her. I did everything to get her attention."

"Where you meet her at, considering she's not Jamaican?" Rick asked.

"I used to do some work for people on her block; at first, she used to look at me like I was crazy."

"Pop, you use the word 'crazy' a lot; are you crazy?"

"Rick, this why I said I should have given your ass away. Damn you, mess up a good thing."

They laughed.

"I'm just kidding; go ahead, man, but I'm telling you, if you hurt my mama, I'm going to get you here and now."

"Rick, if you hit me, I will kick your ass up in here."

"Pop go ahead with your crazy story; I already see me or Tony got to save you on one account already. Shit, you know what? I don't drink, but damn, this calls for some sweet, sweet tea."

"Yeah, and give me my beer."

"Would it be the Jamaican beer in here?"

"Rick, you know what? I really like Tony better than you; damn."

Derickie got up from the table and went in the family room and sat in his favorite chair, staring off with a face of shame.

"Pop, here's your beer, man. Whatever; it was not your fault. If you don't want to see your mother, it's okay."

"She's not my mother," he replied sadly. "She's just the lady who gave me life. That's all she gets from me. Boy, the things she did, I would never have done to my kids; that's why I was so protective of you all. When I got my chance to be with your mother, to marry her, I vowed I was going be faithful to her and have children with only her. No one was ever going to hurt my babies."

Tears rolled down his face, like a stream of water.

"No man or woman, husband or wife better not ever mistreat you all, and damn sure not my grandbabies, none of them. I don't care how old they are, or it's going to be some real trouble, and you know I don't give no damn warnings. I react on the spot."

Rick was speechless for the first time in his life with his father. All he could do was kiss the top of his father's head.

"We love you, Pops."

He sat on the couch across from his father, looking at TV, waiting on his father's next response, but nothing. They fell asleep, in silence.

"Babe, Derickie, y'all fell asleep down here?" Cheryl said the next morning. "Y'all must had a good conversation. I'm glad to see you didn't hurt each other."

"What time is it?" Rick asked.

"It's seven o'clock."

"I'm going upstairs," he said. "Sleeping on that couch was not good. I need to lay down for two hours, at least."

"Well, I'm getting ready to cook you two something to eat; do you feel like eating now?"

"No, I'm going to lay back down too," Derickie replied.

"Were you drinking?" she asked, knowing the answer.

"Drinking what? Rick got drunk off iced tea."

"And how many beers did you have?"

"Two or maybe three." He kissed her on the cheek. "See you in a few hours."

All right, Rick thought when he woke up again. *I feel rested now. Sleeping sitting up can take a toll on your neck. Pops had some very interesting stuff going on with him. I see we got to work on his damn citizenship. What the hell would we do if he was deported? Ma would pass out, but she'll be right by his side. I can only image her reaction; she doesn't curse, but I can hear her. When it comes to her husband, she can act like a crazed woman. Damn, how do I tell Tony? This is more in his field; Pops got to tell me some more. We need to talk with Aunt Malory, see if she has any records on them, but first I gotta call JB to let him know I'm in town.*

"JB, I'm in town," he said after getting his voicemail. "Give me a call back, let me know when you're available; my schedule is open."

Hopefully, he'll stretch this thing out to give me time to think about it, he thought after hanging up. *I haven't sat down yet to put any thought into this.*

"Maria, good morning," he said after calling back home. "Just checking on you. Are you okay?"

"Yes, why do you keep calling me? Take care of your business and make your decision on what you're going to do. I'm all right! Have you seen Karla yet?"

"No, not yet."

"Are you planning on seeing her?"

"Yes, Maria," he snapped. "What is with all the questions?"

"You called me with all the questions, so I'm asking you questions now; so are you planning on seeing her or not?"

"Yes, Maria."

"Good, then go see her and stop calling me; only call me if you got good news, that she's going to marry you. Other than that, I'll see you when you get back."

"Wait, Maria, have you seen Tina around there?"

"Now why would I be looking for that demon?"

"Okay, Maria, I just asked. I'll talk with you later. I was just checking."

"Okay, bye!"

All right, forget it, he thought. *Let me take a shower and get out of here. I need my car, even though I really don't have any plans for today. I need to catch up with Tony and the fellas later on; in the meantime, hit up Big Bro Niki. Maybe I'll take a trip up there while I'm on the East Coast and drag the damn illegal immigrant, smuggle his ass from state to state.*

Derickie knocked on the door and walked in, without waiting on any words.

"Son, what I said last night ..."

"Pops, what you said is fine by me, nothing changed with us; I don't look at you any differently than before. You're still my crazy old father.

"So are you going to take me to get a car or what, or do I need to call my damn brother? Make up your mind; I got things to do today. You can go or stay."

"Man, just hurry up," his father said. "Where you going, anyway?"

"Pops, stop with all these questions; do you want to ride or what?"

"Boy, don't make me ... where you want to get the rental car from?"

"Well, I guess at the airport, so when I fly out, I can turn it back in there."

"Okay, we can catch the train."

Rick laughed at him.

"You catch the train? Since when Pops?"

"Since today; your mother don't need to drive us out there."

"Well, she needs to drive us to the subway, right?"

"All right, let me get dressed, then we can head out to get the car."

"Okay, I'll get some coffee while I'm waiting on your slow butt."

Yeah, neither one of my phones rung at all last night or this morning, he thought. *Damn!* Then his phone rang.

"Hey babe," Tina said. "How are you?"

"Why you calling me?"

"Rick, you know I love you," she said. Let's hook up today and talk about it."

"Nope, I'm done," he growled. "There's nothing else to talk about, but I do have a question."

"What, babe? Anything."

"Why the fuck would you give your family and your girlfriend my damn work number?"

She was snickering her ass off on the other end.

"I didn't give them your numbers."

"Really, Tina? So my numbers just blew into their fucking hands."

"Babe, maybe they called your job."

"And again, how the hell do they know where I work? I guess that just fell in their hands too? Just stop calling me; it's over."

"Rick, it's not over until I say it's over."

"Who the fuck you think you are?"

"Who do you think you are that you can make a call for me about it being over? When I agree it's over, then it's over; until then, it's not over. I'm letting you have your space for now. I'll call you back later on."

Who the fuck she thinks she is? he thought. *It's over when she says; she got me all fucked up! Fuck her. Let me get the hell out of here.*

"Hey, Uncle Rick."

"Hey Nicole, babe; what's going on? Why are you here so early?"

"Today is my day off," his niece explained. "On my days off, I come over here and spend the day with Nana and Pops."

"So you come here to be worried to death by your granddad?"

"Something like that."

"Where's your daughter? How old is she now?" Rick asked.

"She's three and in school, and before you ask, her father is in her life, and we're still together."

"Hey okay, I'm not judging anybody," he said. "I got my own troubles."

"So what you doing home?"

"Girl, you been hanging around your grandfather too long; why I can't come home?"

"Yeah, well, but it's good to see you; how long are you going to be here?"

"Um, two or three weeks, depending on if your grandfather plucks my nerves."

"Uncle Rick, you leave my granddad alone."

"Tell him to leave me alone."

"Rick, you want to eat?" said Cheryl.

"No, but feed your husband over there," he said. "If he wants to hang with me, he needs to eat. I got time; I can wait."

"We can go now, man."

"Ma, go ahead and fix him something to eat; I'll eat with him."

"Nicole, what you have to do today, grandbaby?"

"Nothing, I'm here to chill with you and Nana."

"Good, you can take us to the airport. Rick needs to pick up a rental."

"Okay, sure I'll take you, but I got to move the car seat in the back seat."

"Wait a minute," Rick said. "You still got that small-ass car, right? Damn, this means I'm going to be cramped up, and we're going to look like two clowns getting out that little-ass car. If it was just me, I can do it, but us two in that little car, nope. Pop, can she drive your truck?"

"Hell yeah, she wasn't driving me in that little-ass car."

"Granddaddy, what's wrong with my car?"

"Nothing, babe, it's just enough for you and my little princess, but Granddad can't do that."

"Granddaddy, you're a mess."

"You can say that again, Nicole."

"Uh, Uncle Rick, you're not too far from behind him. I heard about your stories."

"Little girl, after you drop us off, you bring my truck back home and park it," Derickie said. "Don't be rolling around the city, wasting my gas."

"I know, Granddad," she said, laughing. "I'm not taking your truck anywhere. I don't feel like hearing your mouth later on."

"Oh, he gives it to you too?"

"Yeah," she said. "I love my granddad; what would I do without him?"

Nicole drove like a bat out of hell, like she was racing to put out a fire.

"Slow down, girl," Derickie said. "Shit, I want to get there in one piece. It's bad enough I'm hanging out with this knucklehead."

"Nicole, keep driving," Rick said; "you're doing fine. Pops, you should have gotten back here. then you wouldn't see your life flash before your eyes."

"What, is there a shortage out here on cars, and you got to compete to get one? Just slow down; we got time. We're in no hurry."

Nicole got them to the airport in twenty minutes flat, coming from Silver Spring, Maryland to Arlington, Virginia; Derickie was all shaken up.

"Remind me to never ask you to drive me nowhere no more, little girl."

"Why?" she asked, laughing. "You're the one that taught me how to drive."

"Yeah, shit, that was in my younger years. I'm old man now; my damn heart can't take it no more."

"Come on, old man; it's more to come."

"Rick, if you drive like she do … I'm serious. I'm going to slap the shit out of you."

"Okay, come on, man. Pops, did she scare you that bad?"

"Hell, yeah! Stop laughing, man; that shit ain't funny."

"Pop, I'm sorry, but if you could see your face."

"What? I look that damn scared?"

"Man, I never seen you look like that."

"Rick, she's never, ever driving me no damn more. You know, I'm getting old; there was a time I could take that fast driving shit. She must drive at the Indy 500."

"Pops, since you're all shaken up, sit here while I get the car."

"And you better come right back with a big enough vehicle. I'm too damn old, too tall, and too big for some little-ass car."

"All right, Pops; I'm coming back to get you."

"Don't play, now."

"Now, Dad, why would I leave you out here to worry the heck out of someone else? We keep our troubles with us; I'll be right back. Don't you have your phone?"

Shit, Rick thought as he headed to the rental desk, *he's making me wonder about him now; he talking about his heart. Do we need to get a nurse for him? I sure hope he isn't losing it, at least not yet. I need him around for some more years. God, not yet, please.*

After he picked up the rental truck, he walk back down to the terminal but didn't see his father sitting where he left him; he went into panic mood.

Aw, shit, he thought; *where is he?*

He walked back and forth, then he stopped, and as he pulled out his cellphone, Derickie came strolling out the bathroom.

"Man, don't do that anymore," Rick yelled.

"Do what?"

"Leave and don't say anything."

"I'm sorry," his father said. "I didn't know I had to ask for permission to pee. What the hell you all in a tizzy about, son?"

"Nothing," he said. "Come on, man."

They walked outside and jumped in the truck and took off, heading back toward the city.

"So, where're we going now, son?"

"I don't know; where you want to go, Pops?"

"I got nowhere in particular. I'm riding with you, I just want to hang out with you, get in your business. I ain't got nothing else to do. My babies don't come to the house until after school, so as long as I'm home when they get there."

"Pops, it's Saturday."

"Well, anyway, those my babies; you know, sometimes they all stay over on the weekends."

"Yeah, I heard."

"Your sisters bring the grandbabies over to stay with Granddad. They're my weekend dates. We watch movies, eat junk food, after your mother makes us eat dinner first, then we play board games, mostly learning games. They like it, even though a couple of them rascals try to cheat."

"That's good, Pops, got you some company; you sound excited when you talk about them."

"Yeah, y'all gone, so I got my other set of babies, and they act better than y'all; they listen."

"Yeah, that's because you can send them home."

"True; now tell me about this Tina chick."

"What's to tell you, Pops?"

"Erick don't play with me; remember, I'm a crazy old Jamaican man on the edge; I just had the ride of my life, so start talking."

He cut his eye at his father and smirked.

"Is this serious with her?"

"Um, no it's not serious."

"Then why the hell you bring her here to meet us?"

"Pop, I ask myself that all the time."

"Was the pussy that good to you? Was it because she's red?"

"Pop, I don't know why I brought her home, and no, it's not cause she's red."

"It must have been something; maybe you was considering her at one time. She's not a bad looking woman, but something about her I don't like; she's strange. She acts like she never been out in the world before; I've seen them kind one too many times.

"How in the hell did you meet her? Oh, wait a minute; let me ask: Did your dick speak first instead of your mouth? Boy, don't cut your eyes at me; shit, I know. I've seen it with my brother and so many others, and I'm a man too. I swear, sometimes you act just like your uncle in so many ways. He always had the craziest woman too, growing up."

"How do you know, Pops?"

"I heard the story of you and them little girls chasing your ass down; that shit followed you all to your adult life. Man, when you going to settled down? But now if she's crazy, you may want to rethink that one; she'll haunt your ass for the rest of your life."

"Yeah, she's strange."

"Strange, my ass; more like crazy. You always had them ones that created all that drama, fighting each other, cutting your tires, taking you to court. Damn, what's next? Which one is going to cut your dick off? Can you find one that's somewhat stable?"

"Pops, to tell you the truth, I was hooked on the sex."

"Shit, I know you were, son; she looks like she can turn some tricks."

"She really rocked Rick's world."

"Come on, man; at some point in life, everything is not always about sex. Was she a good person? Did y'all share some things in common? Could you make love to her mind without physically touching her? Did you talk about anything without having an argument about who was right? Could you trust her? Could you take her around your friends? You musta had some kind of feelings for her, if you stayed around that long and brought her home to meet us; that there says enough. 'Cause if I didn't care about some woman like that, I wouldn't dare bring her around anyone; she never would've met nobody, and it would have been solely a sex thing and nothing else. Now be honest with yourself, son: This is me you're talking to; what was it?"

"Pops, maybe I did have something for her at one time, for a brief minute. But every time I take her out, she acts a fool with the other women."

"But isn't she a lawyer too?"

"Yeah and the other men that was there, she started flirting with them while I'm standing there, not just talking and smiling, no. The kind of flirting, using her body, leaning up against them, rubbing her breasts on them while their wives were standing there too. I had to pull her ass off them. I was embarrassed. And God knows if I was talking to a female colleague, she rolled her eyes at the woman, making smart comments to her, and then she picked an argument with me in the damn place. Finally, I stopped taking her."

"Damn how many times did you take her before you got the picture?

"Maybe three."

"That's too damn many times. Woman got one time to show her ass, and it would have been over."

"Pops, it gets worse."

"Damn, there's more?"

"Pop, she went off on my doorman, cursed him out some kind of bad, and then she threatened Maria! They got into it verbally. Maria didn't like her the first time she saw her."

"Rick, I was done with her the day you called me from the car; she talked about my damn accent. Then you showed up here with her, she saw me, and her face turned red, looking at me like I was some trash."

"Did she?"

"Yeah, I gave that hussy a glass of wine in my good glass; I should have spit in it."

"Pops!"

"You know she left that glass sitting on the table, looking at me as if to say why did I give it to her. She didn't touch it either, and that bitch never drank it. I told your mother, and she brought her another glass; she took that one and drank it."

"Pops, why didn't you tell me?"

"She was your woman, and I didn't want to say anything, and then what really fucked me up was when my brother came over; she rolled her eyes at him. We heard her say some shit and blurted out, 'Hell, no! Fuckin' Jamaicans.' I wanted to slap her; no, not slap her: I wanted to punch that bitch in her face and throw her ass out my house. After my brother left, I went upstairs and stayed in the room."

"I thought you wasn't feeling well; at least that's what Ma said, so I didn't bother you. Pops, I'm so sorry. I didn't know any of that. I knew you didn't like her. I thought it was because she's a red woman."

"Rick, what else did the nut do?"

"Shit, you name it, and she may have done it."

"Man, when was enough, enough? Come on, man; I know pussy can get us in trouble, but damn. Just say no, especially when you see the signs."

"Yeah, and I had to get a restraining order on her too, just before I left."

"Damn, does she know that you're here?"

"No, at least I don't think so. Does she know about the job that you're going to take as the judge?"

"Nope."

"Well, did you end the relationship with the woman?"

"Yes, Pops, I did, but she called me this morning with some bull-shit, talking about it ain't over until she says it's over. I laughed and told her it's over and to stop calling me."

"You know what, son? This could get ugly. I'm telling you: She ain't leaving you."

"Pops, I'm not with her."

"Yes, you are, whether you want to believe it or not. You're in a relationship with her."

"You know what, Pops? I'm damn good at my job and was good in my football career. I got my own businesses and do well with it, but I can't seem to do well with women; why is that?"

"But that ain't got shit to do with it. Now the question is, do you love that woman?"

"Pops, what kind of question is that? Hell, no. Nowhere near loving her. All she does is cry about me always being at work, and I'm never around her and her family and friends, I don't like them."

"Son, you don't have to like her family and friends, just her. Uh, where're we going? We passed the house."

"We're heading toward the Beltway."

"I don't know; let's just ride around the Beltway and talk."

"Are you hungry or want something to drink?"

"Well, you know I can always take a beer."

"Pop, we're up here in Montgomery County. I seriously doubt if we find any Jamaican beer."

"No, I don't want no other kind of beer, so keep driving."

If I see his damn car out here, Tina thought as she approached his condo, *he's going be sorry. Where is he? Imma go up there and knock on that door. I should kick it in, and if that fuckin' Mexican gets in my way, I'm going fuck her up right quick, before he can save her little old ass.*

She headed toward the front entrance of his condo and saw several LAPD cars sitting out front.

Damn, she thought, *I know that motherfucka didn't call the police on me.*

She walked a few feet backwards to her car, turned around and ran.

I wonder if he been home all day? Let me check the hood of his car; that'll tell me. I just need to get in that garage to see if his hood is hot; if it's cold, then he been in all day, but I doubt that.

She jumped in her car and rode around to the back of the building and parked up the hill.

I know it's an exit back here, nobody uses that one. I checked that out myself awhile back; I got some workout clothes, sneakers, and a cap in my trunk.

She climbed over the wall like a ninja, ducking down between cars and making her way up to level three, to scan the garage.

Ah, there it is, she thought. *I wonder why he has the cover on it; as if I'm not going to know it's his car. I knew it. It's cold as ice; and his damn truck: Where is he? Shit, Rick Tyler. I told you this relationship is not over. Got damn; here come those damn red and blue lights flashing. Damn, somebody must've heard me for them to come up here: nosey people.*

She tried to take off running. but they caught her just as she turned.

"Ma'am, are you, all right?" said the police officer.

"Yes," she said. "Why?"

"Well, there's been some break-ins and robberies in this garage lately."

"Oh, I didn't know."

"Do you live here?"

"No, but my boyfriend does. I just stay here a lot."

"Okay, ma'am; you may want to be careful. The thieves haven't been caught yet."

"Okay; if I see anyone that looks suspicious, I'll be sure to call."

"Yes, please do. Have a good evening, and be careful out here by yourself."

Ah, break-ins, she thought after the police left; *thank you Officer Friendly; good idea. I think I might just need to break in. I'll come back, but not tonight. Mr. Tyler, I'm going to spare you this time, but if I don't see you moving these vehicles, then it's on. And it better not be no bitch up in there, or her ass is mine.*

She walked back down to the lower level of the garage along and climbed the wall.

"Well, well, well, Ms. Tina Black," she heard a voice say. "Or shall I say Diane Blunt."

"Who the fuck is you?"

"Don't worry about who I am. I know who you are."

I don't know this motherfucka; he said that shit before. His face not even ringing a bell.

"Sir, you got me confused with someone else," she replied. "My name is Tina Black."

"Yeah, okay, right, Ms. Black. Now what I could do is turn you over to the police or turn you in later; as you know, there is a restraining order on you."

"Excuse me, for what?"

"For coming within five hundred feet of Mr. Tyler's residence. I just saw you jump the wall from the garage, checking on his cars, and the sign on the wall big as day, says no trespassing or violators will be prosecuted. I would love nothing more than to see them lock your ass up, but I'm going to let you hang yourself, so my advice to you is don't bring your ass back around here again."

"You fuckin' bastard, get off my car," she snapped. "I can come around here if I want to."

"You're right, you can go anywhere you want, as long as it's not within five hundred feet of this building, meaning the whole building, which you just violated."

"Harold, or whoever the fuck you are, if you don't get your ass off of my car, you're going to wish you had."

"Is that a threat, Tina Black?"

"You damn right it's a threat."

He got off her car and walked into the middle of the street, while she got into her car and pulled out of the parking space as she rolled down the window.

"The next time, you won't be standing up if you come between me and my boyfriend."

"What boyfriend would that be, Diane?"

"You know who I'm talking about." She sped off like a wild woman.

"Yeah, okay, Diane," Harold said. "That broad is really crazy."

He walked back around the building, repeatedly looking over his shoulder.

I don't put nothing past that girl, he thought. *She destroyed my sista's life. She took her into that drug world and left her to die alone. She comes from a family of some true nuts. I don't know what Suga did to that one, but wow, she out there. I need to call Mr. Tyler, but I hate to be in the middle of all this. When all the shit hits the fan, I don't want to be called for no witness; they might start digging in my past. I been living a good clean life for a long time; I don't want no trouble. Plus, Rick Tyler is my friend; he looks out for me. I get the hookup with some tickets and passes to some of the best shows in the area; he's good people, but I know that dude still got that street mentality. He ain't nothing but a corporate hoodlum. He sure know how to handle his work business with them white folks, and them Jews love his ass. I know some of them brothers hate him; he a sharp dude, but he got some fucked up relationships. Forget it; I'll rest on it and see if she brings her crazy ass back.*

"So son, sounds like you were going have a shotgun wedding. I love you, man, but you do know I would not have been there. All hell would have broken loose."

"Pops, you would leave me out there like that?"

"Hell, yeah."

They both laughed so hard; Rick hit the accelerator again.

"Slow down, man."

"Yeah, Pops, I will admit I was caught up in the sex. I went to her job to end our sex thing, and she carried on. Pops, she called me gay, bisexual, and said I was fucking the doorman."

"Rick, please stop; you killing me. The shit is funny, but it ain't. What the hell is really going on? She sounds dangerous, and I'm serious. Watch yourself with her, seriously! I'm laughing, but I'm telling you: Shit not right in her head. It's a shame that men fall for the craziest women with all the drama, but we never want the good ones until the end. And when they let us in, we bring all our bullshit. Look here, son, if we can recognize the nonsense up front with our real head, then we need to let the sex thing go or stop it before it gets to that point."

"Yeah, but sometimes we don't know how."

"Son, you can't have all the pussy in the world, but try to get the one who's not going to give you all the drama. We all know relationships are not going to be perfect, but you're a grown-ass man now. This shit here is not looking good for you. Don't let fifty creep up and you still got this young dumb-ass single lifestyle. You know it's rolling up on your ass real soon."

"Wait, Pop, let me take this call."

"Hi, Mr. Tyler, this is Sabrina, calling you to let you know that some lady called here for you; she was very aggressive and demanding."

"What did she want?" he asked. "Did she say what her name was?"

"No, she just asked if you were in the office. I told her no but I couldn't say where you were, and she went off, said she needed information from you; she's a lawyer and needs to speak with you regarding a case. I told her I would get the information to you, if she left me her name and number."

"Did you recognize the number?

"No, it was blocked."

"All right," he said. "I think I know who that was; she can be a bit rough sometimes. Other than that, is everything good?"

"Yeah," Sabrina replied. "We're holding it down."

"Okay, cool; thanks. Give me a call if anything else comes up; if she calls back, put her on hold and call me."

"Will do; have fun. Talk with you later. Bye."

"Shit," he snapped after hanging up.

"So what happened now, son?"

"She's calling my job, harassing my assistant."

Derickie didn't say one word, he turned his head and looked out the window, whistling and shaking his head.

CHAPTER 5
KARLA
THURSDAY, JULY 3, 2008

Damn, she thought after hearing loud knocking on her door; *what now? Who in the heck is it? Alicia or Kareem is not here. I only know one fool that knocks on my door like that*

"Who is it?" she snapped.

"You know who it is."

"Yeah, I do now, but why can't you answer the question?"

"Why you putting me through all this of identification? You know it's me."

"Because I can."

Rick walked in and pecked her on her lips.

"What's up?" he asked. "How are you?"

"I'm good; what about you?"

"I'm much better now that you opened the damn door."

"What if I didn't open it? Were you going to feel bad?"

"No just disappointed you didn't let me in. Why is the music so damn loud? You having a secret party?"

"I might, 'cause I'm in my own house, minding my business."

"You expecting someone?" said Rick.

"If I was expecting someone, I wouldn't have let you in."

"Girl, you wouldn't dare leave me standing out there; if you did, I would have used my key."

"Whatever; you don't have no keys to here."

"Babe, where's Alicia and Kareem?"

"I have no idea," she said. "Why don't you call them? They weren't here, so I turned the music on and cooked me something to eat."

"Wait, wait, hold up; you did what?"

"You heard me. I cooked me something to eat."

"Shit, that's a surprise."

"Leave me alone," she growled as she returned to the sink to finish washing her dishes. "What the hell you come by here for, anyway? To worry me or to check up on me?"

"Yes and yes. I can't check up on you? And by the way, I got your flowers; thank you. They were pretty."

"Good, so what's going on with you? What are you in town for?"

"Nothing, just work: same old thing."

"Yeah, I bet."

"What the hell you mean by that? I know your ass; you got some smart shit behind it."

She threw a hand full of suds at him, and he jumped back out the way.

"You can sit down," she said. "I can hear you talking while I'm cleaning the kitchen."

"Nope, I'll stand. I'm good. I'm still shocked that you cooked."

"Why? I know how to cook."

"I never said you couldn't, babe. I don't know when the last time you cooked; all the times I've come by here, you ain't never cooking nothing. It's always Alicia cooking."

"Is this what you came over here for, to talk about me cooking?"

"No, but woman, I can go on you all day about this shit here; this is a special news break, and I need to send this to the *Washington Post*. Karla Owens cooked today."

They both fell out laughing.

"I'm not even going to ask what you cooked. I might just fall out."

"Rick, you're not funny."

"I know I'm not, but you are."

"So what are you really in town for? You got a date on the East Coast and you stopping through?"

"Nope, meeting with an old friend that's a judge."

"Why you shaking your head?" she asked. "You having a nervous problem today?"

"No, just had a thought about something."

"Oh, okay. So what he do? He wants you to represent him in court to get him out of some trouble?"

She reached around him to open the refrigerator, and her breast brushed against his arm.

"Oh, excuse me," she said.

"You're fine, but now if you do it again, I'm taking it as a sign that you want me."

"I'm just trying to get in my refrigerator."

"Then you should have said excuse me the first time; for the record, you already touched me several times, and the way I see it, if somebody touches you more than once, they are trying to tell you something."

"Man, you got it bad. I sure hope you don't ride the damn trains, freak! You would be in a world of trouble."

"Nah, it's only when you touch me that I'm a freak."

"Well, I'm sorry. I'm not trying to tell you anything; I thought I could squeeze by you. Sorry."

"So on a serious note, I was selected for this position as a judge at DC courts."

"Oh, wow. Rick, that's great. Derickie and Cheryl must be glad; what did they say?

"You know Pops; he always got some smart shit to say, but my mother is happy. In one way, it is cool, but I need to decide whether to take the job or not."

"So you flew out here, without any kind of decision."

"Yeah, and no, I kinda have a decision. I'm just waiting to see how it plays out before I finalize anything. I'm meeting him next week for dinner. So how about you go to dinner with us?"

"Uh, I don't know if that's such a good idea."

"Oh, you have to ask your boyfriend if you can go on a dinner date with an old friend?"

"First of all, I don't have a boyfriend, and second, I don't have to ask anyone for permission to do what I want to do."

"Okay, so I want you to go with me to dinner this week and next week; what's the problem?"

"I don't know; it depends on my schedule."

"You got a schedule doing what?"

"I still practice my martial arts, if you don't mind."

"Nope, not at all; just keep your days open and be ready."

"So tell me more about the job; why is it so hard to say yes or no? How hard is that?"

"It's not that easy to just up and move," Rick replied.

"Since when?" she asked. "You played on what, two football teams, and you had to pick up and move; what's the problem? You've traveled anywhere you wanted at any time; it's not like you have any small ones to move from school to school, or do you?"

"Yeah, true to the first part, but no, I don't have no small ones. But that shit gets old moving around and being single; it's no fun doing certain things by yourself anymore."

"Please, I'm quite sure the things you've done were not always by yourself."

"Okay, maybe not all of them were by myself."

"Yeah, I thought so," said Karla. "All this other crap about being by yourself; that was and is your choice."

"One thing about it: If it was my choice, thank you for accompanying me, because it was you that was always with me."

"But we're just friends," said Karla.

"Friends? Friends; well, we sure did a lot together to be just friends. Tell me who takes his friend to British Virgin Island and other places for weeks."

"Don't go there, Rick; you took other women to places."

"No, babe, never to our special location; it was somewhere else. We went for ten days or more."

"Is something really bothering you," she asked, "or are you unsure about something? Are you dying?"

"Hell, no; at least, I hope not."

"Ain't nobody pressing you to take the damn job, Rick; what's the problem?"

"You."

"What the hell do I have to do with you being a judge?"

"You know what, babe? If I do take this job, you'll be the first one I drag in my damn courtroom and charge your sassy ass with contempt of court."

"Yeah, well, you better have some bail money to get me out."

"Oh, no, babe; don't get it twisted. Your time wouldn't be in DC lockup; it'll be with me, by my side, for a lifetime. That would be your punishment."

"I doubt that; your woman wouldn't let that happen."

"What woman?"

"The one you got," said Karla.

"Babe, it would be none other than you."

"Yeah, right; I need a glass of wine on that one. Matter of fact, I need the whole damn bottle."

Just then, her cellphone started ringing.

"Your phone is ringing off the hook," Rick said. "Is that who you're expecting? I don't want to cause any friction; if that's your boyfriend, I'll leave when he comes. Psych. I changed my mind; if it's him, I'm staying until he gets here. Your friend can see me sitting here when he comes through that door; maybe I'll take my shoes and shirt off; that'll set him on fire."

"Rick, stop tripping; you already have a woman, maybe not Tina, but you got somebody, and furthermore, whoever said I told him about you? He don't know nothing of you."

"Oh, you don't tell your friends that you dating me?"

"I'm not dating you."

"Oh, but you been on trips with me and you slept with me in the same bed."

"Okay, Rick: Define 'slept with you.'"

"I just did: You slept in the same bed with me, and we made love."

"Okay, but I'd just say we had sex."

"Call it whatever you want, Karla Owens; I know we were in each other's inner mind and body; you were my lady during those times."

"Man, I was never your lady."

"Yeah, okay, well, I was almost your man."

"How did we get here? Let me get my phone; it just might be my male friend. Fooling with you; I missed my call."

"Good, I'm glad you did."

"That's not right, Mr. Tyler; do I detect some jealousy and a little unease?"

"Maybe a little jealousy, but never unease."

"Unfrown your face, Rick Tyler; hold on, just stay seated. You're such a trip."

"You know what, Ms. Owens? I really came here to make you my wife."

"Oh really? Well, what if I told you I plan on getting married to someone else, like my man friend?"

"You can't marry him, babe."

"Why not? Now you're finished running women, and now I can be your wife? Wow, picture that shit; after all these years, there's nobody else, and your ass is getting old, so now come marry little old me. Damn, I should feel flattered. What the hell?"

"Babe, it's none of that; never. I always wanted you."

"I should slap you in your damn face right now."

"Why would you want to slap me? I'm asking you a question. I need to know; I'm serious. This has nothing to do with no other women or that I'm getting older. I always wanted you. I really hope you're not marrying him. I will break that shit up, so neither one of us will be married."

"That's just mean," she said. "Why would you do that? Don't you want to see me happy?"

"Yeah, I want to see you happy: with me."

"But you had all the time in the world to ask me, and you didn't."

"You don't think I wanted to ask you so many times, but I had to be somewhat respectful, since you were dating whatever his name is. But you were with me; now you picture that shit."

"So weren't you dating Tina?"

"I was not dating Tina; we were sex partners, and I ended that. Yes, it was wrong on so many levels."

"Whatever; if that was the case, why did you stay in LA and I came back to DC? Now that you're up for a job in DC, all of a sudden, I'm good enough? You are fuckin' kidding me. What the hell is that?"

"Babe, you were always good enough for me. I wanted you with me for many years."

"But you continued to stay with Tina. Was I supposed to stop my relationship for a fuckin' maybe?"

"Look, okay," Rick replied. "We were both wrong."

"True; if it was just for sex and if you felt about me like you say you do, then why didn't you end it a long time ago?"

"Karla, would you have ended your relationship?"

"Yes."

"So do you still love me, like I still love you?" Rick asked.

"What? Are you serious?" Karla replied.

"Yes, I am serious as hell."

She closed her eyes and sipped slowly, shaking her knees.

I feel like cutting his ass into pieces, she thought. *This motherfucka is serious. If he would have asked me a long time ago, I would have said yes, but now, hell no. And yes, I do want someone to really love me and spend the rest of our lives together, but I wasn't thinking of him. I wasn't expecting any of this from him. Why now? After I've raised three children by myself, all the hard jobs running back and forth with children, football, basketball, cheerleading, work, and doctor appointments, while he was in LA doing his thing. I should kick the fucking shit out of him. Ugh!*

"Well, Rick, I really don't know what to say about that now; you really caught me off guard. I'm not sure how I feel about you."

"Let me understand this clearly: You traveled with me, we made love, or fucked, or had sex, whatever you want to call it, and you don't know how you feel about me?"

"Don't raise your voice at me," Karla replied. "Rick, you taking that the wrong way. I don't hate you, at least not anymore. I have much love for you, but I don't think I'm in love with you anymore. I would be devastated if something was to happen to you, but I don't know about being married to you."

The hurt in his eyes showed more than the pain in his heart; he leaned over and kissed her on her lips, pulling her close into him. He pulled her into him and thrust his tongue down her throat and kissed her so passionately he felt his dick rising, as if it was going to bust the zipper off his pants.

"Rick, stop; let's not do this."

"Why not? I just want to kiss you on your lips."

"That wasn't a kiss on the lips."

"I know, but your lips are so sweet, and I thought it was a forgiveness signal. I know you want me as much as I want you. I know your body is throbbing for me; you want me inside of you just as much as I want to be inside of you. I felt your heat."

He kissed her on her neck, nibbled on her ear, softly kissed up and down the back of her ear, whispering, "I know you too well. I know you're burning inside. I want to taste you and get deep down inside of you and feel all of you."

Her nipples were hard as raisins; her heart was pounding, and her body heat was flaring. She couldn't resist his touch. She was so close into him, she was a part of him.

"I know you want me mentally and physically, but you just won't give in to me emotionally. I'm not going to stop trying. Babe, I want you to come with me, whether I go back to LA or stay here; wherever I go, I want you with me in my life."

She didn't say a word; she just let him lead her to her room. His six-foot, four-inch body towered over her, weighing in at least 210 pounds, cut into a lean piece of fine, expensive meat, and chocolate as a Hershey candy bar. He undressed her slowly, lifted her up, and sucked her breasts and softly bit her nipples; she moaned, with her legs wrapped around his waist, kissing him from his neck to his lips. He then laid her down slowly, kissing all over her body as she slowly unbuttoned his shirt, taking it off his shoulder, kissing his chest.

He pushed her legs open as wide as he could and then licked her and sucked her inside out, tracing her outer pussy. He nibbled on her clit until she hollered, then stuck his tongue inside of her until she came like a flowing river, as he moaned with satisfaction and pleasure.

He gently pushed her back, and she rolled over and unzipped his pants, pulling them off along with his underwear. She straddled him and kissed him the same way, nibbling on him and rubbing her body against his.

"Babe, I love you," said Rick.

Karla didn't say anything; she continued to kiss and lick, allowing his dick to flop in her mouth, licking him like a cream pop. She then slid up and down on his body like a snake, with her breasts gliding up his legs to his chest, kissing him until her nipples pressed deep into his chest. She finally rested her hips across his dick; he entered her and watched her movement as tears rolled from her eyes.

He rubbed her ass and her back, lifting her up and down slowly on him, moaning and whining uncontrollably. She rode him like a black stallion, rocking on him back and forth while he sucked her breast until she was soaking wet again. He then flipped her over like she was a piece of paper and entered her from the back; all you could hear were screams of satisfaction from them both.

"Stop," Karla finally cried. "This is not good."

"No, I'm not stopping," he said. "You're going to understand we don't have sex; we make love, and I love you, and I have been in love with you for so long."

He gyrated his hips back and forth, in and out of her, pushing his hips deeper into her, licking and biting her back, up to her neck.

"Rick, please stop."

He slowed his motion, stroking her slowly until they both reach their climax again and fell back to the bed. He lay on his side, still inside of her, holding her against him, until he slipped out.

"Babe, did I hurt you?"

"No."

"You know, if you wanted me to, you could have said something long time ago, as well. I'm sorry I didn't ask you then; I should have asked you anyway. My life in LA was not that great, if you really want to know. You don't know how many nights I sat up, thinking about you. I'm sorry things didn't go as we planned. I can't change that, but I can sure as hell make up for that time, if you give me the chance.

You can have all of me, mentally, physically, emotionally, as well as spiritually; you can have all of my money, but in return, I want you. I want to have the glory and the stars that twinkle at us at night and the sun that shines on us in the morning and the moon that we dream on together. I want us to share all of that. I want you."

"I don't mean to laugh, but damn, you sound like you were about to start singing."

"I know, it did sound like that, but seriously, babe, I am going to stop here because I feel like I'm begging you. I'm going to leave it alone for now. I'll just let it play out."

"Damn, you talk about my phone," she said, laughing again. "Your phone vibrating like that."

"Babe, this Tina; please call me. I'm sorry for what happened. I went by your place and did what you told me to do; where are you? Babe, please call me. I need you; please, babe."

"Wow, and that's over?" Karla snapped. "You said you ended that relationship."

"Yeah, babe, it's over; I'm serious."

Karla laughed in disgrace at herself for believing him; she got out of her bed and went straight to the bathroom.

"Well, you might want to call little Ms. Pumpkin Pie back, cause it ain't over. This the shit I'm talking about; I was just lying there, thinking about how this was going to play out, and sure enough, my thoughts exactly. Every time you come to town, we do just like I said: fuck, and yes, even on our excursions, we fucked. Now I would have been a fuckin' fool to give in to your bullshit."

"We didn't just fuck," he said. "We just made love."

"No, you made love. I fucked, and it was great, but now I'm going to take a shower, and you need to leave, so you can make your call at your damn place or wherever the fuck you're staying. So get the hell out my house and do what you need to do."

He jumped out the bed, standing naked in the middle of her floor. "I ain't going nowhere."

"Rick, don't make me call your cousin to come get your ass out my house."

"So you want me to leave because my phone rang."

She walked back in the room and stood in his face.

"Rick, do not play on my intelligence. I don't give a damn about your phone ringing, but you just sat downstairs, claiming, 'Oh, I'm so serious; it was just a fuck thing. It's over.' Really? 'Cause that didn't sound like it was just a fuck thing; that shit is a relationship, and you're not finished with her. That's probably where you should be … in LA with her. I don't want to play your game anymore. I'm out. I'm done with you. Today was our last fuck."

"Babe, it's the truth; let me tell you."

"Rick, I don't care what happened. I don't want to hear it. You came over here with this bullshit-ass story, I'm so lonely, and I want a family. Well, you got one in LA, waiting on your ass to get back. With all the damn women you had, you telling me not one of them from the West Coast was worthy to marry? I'm sorry that didn't happen for you, but I got a family. I might not have a husband, but I got children and your son too. Get the fuck outta here."

"I don't have a family in LA," he said. "My family is here in DC; don't you know I wanted a family with you?"

"You didn't want shit with me. Blab blab blab, bullshit. I'm cool now with the things that didn't happen as planned. I got over that. You know you almost had me again, but fuck you. I don't care what happens and hope you fuckin' get VD or some shit. I don't care; leave me the hell alone."

She pulled away from him and slapped him so hard.

"Fuck you," she repeated, stomping into the bathroom and turning the shower on. He picked his clothes up off the bench and got dressed, and his phone rang again.

"Yeah?"

"Hey, babe, it's me, Tina; we need to talk. I'm sorry; I was just having a moment. You been acting so strange, and I'm on edge; where are you? I came by your place, Maria said you were not home."

"That's right, I'm not."

"Well, where are you? I can come wherever you are so we can talk; let's straighten this thing out. I love you, and I'm in love with you."

"Look, let me call you later.

"Karla, let's talk about this," Rick said as she came out of the bathroom.

"No, we don't have to talk about nothing; the person you need to talk with is on that phone, which you didn't hang up."

She was screaming so loud through the phone:

"You son of a bitch, you must be in DC! I'm catching the next flight out. Who the fuck is she, and why are you with her? I knew you was cheating. I'm coming to see who she is."

He finally hung up on her.

"I'm sorry, Karla," he said; "this not what you think. I did not come over here with the intent to make love to you."

"No, we had sex," Karla replied. "Get it right."

"What the fuck ever. It just happened." "So I kissed you, but you didn't resist either, now did you?"

"If that wasn't your intent, Rick, why did you pursue it?"

"Because I wanted you, babe."

"So you think having sex with me was going to make me change my mind?"

"No."

But his devilish mind was saying yes. He had to catch himself; he almost smiled.

"Look, you need to leave now; your business here is finished. We are done."

He felt like she just donkey-kicked him right in his chest with that remark, but he took the blow.

"Go to your parents' house or somewhere, so when Ms. Tina gets here with her drama, you need to be there to greet her and not here."

"Tell you what," Rick said angrily, "call Derickie for me; have him come get me. I'm going downstairs. I'll be downstairs watching your TV to calm down from not wanting to grab your ass for slapping me that damn hard, then I'll leave … maybe."

"What the hell you mean, maybe?" Karla replied.

"Like I said, maybe!"

She lucky I truly love her, slapping me that damn hard, he thought.

Is she crazy? Then telling me I need to leave; she must be out her fuckin' mind. I thought her ass was taking a shower. I don't hear no damn water running. I should go up there and get in, just for the hell of it. Naw, that might not be good; she might really start hitting me, then I have to restrain her ass.

Forget that shower, she thought. *I'll take one when his ass leaves.*

"Rick, I don't hear you leaving," she called down. "I don't hear the door opening and closing behind you. What's taking you so long?"

"Yeah, well, I don't hear you taking no shower, either. I'm not leaving, so what you going to do, call the police?"

"I might."

"Well, if you do like I said, call Derickie. I've been trying to reach him anyway."

"Look, Rick, you know I'm not calling the police. I don't want to hinder your sorry ass from getting your job as the judge. That wouldn't be a pretty scene, and I don't want to be the reason for you not getting it, so just leave."

"Babe, go take your shower; leave me alone. I'm not going anywhere yet."

She flung herself across her bed.

Ugh, this bitch, she thought.

She turned on the TV without intending to fall asleep. After a while, he went back upstairs, took his clothes off, and got in the bed with her, pushing himself up against her.

"Why are you still here?" she asked, shaking and punching him in his chest. "Rick, it's time for you to leave."

"Babe, leave me alone. I'm sleep."

"You fucker, you ain't sleeping."

"Yes, I am, and you love me; you can't stay away. You keep coming back to me, and if you hit me again, I'm hitting your ass back."

She hit him again and again; he turned the other way to keep the peace and laughed softly to himself.

Why doesn't he just leave me alone, she thought angrily. *Why does he keep coming back to me?*

"Babe, babe, I know you're not sleep," he said. "If you were sleep, your ass would be snoring. I hear you crying. What do you want? You keep touching me; just lay your butt over there and leave me alone and get your story together for Tina, cause the way it sounds to me, she's coming here looking for your ass. It seems to me you got some explaining to do, and you need to get that story in place."

"Babe, I'm sorry that you feel that way," he replied. "Everything I told you is the truth. I really do love you."

"You don't love me; you love her, and since you're the lawyer, you know how to do it: work it out with her, bro, and leave me alone."

He wanted to laugh at the way she said it, but he also knew Tina would be at his parents' house first thing in the morning, waking them up with this shit.

"All right, babe, I'm going to leave you alone for now. We'll talk later."

He kissed her on her shoulder, lay his head on the corner of her pillow, and went to sleep.

"Thank God it's morning," she said after waking up. "You can leave now."

"Good morning to you too, babe; you were snoring."

"So what? My house, my bed; I can do that."

"Damn, you still mad?"

"Yeah, and I'm still waiting for you to leave."

"When I feel like it, I will."

She threw the blanket back and jumped up out the bed, heading for the bathroom.

"Why, Lord, why is this man doing this to me?"

"Lord, for the same reason she's doing it to me."

"Rick, I'm not playing with you; seriously, what time are you leaving? I can't look at you anymore."

"When I am ready; we really need to talk about last night,"

"No, dude; we talked last night. What else is there to say?"

"No, we didn't, you fussed and carried on. I never got a chance to explain; you tried to throw me out, and that's why I'm still here."

"What is it that you have to say that wasn't said last night? Say what you need to say and leave, but please don't tell me no more bullshit. I can't take it."

"As soon as you give me a toothbrush, so I can get all in your face; where are your extra ones? I know you got some, so don't play with me."

"Like you don't know where they are. Could you please move so I can leave out? I don't want to see you brush your damn teeth."

"Nope; wait until I finish."

He blocked her in the bathroom, knowing she couldn't move him; he stood there looking at himself, taking his sweet time doing everything, while she sat on the side of the tub, looking down at the floor.

"What the hell you doing?" she snapped. "You should be finished; keep checking yourself out in the mirror. No worries; I didn't leave any marks on you. You're okay; it's safe."

"You should have," he said, laughing. "I would love to see your love marks on me; that would make my day. I left some on your back, your neck, your ass, and one big one, all over you."

"Got damn," she growled. "Shit, I agree with Derickie: He should have given your ass away; your black self is out of control."

"Babe, this black man is crazy in love with you, and if Derickie had given me away, then I wouldn't have met you and fallen in love with you."

"Shit, that would have been fine by me."

He leaned down her and tried to kiss her, but she pushed him back out of her face.

"Get away from me, creep. I don't see anything funny."

"No, it's not funny, babe, but your remarks are funny. I'm leaving."

"Good, hurry up."

"Why you going back to bed? You want some more?"

"Hell, no. I'm waiting on you to get dressed so I can lock my door."

He snickered.

"Okay, look, babe. I'm sorry: sorry for what I did in the past, present, and one for the future. I should've asked you to marry me a long time ago, but I didn't. Truthfully, I didn't think you wanted me to. You might have said no, and my heart would have been broken; our time together was going so well, I didn't want to take that chance. I guess it was just like you said: It was a sex thing. But admit it: We both enjoyed each other, so was I wrong for wanting it to be more than just a sex thing? Am I wrong for still being in love with you?"

"Yes," Karla replied.

"Okay, fine; if that's how you feel, then I'll take that. It's just a fuck thing from here on out then. And as far as Tina, I did end that relationship before coming here."

"Wait," she snapped, "so you just ended your relationship like when? Boy, I tell you: You're too got damn funny. Do you seriously think that woman is going to let you go, just like that? You just ended it right before coming here? Yeah, right."

"Karla, I've been here for a couple of weeks; why you making it seem like I just ended it a week ago?"

"You know damn well you don't end a relationship in a week's time; I told you don't come with no bullshit, and what the hell is this bullshit? You must be fuckin' smokin' drugs, 'cause you're crazy as shit. What makes you think because you said it's over, then it's over? Oh, I'm sorry, you're Erick Tyler.

"Babe, stop fooling your damn self," she continued. "That takes time to heal, but you here in DC in my damn bed, and she calling you, begging your black ass to call her, and you think she's going for that."

"First of all," he replied, "I never said it was a week ago. I said I ended the relationship before coming out here, so that was already done."

"If I was her, I would slap your face when I see you. For real, I should be cutting or stabbing your ass up right about now. I should pull my sword out and slice your ass up."

"Karla, if you pull that damn sword out, we will most definitely be done, because I would kick your ass."

"I doubt that," she replied.

"Well, I tell you what," he said. "We would be tearing some shit up in here, if you think I'm going to let you do that shit on me."

She leaned over the side of the bed, holding onto his arm, looking under her bed for her sword.

"Karla, I'm telling you: I'd hate to throw your little ass around up against these walls, at least not like that."

"Shut up," she snapped. "I'm not reaching for that. I was checking to make sure it's still there, just in case I really do need it."

"Whatever; you better leave that damn sword under this bed. I'd hate to smack that ass."

"I should go around to the house just to see her slap the mess out of you," she said. "I want to know what's going to happen to you."

"Ain't nothing going to happen to me," he said, "and she's not going to slap me, either. I can tell you that much."

"Yeah, Erick, I really want to see how this one is going play out for you, but what if she asks who I am?"

"What if she does?" Rick replied.

"Then what you going to tell her, player?"

"Look, I'm not going through this with you. I already told you: I'm not lying. You don't want me; you said it was about sex, so fuck it. You said as of today, this is it; we're nothing, and we not having sex anymore. I'm done, just like you are."

"Mr. Tyler, you only control your feelings; you can't control mine. You refuse to see the whole picture of this situation."

"Maybe I don't, Karla; please share the picture."

"Rick, so far you hurt three people's hearts in less than twenty-four hours."

"Who are the three people I hurt?" Rick asked.

"Me, Tina, and yourself. Why you acting like you don't know? It's always about what you want. You cut one person loose to pick up another person. Fuck the other person's feelings, like Tina, because you're Rick Tyler. You really need to stop and think about it, seriously. If I did that to you, you would be hurt; try putting yourself in our shoes. If you had asked me a year ago to marry you, I would have dropped whoever I was seeing to marry you. I did love you because of our past relationship; we share love for our children, but as of today, I gained more pain than anger. I can't give you all my love, and you're still sharing your love with someone else; that's not happening."

"Hold up," he interrupted. "So you tell me, Ms. Owens, how you not going have love for me, but you were seeing someone else too, and you trying to attack me on relationships status."

"And I said to you last night: Do you think I'm giving up my thing for you, but whether I'm in a relationship or not, I didn't bring him into anything."

"What if he comes over here this morning? What you going tell him then? I want to hear it."

"I doubt that."

"Okay, babe. That relationship wasn't for me. I really do understand what you're saying, and yeah, I would be hurt if it was me. I will say in the last year, I almost settled for her, since I couldn't have you, but I didn't want to be with her. I just liked the sex. She's not my soulmate, and we didn't have nothing in common but the sex."

"Well, they say opposites attract," Karla replied.

"And babe, we definitely were opposites. Listen, I really did come over here to talk to you; it was not my intent for us to make love. But let me ask you: All the times we were together, what was it for you? Was it just something for you to do, or because your man didn't take you places?"

"Uh, Rick, don't go there. I could've gone many places with him and not you, and yeah, it was about the sex with you. I kept it at that level. You were a great lover, and with the sound of things, you are a great lover to Tina. You don't need me in your life. You'll heal, and I hope you can handle that and move on."

"Well, know this, Karla Owens: He can't love you like I can, or could have; he never will match up to me with you."

"Maybe or maybe not, Mr. Tyler, but it's your loss. Rick, what if you were my man, and I was creeping with another man; how would you feel?"

"Fuck the bullshit about what if. You wouldn't have time to creep with another man; your interests would be with me, and I would make sure of that."

"Rick, it's not about sex."

"I didn't say it was, Karla. I'm interested in you in more ways than sex. Your thoughts wouldn't be on any other man; so that shit you just said, I don't want to hear. Just know this: I got your mind, your heart, and I had your body, without a doubt, so if you go to that bamma, then so be it. I know where I stand in your heart."

"I swear you give good words," she said, "but some bad action; hurry up and get out. I'm sleepy. Your chick is probably out this morning, looking all over DC for you. You need to find her and handle your business."

"Why the hell I need to find her?" he asked. "I didn't invite her here."

"No, but you said yourself, she'll be here. If you weren't that into her, as you said, and she wasn't for you, then tell me why the hell the relationship has been going on for so damn long? If it was me, at some point, I would cut it off, just for the sake of peace."

"Babe, come on. I thought you were getting dressed to go with me," said Rick.

"Don't change the subject. I'm not going nowhere with you. I'm not messing with you and Tina; she sounds too damn crazy, screaming like a mad woman. I ain't mad at her that your ass is cheating, but because you lied."

"Yeah, she's a little crazy!"

"No more than you," she said. "You stayed with her, so she couldn't have been that crazy. Now hurry up and get out; I need my sleep."

"Why are you going back to sleep? Are you pregnant?"

"Yeah," she snapped, "and it's not yours."

"Um, well, I enjoyed your pregnant ass," he replied. "That was hotter than hot, and I hope it comes out looking just like me, to remind your ass of everything about me. So tell that man of yours his pregnant woman got some hot sex and ask if I can have some more, before you have the baby."

"Get out, Rick! We talked but not much changed. I still feel the same way; it's almost noon, and you haven't made it around to your parents' house yet."

"Who said I was going there?"

"Wherever you or she goes, VA or DC, just not here."

"She don't know nothing about my place in Virginia."

"Whatever, but I'm sure she is here by now, and I'm sure she knows where your parents live, right?"

"Yeah, she knows."

"Oh, she's not your woman, but you brought her to DC to meet your family; um, I would think you would only do that if you were really in a serious relationship, not somebody you're just having sex with. Man, you are not funny! I know one thing: If Derickie is home, she'll get a nice warm welcome."

Just then, Rick's phone rang again.

"Oh, see? Your woman is calling you now."

She threw his phone at his head, and he caught it just in time.

"You didn't have to throw it at my head."

"Listen, Rick, you're a very intelligent man. You understand very well; you just don't want to. You don't need my advice, but why don't you handle what you have going on now, before you try moving to someone else? You've held me up long enough; get out of here with your foolishness."

"Okay, I'm leaving this time, but the next time, I won't."

"I know, so you need to stop," she said. "How long is this saga going to go on with you?"

"As long as you want to, babe."

He pulled her off the bed by her robe so quickly, she didn't have a chance to react. He thrust his tongue down her throat and rubbed his body up against her. He untied her robe and threw it to the floor, pushing her back down onto the bed, straddling his body on hers as he took off his clothes.

"Rick, get off me."

"Nope," he said. "Call the police. I told you before, I'm sorry, and I'm not here to hurt you by any means."

He smiled real hard, showing his pearly whites.

"Whether you like it not, I'm coming back to you."

"And it's not a guarantee I'll be here for you," Karla replied.

"I'll take my chance on that. And for the record, we will not be having this bullshit pillow talk anymore, after today. I'm leaving now; my business is finished here for now. You can tell Mark I left marks of my own on you."

He was smiling his ass off, putting his clothes back on.

"You know you just raped me."

"No, I didn't," he replied. "You didn't say no."

"And I didn't say yes either."

"Yeah, but you didn't try to stop me, either, now did you?"

"You're really an ass."

"I know, babe; that's what you always say when you're mad at me."

"You know, I do hate you. Hurry up and get out of my damn house."

"I'm leaving. I need to get out of here anyway; oh, and call Derickie for me. Tell him to hit me later; that's if you still want to call the police to come for me. I don't know what you're going tell them, but call me later so we can be on the same page for our story. As an attorney, I can keep you out of trouble."

"Take your ass out."

He grabbed his phone and ran down the steps, pulling his wallet out of his pocket. He threw some money on the couch and then walked out the door.

"You want to come down and lock the door?" he called back.

"Just close it," she snapped. "I'm coming. Just get out."

Should I say fuck her and move on, he thought, *or do I try a little harder? Fuck it; not a problem. Um, who's that bamma, just sitting in the car, staring over here? I wonder if that's her friend Mark. He probably saw me coming out her house. Oh well, if he did, so what? She says she don't want me anyway; that's her problem. A shower would've been good, but I got to go around here first.*

Shit, Karla said to herself as she looked out the window, *what the hell is he doing here? He didn't call me to ask if he could come over. Damn! I'm sure he saw Rick leaving my house, and I know that fool saw him sitting in the car; knowing him, he took his sweet time, so he could get a good look at him.*

She ran around her room, picking clothes up off the floor and pulling the sheets off the bed, throwing them in hamper in the closet.

Got damn it, she thought. *Ugh! Why? I don't like no shit like this!*

"Oh, my God," she yelled when she came out of the bathroom and saw Mark standing there. "What the hell you doing in here? You scared the shit out of me; how you get in here?"

"Your front door was open," Mark said, "so I came on in."

"What? You can't just walk into someone's house without permission; you should've rung the bell and waited. I don't care if my door was open."

"Well, I knocked, Karla. Sorry, I thought it was okay. And who the hell you talking about, he gets on your nerves? I heard you in the shower fussing; who you talking about?"

"I was just talking out loud about something I saw on TV; let's get back to you."

"Look, I knocked on the door," he said. "I saw your car outside and thought something was wrong. I looked in the window; I went back to my car to call you, and when you didn't answer, I checked the door again, and it was unlocked. Did you see the news last night?"

"No, what the hell the news from last night have to do with you walking in my damn house? What happened?"

"There was a big shootout around here last night, and they were running up in people's houses; a couple of people got killed from them busting in their houses."

"Oh, so what made you think I was one of them people? My door is still on the hinges, right? And when you pulled up and saw my door was not kicked in, you should have known then; if something did happen, I do believe the yellow crime scene tape would've been wrapped around my porch, and the police would've been outside, right?"

"Maybe," Mark replied, "but they could've come through the back door."

She was standing there with her towel wrapped around her, looking at him with her face twisted.

"Dang, Karla," he said, looking around, "your room looks so fresh and clean."

"What? My bed is made up, that's it, and how you know what my room looks like when you never been in here?"

She grabbed her robe and walked back in the bathroom; when she saw the other toothbrush in the holder, she snatched it out and put it in her pocket.

"Mark, sit right there," she said. "I'll be right back; I'm running downstairs."

I know he didn't throw money on my damn couch, she thought when she saw the bills he left on the sofa, *like I'm his private whore.*

She picked up the money and the mail off the floor and ran back upstairs, placing the money between the mail.

"So how come you came here, Mark?" she asked.

He stood up and reached out for her.

"Hmm, sweetie, since you in your robe, let's say we get it on."

He began kissing her and stroking her body.

"Uh, no. I don't feel like it, plus I just came on my cycles."

"Really? Then why you don't have no panties on?"

She pulled some clothes out of her drawers and went back in the bathroom.

"Damn, cause I got a tampon on, and I'm putting some on now, thank you."

"Karla, how long does it takes to put on clothes," he called after a few minutes. "What are you doing in there? Do I need to come in there?"

"I'm coming out; listen, I have some things to do today. It's nice to know you were concerned about me, but I have to take my mother and grandmother out on some errands."

"Can't we do it together? I want to spend the day with you."

"Uh, I'm sorry, but when I talked with you yesterday, you didn't say that you wanted to hang out, so I made plans."

"I didn't think I had to put in a twenty-four-hour request to hang out with you," he complained. "Now all of sudden I have to request your time?"

She strolled out the bathroom and flopped down on her bench, trying to give him her attention when the phone rang.

"Hey, Karla," Cheryl said. "How are you, girl? I'm going to make this quick: Is my son around there?"

"No, why you ask?"

"His friend flew in from California this morning, and she's here looking for him, and it's ugly."

She stood up and walked out of the room, trying to be discreet as she answered her questions.

"So what do you want me to do?"

"What's wrong, sweetie?" Mark asked.

She waved her hand at him to be quiet.

"Is that your friend?" Cheryl asked.

"Yeah."

"Where is he? He need his butt here; this is not good at all. Derickie is acting like a fool in here, hollering and fussing, and I don't want to hear this mess. It's not his business."

"I don't know, but I have got to take my mother and grandmother to the store anyway. I'll call you later on; let's talk then."

"Okay, Karla; if he comes back there, tell him to get his butt around here now, but don't you come with him. Bye."

"Honey, what's wrong? Is everything okay? Who you talking to?"

"A friend, Mark. I need to meet her 'cause she's having a problem and needs my help."

"Oh, but you can go be with her at the last minute and change your plans, but you can't make time for me? What's that about?"

"Look, I think you better go," she snapped. "No, I know you better go. I spared your ass after coming in my house like you did. I said I got something to do."

She led him down the downstairs to the front door and escorted him out.

"Yeah, okay, he said. "Not a problem. I'll let it go this time, but you owe me."

He kissed her on her cheek.

"I'll call you later, then."

Rick finally came strolling through the front door of his parents' house; he saw his mother standing in the doorway of the dining room, smiling and stretching her arms out to him.

"Hey, son," she said. "Come give your mother a hug. Your woman is sitting in there on the couch; why is she in my house?"

He looked in the door and saw Tina, sitting like she was the first lady of a church, with her hand folded and legs crossed.

"Look, you're a grown man, but this here is not happening; your father already told me a little of it in between him fussing and cussing, and I know you, so handle this mess somewhere else before your father hurts somebody."

"Tina, let's go now," Rick snapped. "Get up."

"Where're we going, babe?" she asked sweetly. "I just got here; let's stay awhile and visit your parents."

"No," he said, pulling her up, "let's take a ride."

"You're getting the hell out my house," Derickie growled. "Take that shit somewhere else, Rick, and Tina, nothing better not happen to my damn son, or I'm coming after your ass."

"Pops, sit down, man; it's okay. I got this."

"Boy, then why she here? I told you don't bring that bitch back to my damn house."

"Pops, I didn't bring her to your house! She flew in on her own!" He turned to Tina and asked, "When did you get here, and what the hell you come for? I told you it was over before I left; what part are you not getting?"

"I got here not too long ago," she said. "Derickie let me in."

"Hold up, lady," Derickie said. "For the record, my name is Mr. Tyler, or Mr. Derrick to you; I only let people I like call me Derickie.

"Son, I know you not a youngster anymore, but if you don't get her out my house, this shit going to be very ugly. Somebody is going to be embarrassed. How you want it?"

"Derickie," Cheryl said.

"What?"

"Come in here and stay out of it."

"Cheryl, I'm not coming in there. I'm not having his bullshit mess at my damn house. If it ain't him, it's the other fool! Take that shit and keep it at your house. Just tell me the damn story later. Get the hell out of my house with this shit!"

"Really, Pops?"

"Rick, take her ass out of here."

Rick grabbed Tina by the arm; she tried to take his hand, but he snatched it back and pushed her toward the door. Derickie was walking behind him, poking him in the back and mumbling.

"What, Pops?"

"Your shit is getting raggedly as hell," he said. "Soon as you finish with her ass, bring yourself back here; we need to talk."

"Pops, I'm not a little boy or as you say a youngster. I think I can handle this."

Derickie fell out laughing, waving his hands in the air.

"Boy, please. That woman is crazy. I told you that before, and I'm telling you: You can't handle that one. You ain't got this one, trust me, son. She's like a pig. To get rid of her, you got to kill her like a pig; you got to shoot them in the middle of their forehead or crack them with a shovel as hard as you can. Now you better end this one before she kills you. Tina, since you got your hand on my doorknob, you can open it and go outside, or I gonna throw your skanky ass out."

"I got this, Pops," Rick said, walking out and slamming the door.

"Derickie, did you have to act like that?" Cheryl asked.

"Yes, I did," he said. "She don't just show her ass up at our house for him; take that shit to his place."

"I don't think she knows about his place in Virginia."

"Well, I tell you what, Cheryl: If this shit keeps up, she soon will know; fuck with me, and I'll give her ass the complete mailing address and phone number, and she can ship her ass there. His ass don't live here. I'm putting a fuckin' sticker on him: 'Return to sender.'"

"Derrick, you should be ashamed of yourself."

"Well, I'm not," he snapped. "I'm going upstairs; they get on my damn nerves. I swear I'll be glad when he finds a got damn wife, one that ain't crazy. Acting like a wild fuckin' dog; he should've had all the damn pussy in the world by now, but no, he got to get one last one, which happens to be a fuckin' crazy woman. Got damn, those sons of yours."

"Look here, Tina," Rick said outside, "I told you this relationship is over; it's been over. Why you trying to drag this on?"

"It's not over," she replied. "I can change, and I said I was sorry. I love you."

"Tina, seriously, stop doing this to you and me; all you doing is making matters worse."

"I am not, and why are you here? Who's that woman you were talking to? Is she your girlfriend?"

"Why I'm here is none of your business, neither is who I was talking to. Our relationship was solely sexual, and that's it; it's over."

"If it was just sexual, why you bring me out here to meet your damn family?"

She repeatedly punched him in his chest, like she was beating on a drum.

"I know you love me; say you do."

He slapped her hands so hard she nearly fell to the ground.

"I told you before," he growled, "don't put your hands on me."

She tried to slap him in his face, but he blocked her hand and pushed her back again.

"If you ever try that shit again, I will forget you're supposed to be a lady and fuck you up. Don't you dare make no damn scene out here and start that got damn screaming and crying. We can end this on a good note, be cordial to one another in passing in the courthouse. Other than that, you don't need to say shit to me."

He started walking up the street away from her; she took off running behind him.

"You better grab your suitcase."

"You're not going to carry it for me?"

"Nope. I didn't bring it out the door, nor did I carry it from the airport, so however you got it here is the same way you're taking it back, you got it?"

She went back to get her suitcase and dragged it toward the car; just then, she realized people were watching from their porches, and she started screaming and crying out loud.

"You can be so rude, Rick Tyler."

He stopped in his tracks and yanked her by her arm.

"I told you don't start that shit."

He opened the car door, pushed her inside, and threw her suitcase on her lap.

"I should punch you in your motherfuckin' head," he said.

"You ain't going to do shit to me," she warned. "I wish you would put your hands on me; my brothers will be out here to kick your ass."

"Girl, you know nothing about me, so let's keep it that away. I know you can't beat my ass, nor can your brothers, so don't you ever think you can."

"Where are we going?" she asked as he got into the car.

"I know where I'm going: I'm taking your ass back to the airport."

"You're so wrong," she cried. "This is not right; how could you do this to me? I know you hear me talking to you; why you doing this to me?"

"Doing this to you?" he snapped. "You're doing it to yourself. I moved on; it's you. It was over then, and it's still over. We're never having sex again, so call the airlines now and get your ass on the next flight out of here."

"You know what, you motherfucka?" she growled. "You bastard, you don't need to take me to the airport. I can get there myself."

"That's good," he said, "but only one thing: There's no cabs running up and down this street; you have to walk a couple of blocks for the bus, so at least I can take you to the airport. Or I can put you in a motherfuckin' cab, or you can catch the damn bus, so pick one now. I don't give a shit what your ass does. This is some insane shit."

"Who you calling insane?" Tina replied.

"I didn't call you insane, girl, but now if you want me to call your ass insane, then you got that. What airport did you fly into?"

"I think it was BWI or Ronald Reagan; I'm not sure."

"Uh-huh, you think."

"Why do you care?" Tina replied.

"Because I'm not riding all over the damn city with you. How about this: I take you to Ronald Reagan Washington National Airport."

"I thought we could make it work and I would hang out here with you for a while, and then we can fly back together."

"Nope, that won't be happening," he said. "I'm not entertaining you today, tomorrow, or any other day. I'm taking you to the airport; if that's the wrong one, they got a shuttle bus to take you to the right one. If you choose to stay here, you on your own. I can't make you get on that plane; you're free to do whatever you want to here, but I'm dropping you off at National Airport. Don't go back to my parents' house, do you understand? You already saw how my father carried on, and trust me, the next time, he will not be this gentle."

"Why's your father so mean to me, anyway?"

"Okay, Tina," he said, ignoring her question as they approached the airport, "you're here; this chapter is closed for good and forever. It's done. I wish you well in your life; good luck with your new love, now get the fuck out my truck."

"I'm getting out," she said. "I got it then, and I got it now."

She leaned over to grab his crotch, and he slapped her hand away.

"I just thought if you saw me one more time, you might change your mind."

"Tina, don't touch me," he said.

"Why not?" she asked. "Isn't that your weakness? You might give in, like the first night I met you."

"Girl, please: I told you before, I've had my dick sucked more times than I care to count; trust me, babe: Your sucking and licking ain't no damn different."

"So why did you give in that first night?"

"Damn good question. I guess because you were free and fun."

"Well, damn, you could at least help me out and with my bags."

"I didn't help you bring them," he snapped. "I told you that; you got it. Somebody inside will help you."

He sat in the truck, watching her walk through the double doors.

I know she's probably not going to get on that flight, he thought, *but hell, I can't worry about her ass. I got other shit to worry about. Damn, I might have to lay low at home a day or so. In the meantime, Imma turn this truck in and get another one; she probably got the tag number; let me take my ass to Amtrak.*

Fuck, he thought as he drove to the train station. *I can't take this job; it'll be a fuckin' heartache. If I stay in LA, that'll be a fuckin' nightmare. Got damn! All for pussy! Shit.*

He drove all the way back to DC with no music, thinking. *Damn, she did have a good question: Why did I give in? The only thing I came up with was she was looking hot that night, and I wanted to fuck her, but I fucked up. I let it go on too long. Damn. Oh, well, it happened. I got to live with that mistake. Shit, you win some and lose some, and so far, I'm losing this one.*

He took the D Street exit and went to Union Station; he pulled into the garage and went down to the rental cars.

"Afternoon, sir; how can I help you?" the attendant asked.

"I need to trade this truck in for another truck, now."

"Sir, we can't just take your vehicle like that," he said. "You need to go upstairs and make the transition."

"Okay," Rick said, "not a problem, but I need to know if you have any trucks ready to go before I do all that."

"Sir, you need to go upstairs."

"Man, I got that; I just want to know before I go up those stairs. Can you tell me, since you work down here with the damn cars, if you have any trucks ready to go? Otherwise, I'll go to someone else."

"Like I said, man: You need to go upstairs."

"Man, I'm not doing all that running back and forth," Rick said. "You telling me you can't pluck your damn finger on that damn keyboard to see if you have any trucks available? What the hell do you do, just sit here looking crazy?"

"I could look for you, but now I won't."

"Man, not you too. I know you don't give a damn about my day, but in the next few minutes, this shit is going be ugly. You can look on that got damn computer now or call your manager if you're not going to do your job."

"I'm not checking nothing for you," the attendant snapped. "You come up in here like you all that. Man, fuck you! I know who you are, you that bitch-ass nigga."

Rick swung and hit the guy in his face; out of nowhere, the manager jumped in between them.

"Oh, my God," he said, "it's Rick Tyler. Sir, I got this. Ellsworth, step back."

"Imma bust that nigga in his head, Mr. Wiggins," Ellsworth said, "punching me in the face."

"Ellsworth?" Rick said, laughing. "With a name like that, I'd be mad too, little punk."

"Fuck you, nigga; you the punk."

"Ellsworth, calm down," Wiggins, the manager, said. "What happened?"

"He brought his ass in here like he's running shit, talking 'bout he need a truck now. I told him he need to go upstairs."

"And you did, punk, and I asked you to look in the system first to see if you had any trucks available, ready to go, now."

"Mr. Wiggins, that's the damn cop that locked me up last week for nothing."

Rick stepped back and wanted to laugh.

"Man, I couldn't have locked your ass up two week ago," he said. "I wasn't here two weeks ago."

"Oh, now what? You got a lack of memory? You fuckin' DC cops all alike. Think you can do whatever you want."

"Ellsworth, that wasn't me," Rick said. "That was my cousin. He's a cop, but now if you come across my courtroom, I'll be the one that will lock your ass up for a long time, 'cause I'm the new judge in town."

Ellsworth's mouth dropped, and so did Wiggins's.

"Oh, shit!" said Ellsworth.

Wiggins kept apologizing, but Ellsworth kept saying, "He still a bitch nigga."

"You know what, little man?" Rick said. "I could file charges on you and have your ass locked up for sure, but I'm going spare your dumb ass, since I was a little wrong. Mr. Wiggins, you may want to sign him up for some customer training classes. And write his ass up and maybe suspend him for a few days, and let's see if he likes those missing pay days. He's going to mess around and have this company in court for his stupid attitude.

"Ellsworth, you get yourself some anger management and get yourself in an educational program, and when you finish, get back with me, and I won't file charges against you for slander or sue this company. In the meantime, I still need a truck."

"Sir, we have a truck available," Wiggins said. "It will be ready shortly, give me ten minutes."

"Thank you; should I go upstairs now?"

"No, Mr. Tyler, no need to go upstairs. I'll take care of it here."

"Man, my bad," said Ellsworth.

"That's all you got, is 'your bad'? Look, I apologize for coming in here the way I did, but you need to be professional and respectful; don't let nobody take you out of your character on your job."

"So you're Rick Tyler, the football player, and that other dude is your cousin?"

"Yeah, but fine time to ask."

"Damn, man, can I get your autograph?"

"I'll give you one you'll never forget, for calling me a bitch nigga. You should be here when I bring this back; if not, here's my personal card. If you get in any more trouble, call me. I might can help you out, punk. You better not give my number out, or Imma give you another autograph you won't forget."

After Wiggins finished the paperwork and they brought his new truck down, Rick gave the manager and Ellsworth that brotherly love hug and rolled out.

I'm going home first, he thought as he drove his new rental truck away. *I ain't going back uptown fooling with Pops now. I'm getting me some rest and relaxation. I might go out tonight, and besides, if I go up there, he might get a hit upside his damn head for acting like a fool. I swear I wanted to punch his ass.* Just then his cellphone rang. *Got damn, who the hell is this now? This better not be Pops with his mouth; all I want to do is go home.*

"Yeah?"

"Man, what the fuck is going on with you?" It was his brother Tony. "Pop just called me, fussing; you know he told me all about it. So she showed up at the house; was you there?"

"Man, hell, no!"

"Where were you? Oh, let me guess: over Karla's? That explains why I haven't heard back from you. Damn, you got one chasing you, and the other one fighting you off. What the hell, is she still here?"

"Man, I don't know," Rick said. "I just dropped her ass off at the airport. I saw her go through the door, but that don't mean she got on that damn plane."

"Lil' Bro, do you think she's going to hang around for a while?"

"Hell, yeah, at least for a couple days or so."

"So what you going to do later on?" Tony asked.

"Man, I got to some moves to make, and I need to meet with JB this week coming."

"You need a chaperone?"

"Fuck you, Tony; but wait a minute, that don't sound too bad."

"Hold up! Now, if you want me to chaperone your ass, nigga want a fee; my services ain't free."

Tony was laughing so hard he was almost crying.

"Never mind, then. I'll take my chances on being stalked."

"You can always call Derickie."

"Shit, which one, big or little? Neither one is going to be a perfect fit."

"Man, you right. Pops be cursing, and she might get a punch or slap, and then he'll be locked up, but with fuckin' with cousin Derickie, he'll be trying to fuck her. He'll say some crazy shit that she might fall for, like they normally do: 'Come be with me, babe'; he'll lay his accent on her and feed her more bullshit lines, and the damn woman be in a bed with him."

"That's the truth, but Tony, she don't like Jamaican men."

"What? Man, you kidding?"

"Naw. I'm not so sure Derickie would stand a chance."

"Don't she know that's what you are?"

"Yeah, she do!"

"Um, wow, and you dealt with her that long? Why?" said Tony. "Anyway, where you coming from?"

"Coming from Amtrak," he said, "and I just got another truck and got into with this little dude name Ellsworth, giving me all kinds of attitude."

"Man, this not going good for you at all today, is it?"

"Hell, no."

"What happened down there?" Tony asked.

"He called me a bitch-ass nigga."

Tony hollered, "What? What you do, Rick?"

"I punched him in his face, only to find out he thought I was Derickie."

"Aw, shit; man, I'm glad it's you this time and not me. I think I would've kicked his ass. I'm so tired of people mistaking me for that fool. I don't look nothing like him, as much as you do."

"Tony, if I come back on this end, I see this is going to be some shit; it was okay when we were young, but as adults, hell no! I got enough of my own shit."

"Yeah, you do, man. Are you heading home now?"

"Yeah, I'm going in to VA."

"But seriously, man, you sure you'll be okay by yourself? You know that stalking shit is serious."

"I'm good."

"All right, I'll be home; if you come over, bring my babysitting money, nigga. Talk with you later."

I feel dirty and stinky, he thought after hanging up. *I made love all night and this morning, been in three mental fights, one almost a physical fight; damn, what a day. Tina, you can get yourself around if you want, just don't be in my space.*

Damn, he thought after he arrived at his house in Virginia. *I came here to take care of one small piece of business, and it's turning into a freakin' disaster. Karla is mad as hell at me, but it wasn't my fault; she took it out of context. We could've continued on with today, but no. Forget it; I ain't going out this door, until I meet with JB, and I'm not making no calls. I'm keeping my ass in here, laying low.*

Damn it if I don't feel like a crazy woman, Karla thought recalling Mark popping inside without knocking, *running back and forth through my own house, checking shit before leaving my own damn house. This is about to be O-V-E-R; I see where this is going. I'm not even keeping him for a playtoy. Him and that got damn Rick Tyler, with their shit; if I added up each one of their lists, I think Rick just might win, but he don't care. he just do it and pay the price later, like now. I been fucked two times in less than twenty-four hours, by one fool man. I must say it was great, almost better than before, but damn.*

She slammed the door shut and skipped down the steps, switching off across the street like she was on Hollywood Boulevard before getting in her car and heading out.

Ugh, sweet Mark, she continued thinking, *you're a nice piece of eye candy. I could've trained you, but you messed that up. Um, that first day I met you, over at Pentagon City Mall in the Swarovski store; you were so sweet. I was checking out a pair of those Charlie sunglasses that was calling my name and saw you coming through the door; you spoke and I spoke. Oh, boy, that cologne he had on was a breathtaker. He was well groomed, almost like an Almond Joy, then he commented on the glasses. "I like the look of those glasses on you," he said. "Very sexy, you are." Now what girl don't want hear that? I should have stopped right there. But no, I tried to act like I was deaf, but considering I already spoke, I had to finish out the conversation, and then I walked away.*

She pulled up to a light and looked over at the next car, which had two women in it; she shouted over to them, "Ladies, good looks draw us in every damn time, don't they?"

"They sure do, and we always fall for it!" said one of them.

They all laughed and pulled off.

And that damn cashier had to stopped me before I could get out the store to say, "Ma'am, that gentleman you were talking to asked me to give you this; this is so cute." I felt like it was the prince that found Cinderella. I opened the gift box and read the note; it was sweet and cute: "Those glasses were hot, like you! I hope to see you again or hear from you soon. If not, at least I'll be able to pick you out of a crowd with those sexy glasses." He left his number on the note; I figured I'd keep the glasses and at least call him to thank him; that was the right thing to do.

She looked at herself in the mirror and smiled.

And I'm wearing the hell out of them now, she thought. *Even Mr. Tyler liked my glasses, asking me where I got them from; none of his damn business, and of course he was in his feelings for a minute, until I burped the bamma on his back so he would stop crying. It's a got damn shame, crying-ass men; if I thought about it today, I would've put my sunglasses on, just for the hell of it. Anyway, let me call Cheryl to see what she wanted.*

"Hey Derickie," she said. "Is your wife there?"

"No, troublemaker!"

"Excuse me? What did I do?"

"I know he was with you last night, girl."

"What makes you so sure he was with me?"

"Don't lie to me; he told me he was going to see you, and he didn't come back around here until this afternoon sometime, with the same clothes on."

"And I'm the troublemaker, why? Because he had on the same clothes from yesterday? Look, I was just calling to see where your wife is. I don't have nothing to do with Rick and his girlfriend or whatever; that's between them two."

"You know, I'll be glad when you two work out your differences; at least be friends without benefits, that might resolve some of the drama with him."

"I did nothing; don't drag me in on his mess."

"Well, you know what, Karla? You are in it whether you want to or not, because it always reflects back to you."

"Derickie, I'm going to assume Cheryl isn't home, so I guess I can say goodbye. I'm hanging up. Bye."

That Derickie, she thought. *You gotta love him. But got damn, you don't what will roll off his tongue. He don't give a darn whose feelings he hurt; you got to be a strong person and get used to him; otherwise, your feelings will be crushed.*

She pulled up in her sister Sherri's driveway, got out, and banged on the door.

"Ri, open this door, girl; it's hot out here. I know you're in there."

"You can stand to be a little darker," Ri said, "and why you calling my name all loud? You need to seek some help."

"I will only if you can you join me. I got a two-for-one deal coming up."

They hugged and kissed each other on the cheek. "What's going on with you?"

"Girl, where you want me to start?"

"Do I need a cocktail for this story?" Ri replied.

"Yeah, make it two. I just got off the phone with that Derickie, and I tell you, that man is a beast when he gets mad."

"Derickie is a beast when he ain't mad; what he do? Please share."

"Derickie is pissed with Rick."

"Girl, what Rick do now? Is he still chasing women? They drive his ass crazy."

"Yeah, and still chasing me, driving me crazy."

"Girl, please; you allow it. You fall into him every time, so what's new?"

"No, Ri. I had enough this time; seriously, he's too much."

"Sis, you say that all the time, but somehow you manage to be back in his arms again. Where was the last trip y'all went to? British Virgin Islands. And before that? Come on, Karla; who you fooling? Nobody but yourself."

"No, Ri! We just friends."

"Karla, if you tell me that friend shit one more time, I'm throwing your ass out. Don't no friends take elaborate trips like that; he wines and dines you. I know damn well he got to be more than just a friend. Come on. You know and I know; who in their right mind is going to do all that and not have some type of feelings for a person? I'm not talking about just going to the West Coast; these were trips outside the USA. Girl, come on; be for real. Let me call my old boyfriends; see if they take me on trips like that more than one time. Some feeling is going to flicker."

"Whatever, Ri."

"Whatever, my ass, Karla. I know you; if you didn't have feelings for him, you would not be spending time with him. What about that guy Mark? Is he still around?"

"Got damn, Sherri; is this Twenty Questions?"

"Yeah, hussy. I'm waiting for an answer."

"Anyway, Rick's girlfriend came in town today; she went to Derickie and Cheryl's house. I guess some shit kicked off, and Derickie is blaming me."

"Let me guess: He was with you last night."

Tears formed up in her eyes.

"Yeah, telling me his bullshit story, that their relationship is over, and that he ended it before he got here. I still don't know for sure if or how long ago. I don't know what to believe."

"Wow, sis. But you say you just friends; see what I mean about feelings? That must have been a mind-blower. Look, if you want to stay here for a few hours and weep, I understand. Ain't no need to pretend it doesn't hurt and it does. I know you trying to be strong; just let it out. Go lay across my bed; I'll join you in a little bit."

She lay across the bed for the rest of the day, balled up like a fetus, with all kinds of thoughts racing through her head.

Why do I feel like I just been played and used up in his bullshit?

she asked herself. *Why is my heart aching? Maybe I haven't had enough; maybe I'm just a glutton for his punishment, acting like I don't know my place in his life. I know I'm second fiddle to his other women.*

"Okay, Karla," Ri said after a while, "get out of his second bullshit lane; you've been hit too many times, and I know it's not feeling too good. Move over and give me a pillow."

"I miss you, Ri," she said, "coming out here, lying in your bed, listening to you give me lectures about nothing, trying on your clothes that you made, and paying you no attention. I wonder what happened?"

"Don't know, Karla. I guess we grew apart for a while, but it's okay. You're older now; you don't need me anymore. I got my family, and you got yours, but at the end, we still got each other."

"You know, Ri, when I was pulling up, it felt like I was a runaway and was creeping back home; it felt funny coming back here."

"Girl, you're always welcome back home anytime, but not anytime of the night: I got enough of own my two running back and forth all hours of the night."

"Well, what's the cutoff time for me to be in?"

"Girl, before midnight!" Ri replied.

"Well, shit, I might as well stay out like them, but thanks for the curfew."

"So what you going to do now? But before you fill me in, let me update you on Matthew: He's still overseas. His tour ends in a month or so; he'll be home in six months, with plans to retire."

"Good," Karla replied. "Billy-Bob be coming home, still talking much more smack again. I miss that fool."

"Yeah, me too!"

"Sherri, you think he's been faithful to you?"

"Well, my situation is a little different from yours. I can only go with what my heart says. I never wanted to put that thought in my head. Once you plant that seed, then it sticks, but all I can say is that I've been faithful to my husband. If he hasn't been faithful to me, time will tell. Now you, on the other hand, have a choice to walk away;

you're not married to Rick, but you do need to stop leading him on and cut your sexual relationship with him if you're not for real. Now tell me about that other one."

"I got to end this relationship with Mark, like real soon."

"Why, what he do? Oh, he don't measure up to Rick?" said Ri. "He seems like a nice guy, at least of what you said, even though you never brought him around. I wonder why."

"Yeah, well, I haven't been around myself; he's a nice one, but just not for me, and girl, the sex is awful. He ain't got two out of three."

"What the hell is two out of three? I never heard that one before; is this some new shit you made up?"

"One: He can't fuck; two: he can't eat pussy; and three: he has no damn romance."

"So he's nothing that excites you?" Ri replied.

"Correct; he's nice but kind of creepy and insecure too; he needs a needy woman that needs him, and I'm not that one."

"Is he caring?" said Ri.

"Sort of, but I think it's nosier than caring."

"Okay, sis; well, tell me 'bout this morning."

"Ugh, Rick really needs a reality check; he been over in LA with the rich folks a tad bit too long."

"Karla, what's that got to do with it?"

"I don't know, Ri; it just sounds good to say. He can dish the shit but he can't take it; we went toe-to-toe this morning."

"Oh, so he really was with you?"

"Yeah, I never said he wasn't. He showed up at my house last night, uninvited, so we talked for a while; everything was going good, and then it happened."

"What happened, Karla?"

"He reached over and kissed me, and it went from there."

"Oh shit."

"Yeah, Sherri, oh shit. I told myself after the last trip, I was not dealing with him anymore, but he keeps coming back."

"Okay, well, but you did; so what happened this morning?"

"The girlfriend called; it was ugly."

"Girl, stop playing; what time did this happen that she got here so damn fast?"

"I don't know; she must've caught a red eye, or maybe was already here; who knows? At least I don't."

"I don't mean to laugh so hard, but when did he end the relationship again?"

"Girl, I'm still not sure; he said before he came here, and I'm not sure how long he was here. I just saw him last night."

"Imma ask this question again: How do you feel about him, truthfully? Either you're going to be with him or not."

"Sherri, I'm fighting myself for being in love with him. I love everything about him, physically and emotionally. We talk, we laugh, and we play, and our communication is great; he is caring, but he's not understanding to certain things, and he's a damn good lover. He got all three points, but he also got bullshit. I don't know what the hell the truth is."

"Did you ever believe him on anything?"

"Sometimes," Karla replied.

"So what, you think he's a liar? He never lied to you before? He never told you certain things, but he didn't lie to you?"

"I think we all lie, to a point, but I think we both are struggling with our feelings about a relationship that neither one of us wants to be in."

"There could be some truth to that. I think you both need to put closure to the relationships that you're in, and not deal with each other until you know yourselves again. Then you both will have clear minds and hearts, hopefully."

"I know; I told him that this morning."

"What did he say?"

"He didn't say anything; he just looked at me crazy."

"Um, well, what about you?" Ri asked. "When you are going to end yours?"

"I don't know."

"See, this is what I'm saying: Neither one of you wants to let the other person go; if you don't like the guy, then let him go. End the damn thing. It's not like you're married to him."

"But when I end mine, it's not to be with Rick. I'm just ending it."

"You sound crazy now; I never said you had to be with him. You know what, baby sister? I love you to death, but I'll be damned if you going to drive me crazy with this. I think you want to be with him, but you are scared."

"Scared of what?"

"I don't know of what, but considering you been out the damn country with him and everywhere else, you just need to give in to his ass. You need to decide. I can't help you on your feelings."

"Why you mad at me?" said Karla.

"I'm not mad at you. I'm disappointed that you two still going through this after all these years; either you're in or you're out. Damn, this is stupid: You creeping around with him like you married to someone, but it's your damn lover, and nobody cares. Look, Karla: That man did nothing wrong; he offered you a bite, and you took the offer. You're the one who keeps going back, and I'm sure he didn't set out for his phone to ring with her on the other end. Maybe he thought he hung up and he didn't; it was a stupid mistake on his end. Now, yes, it was wrong of him, but you went along with it. You were in control of the whole night and morning, so if you're mad at anybody, be mad at yourself."

"What, you're taking up for him?" Karla replied.

"No, and I'm not taking your side, either. I like Rick, always have, and yes, he got some shit with him, but you do too. So you're just as guilty as he is. All I'm saying is today's relationships are crazy. Nobody wants to be faithful anymore; if you're in love with that person, then stay there; it's no need to look for someone that'll cause you pain. What I'm saying is, you two are hurting the other person, as well as yourself.

"Look I'm not ragging on you or anybody," Ri continued, "because my husband is a million miles away. I'm just saying, if he don't want me anymore or I don't want him, we got to be strong and deal with the hand we dealt. There's no need to lead each other on. All of that was not necessary; you're acting like a spoiled child. That shit was stupid but funny as hell."

"Maybe I should not have taken those trips and gifts."

“Uh, it’s too late for a maybe,” Ri replied. “It’s done.”

“Oh, and this morning, he left me some money on my couch.”

“What? How much?”

“I don’t know; I put it in my draw. I never counted it. I do know it was over a couple hundred dollars.”

“Girl, give him his money back; this what I’m talking about: Stop leading him on. Why are you doing this to yourself?”

Karla walked over to the window and pulled the curtains back.

“I know he didn’t follow me over here.”

“Who followed you, Rick?”

“Now you know if he followed me, his ass would’ve been in here by now. No, Mark.”

“Oh my God, has he’s been sitting out here all this time?” Ri asked.

“I don’t know, I just looked out the window. I ought to call this fool, or maybe I should walk out to his car and surprise his ass.”

“Karla, don’t go out there; what made him follow you out here, anyway?”

“I don’t know.”

“So you telling me you don’t know why he followed you; it must be a reason. Don’t nobody just follow people for no damn reason. What did you do? See, this is what happens when you lead a person on.”

“I’m not leading him on. I didn’t do anything.”

“You need to end the shit if you’re not going be with him; don’t start that damn drama shit, having him follow you to people’s houses. This is how innocent people get caught up.”

“Girl, calm down; you making something out of nothing.”

“Calm down, my ass. I’m starting to feel you and Rick do deserve each other’s bullshit.”

“Look, I’m going home,” Karla said. “It’s late anyway, and you all jumpy, and neither one of us would get any sleep because of you. See, I told you he’s insecure.”

“Insecure, my ass; what the fuck happened with him that he has to follow you out here?”

“Nothing. I just told him I had to take my mother and grandmother to the store. Apparently, he was sitting somewhere, and I didn't see him, and he followed me here. Shit!"

"What? That shit don't sound right, and you talking about Rick. You sound like him and his shit; I swear you two are made for each other. Fuck, I can't believe he followed you for that story. I know something else happened. What? Start talking, you brat. You can roll your eyes all you want."

"Okay, when I got out the shower, he was sitting on bed. I think he might have seen Rick leaving my house this afternoon. He said he thought something happened to me. He claimed something happened in my area, a big shoot-out, and people were running through their houses, and he thought I was one of the them."

"When did that happened? I saw the news last night; I didn't see any of that."

"Yeah, and neither did I. Look, I'm going home. I'm okay."

"Well, I can't make you stay, so if you're going home, will you please try to be careful? Here's my advice: If you say you're going to end the affairs with Rick and Mark, then you really need to give Rick his money back. It's not like you need the fuckin' money. And end it with Mark, okay?"

"Ugh, Sherri, I hate him."

"Which one? I can't tell that you hate either one of them."

"Sherri, I didn't ask what you think."

"I know you didn't, but I'm telling you anyway. Now, take your butt straight home."

Sherri walked Karla out the front door, gave her a hug, and kissed her on the back of her head.

"Is that him sitting over there?"

"Yeah."

"Call me when you when you get home."

She got in her car and pulled off, thinking about what her sister said. Just then, her phone rang.

"Oh, hell, no; not now. What do you want? Leave me alone. Just leave a message. Why aren't you with your woman, satisfying her or letting her scratch your damn eyeballs out? FUCK!"

It was Sherri.

"Karla, I thought you were calling me," she said.

"I'm not home yet; dang, I just pulled off. What is wrong with you? Why are you so paranoid?"

"Hang up, girl; he might think you're talking to the police or something. He may know you saw him. Girl, people are crazy."

"Okay, Ri; damn, you so damn jumpy. I'll call you when I get home." *What the hell is wrong with her? I swear, and she's a Lombardo!*

She pulled her gun from the glove compartment and placed it between her legs.

Now this fool can act crazy if he wants to.

Mark flew past Karla, never looking her way, and she acted as if she didn't see him, either. Then she decided to call his cell.

"Hey Mark, what's going on? I'm finished with my mother and grandmother; they wore me out today."

"Oh, okay, sweetie. I'm not doing nothing, just sitting here in the house, watching a little TV, flipping the channels. Where are you?"

"Oh, I'm just leaving my sister's house. I stopped here before going home."

"Uh-huh, your sister? I didn't know you had a sister; do you have brothers too?"

"Uh, yeah, I got seven sisters and six brothers; why you ask?"

"Oh okay; wow, you got a large family. I guess I'll never meet them, huh? So where're you heading to now? You could come by my place for a nightcap."

"Uh no, it's late. I'm heading home and going to bed, alone. I'm tired. I've been running all day."

"What if I come over there? We can lay together. I promise I won't touch you. I just want to be beside you and talk."

"I'm going home alone, and I'm almost there."

"Already? You must be flying."

"No, I'm driving the speed limit. I'll talk with you tomorrow."

"Okay; wait a minute, how about Sunday morning breakfast to start your day? I'll call you around eight."

"That's good; good night."

Good, she thought after hanging up, *then I can break this off with him early. Um, looks like nobody home again. I don't think he followed me, at least I don't see his car, but let me circle the block real slow, just in case. Good, I don't see Mr. Tyler's truck, either; that's a good sign, but I don't put nothing past him. He could've had somebody drop him off and be waiting in here in the dark, on my damn bed, knowing him. Anything is possible when it comes to him.*

As she got out of her car, she saw her neighbors.

"Hi Hamiltons," she called. Y'all out late taking in the night air?"

"Yeah, babe," Mrs. Hamilton replied. "Trying to cool off; it was a hot day. It cooled down a little tonight."

"Hey, did you see anybody come by my house tonight?"

"No, we been out here for a while; we haven't seen nobody. Were you expecting someone?"

"No, I just asked. Good night."

She went inside, turned the light on, and locked the door.

Shoot, she thought, *right about now, I don't trust Mark or Rick. At this point, I'm feeling a little weary of them both; at least with Rick, it won't be too much of a damn surprise. I know he's near, but let me leave some lights on in here tonight, just in case, since I'm in here by myself. I know what I'll do: I'll fix his butt if he tries to come through my basement door. He'll get snapped like a damn mouse getting caught in a trap, and that goes for anybody that comes in here without my permission. Hopefully, I'll hear them.*

She picked up the house phone and called her sister.

"Hey Sherri, I'm home; what the hell was that about? What's the problem?"

"I figured if he followed you, it's possible he could have your phone traced; you never know with these new phones."

"What? Come on, Sherri, you watch way too much TV. I swear."

"Seriously, anything is possible; you never know. Just be careful talking on your phone; you should get another cellphone and let that one play out."

"All right, you may be right, but I really don't think it's that serious. Stay off the TV, please; you are being creepy."

"Come on, Karla; did you forget how it was living with the Lombardos?"

"No, I didn't, but damn, we haven't lived that lifestyle in a long time. I don't want to think about it."

"Well, you better rewind those memories; stop sleeping on shit, girl. Be careful, baby sister; love you. Call me in the morning, but think about getting another phone. Are you sure you're going to be okay?"

"Yes, Sherri, and whatever you do, please don't call any of them Lombardos, especially not Felipo, okay?"

"Okay, but if this gets out of hand, I'm calling Kimmie, even though she ain't no better than Felipo."

"Okay, 'cause Felipo don't give a damn; that gives him a reason to shoot to kill. And Kimmie needs a damn man; I swear she's a got damn Calamity Jane."

"Leave our sister alone; she got a man already."

"Who? I know I haven't talked with her in a while. She never said anything about no man."

"You'll meet him soon; let me just say he's a fine-ass white boy."

"Oh shit," said Karla. "Did Georgie and Ma meet him yet?"

"Nope, and I can't wait to see Georgie's face."

"What you know about him, Sherri?"

"A lot; you'll see him, but in the meantime, mind your business and handle them crazy men you got. Goodbye."

Got damn, Karla thought, *she can be so scared sometimes. No wonder Dakota call her Ms. Prissy; she ain't never did no fighting, only Calamity Jane and me, but I love her to death, damn scaredy cat.*

She turned the TV on and lay across her bed, wrapped in her comforter, until she fell asleep.

CHAPTER 6

SATURDAY, JULY 5, 2008

Karla lay in the bed, watching the clock, thinking about the conversation she and Ri had last night.

Well, she thought, *I'll get up in a few minutes and take a shower. Today, for sure, I'm ending this with him and Rick. I promise myself: I'm not sleeping with him no more. I'm done. Great for Rick if he gets the job; hopefully, he'll find someone new, and he can move on, and so can I.*

A noise came from outside her window.

What the hell was that?

She jumped off the bed and peeked out the window. She snatched her gun from under her pillow, grabbed her cellphone, and tiptoed to the top of the stairs, then she crept down the steps, went into the kitchen, and jumped behind the door.

"You may want to turn around real slow," she warned. "The choice is yours."

She cocked the trigger, and the man turned around slowly with one hand in the air; with the other hand, he pulled off his hood.

"Good morning, sweetie." It was Mark.

"Motherfucka, good morning? What's so good about this? You just broke into my house again; what the hell is wrong with you?"

"I didn't break in."

"Then what the fuck do you call it?"

"I got a key."

"How in the hell did you get a key to my house?"

"Does it matter? I'm in here now."

"Yeah, it does matter. I didn't give you no key to my place, so this isn't going to matter either."

She raised her gun and shot him once his arm and once in his upper leg.

"Ow!" he cried. "Look, sweetie, put the gun down. I'm not going to hurt you, I promise."

"I know you're not," she replied, "but I'm going hurt you again, and trust me, the next shot will not be in your arm or leg. You going to be close to dead. So I suggest you do what I say."

He took four steps back, limping away from her, blood pouring from his arm and his leg.

"Karla, can you put the gun down? My arm and leg is killing me; what can I do with a wounded arm and leg."

"Um, let's see," she said. "That would be a hell no! You came into my house, uninvited, and I'm supposed to put my weapon down? You must be a fool if you think I'm going to lower my shit. If you make another fucking move, Imma kill you. Now if you choose to die, that would be on you."

"Karla, just tell me the truth: I've been following you for quite some time, and I couldn't find too much on you, til recently. I seen your children come and go, and I seen men come and go out your house. I'm not sure if you're running some kind of trafficking or drugs or maybe prostituting. Every time I came by here, there was a different man coming or going."

"Excuse me, what the hell you doing, watching my house?"

"I called you that night, and you didn't answer, so I stayed around. Once I saw that guy going in your house the other day, I wanted to get a good look at the guy, because he looks familiar."

"So that identified me as a prostitute?"

"Then I saw him in the daylight, coming out your house, and to my surprise, I know him. We locked eyes."

"Mark, you need to leave my house now. I don't owe you nothing of what's going on in here."

He took a step toward her, and she fired off again, hitting the wall, missing him on purpose.

"Karla, hold up. I know who he is: He's the guy that slept with my wife."

Her mouth flew wide open, she lowered her gun, and then reached in her kitchen draw and gave him two cloths to wrap his wounds with.

"He did what?" she asked. "When did this happen?" *Um, so he was seeing someone else in DC beside me,* she thought. *He ain't shit, that lying ass.*

"Mark, I don't know what to say to you on that, but out of curiosity, how long ago did he sleep with your wife?"

"A year ago; he was the one that broke up my family. She had a baby girl by him, and when I saw him coming out your house yesterday morning, that made it even worse. Now he's sleeping with my girlfriend."

He lowered his head in disgust as if he wanted to cry.

"How much can a man take? Before I saw him, I actually was calling you to break it off, but you didn't answer. I had to know why you weren't taking my call, so that's why I came inside."

"Mark, by the time I got upstairs to the phone, it stopped ringing. There was no message, and the number was blocked, so how was I supposed to know it was you?"

Karla was glad to hear he was about to break it off first. *He don't even know he did me a favor,* she thought. *but I wasn't expecting it this way.*

"Okay, hold on, Mark. So you saw him coming out my house, so what? If your plans were to dump me, then why didn't you just leave? Why did you sit outside my house all night? What was your plan?"

"My plan was to hurt him, like he hurt me with my wife; he destroyed my home. I just got over all that, but when I saw him, it brought back memories and pain; now I can't let this go."

"Wait, is she your ex-wife?"

"No, she's still my wife. I can't find her to get the divorce, and to top it off, I'm paying child support for a child that's not mine; she told me after I signed the birth certificate. I was messed up behind that.

I saw a picture of them two; I saw him in his marked police car, but the other day, he was in a truck."

Oh, shit, she thought, *is Derickie's women's men catching up to him now? This must be the Tyler boys' lucky day.*

"Mark, I don't know what to tell you. It's fine you ending this relationship; I'm good with that, but as far as you coming in my house like you did, that's unacceptable. I'm not cool with that."

"Sweetie, I'm sorry for coming in here like this and following you; it hurts when someone you love hurts your heart the way she did. You lose your mind and always feel insecure in relationships. Maybe I'm not ready for a relationship. I'm still hurting inside. I'm so sorry."

"So how you get a key to my door? How many sets do you have?"

He threw the key on the counter and walked toward the door.

"I only got one key," he said, "and it's to this door. Karla, this not me at all. I don't do this kind of stuff. I'm shocked at myself; do you accept my apology?"

"No, but I do sympathize with your pain. So what's your plan now?"

"Well, I'm leaving DC next week. I'm going back to my hometown."

"Now what happens if you run across him again before you leave?" she asked. "Do you plan on confronting him?"

"I'll probably try to hurt him really bad, like he did me."

She opened the back door and escorted him out; as they stood on the porch, she watched him soaking up the blood from his arm to his leg.

I guess I better tell this fool who he is before he kills the wrong person, she thought. *If anybody kills Rick Tyler, it's going to be me.*

"Look, Mark, let me warn you: Before you kill him, you need to make sure you have the right person. The guy you saw yesterday is Erick Tyler, not Derrick Tyler. They're cousins, and people have made that mistake with them for many years. I strongly suggest you leave it alone. I know you're upset, and he destroyed your family, but I beg you to leave it alone. Just leave the area if you're done with her; it's not worth it."

"Well, since you seem to know so much, where can I find this Derrick Tyler?" he asked. "I'm done with her, but I want revenge."

Karla was almost in tears; she begged, "Mark, please don't jeopardize your life for him; it's not worth going to jail over it. Just keep living your life; make a new start on your move, please."

"If he crosses my path before I leave, he's mine, Karla. I'm just saying it."

He walked off the porch, with his blood trailing behind him. She ran back into the house, slammed the door, and locked it.

Okay, she thought, *that's it: I'm calling a locksmith to come out and change all these locks and reactive my ADT. Where the hell did he park? I don't see his car in the alley.*

She ran to the front of the house, looking out from window to window, then ran back upstairs to her bedroom and flung herself across her bed.

Answer this phone, she thought as she called her sister. "Sherri! I know it's early, but I have got to tell you this: Oh, my God, girl, he had a key to my back door."

"Who did?" Sherri asked. "And how in the hell did he get a key?"

"Mark, and I don't know; he never said how he got it."

"You got to be kidding me."

"Nope, I'm not kidding. I was totally shocked that he would do something like that."

"Are you all right? Were you still asleep? Oh, my God, girl I would have shot the shit out of him."

"Yeah, I'm good. I did shoot him, twice; he lucky I didn't really wound him. I wanted to blow his head off, walking up in my damn house."

"Girl, that's scary."

"But Ri, there's more; you're going to die on this. He's been watching me for a while; he saw Alicia and Kareem, and he thought I was a prostitute and running a drug ring."

She couldn't help but to burst out laughing and so did Sherri.

"What, so you're a prostitute now and a drug dealer? Wow, that's a new one. Do Georgie know about this? Girl, he would beat you senseless."

They were laughing so hard, they were crying.

"I guess that's why Rick left me some money, huh, and there's more: He did see Rick leaving out yesterday, and he also saw him coming in that Thursday evening; he sat outside in his car all night watching my house, but he thought Rick was Derickie."

"What? Oh, my God. Girl, I swear I feel like this is a Lifetime movie; what the hell did Derickie do now?"

"Sherri, come on; are you serious? We all know Derickie's track record. Stop laughing; it really isn't funny. I wanted to fall out laughing too when he told me, but I couldn't let my guard down. Apparently, Derickie slept with his wife; the chick got pregnant and had a baby girl. He thought it was his baby, but to find out it's not, and then she left him."

"Wow," said Ri. "What else?"

"I don't know, but he said if he ran across Derickie again before he leaves town, his ass is his."

"Uh uh, girl; you got some drama with you. What's that dumb saying the kids got: "No speed bump, no punching back." You got it, sista; way too much."

"I know, I'm calling a locksmith and ADT to reactivate my account today. Oh, Sherri, and by the way, before he came inside and got his ass shot, he was calling me to dump me."

Sherri burst out laughed again.

"So he dumped you? Good; good for you. He should have. So now that he thinks Rick is Derickie, you may want to tell him, just in case he comes back to your house."

"He might," she said, laughing. "It would serve him right."

"Karla, that's not nice; Mark probably is laying low for him or Derickie. He may shoot one of them, not knowing who is who. That's means if you don't say anything and one of them gets shot, then what?"

"Uh-huh, I know then he'll think it was Tina, paying his ass back."

"Yeah, but girl, he may kill him, then you'll be messed up in the head; at least warn the two fools."

"Wait, then that means I have to talk to him."

"Karla, you gotta tell them both before somebody gets hurt."

"Okay, damn it; can I wait a few days?"

"No, Karla; even though it does sound funny. I can picture it too, but no."

"All right. I'll talk with you later. I got to find a locksmith; bye."

She lay across the bed, looking up at the ceiling, giggling to herself, plotting on whether to tell him or not.

I shouldn't tell his ass nothing, she thought, *but I guess I better, for my heart's sake. I'll be the one walking around messed up, all because I knew. I'm still in love with him. Ugh.*

She made her phone call to reactive her home security then headed out for a ride.

Mark got me all paranoid, she thought as she walked out the door, *and my neighbors probably think I'm crazy, out here checking my windows and doors and now looking under my car, like a crazy person.*

I don't think the man is a total fruit loop, she thought; *poor thing is just emotionally messed up. That's probably why he couldn't perform in bed; he was so messed up, and I didn't know it. I guess that's enough to set a person off on the deep end. If my man came home and told me he had a baby with another woman and left me for her, I'd be messed up too. I wouldn't try to hurt her, but I haven't been in that situation.*

She let a whole week go by before she said a word. She went on with her everyday life, without speaking to Rick all week, but also was silently hoping Mark didn't catch up with him either.

Well, this the weekend again, she thought on Friday, as she drove home from work; *so far, no news is good news. I didn't hear about neither one of them getting hit upside the head. Let's see, who do I tell first? Derickie, since he's really after him, or Rick, to watch his ass act a fool; he'll be pissed, fussing because he got to walk a thin line 'cause of Derickie. They thought that shit was funny when they were growing up, but ha ha, the joke is on them now. I bet they never thought this would come back to haunt their chocolate asses. I think I'll tell Mr. Smart Ass Rick Tyler, first; see his face and reaction on this, but knowing him, it's not going be about Mark is out for him. He's going to interrogate me about the relationship first, but oh, well. Imma go to the mall with his money, and while I'm there, I'll check out changing my number. I just can't believe Wheaton Mall is this packed; what's in here that makes it so crowded? Nothing, damn it.*

She sashayed through the mall entrance double doors as if she were on the red carpet; her cutup jeans showed off her small curvy figure, and she had on a fitted tee-shirt, a pair of her favorite mules, a flop hat, her big LV purse, and a pair of sunglasses.

"Good afternoon, ma'am," a salesman said. "Can I help you with something?"

She sashayed over to the counter and spoke very softly in her sexy voice. "I was wondering if I could change my number on this plan."

"Well, if I change your number, can I call you?" he asked, flirting.

"I don't think so, babe; that's why I'm trying to change it now."

"Why, too many boyfriends? Can't you keep up?"

"Well, let's see here; I don't have boyfriends. Boyfriends are playtoys; I like to have a man, but the answer to that question is yes, that's why I'm changing my number."

He was leaning across the counter, smiling as he checked her out, up and down.

"Um, you might want to get a boyfriend again," he said. "I promise you I'll play right. I can walk, talk, and take you to wherever you want to go, and I'll never stalk you."

"What's your name?" Karla asked.

"Justin."

"Yeah, well, Justin, that's what they all say in the beginning."

"I'm not them all," he replied.

She leaned a little closer into him, giving him more breast to look at.

"I tell you what, if you can make this happen for me, we can talk about it."

Karla pulled her glasses off and twirled them around on her fingers watching his moves.

Um, he does have a sexy walk, she thought, *long and tall like a peanut butter cookie; he must be early to midthirties. Yeah, he could be a playtoy and definitely good eye candy. I might run circles around him, but he's talking a good game. It might be fun; I might let him come to the playground for an hour or so, that's it, no more. If he's good and well behaved, then he can stay and take me downtown; um, hell no, Karla.*

"Ma'am," Justin said, "I spoke with my manager; he said you would have to get a new plan. He can't change your number otherwise."

"Really? Okay, but no thanks. I won't be doing that; thanks for trying."

"You're welcome; now does this mean I can't call you?"

"Justin, I'm sure you have some justice with you, but the timing is not good. I tell you what, Justin; why don't you give me your number, and I'll call you for lunch one day."

He leaned across the counter and got up in her face, looking into her eyes.

"I only give my number out when it's a for sure thing," he said. "Why don't you come back when the timing is right?"

"I might, but now you never know when anything is for sure, do we, Justin? If that's how you feel, not a problem, sweetheart; you look like you could've been fun."

Karla winked her eye, took her phone out of his hand, and sashayed out the door.

"You have a good day, Justin."

Good, she thought, *'cause I don't need another sheep in my stable. Okay, that didn't work; forget it. I'm going to Macy's and spend some of this bamma's money for my troubles.*

She headed straight to the shoe department and bought several pair of shoes, then over to the handbag section and brought a new purse, and then to the perfume counter, looking around.

"Andriano and Paulie Lombardo," she said, seeing her uncles in the mall, "what you two doing down here?"

"Hey, my babe," said Andriano.

"My babe, my foot," she said. "You didn't call or stop by the house to let me know that you were in town?"

"We going to a frat party tonight in VA," Andriano said, "meeting up with Troy, Aton, and the other fellas."

"I might want to go," she said hopefully.

"No, we are not dragging your ass with us anymore."

"Hey, I heard Rick is in town," Paulie said. "Is that where you're running to?"

Karla threw her hands up in the air and put her perfume on the counter with their stuff and walked off.

"No, I see you when you get to the house; bye, and thanks. I got somewhere else to go."

Dang, she thought, *where did the time go? It's six o'clock already; wasn't no fun shopping today. Been to two malls and nothing. I'm taking myself back to my side of town.*

By time she got home, Andriano and Paulie were sitting on the porch.

"Dang," she said, laughing, "what'd y'all do, run the lights? I know I made a couple more stops, but dang. I'm glad I don't have a husband; he'd be mad as heck to come home and see y'all on his porch."

Paulie mumbled, "You do have a husband; he just not here yet!"

"What you say, Paulie?"

"Nothing."

They all went inside and got comfortable. Andriano went straight to the kitchen and starting cooking; they all sat around for hours, talking until Troy and Anton walked through the door, talking loud.

"Troy, don't start that stepping shit in here," Karla said. "Not today. I don't feel like hearing that."

"Why not? I'm sure you don't say that when he starts stomping; let's see if you going to tell him to not start that stomping."

He laughed in her face and kept stepping.

"Okay, Troy, but this pussy cat don't want to hear that, and how did we get there? All I said was that damn stepping, and anyway, I wasn't invited."

"Since when you wait on an invite with him?" Troy asked. "You automatically got a ticket."

"Shut up, Troy," Paulie said. "Did you talk with him yet? I want to know if he's coming up this end."

"No," Karla said. "I need to go call him anyway."

"What's going on with you two lately?" Paulie asked. "Let's hear it."

"Nothing."

"Oh, it's not nothing; what, you pregnant and y'all secretly got married?"

"No, something a little more serious," Karla said. "Their fun maybe on hold for a while."

"What you mean by that? What's up?" Paulie asked.

"Well, they may want to lay low for a few days."

She started fumbling for words and then poured a glass of wine and took a seat at the dining room table.

"What the hell you talking about?" Paulie asked. "Who is they? Is there something you need to let us know? What's wrong? That shit coming out your mouth don't sound right.

"Somebody wants to kill Derickie."

They all hollered, "What? For what?"

"Well, apparently Derickie slept with some man's wife."

"Karla don't start that bits and pieces of shit," Andriano said. "What happened?"

"Look here, Andriano," Karla snapped. "Don't holler at me. I'm not your child or a dog. You talk to me like an adult. Now if we can't have adult conversations, then we don't have shit to talk about."

"I'm not hollering at you, but this is serious, and you giving bits and pieces. What do you know?"

"I'm not given no damn bits and pieces; what I said is the main point."

"Got damn it, Karla. Rick taught you well," Troy said. "Spill the shit, and answer one damn question. That nigga don't give no information unless you ask; otherwise, you get what you ask for!"

"What else happened, girl?" said Andriano.

"But how did all of this come about with Rick?" Paulie asked.

"Okay, Karla, are you going to call either one of them about this?" Troy asked.

"I was going to call, but y'all keep stopping me."

"We didn't stop you," Troy said. "So what's taking you so long? Do I need to call myself?"

"You need to call him now," said Andriano.

"Why are you yelling, Andriano? Damn."

"You can handle it," Troy said. "Look who you been dealing with over the past years."

"No, I haven't been dealing with him lately."

"Girl, please," Andriano said, laughing. "We all know you and Rick still see each other; who you fooling but yourself?"

"Karla, are you serious about this?" said Paulie.

"Yeah, you think I just made this up?"

"Okay, but again, how do Rick fall into this with Derickie?"

"Well, a friend of mine saw Rick and thought he was Derickie, but I told him it wasn't him." She kept hesitating and taking long sips of her wine. "A year ago, Derickie had sex with my friend's wife, and she got pregnant; they broke up, and now he's paying child support for a child that's not his."

"Here she go again," Anton snapped. "A half-ass story; you may want to share that half-ass story with Rick and Derickie tonight, so they can be on the lookout for this guy. So how the hell did all of this come about, Karla?"

"Why you ask me like that? Dang, you making it sound like it's my fault."

"Well, is it?" Anton replied.

"My friend had been following me," Karla said, "and spotted Rick coming outta my place."

"Following you? For what?" said Anton.

"I didn't know until today."

"If this man has been following you, then why in the hell was you at the mall?" said Paulie.

She sucked her teeth, rolled her eyes, and took another sip. "I went to the mall to see if I could change my number."

"Well, are you okay?" Anton asked.

"I'm good. I don't think he's going do anything to them. I told him I understood his pain and said not to put himself in any trouble; it's not worth it."

"Girl, please," Anton replied. "That man is hurting. You think he's going to listen to you? Don't take that shit lightly."

"He said he was leaving the area soon, but he wanted revenge."

"Okay," Anton said, "I do think Derickie need his ass kicked, but not killed."

"I agree," Karla said. "My feeling exactly, so could you tell them for me? Neither one of them is answering. Imma leave a message on their phone."

"Just make sure they get that message."

She nonchalantly got up, took her glass of wine, and went downstairs. She turned on some music and parked herself on the couch, watching TV.

Within an hour, Derickie was walking through her front door.

"What's up, man?" he said. "I got the message. I figured I'd stop by since I was already on this side of town."

Troy blurted out, "Man, somebody is out to kill you."

"Man, please; who?"

"Don't you be taking this lightly, considering you a cop; you know some people are ready to knock one of you DC cops off the block, anyway."

Karla hit the top of the steps and stood in the door, pointing her finger.

"See what I mean?" Karla said. "He don't listen; for once in your freakin life, just listen. Damn; you all over yourself, so sure ain't nobody going to do nothing to you. Well, let me be the first to tell you, Derrick: Somebody is out to get your ass."

He stepped back and looked at her without a smile on his face.

"Who is it, Karla?" he asked. "You never talked to me like this before, raising your voice at me. If we was on the streets, girl, and you raised your voice at me…"

"And what? Derickie, what would you have done?"

Karla stepped closer to his face, probably more so to his chest.

"I'm trying to save you," she said, "but if you don't want to listen, then don't save your own tail. By the way, you got your twin cousin hooked up in your mess, so it's a possibility that one of you just might take a licking soon."

She stepped back off him and walked in the kitchen. Derickie pulled her back by her arm.

"Wait a minute," he said. "Tell me who this guy is."

"Karla, Rick is on the phone," Anton said. "He wants to talk with you."

"About what?"

"Girl, get on the got damn phone," Anton snapped.

"Put him on speaker."

"What the hell is going on?" Rick asked. "Are you all right?"

"Yeah, I'm fine."

"Well, stop with all the attitude. I got it already: You mad at me, so what? Now what's going on?"

"You think I have an attitude?"

"Rick, you're on speakerphone," Anton said.

"I don't give a fuck, Anton; she needs to stop this shit. I got it already; what's wrong? What's the urgency, since she acting all crazy? What's going on?"

"Karla, are you going tell him?"

Silence filled the room; you could hear a pin drop.

"Some-motherfuckin'-body better start talking," he snapped. "What's up?"

"Uh, a friend of mine is out to hurt Derickie," she said. "He saw you coming out of my house and thought you were Derickie."

"What friend, Karla? Was this friend somebody you were dating?"

"Uh, Rick, this is not the time."

"Why not? Everybody knows we been seeing each other on and off; our affair is no got damn secret. I'm on my way up there, and when I get there, you better be ready to talk."

"You don't have to come up here," she said. "Derickie is here; he can fill you in on the rest if he chooses to."

"Fuck you mean, he can fill me in? No, you going to fill me in, so don't you make a fucking move. I'm on my way, and you gonna tell me the rest of this story."

"Mark is out to kill him," she said.

"Mark? That bamma that you was fuckin' with?"

She blew, and they had a look of surprise.

"Really, Rick," she begged, "let's not go there. Damn."

"Yeah, let's go there, got damn it."

"Wait a minute," Anton said. "You two can you fuss about your love affairs at a later date; the point to this, Rick, is that he wants to kill Derickie; he thought you were him."

Then Troy chimed in, saying, "I have a question for the both of you: What the hell is the big secret of y'all seeing each? I don't give a damn; then and now, if you choose to see each other, good for you. All I say is don't pull people in y'all's love triangle."

"Derickie, tell your cousin, man," said Anton.

"Rick, don't come out, man. Lay low for a few; let me see what she talking 'bout."

"What? Are you fuckin' playing? I'm coming out now, and I'm on my way up there."

"Rick?"

"What, Troy?"

"What the hell Derickie get his self into now, damn it?"

"I don't know, but he needs to stop. I just got here."

"Um, look at the pot calling the kettle black," Karla said.

"Karla, don't go there," Anton snapped. "Your shit ain't looking too bright, either."

"Hey Rick, once she takes you back, you need to beat her," Derickie said. "Put her in place; she too damn sassy."

"Derickie, this is not the time," Rick said. "I'm hanging up, man. I'll be there shortly."

"Man, this is some shit here," Anton said.

"Derickie, you have no idea who she is?" Troy said.

"Man, I don't have a clue."

"Well, she got your baby, and dude picked you out through Rick."

"He must've been following his wife and did some picture snapping," Troy suggested.

"Man, I don't know."

"Damn, Derickie, how many women you sleeping with?"

"Man, to be honest with you, I haven't been with anybody lately. I've been too busy at work."

"What, you're on strike?"

They all laughed.

"Paulie, you got jokes, man, but I need some clarity on this story."

Karla crept off back downstairs.

"Hey Karla," Derickie said. "I know you hear me calling you."

"Derickie, you might want to leave that alone until Rick gets here," said Paulie.

"I guess you got a point there; it might be ugly."

"Derickie, she might need to be beat," Andriano said, "but the only beating she get is from me. I love you to death, and the way this is going, that could soon be a possibility, but if you think I'm going to stand here and let you put your hands on my niece, that won't be happening."

"Come on, man, I wouldn't do that, Andriano. I love her too. I might throw a few water balloons, fuck her hair up; she'll be mad as shit, but she'll get over that."

"Yeah, but then we got another problem with your damn cousin," Andriano replied.

"Look here," Paulie said. "I'm going to take a shower, so by the time Rick gets here, at least somebody will be dressed."

"All right, but you still want to go to this party?" Troy replied.

"I don't know, man, I'll play it by ear," said Paulie.

Rick was driving faster than the cars on the Indianapolis 500 raceway, mind racing faster than he drove. *I knew they were quote unquote lovers or whatever she calls it*, he thought as he sped along. She was so nonchalant about. So that was the guy sitting across the street in that car; I got a good look at him. I should've snapped his picture just for the hell of it, but I remember what he was driving, and she said she was dumping me for his crazy ass. I should slap her ass; she plays too many got damn games. I'm not playing with her anymore; this is it. When I get up there, Derickie better tell me every damn thing; fuck this damn ducking. I got to meet with JB; all this nonsense drama has to end as of now. Ha ha; it's not funny anymore.

He reached Karla's house in twenty minutes flat.

Damn, he thought, *it ain't never no parking around here!*

He rode around back and parked in her driveway, then got out and ran up the stairs and walked in, looking mad as hell; he caught all of them off guard.

"Damn, he scared the shit out me," Paulie said.

"Me too," said Troy.

"Derickie, we need to talk," Rick said, "but after I talk to Karla; where the hell is she?"

"In the basement," said Troy.

He closed the door behind him and stomped down the stairs with all his weight.

"Karla."

"What?"

"We need to talk, and I don't want to hear no shit from you about later, or you don't want to talk to me; none of that shit. I didn't come here for your nonsense or to play any games with you. I want you to talk to me, so first tell me about Mark, trying to kill Derickie."

Karla laid on the couch with her feet up on the arm rest, sipping her wine. He picked her feet up off the arm rest and laid them on his lap.

"Don't cut your eyes at me," he said. "Start talking; what happened?"

"I don't know where to start with this."

"Well, start backwards, or start with Derickie."

"Well, apparently Derickie slept with his wife, and he wants revenge. He saw you come in the other day. He was sitting outside my house all night; that was him calling me on the phone to dump me, by the way. Don't you even smile."

"I didn't say anything or smile. I'm listening."

"I saw your face."

"Go ahead, girl; keep talking."

"Anyway, he stayed out there all night; he said he wanted to get a good look at you. He followed me to Sherri's house and then followed me halfway home."

"When did you notice him, at Sherri's house?"

"Rick, why do I feel like I'm one of your clients? Stop interrogating me."

"Babe, how do you want me to talk to you? Keep going."

"I noticed him when I was getting ready to leave. I saw him out the window. I called him that night, as if I didn't know he had followed me, and he asked me to go to breakfast the next day."

"Babe, I should punch you in your head; why the hell would you go to breakfast with him after you knew he was following you?"

"I don't know. I was going to call it quits."

"So you had to go out with him to do that?"

"Well, we never made it," she explained. "He came here Sunday morning."

"He did what?"

"He came through my back door, he had a key made."

"He had a key made? What the hell, Karla! You gave him a key?"

"No. I didn't know he had a key until that day. Rick, calm down."

"Calm down? Are you for real? He could've hurt you and did whatever he wanted to you."

He was staring in her face, shaking his head.

"Well, I slept with my gun under my pillow, and the sword was under my bed."

"Karla, that dude look pretty big, almost as big as me; he could have handled you."

"Well, that's a chance I had to take."

"What the fuck? Why didn't you call me?"

Karla rolled her eyes and sucked her teeth.

"Oh, that's right: You're pissed with me, so you wouldn't dare. Look here: I don't give a damn how mad you are at me, you call me next time."

"Please; you got your own troubles."

"Karla, you are my troubles, good and bad."

She sat up on the couch and swung her feet to the floor. He looked down into the palms of his hands, shaking his head.

"Karla, just keep talking," he said. "What else happened?"

"By the time I got downstairs, I saw the doorknob turning. I stepped back behind the door with my gun drawn."

"Did he come in?"

"Yeah."

He shook his head again and grunted. "Go ahead; what else?"

"He didn't expect me to be at the door. I told him if he moved, I was going to shoot him."

"Well, did you?"

"Yeah."

"What? How many times, babe?"

"Once in his arm and once in his leg, then there was a few other words exchanged. That's when he told me about you, or shall I say Derickie."

"Go ahead; I know there's more."

"Supposedly, Derickie slept with his wife; she got a baby, and he thought it was his daughter. The woman came home, packed up her belongings, and left the house to be with Derickie. I told him you weren't Derickie. I asked him did he know who you were; he said yes."

"Babe, when did all of this take place about the affair with his wife?"

"He said a year ago; for a minute, I thought maybe it was you that had the affair with her."

He lifted his head up and looked over at her.

"I may have had my share of some crazy stuff, but I would never mess with anyone's wife. When we get married, you better not be out here with no other man, and I most definitely will not be out here with no other woman."

Karla rubbed his back, he leaned in and pecked her on the lips.

"Damn, that's all you got?" she asked.

He cut his eyes at her, with a frown on his face.

"I'm not going there with you now. You need to tell Derickie this."

He stood up and pulled her off the couch by her hand, walking over to the steps.

"You can go first," said Karla.

"Why does it matter who goes first?" he asked. "Just go."

"Yeah, I don't want you looking at my ass."

"But you're going look at mine." He shook his head again. "Come on, girl. I'm not playing with you."

"Okay, Derickie, you need to hear this, and listen, man: Our lives are on the line for now; you need to know who this man is. Babe, do you want me to tell him or you?"

"You can tell him," she said. "He's not listening to me."

"I do listen," Derickie said. "You didn't tell me anything."

"I told you someone is out to kill your ass, but you acted so uncaring, so there was no need for me to go any further."

"Babe, stop all that hollering," said Rick. "Okay, Derickie, this is what it is: You supposedly slept with Mark's wife, and she had baby girl by you. Came home, cleaned out the house, and told dude she was leaving to be with you. All of this supposed to happen a year ago."

"Rick, who the hell is Mark?"

"He's a friend of Karla's."

"Is there anything else I need to know?" Rick asked. "This shit is getting crazier by the minute."

"Yeah," said Karla.

"What is it?" Rick asked.

"I love you, and I'm still in love with you," she said. "Always have been. Now there you go, I said it."

He nodded his head in agreement with her.

"Uh huh, and I love you too. I'm still in love with you, so why in the hell you putting me through all this shit?"

They stood face to face; tears were rolling down Karla's cheeks.

"I'm sorry," Karla said, "but you put me through shit too. Look what happened in the last week; all you had to do was tell the truth."

"Look, I had no control over that," he said, "and I told you the truth. Nothing I said to you was a lie; I've never lied to you."

"Um, excuse me," said Derickie. "I thought this was about me getting killed."

"Got damn, I swear I feel like I'm watching a real live Lifetime story," said Troy.

"Damn, you watch Lifetime?" Derickie replied.

"Hell, yeah, man; my lady and I lay in the bed watching it. Whatever she wants, man; you better know it. Know where your real love comes from; that's the one that takes care of me, fool."

"Derickie, when you settle down, you will be watching Lifetime too," said Anton. "Watch Rick: He gonna be watching Lifetime too."

"Yeah, whatever! Back to you, Derickie; do you recall that woman?"

"Man, I have no idea who she could be, really. Karla, do you know her name?"

"No, and I'm not calling him to ask. I told him to leave it alone; there's no reason for revenge. The damage is done; ain't nobody living with you."

"Well, damn; what, I can't have a woman living with me?"

They all looked at Derickie as if he was really crazy.

"Unless you living in Africa in one of those tribes, or you got some sex slave mess going on at your house, then she could be living with you."

"Karla, call him and ask him his wife's name, please?" said Derickie.

Karla looked up at Rick for his advice.

"You may have to, babe; that's the only way we gonna know."

"Ain't no way I'm calling him to ask for his wife's name. Derickie can talk to him."

"Girl you sound crazy. I'm not calling that man to ask him his wife's name; fuck it!"

"Derickie, man, you need to stop all this sleeping around shit. Man if I take this job, all this crazy mess has to stop, or I'll be fired before I take an oath."

"Oh, wait," Karla said. "My phone is ringing. This may be him." She ran downstairs and then came back upstairs. Rick was looking dead at her.

"Was that him?" he asked.

"No," she said, with a smirk on her face.

Rick cut his eyes at her again.

"Derickie, what if I call him, ask him to meet you somewhere?" Karla asked. "You can ask him yourself; you a cop, take your partner with you."

"Okay, people, it's late," Troy said, "and I don't feel like getting dressed now; it's after midnight. Shit! I ate, I drank, and I saw a real Lifetime movie. I'm going home. Karla, I love you babe, but this here was not good; you should have told me at least."

"Yeah, I probably should have. I just didn't."

"Fellas, what y'all gonna do?" Rick asked. "I'm going home. Karla, let's go; you not staying here by yourself tonight, or the next few days. Where's Alicia and Kareem?"

"I don't know," she said. "I've been calling them all weekend and left messages; no response. I'm okay, I can stay here."

"Karla, get your big-ass bag and let's go," he said. "You coming with me."

"I'm not going to no frat party."

"And neither am I."

"Well, I need to get some clothes together."

"Like what? You got stuff at my house."

"Why do we always have to have a personal conversation in front of everybody?"

"What's personal about it?

"What clothes? I haven't been to your house since you been here."

"I brought you some things back from LA; stop rolling your damn eyes and just come on."

"I have to turn out the lights upstairs and check the doors downstairs."

"No, you don't," Paulie said. "I'll do it; just go. Y'all making me tired. Shit, I was ready to party and meet some new chicks, but after all this shit, fuck it. I'll keep what I got; she's a good woman."

"Andriano, what you gonna do?" Karla asked.

"After y'all leave, I'm making a call to my friend, see what's going on with us, and work it out."

"I'm crashing here tonight," Paulie said. "If that dude come up in here tonight or tomorrow, he's gonna be short."

She and Rick left first, out the back door. Troy, Anton, and Derickie went out the front door, and Andriano and Paulie stayed.

"If this motherfucka is out here," Rick said, "he better kill me because if I can get up, I'm fucking him up."

"Babe, is there anything else I need to know?" Rick asked as they walked to his truck.

"I already told you everything."

"All right, let's go!" he replied.

"Since you carried on like I said you would," Karla said, laughing.

"What you mean, carried on like you said I would; who did you tell that to?"

"Ri."

He laughed.

"No I didn't. But if he brings harm and fear to my family, you damn right. Imma be a fool. I know one thing: You better not ever do no more dumb shit like that again. But you won't have to; you'll be with me."

"Rick Tyler?"

"What, babe?" he asked.

"Can we make love tonight?"

He stopped the truck in the middle of the alley, leaned over to her seat, and kissed her like he hadn't touched her in years.

"Yes, babe, we most definitely will be making love tonight."

CHAPTER 7
THE FIGHT
MONDAY, JULY 21, 2008

A few weeks later, Rick and Karla finally met with JB for dinner at one of the finest five-star restaurants in Georgetown. JB adored Karla and directed all of his attention to her. Rick finally got JB's attention and finally got a word in.

"Well, JB, I made my decision," he said. "I'll take the job, if it's still available."

"You know what, Rick Tyler? You lucky I held this out for as long as you dragged it out, but you made a good choice and a wise decision. I'll let the board know as soon as possible, so they can start the process and get you onboard. Let me be the first to say congratulations. You'll make a fine judge, and I'm glad to meet this beautiful lady you're so happy with. I wish you all the best, but more so you, young lady; he's a piece of work."

Karla returned the smile, softly touching his hand.

"JB, you are so right," she said. "He is a piece of work, and I know he'll be a good judge, another one of DC's finest.

They finished out the night eating and talking; JB told Karla about his friendship with Rick over the years.

"JB, we must end this wonderful night with you," Rick said. "We had a great evening, and as usual, my friend, I enjoyed rapping with you, but we got to go. I need to fly out of here this week. I'll be back in LA for about a month, and I got some business plans to wrap up tomorrow. I'm saying good night, and we will most definitely talk later on."

"Okay, young man," he replied. "You have all you need for now, and I'll see you at the ceremony. Ms. Owens, it was my pleasure to have met you. I hope to see you again."

They all left the restaurant together; JB shook Rick's hand, kissed Karla on the cheek, and left for his car.

"He's a really nice man," she said. "He's funny"

"Yeah, very smart man too. I learned a lot from him."

They walked around Georgetown for a while and then headed back to the garage for the truck. The next day, after they woke up, they lay in bed talking.

"Babe, are you ready for this ride?" Rick asked. "Can you handle me being a judge and whatever comes along with it? I don't want to hear it later down the road, about me always at work or I don't give you enough time."

"Well, babe, my choice is to take this ride with you. I'm ready. Let's do it, but I still want my time, all the time, no matter what; just don't forget about me."

He hugged her tight and gave her a big kiss on the lips.

"I love you," he said, smiling and squeezing her body against his.

"I love you too," she said.

"All right, babe; you know, I've been gone for two months. I got to handle some business on this end, so come on take a ride with me. I have a meeting with a consultant today in Annapolis."

"Do I have to go?" she asked. "I just want to lay here and rest. I'm really tired. I'm not used to that kind of romance; my dates are quick and to the point. I'm a single lady."

Karla burst out laughing, rolling herself up in the sheet.

"Yeah, sorry to break the news to you, but you're not single anymore."

He snatched the sheet off of her and was pulling her out of the bed by her feet.

"Come on, get up; let's get dressed. I need to be there on time."

She followed him to the bathroom and stood in front of the mirror, looking at herself.

"What you doing?" he asked. "You're still in one piece. I didn't break nothing; if anything, I mended our hearts back together. You all right?"

He pulled her into the shower with him and rubbed his hand down the front of her body, massaging her clitoris with the flow of the water.

"Babe, how you feeling?" he asked. "I know I picked a fine time to ask you, but tell me how you really feel?"

"I feel fine," she said. "Why? How should I feel? Did you poison me with something and you trying to find out if it's kicking in?"

"Girl, if I was going to kill you, I would've done it long time ago, but I did poison you with my love, and so far, the formula is still working. Let's see how it plays out later down the line, 'cause you're still on a trial basis."

"That's fine too, Mr. Tyler; if I'm on a trial basis, so are you."

"Whatever; you just hurry up, Ms. Owens. I have to put my stamp on this deal soon."

"What deal you got going on now?" she asked. "What are you buying now, or shall I say what investment are you making?"

"Just hurry up, babe; you're going to like this. It's a surprise."

He slipped on a pair of jeans and a rust color Armani Collezioni sportcoat with a chocolate pair of Armani penny loafers. He grabbed his keys and wallet off the dresser and walked out the room, waiting on her.

"Wow," he said, watching her stroll past him in an all-white maxi dress with a pair of tan Tory Burch thong sandals, her flop hat, and her favorite shades. "You're looking sexy."

"Thank you," she said. "So do you, babe; you don't look too bad yourself."

"Wait, sexy. I left my phones on the counter. I need them."

"No, you didn't," she said. "I grabbed them off of the counter, while you was flying out the door like Superman."

He playfully yanked her hand.

"Who you calling Superman? Well, on that note, thanks Lois Lane; now we can move."

"I got your back," she said, kissing him on his lips, and they headed for the truck and rolled out.

"That's what I'm talking about," he said as they drove past the Naval Academy. "It's the small stuff that counts. I must be the luckiest man in town."

"Yeah, you are; so what kind of business you have out here in Annapolis? What you got going on that you haven't told me about yet?"

"Nothing, just a small project; meeting my foreman to walk through some floor plans, that's all."

"Okay, that's cool, but I have something that has been bothering me for a long time, and I got to ask you this question. It comes and goes, and I've tried to answer to find my own closure, but why did you leave me when we were teenagers and have a baby with someone else?"

He nearly slammed on the brakes in the middle of traffic.

"Karla, why are you bringing that up now? Things are going so well; let's not mess the day up, okay?"

"I just want to know," she said. "We never talked about that; we talked about everything else but that. Why?"

"Babe, I don't have an answer; it was so long ago. Let it go."

"But why didn't you ever come back for me? Did you really love me like you said you did back then, and like you say you do now?"

"Karla, where you going with this? I swear I don't want to revisit the past. Just let it go."

"But I want to. I was so hurt that Angela had your baby; you moved on with your life and never looked back. You never came to talk to me to say anything; you said nothing, even until this day. I hurt for a long time behind that. I was so in love with you."

"Look, Karla, I don't know what to say at this point. Do I say I'm sorry? That was almost twenty-five years ago; damn, let it go."

"Hell, yeah," she said. "Say something; that would at least help. I'd feel better with some type of explanation."

"Babe, why now? Does it matter at this point? Ric's here, and she's gone on with her life, and we are together, trying to move on with ours."

"Come on, babe; give me something an answer. Why?" Karla said, "We talk about anything and everything; why not this and now? You're gonna be a judge, and you telling me you can't be honest and answer the question?"

"That's different, babe."

"How? Tell me how it's different; a truth is a truth, correct?"

She turned completely around in her seat, staring at him.

"Well, will you at least look at me?"

"I can't look at you babe," he said. "I'm driving."

"Really? You look over me at any other time; now I'm asking you a question, and you can't look at me. Why not?"

"Babe, I really don't have an answer to what happened, okay? Why the hell are you bringing this up now? Does it really matter?"

Damn, he thought, *she raised the boy with her children, and Angela and I haven't talked in many years. I don't even know where she is. Fuck. I don't even think Ric knows where she is.*

"I just feel I need a final answer."

"What's the final answer are you looking for, Karla? What?"

"You left for college and never looked back for me at all."

"Babe, we were young; nothing was promised, okay? Damn."

"Young? Shit, you wasn't that young; you had the baby your sophomore year; you didn't write or call. You never said anything. I found out from Sandy."

"Oh, so Sandy was the one that told you? She said she never told you. I knew she was lying anyway."

"Yeah, she told me one night when we were hanging out; my heart broke that night for the first time. The love, trust, and honesty I had for you went right out the door; that night, I tried to keep a straight face, but my heart was in little pieces. When I got home that night, I cried and sheltered myself for days behind that."

"Look, Karla, like I said, I don't know why it happened; it wasn't in my plan to go away to college, meet someone else, and have a baby with her. I don't have an answer, except for maybe being young and immature, away in school, first time away from home by myself with no parents, doing what I wanted to do; maybe my head got big. I was the hot man on campus. Things became different for me."

"Different? How? Please explain."

He began to feel pressured and yelled, "I just told you, babe! It just happened; it's not like I planned it, okay? And let me just say for a final closure, I'm sorry for hurting you and breaking your heart, your trust, and my honesty. I'm so sorry. I can't go back to that date and time; if I could change it, I wouldn't, because I wouldn't have my son or the other things in my life, okay? Look, sometimes, things happen for a reason, whether it's good or bad, and it makes us grow up faster than we want to. We sometimes make decisions that we don't want to make, okay? That's all I got; take it or leave it."

"You don't have to yell at me; I'm sitting right here."

"I'm not yelling at you, babe; you trying to make me give you a reason that I don't have, an answer why I never came back for you. It's not that I didn't want to. I didn't think you wanted me. I didn't have the heart to come back to face you, knowing what happened and how it happened. Damn, are you satisfied with that answer?"

"No, because that's not an answer."

"Well, babe, I don't know what to tell you then. I'm done with that story."

"Whatever, Rick."

"What the hell does that mean, whatever? Shit, you asked me. I didn't bring it up; now you mad. I should be mad."

"Just like I said, that's a bullshit answer," Karla replied.

"Karla, what the hell do you want? Okay, I apologize for my actions as a teenager and maybe for some of my adult actions, but damn, are you ever going to forgive me? Oh, so now you can't look at me; picture that shit: You turn your head, and you ain't even driving, but you can look out the got damn window. Wow. Look, I love you now. I always loved you. I am in love with you, and I hoped one day you would forgive me, marry me, and maybe one day, we could have our own children together. I'm sorry for the hundredth time; if I wasn't driving, I would get down on my knee and apologize. What do you want me to do? I'm sorry, babe; that's all I got."

She didn't respond the whole ride to Annapolis; he kept touching her face and stroking her hair. She ignored him, as if she didn't feel his touch.

"I'm sorry, babe, and I am not going to keep taking these daggers much longer. I'll play along for a little while, but don't make me check your ass. Look, we here; are you getting out the truck or you gonna sit over there with your arms still folded, looking pissed?"

"No, and I'm not pissed. I'll get out in a few minutes."

"Okay, we'll sit here together. I'll wait with you; we a little early anyway."

"You don't have to wait for me; if you supposed to meet someone here at two o'clock, then go inside. It's 1:45."

"Look, babe, I asked you to come with me for a reason, for some suggestions; don't act like that."

"No, you didn't. You ask me to take a ride with you; you never said anything about my suggestions, and my suggestions don't mean a hill of beans. I'm not your wife; I'm just your woman."

"Girl, you need to stop being so damn mean."

"If this is one of your clients' houses, why aren't they here to give you suggestions?"

"All right, Karla, just forget it; stay here til you ready. I'm not entertaining you."

He rolled the windows up on purpose, turned the truck off, got out, and slammed the door.

Then she'll sit her ass in there with no damn air, he thought. *I bet she'll get the fuck out then.*

He was shaking his head as he headed for the door.

She don't hear me holding her responsible for my pain when she had that abortion; she never asked me how I felt about it. It was a done deal when I found out. Shit.

Just then the man he was meeting walked over.

"Good afternoon, Mr. Tyler; how you doing on this fine day?" the man asked.

"I'm okay, Mr. Broom, and yourself?"

"I'm just dandy. I'm ready to go over your plans."

"Well, sorry that you had to take time out from your personal schedule today, but this is on hold for now," Rick said. "Just finish all of the plumbing and electrical work; once that's done, let me know. Put all contractors on hold after that."

"Are you sure, Mr. Tyler? This is going to be a nice house."

"Yeah, it is, but I'm not living here by myself; too much space. I'll sell it first, even if it means I lose some money, but that's cool."

"Okay, will do."

"Just keep me posted on the updates; I'll be out here to check from time to time; send me all confirmations that work has been completed."

"Yes, sir."

Just then, Karla came walking toward the two men.

"Oh, you can stop right there, Ms. Owens," Rick said coldly. "No need to come any further. Let's go. I'm finished with what I had to do."

They turned around and walked out the front door. She was walking behind him; he opened the truck door for her and slammed it behind her.

"Dang, good thing I pulled my dress in and moved my leg; you slammed the door."

Mr. Broom came running out and caught him just as he was pulling off.

"Mr. Tyler, did you lock the doors or put the sign out?"

"No, I didn't; would you do that, please? Lock up and make sure the No Trespassing sign is out; make sure it's visible."

He pulled out of the lot, with the radio blaring, then he turned it off.

"You know what? We started out good, but somehow it took another turn, so since we took that wrong turn, let's go. I didn't want to go down memory lane, but let's just go there anyway for the hell of it. None of that old shit counts; I don't give a damn about your past relationships. I knew about some of your bullshit relationships, but who the fuck was I to step into your relationships? I hated to hear if they were good or bad; I wanted to be there for you, but I couldn't. I just thank God nobody killed your ass."

If looks could kill, he was a dead man.

"Oh, now you can look at me, as if I said some wrong shit. Let's fuckin' go there, babe. I got a question that haunted me for years, but I never said anything about. I just let it go, and to this day, you never said anything about it either, not one got damn word. When we did finally start seeing each other again, you still didn't say anything, so now let me just ask you something, since you want to be the innocent one. I'm searching for an answer too. Oh no, don't huff and puff. Picture that shit; you still think you can do and say what you want, but now I want some answers. You looking at me like I'm crazy. Georgie ain't here, and none of your uncles is here to protect that ass this time."

"I don't need them here to protect me."

"Really? I'm quite sure when this is all over, your ass will be texting or calling somebody, but I don't give a damn."

"I can call or text anybody I want."

She pulled her phone out of her purse, but he snatched it out of her hand.

"Give me that motherfuckin' phone."

He rolled the window down, contemplating on throwing it out the window; instead, he threw it in his side door.

"After this, I don't give a fuck who you call, or what you do, but I want my answer today, before you get your ass out this truck."

"What answer?"

"Why didn't you tell me about the pregnancy?"

"What pregnancy?"

"Don't fuckin' play with me, Karla; you know just what the hell I'm talking about. I damn sure ain't talking about Alicia or Kareem or Ric! Let me refresh your damn memory."

His voice was so deep that she really was scared for the first time ever.

"The one when we were seventeen years old, and you were pregnant by me; that is correct, right? It was my baby, right?"

"Oh yeah; yes, it was your baby."

"So tell me why the hell I never knew about that."

She couldn't answer the question; all she could do was shed her tears.

"Oh no, answer the got damn question; don't cry now."

"I don't know why I didn't tell you."

"Really? You don't know? Well, what a fuckin' coincidence, because I don't know why either. When I found out about the baby, you had already had the abortion; now tell me why. Well, let me tell you how I found out. Georgie made it his business to secretly come into town and come by my parents' house one weekend. I just happened to be home, and he let everybody that was there know that you were pregnant and you had an abortion. My mother and father was fucked up from the news; they were looking at me like I was crazy, and I was looking crazy because I had no idea of nothing. You never told me shit."

He was beating her with his tone of voice; she couldn't fight back, at least with words.

"So not only was I getting laid out from Georgie, but from my parents too. Georgie so nicely told us I wasn't shit, that I got you pregnant, and I was going on to college, and there was nothing I could do for you. I didn't have shit and never was going to be shit. I wasn't going to amount to nothing. He read my ass so bad that he and my father went to blows in the house that day.

"Do you recall any of that, Karla?" he asked. "That's the day my father pulled out his gun, and Georgie pulled out his, and they drew on each other; it was about to be some blood shedding. My mother was upset, crying and screaming and, at the same time, slapping the shit out of me; the whole damn house was in an uproar. My father told Georgie he would blow his fuckin' brains out if he ever disrespected me and his family again; maybe that's why I didn't call you and moved on. It may have had something to do with that, until years later, I let it go."

"Oh, my goodness," Karla whispered. "Are you serious?"

"Yes, I'm serious; you think I'm just making this up as I'm talking?

Why didn't you tell me about the baby, Karla? You want to talk about pain? I hurt for a long time behind that. One, you never told me, and then, how I found out was even more fucked up, so Karla, why? Why?

"No, don't cry now. All of your crying should be done and over with. You said I hurt you, but do you think you hurt me? I'll accept that I hurt you, but it was not intentional, but here's the thing, Karla: If you wanted to be with me, you could have just as well reached out to me too.

"When I came home," he continued, "you never said anything; instead, you distanced yourself. I guess for real that's been the whole damn problem: Your ass was too fuckin' spoiled. Karla could do whatever she wants, and nobody better treat her wrong. Yeah, right! If Georgie's babe don't get what she wants, she cries to her daddy! Oops, shit; I'm sorry, it's the granddaddy Felipo Lombardo; he's the one that really makes shit happen for you, and to anyone that fuck over babe …"

"I'm not spoiled."

"Shit, maybe not now; what happen? Who cut who off? Did Georgie cut his baby girl off? Aw, too sad. So that explains why your ass chose to struggle for no damn reason, and why you had these fucked-up relationships, 'cause them motherfuckas only wanted to get in your pockets, especially when they found out who you belonged to, and you do know the streets talk, babe. You do know you had a couple that wasn't impressed with you, but they had other motives, I know all about it."

He was riding her ass so hard, he forgot himself who he was talking to.

"Why are you talking to me like this?"

"Because I can, damn it. You talk to me any kind of way you want to, and it's cool; how long do you think I'm going to let you keep throwing daggers at me and stabbing me in my damn heart? Are you serious? Shit not happening."

"We don't have to go no further," she cried. "We can end this for real here today; say the word. Shit, I tried."

She cried and cried, trying to explain what happen, but her tears were flowing like a river. By this point, he didn't give a damn; he was so angry and hurt, he stopped trying to explain.

"Look here, Karla: All that crying shit ain't working with me; at this point, I've expressed how I feel for you. I left all that old shit behind; it was history. I don't have an answer for you of what happened then. You pushed and pushed into some bullshit that didn't have to go this way; I love you, and I want you in my life. Here is my response to your stupid ass question: I have one son, and maybe one day a couple of stepchildren. My son, I love as much as myself, but my son is now grown, and you know he loves you dearly. Even though he knows his biological mother, he doesn't call he 'Ma.' He calls her Angela. Even though we were not together then, you always looked out for my son, and I never knew why. You treated him as your own child, and I always loved you for that. Babe, I don't see why an answer is required after all these years; if you did all of those things for him and me, and it was from your heart, why is an answer needed now? What the hell are you searching for?"

"Whatever I did for him is because I wanted to," she said softly. "It had nothing to do with you. Your answer is not required."

"Oh, now my answer is not required." He laughed. "But let me understand: A fuckin' answer was needed when you were asking me the questions; ain't that some shit? Your ass is still so damn spoiled, and you think people supposed to respond to you with an answer, but you don't have to respond to them with an answer; what kind of shit is that?" He laughed and shook his head. "And just think, I still love you. So what you want do: go home, or go with me?"

She mumbled, while wiping her face, "I'll go with you."

"Is that a yes with me, or what? I didn't hear you."

He heard exactly what she said.

"Just because your ass is mad and I said a few things, and Lord knows you said some shit to me, don't pipe down now. I should just drop your overgrown spoiled ass off; do you want me to?"

"You can take me home to my house," she said. "I got a damn headache anyway. I need to lay down."

"Do you want to lay in my bed with your headache?"

"Now why would I want to lay in your bed, after you blasted me out; are you crazy?"

He snickered.

"There you go again, smart ass, can't just answer the question, but if that's what you feel, then so be it, Karla Owens. Fuck it. I'm done. I'll take your ass to your house, not a damn problem."

When they reached the Davidsonville exit, he changed his mind; with a smirk on his face, he shoved her shoulder.

"You know what?" he said. "Instead, that's a hell, no. I'm not driving to DC. I'm not taking your ass home; your ass is going to suffer with me tonight. You just sit your ass over there and get yourself together; you're out of control. Your ass is on punishment. I'll take you home another time; until then, you're coming with me, and don't be flinging yourself against my seat; what's wrong with you?"

"Rick, leave me alone," she cried. "I got a headache."

"You should have an ass ache."

"I want my phone back; it's ringing. It may be one of my children. Why are you answering my phone?"

"Alicia, what's going on," he asked. "Where are you, babe?"

"I'm at the house," she said. "Kareem and I in here cooking, or at least I am. How you get my mom's phone?"

"I'm with your mean-ass Mom."

"Cool, okay, well, Ric is in town; he said he on his way by here. He asked for Ma."

"Well, he knows how to reach us. I wonder if his mother knows he's in town."

"Yes, I do."

"If you knew he was coming in town, why didn't you tell me?"

She snatched the phone from his ear. "Hey Alicia, I'll be home tomorrow; call me if you'll need me."

"I will, Ma; love you."

Damn, he thought, *I hope I really didn't hurt her feelings, but we were young and neither one of us knew what was really right or wrong. All we knew was we loved each other. I guess the question now is, do we love each other for real, or are we really just comfortable with each other? Uh huh; naw, I really do love her. She's always been my soulmate; she's a sweetheart, just set in her ways sometimes. I am too; oh well, we'll just play it out and see where we go from here.*

She lay her head back against the headrest and closed her eyes; she stayed like that all the way back to his place. He parked the truck and helped her out by holding held her hand; he stroked her back as they walked through the lobby doors. The concierge was smiling as he spoke to them both, but more so to Karla. She smiled back, and he was taken by her sensuous smile and the glow of beautiful, bright brown skin.

"Man, what's up?" Rick said to the concierge. "Why you smiling so hard at my woman? You can't have her; nobody can, but me."

He yanked her hand as they continued to walk toward the elevator for upstairs.

Shit, she thought after they went inside his condo, *he gave me a headache. I didn't know Georgie did all that. I guess I better leave well enough alone then; ain't no telling what may come out next.*

He burst into the bathroom, just as she was climbing in the tub.

"Babe, Imma make something to eat; what would you like?"

She closed the door in his face and slid down in the tub.

"I know you heard me," he said. "How long are we going to do this, for the next five minutes, right? Because that's all you getting."

"What?" she asked. "What did you say? The door was closing as you were talking."

He pushed the door opened again.

"I said, what you want to eat? I know you heard me."

"Nothing," she replied. "I'm not hungry."

"Girl, I know you're hungry by now; you haven't eaten anything all day. All you ate was some junk food."

"No, I'm fine really."

This is going to be a hard case to crack, he thought. *She making me work for no reason at all.*

He closed the bathroom door and walked back into the living room.

Fine, he thought. *I got some things to look over, anyway.*

He sat on the couch, pulled out his laptop, and started reading over some documents that Whitey's secretary forwarded, marked "Urgent."

"Whitey, man, you lucky I like you," he said aloud. "I'm closing out my own cases, and now you want me to help you on some damn murder case.

"This woman has been missing for years, and her family just realized she's been murdered. Um, I wonder if this is Sabrina's friend's cousin she was telling me about; what a coincidence that Whitey got this. I wonder if he will be flying out here, or do I have to make a quick run back to LA. I know it's the wee hours of the morning over there, but I need to talk with him, see what's up."

He picked up his phone and dialed Whitey's number.

"Hey, man, I would say I'm sorry for waking you up. I was planning to leave a message. I didn't expect you to answer, but what the hell? You're up now."

"To what do I owe the pleasure of you calling me so damn early, Chocolate Man?"

"This case you sent me is crazy. I read the first ten pages, and I think this is Sabrina's friend's cousin."

"How you figure that?" Whitey replied.

"Man, she told me about her long before I left that she was missing, but we never talked about it anymore; time got away from me, and she never finished given me the details."

"You sure?"

"Not really, but I need to read more and then touch basis with Sabrina to get the details of what she knows."

"All right man, so when are you going to finish reading it?"

"Maybe tonight or tomorrow. Karla is here."

"Okay; how's the house coming along and Karla?"

"Not so good; that's a whole other story on them both."

"Okay, I'll leave that alone. I'm planning on coming to DC in a few weeks or so."

"Oh yeah? What's going on out this way, or shall I say, who you coming to meet?"

Whitey laughed.

"My parents are heading that way. I told them I'll fly out and hang out with them a few days; they said they want to surprise you to say hello."

"I won't be here," he replied. "I'm heading back that way soon for a couple of months."

"All right, cool, Chocolate Man. I'll get up with you then; until then, I'm out. Peace."

"All right. Peace!"

Well, let me cook my babe something to eat, he thought. *She's going to eat; she just being a butt. She still in her feelings; maybe I'll apologize for laying her ass out, before this goes on the history list, then she'll bring this up twenty years later. Jeeze!*

He prepared one of his favorite dishes for her: pan-seared scallops on linguine with tomato cream sauce, served with a chilled bottle of Riesling. He set the table for two out on the balcony, with candles, the fine china, and wine glasses on the table, overlooking Arlington and the city of DC.

I must say so myself, he thought, *this really is a romantic setting.*

Oh, thank goodness my headache is gone, she thought after her shower. Thank you, Lord; this has been a crazy day. I guess I do owe him an apology for bringing up the past. I just wanted to know. I guess sometimes it's best that you don't know and move on; look at it like this: If we did get together back then, we would probably be divorced by now, and Lord knows how many children I would have. I'll do the right thing and apologize.

"What the hell are you screaming about?" Rick asked.

"I don't know," she said. "You caught me off guard."

"Really? Good. I'm glad to know I can still catch you off guard."

She smacked her lips and pushed past him.

"You always think everything is funny, chocolate ass self."

"You love it, though, don't you? Now, bring your ass on out here and eat. I prepared a peace offering dinner. Hey, why do you have PJs on so damn early?"

"Why?" Karla asked. "Are we going somewhere?"

"Maybe."

"Okay, then, I can change when we finish."

He opened the vertical blinds, and her face lit up when she saw the table set on the balcony.

"Wait," he said. "Don't go out there yet! Listen, babe, I'm sorry for today; it went too far on both our ends. I don't want this to come up twenty years later, so I apologize for what I said, okay?"

"Apology accepted," she began, "and I apologize too. And ..."

"Karla, stop right there," he interrupted. "Don't say anything else. I got it, okay? And please don't bring this up ever again; are we clear? Can we agree on that?"

She nodded her head in agreement and pecked him on the lips, then he poured her a glass.

"Hold tight, babe; sip slowly while I get the food."

"Wow," she said when he brought the plates out. "That smells and looks good, babe."

"Yeah, it does," he replied, "but not better than you. Since the midday didn't turn out to be so great, let's see how the late evening goes."

"You know, I never knew how beautiful it was sitting out here at night," Karla said. "It's terrific, isn't it?"

"Yeah, it is," he agreed. "I've sat on the couch many days, watching the sun come up and the moon go down, by myself. Yes," he repeated, "by myself."

"Shut up," he replied. "I didn't say anything. I just was looking at you."

"Yeah, okay, Ms. Owens, but I saw your face; you're the only woman that has ever comes to this place."

"But we're not going to talk about our past relationships, are we? No, 'cause we both can get a little jealous, so leave it. One day, maybe when we can handle it; we'll laugh about it then, but now, hell, no."

They finished eating and stayed out on the balcony, talking and laughing until the moon was high and darkness had slipped upon them.

"Babe, when I come back, I have a really serious question for you."

"About what?" she asked. "I don't want another surprise."

"No, it's nothing like earlier today, but you better answer this, and I'm not playing with you."

"Let me help you," she said, "so we can get this question out the way."

"Nope, I got this," he replied. "Just relax. I'll be back shortly."

There was a hammock on the balcony, and she climbed in with her glass of wine, sipping as she swung back and forth; Rick came back and climbed in the hammock with her.

"Why you staring at me?" said Karla.

"Okay," he said, "I'm just going to come straight out with this: I need your help."

"Will you get to the question before I get mad?"

"You get mad all you want," he said. "That doesn't bother me; I'm so used to it."

He leaned out of the hammock and picked up a silver box from the ground.

"Why the hell are you crying now?" he asked. "I didn't say this was for you."

"Oh, well, what's the question?" Karla asked.

"My father asked me to pick something up for him, so I did. You know him; I got to make sure it's right, or I'll never hear the end of it. You know, their anniversary is coming up, and he wanted something special for my mother."

"So why you asking me about it? Why don't you show your sisters and brothers?"

"I did, all they said was it's nice and they like it, but I want your opinion. I know you two are close; you'd know if she'll really like it or not."

"All right, let's see it, then, but you could have asked Sandy too."

"Just take a look at, babe, tell me what you think."

She opened the box and her mouth was wide open; she didn't

know whether to cry, holler, or hit him. She kept staring at the ring in the box, with tears rolling down her face.

"Oh, my God," she cried.

"Babe," he began, "will you marry me? Will you spend the rest of your life with me? Stop crying and answer me."

"Shut up," she said. "Stop it! I do have an answer."

"Well, if you have an answer, when you going to let me know? I'm the one that asked the question."

"Yes, Erick Tyler, I'll marry you."

She leaned over and hugged him, then gave him a long kiss.

"I do love you."

"I'll be," she said after they went inside; "here we go again! Your phone is ringing off the hook; who's sending you a text this late?"

"What the hell?" Rick said, looking at this phone. "Aw shit; come on, babe, we got to go. Derickie just been shot, and they taking him to Washington Hospital Center."

They both jumped up; Karla quickly changed her clothes, and Rick slipped on a tee-shirt and grabbed his keys. They rolled out, heading for DC. By the time Rick and Karla got there, everyone was there, waiting to hear the news. Derickie's partner and other policemen were all standing around. Ricky, Derickie's father, was standing outside the operating room, pacing the floor and crying for his son.

"Babe who texted you?" Karla asked.

"I don't know, but the strangest thing: It came from Derickie's phone. If he's laying up in here, who knew to text me?"

He gave Karla his phone, and her mouth flew wide open.

"Rick, was Derickie somewhere he shouldn't be?" she asked. "This is crazy; you didn't read the whole thing, did you?"

"No, why? Is there more? I only saw the first part of the text."

"Yeah; it says, 'Come get your cousin or brother; he'll know the next time he lay up with someone else's woman. He lucky I didn't chop his shit off, and the next time he wants to have an affair with two others, he needs to include me and make a foursome. Good luck. I hope he make it to safety."

"What the hell?" Rick said. "Who knows with Derickie? I just hope the fool is alive."

The doctors came out to talk with Derickie's father; he braced himself for the news.

"Give it to me straight, Doctor," Ricky said. "He's my only son; is he all right?"

"Sir," the doctor began, "your son is alive; he'll be in some pain for a while, but he'll live. Miraculously, one bullet bypassed his lungs, and the other just missed the main nerve in his back. He's going up to a room now; you'll be able to see him in a little while."

All of the Tylers were standing around, listening. Derickie's cousins weren't shocked at all; they seemed to look at each other, as if someone had an answer.

"Don't look at me," Rick said. "I don't know nothing."

"I know you know," Aunt Malory said. "You're closer to him than anybody; who was he with?"

Rick yanked Karla's hand and dragged her down the hall, and out the door they went.

"I'll come back later when he comes around and find out where his ass was, but I'm not telling them. Do you think Mark may have something to do with this?"

"I don't know, just wait until you talk with him. I'm sure it will come out sooner or later. In the meantime, we got a wedding to plan. Derickie ain't going nowhere, not for a while."

CHAPTER 8
THE BIG WEDDING
ONE YEAR LATER
SATURDAY, JULY 25, 2009

Thank God, Karla thought. *I'm so happy this day is here. it must be some real love.*

She slid on a pair of white satin Vera Wang slingback shoes, then stepped into her strapless satin gown, with a chapel-length embroidered train. Laying against her collarbone was a two-carat diamond pendant necklace. Her hair was pinned up in a bun with small flower clips.

"Ri, not today," Karla said. "I didn't ask you for your opinion."

"You never do, but I gave it anyway. You two don't have a clue how happy we all are; we were tired of you and him. We're happier than you two are."

"Karla, are you ready?" asked Charlotte, the wedding coordinator. "The car is here; it's time, so let's go, ladies. Chop, chop. We can do a few pictures as we head out."

Alicia came down first; she was the maid of honor, and her dress was similar to her mother's: a soft pink chiffon strapless gown and pink slingbacks. She was as beautiful as her mother.

"Wow," Charlotte said. "You and your mother look so beautiful. I like that style on you both."

Sandy and Kimmie wore lavender chiffon strapless gowns with cream petals. Cerise and Patsy wore halter knee-length dresses, with pink and lavender petals, and Renee wore a plain lavender knee-length dress, and Gail wore a soft pink one.

"Okay, ladies," Charlotte said. "Let's get in the car; we got enough here. We're on a schedule; please come on."

"Come on," Karla added. "I can't be late; today is the day. I got to go greet my husband-to-be."

"Yes," Cerise said. "Please let's get her there; if we're late, we'll never hear the end of it from him."

They all piled in the car, one by one; not long after the car pulled off, it started.

"Well, Well Ms. Thing," Renee said, "you finally got him. So what's your plans now that you're marrying my brother?"

"First of all, Renee, my name is not Ms. Thing; it's Karla Owens, soon to be Karla Tyler, and where you going with your question?"

"I just asked, now that you marrying someone with lots of money, do you plan on continuing to work, or are you just going to live off him?"

"Renee, why don't you shut up?" Sandy said. "Stop trying to start stuff; it's not your business, anyway."

"You shut up, Sandra. I'm just asking her a question, since she doesn't have any money of her own. I'm just saying, it's funny that all of sudden, you now marrying him, but not long ago, you didn't want any part of him. Now you're so in love with him; what's that about?"

"Renee, it's not your got damn business," Karla snapped, "and furthermore, why you're so concerned about your brother? Are you scared that he's not going to support you and your sorry-ass husband anymore?"

"You bitch; my husband is not sorry, he got a job, and we good."

"Really? When the last time that husband of yours had a real job and kept it for more than a week? Does the fucker pay any mortgage? Oh that's right, y'all pay rent, right? He fucked your credit up; it's so got damn bad, you can't even get a fuckin' toilet to piss in. Your damn brothers have been bailing your ass out! aren't you tired of that?"

"Fuck you, Karla."

"No, fuck you, Renee; the only reason I asked you to be in our wedding was to keep peace with him; remember one thing, boo: I don't owe you no explanation of our relationship. What Erick and I do is our business; that's a piece of information for the front of your little stupid-ass mind."

"Wait," Kimmie interrupted. "This is going way to far; stop it!"

Renee took a swing at Karla but hit her sister, Cerise, instead.

"I know you, bitch."

"Renee, you don't know me," Karla said. "You been seeing me for years, but you know nothing about me. You don't know my life, only of what you may have heard, but if you were not there firsthand, you know nothing of me."

"Hold up," Sherri said. "You don't have to explain yourself to nobody except to your husband. Renee, you're way out of line."

"You know exactly how your brother feels about her," Kimmie said, "and we all know how she feels about him. They both talked our ears off. I'm not going to paint a picture for Karla and Rick, because they both deserve each other today. Got damn it, I'm sick of them; they're going to be together forever, whether you like it or not, so just stop and sit back. Don't you throw another punch."

"Ok, hold up, Kimmie," Cerise said. "I know she can take stuff way too far. Renee, you're wrong; mind your business. If you feel that way, then why did you agree to be in their wedding? You could have declined. I don't know what your motive is, but today is not the day, okay?"

"Cerise, I was just asking. I just want to know 'cause all of a sudden, she decided to marry him; seems strange to me. Two years ago, she didn't want anything to do with him."

"Enough, Renee; so what? Rick ain't a little boy; he's a grown-ass man, so enjoy the day for him. Damn."

"But Cerise, he was supposed to marry Tina."

"Who the hell is Tina?" Kimmie asked. "Evidently, he didn't want to marry her, because he's marrying my sister."

"Look Renee, I'm sure your brother still loves you," Sherri said, "and I'm quite sure he will help you from time to time, but he now is making his own family. You have to accept that; stop tripping over nothing."

"Renee, I've tried for years to be cordial with you," Karla said, "but it's still not working. I don't give a damn about you. What I really want to do is reach over there and punch you in the fucking face for bringing up her name on my day, but that wouldn't be right, now would it?"

"Do what you feel, Karla; let's do it. Get it off your chest, bitch. I have never liked your ass from day one, and I still don't."

Karla punched Renee in the face and then pulled her hair, shaking her head like a piece of paper. Renee screamed, trying to hold her head up, but Karla kept shaking her head even harder.

"Oh my goodness, stop," said Sandy. "Renee, that's enough of your mess. I swear, I feel like slapping the shit out of you myself. Once this is all over, you and I are going to have a serious talk."

"About what? She hit me; you're my sister. You ain't said shit to her ass."

"Renee, what the hell is wrong with you?" Cerise said. "Do you want your own brother, because that's how you sound: like a jealous old girlfriend."

"No, now you sound like a fool; why would I want my brother? I just don't like her ass. I wish he would have married Tina or anybody else, except her ass over there."

"Ladies, can we pull this together?" Charlotte said. "We're almost there. I don't want you all getting out like you've been in a mud fight."

"Ms. Renee," Charlotte said, "if you do not want to be in this wedding party, please tell me now, so that I can make arrangements with the groomsmen. I'm not having this mess out of you; this is not your day. I have a job to do, and if that means having you removed, that's what I'll do."

"I'm not going to say anything else. I'm only doing this for my brother."

"Oh, my God, Renee, just answer the question," Sandy said. "Do you want to be in the wedding or not? All this shit about your brother; please. You got two other brothers and two sisters; we all have families and haven't stop loving you no less. This here is stupid, and you know it. Yes or no: What's your answer, Renee?"

"Yes."

The bridal party got out the car and walked through the side door of the mansion; they all looked agitated and pissed as hell.

"Oh, my goodness," Cerise said. "It's sure a lot of people here."

"Yeah," Kimmie said. "They're all here to see this marriage for themselves, just like we are."

Gail pinched Karla's her arm and burst out laughing.

"So how many people are here for you, Karla? You don't have no friends."

"It may appear that way," she said, "but I got a few out there."

Renee purposely brushed up against Karla and bumped her arm on her way up the steps.

"I bet my brother kicked out a lot the money for this place for you."

"Ladies, please go upstairs," Charlotte said. "You can freshen up and rest for about thirty minutes; we're on time. Just sit down and relax yourself and no arguing."

"Karla, don't look so worried," Sandy said. "He'll be here soon; trust me, girl: He'll be here."

"Baby sis, I am so proud of you," Sherri said. "One, for being the person that you are, and second, for being placed in my heart and my soul for all these years. You and Kimmie have made my life, and I thank you so much for being my sisters. We share the same love that travels from our hearts to our soul, and lastly, thank God, you're finally doing it. I love you."

"Hey, what's going on over there?" Kimmie asked.

"I was just telling our baby sista how much I love her for being who she is."

"Yeah, she's all right sometimes," Gayle said, laughing.

"Sisters and sisters-in-law, can I have your attention for a minute?" Karla said. "I want to first and foremost thank each of you for joining our celebration and to stand with us to witness our confession of love."

"Girl, none of us would dare to miss this," said Patsy.

"Shut up, Patsy. I would like to give thanks to my almighty

heavenly Father for blessing me with my daughter, who is my matron of honor. Alicia, you are my soul and everything. You are my first born; you and your brothers are my everything. Without you three, I would not be here today."

What is this bitch talking about? Renee thought angrily. *Ric is not her son. She makes me fuckin' sick, always calling him her son; got people thinking that bullshit, and she's not his fuckin' mother.*

"Renee, why are you looking so mad?" Sandy whispered. "Your face all turned up; what's wrong now?"

"I'm sorry, Sandy. I was thinking about something else." *I wish she would shut up. I don't care what she has to say; let's just get this over with.*

"Kimmie, you have taught me so many different things, and you took me places that if Papa knew we were there, oh my goodness; you would be in a world of trouble, then and now. I love you."

"Yeah, I know," Kimie said. "Thank God he don't know, or we would still be grounded, maybe. I love you too, Karla, but now if you ever tell Papa, I'll have to hurt you."

"Patsy, you're my blood sister, and I couldn't have asked for a better sister than you. We spent many nights laying in the same bed, laughing, chatting about people, and just talking about everything, including relationships. When we were teenagers, we spent so many nights talking about you-know-who."

"That darn Rick Tyler," said Patsy. "I love you for those days and nights; we had many jokes on him, didn't we?"

Patsy winked her eye at Karla and smiled.

"Gail, my troublemaker sister: I love you just as much as the others. Patsy and I used to lay in the bed and think about how we could duct-tape your mouth shut, but we knew if we did, we wouldn't have anyone to tell us bullshit stories. I love you for that, because you keep our lives full of laughter."

"I love you too, Karla," Gail said, "but if the truth be told, I thought many nights myself of how I could duct-tape you two. I knew if I did, I'd be the one that got in trouble."

"Sandy, my soulmate of a girlfriend, we have been through a lot together: parties that we weren't supposed to go to and places we shouldn't have been in. I love you, girl, and hope we can continue our journey in life now as sisters-in-law."

"Cerise, you are the peacemaker of your family; those same soft-spoken words you said to me is how I feel about you. You are my heart, and I love you so much."

Renee was standing in the back with her lips turned up, rolling her eyes up in the air.

"Look, Karla," she said, "before you say anything, I know we are close, so keep your memorable speech to yourself."

"Okay, ladies, that was all good," Charlotte said, "but it's show-time now. On my count, one by one, go."

The sax player was blowing so beautifully; it sounded like birds singing. They floated out gracefully, marching to the beat of the music. The doors opened, and there was Georgie standing in his black tux, waiting to escort his daughter down the aisle.

"Hi, my babe," he said when she appeared. "You look so beautiful."

"Thanks, Georgie," Karla said. "You look pretty darn handsome yourself, as always."

Karla and Georgie made their entrance; he wrapped her arm around his, and they glided down the aisle to where her groom was waiting.

"Who gives this woman away?" the preacher asked.

"I do," Georgie said. "I hope this isn't the last time I get to hug my babe."

"No, Georgie," Rick whispered, "it won't be." He winked his eye with a big ole smile and said, "Hey, babe."

The preacher had the perfect sermon for their ceremony: Adam and Eve. Rick said his vows first, and then Karla. He placed the ring onto her finger, and then she placed his matching band on his finger.

"I now pronounce you Mr. and Mrs. Erick Tyler."

As they were kissing, the sax player hit it again, playing "Love Is in the Air."

"Congratulations, Mr. and Mrs. Erick Tyler; now please follow me," Charlotte ordered. "Remember now, we're on a schedule."

"We're coming," Rick said. "The main part is done for me, so if we run off the schedule, don't worry about it. You'll still be paid for your time."

"Thanks for that information, Mr. Tyler, but I am not scheduled to be here all night. Let's stay on track; it's picture time."

Karla interjected before he could respond: "We'll be there in fifteen minutes; have the photographer meet us in the courtyard with the wedding party. Thanks, Charlotte."

Charlotte rolled her eyes and mumbled under her breath, "Smart ass; ugh."

"Babe, is she going to worry us the rest of the night?" Rick asked. "Damn, I know she's the coordinator, but she acting like the warden."

"Rick, leave her alone and let her do her job, okay? Just follow the program; come on, relax. You got me now, so stop acting up; anyway, I need to talk to you."

She dragged him into a side room.

"Aw shit, here we go again," he said. "Is this about some old shit?"

"No, it's not any old shit."

"Then what is it?"

"Babe, what the hell is wrong with Renee?"

"I don't know; you brought me up here to ask me that? You could have asked me that outside as we were walking."

"No, she and I got into it as soon as we got in the car; she started mouthing off about me marrying you."

"Where is this going?" he asked. "Go ahead tell me; I'm listening."

"The first thing, she asked was I going to continue to work and said that I was only marrying you for your money."

"Karla, that's none of her damn business; why do you care what she says now after all these years? You don't care; come on, are you serious?"

"Do I look like I'm playing? She was so serious; I already know she can't stand me, but then she said you should have married Tina or anybody else except me."

"Okay, stop, babe; stop. Let me put an end to this shit before it goes too far; don't tell me anymore about what Renee said. Here's it is: You are my wife now, and if you don't ever go back to work again, that's our business. Don't let Renee get under you; stop entertaining that shit. She don't put nothing in my pockets or our household, let alone run my life; are we clear on her?"

"Yeah, but what if she acts out during the reception?"

"Babe, if she does, I'll handle her on the spot; just keep being you. You don't owe her shit, and the next time you pull me upstairs like this again, it better be because you want my body. Now let's go take these pictures and enjoy the rest of the day."

"Well, wait," she said. "Since we're alone here, can we go for a quickie?"

"Uh, woman, no. Let's go; we'll be all day."

"Man, you finally did it," JB said. "Thank you, Lord. I thought this day would never come. You were making me a little nervous there for a minute."

"Nervous from what JB? You thought I was going to be an old whore?"

"Yeah," he said.

"Congratulations, Erick," Octavia, JB's wife, said.

"Octavia, you don't have to hug the man that hard," JB said, laughing. "Let him go."

"JB, I know you're not jealous," she said. "You still as handsome as he is. I'm still going home with you, plus you're broken in. I'm too old to train a new man now."

"How you doing, Ms. Octavia?" Rick asked.

"You still call me Ms. Octavia, after all these years?"

"Yes, and I'm going to continue to call you that."

He peeled himself away from her and stepped back.

"Where's your bride?" Octavia asked. "I like to meet her."

"She's walking up behind you now."

"Oh my, you look so beautiful," she said.

"Congratulations, Mrs. Tyler," said JB.

"Thank you, sir; it's a pleasure to see you again."

"Rick, she's a doll! I can see who's the boss now."

"You ain't in control of nothing except the courtroom, my brother."

Karla turned toward Octavia, greeted her with a smile, and extended her hand.

"Hello, and how are you? I'm Karla."

"I'm fine, darling; you look so beautiful today, and like my husband said, congratulations. We are so proud of Rick."

"Rick, she's a cutie, and she has a cute little shape."

"Thank you, Ms. Octavia."

"JB and Ms. Octavia, excuse us," Rick said. "We'll catch up with you all later; we need to find our children and take some more pictures."

"Children? Honey, aren't you a little old to have small children?"

"Ma'am, we have three grown children." Karla kept a smile on her face but clenched her teeth.

"Oh, I thought you was toting around some youngins you had by another man before marrying Rick."

Karla looked her up and down, without a smile on her face.

JB grabbed his wife by her arm and quickly walked off.

"Come on, Octavia," he said. "Let's find our seats; you don't know what to say sometimes, woman."

"Don't you say a word," Rick said.

"I wasn't going say anything," Karla replied. "She needs some attention; she's fat and old now. If my mouth gets like that, please put me out of my misery."

"You can rest assure on that. I'll probably hit you upside your damn head to bring your ass back around. JB likes you; that old man don't like too many people."

"Oh, he's just an old stubborn and stern man," she said. "You just need to know how to stroke him, that's all."

"Well, you keep up the good work in stroking him." "Whatever, foolish; one day, your ass will be old, and I will have to stroke your ass."

"And when you stroke my ass, make sure you stroke everything else too; don't miss a spot."

"I swear, you are such a freak."

"I know, and so are you."

"Mr. and Mrs. Tyler, over here," Charlotte called. "We're waiting on you two."

They took about twenty pictures or so, before Rick blurted out, "It's too hot. That's enough for now; let's come back later."

Renee caught up with him as he was walking across the lawn.

"So, brother, now that you're married to your so-called sweetheart of a wife, is she going back to work or what? I don't even know why you married her ass; she's not the one for you."

"Renee, hold the fuck up," he growled. "I already got the fuckin' story of what happened this morning; what the hell was all that about? Why is our business any concern of yours? You don't tell me who the fuck I should marry or how to do any got damn thing I'm sick of your ass."

"Dad, Dad, lower your voice," Ric said.

"Lower my ass? Ric, I'm sick of Renee's shit, coming over to me with that stupid nonsense."

"Aunt Renee, not today," Ric said. "If you don't like my mother, that's fine; she's not your wife."

"First off, Ric, I'm not talking to you, and second, she's not your mother."

"Hold up," Rick said. "If he wants to call her his mother, he can. Who the fuck is you? If you got a damn question about my household, you ask me, and I'll tell you just what I want you to hear."

"Rick and Renee, stop it now," Cheryl said. "Renee, what the heck are you doing now? I told you before to mind your business; you just keep pushing. You know how he is; now let it go."

It was spinning out of control; Karla lifted up her gown and started scooting across the lawn as fast as she could.

Renee screamed, "I didn't ask to be in your got damn wedding anyway; remember, you asked me."

"You right, Renee, I did. I tried to keep the peace with you, but fuck you. I don't give a damn any more about peace with you. I don't owe you shit."

Cheryl was pushing Renee away, but she kept coming after Rick.

"Excuse me, stop. Wait! Babe, stop; not here. Let it go for now." Said Karla.

"Your bitch is here for you."

Before anyone knew it, Renee punched him in his chest as hard as she could. Rick reached around his mother and Karla and slapped her so hard her whole body shook; blood flew out of her nose and lip from the slap.

"Rick, you didn't have to hit her that hard."

"Yes, I did."

"Renee, what is wrong with you today?"

"He hit me."

"Renee, you deserved that lick," Cheryl said. "Go inside and clean your face and hold your tongue ."

"I know; everything is not okay. Maybe I shouldn't have said anything."

"Whether you did or not, she came to me with that shit, and it wasn't okay then, and it's not okay now. I want to kick her ass, but that's my sister."

"Come on, let's walk over here and sit down on this bench. You need to calm down," Karla said. "Today is our day; don't let her destroy it. Isn't that what you told me? Don't act up."

"Babe, she called you a bitch in my face, and then she punched me in my chest. Her damn hand hurt."

"Okay, that's not the first time she said that, but did you have to hit her out here, today of all days?"

"Yes, I did. I'm sick of her shit talking."

"Get yourself together, Erick Tyler; let's finish taking the rest of these pictures please. That was your only show-off for today; no more. Do you understand me, sir?"

"Yeah, babe. I'm sorry, but if she comes back, I can't promise you anything."

She sucked his bottom lip and then kissed him.

"You get the rest later," she purred. "Let's go and have a good time."

"Renee, you were wrong in so many ways," Cheryl said. "You are too old to be still picking fights."

"Ma, I didn't start anything. I was just asking him a question, and he started yelling at me."

"Renee, you called his wife a bitch in his face. I heard the whole thing; why are you so worried about what goes on in his life and home? You're just his sister; you have no control over his life."

"Ma, but you don't know the things she said to me in the car."

"Renee, first of all, this is their wedding day; this isn't no house party. Why would you do that here? Why you trying to put him on a spot or something? Where were you going with that? Never mind, Renee; don't even answer because I can only imagine with you."

"Pardon me," Charlotte said, "but do you all plan on finishing up the wedding pictures?"

"Yes, we're coming now."

"Thank you, I'll gather the party up again for the rest of the pictures."

"She better make these the last set of pictures," Rick grumbled. "It's too hot to be standing taking pictures; if she brings us inside, I'll take all the pictures she wants."

"Babe, what did I say?"

"I didn't say anything"

"Um, now that I'm married to you, I see for real this is going to be some work."

"What's the difference from before to now?" Rick replied.

"Before, I didn't live with you," Karla said. "I could close you out, but now I can't. I'm with you in more ways than one."

"Yeah, well, you got work to do; in the meantime, let's just finish up these pictures and go into the reception."

Karla and Rick and the rest of the wedding party stayed outside for almost two hours, taking pictures.

"Okay," he finally said. "That's it; that was the last click. We out; let's go inside, babe."

"Wait," Charlotte said. "I know you're not in a hurry to enter; I've been trying to keep everything on schedule. You two just have to wait until everyone is over here together, so that I can make the introduction."

"Babe, is she yelling at us?"

"Yup, and don't you open your mouth; you just take it."

Rick didn't say a word; he stood there with his mouth closed, waiting on Charlotte's command to move. Karla looked back at Charlotte and winked her eye, then looked at him and snickered. Charlotte winked back and cracked a smile too.

"Ladies and gentlemen, I would like to introduce to all of you for the first time, Mr. and Mrs. Erick Tyler."

"OMG, is he always that direct?" Charlotte asked after they took their places in the reception hall.

"Yeah, sometimes, but he means well."

"Girl, God bless you; um, I could not do him. I'm too controlling; we would bump heads on a regular, bless you."

There were even more people at the reception than the wedding: athletes from different arenas, law officers, senators, lawyers, judges, and Rick's staff from the old firm. They partied the rest of the evening until almost midnight.

"Karla, we went past our time limit," Charlotte finally said. "I need to wrap this up."

"Yes, we did," Karla said. "I realize that; it is late. Charlotte, I thank you so much for your patience; from the bottom of my heart, I do apologize for today."

"Excuse me," Rick said, taking the microphone and getting everyone's attention. "I want to thank all of you for being a part of our wedding celebration; a lot of you have traveled a good distance to get here, but we have to shut it down now. Those of you who can't drive home or to your hotel, get a cab or let someone whose sober take you. We don't want any mishaps."

Karla snatched the mic out his hand, before he went on and on.

"Yes, thank you again for joining us on this day; we all know Mr. Tyler can go on, but we need to get out of here. Thank you all for your love and support and the cards and gifts. We will be local for a while; you know how to reach us. Please drive safely; until we see you again, good night. We love you all."

"Look, Charlotte, I'm sorry for my behavior today," Rick said. "In the meantime, you can wrap up on your end; we'll stay around to help you. Thank you for your help today."

"You're welcome," she said, "and thank you for your business."

He slipped her an envelope of cash. Rick, Karla, and the wedding party stayed around to help her and her team clean out the mansion.

CHAPTER 9
A WEEK LATER
SATURDAY, AUGUST 1, 2009

"All right, Mr. Tyler, we're opening up these cards and gifts today, so we can get back with Charlotte, so she can send out the thank you cards."

"Yeah, I don't want to be late on that with her; she'll be calling giving orders."

The phone rang, and Karla listened to someone speaking before hanging up.

"Who was that?" Rick asked.

"I think it was Renee; all she kept saying was 'Let me speak to my brother.' I kept saying 'Hello'; she didn't say anything else, so I hung up."

"I'm ain't fooling with Renee; all was cool until last Saturday, then it got real ugly."

"Did you really have to slap her that hard?"

"Yeah, but that wasn't hard enough. I should have blacked her eye. I don't know why you always shaking your damn head."

"Because, babe, you are a mess; the shit that still come out your mouth."

"I know you're not talking to me," he said. "When did you become so righteous?"

"Since the day I married you. One of us has to be righteous; crazy man."

"Whatever, babe."

"Yeah, whatever, Rick Tyler; your sister is calling you again. Do you want me to answer it?"

"Nope, I'll get it this time. Hello?"

"Hey, Rick."

"Hey, Renee; what is it?"

"I need five thousand dollars, or whatever you can help me with."

"Okay, so what you calling me for? Ask your husband."

"He doesn't have it, and I need to pay my rent and car note."

"Renee, I just got married."

"So? I know you got it; you can have it back in installments."

"You're right: I do have it, and it's my money that I'm keeping."

"Rick, come on. I'm giving it back."

"You don't really think I'm really going to give you my money, after you showed your ass with me on my wedding day? You have got to be fuckin' kidding me. Do you smoke that shit too? 'Cause you sound crazy."

"I said I'm sorry."

"Renee, you didn't say shit; the only thing came out your mouth was you need $5,000. Anyway, I need to talk to my wife to see if that's cool, because it's our household; remember, she ain't working no more. And in case you forgot, I said I'm done with you. I told you that I'm not trying to keep peace with you anymore, so you handle your own business. I'm handling mine. Bye."

"Babe, does he have the money?" Karla asked after he hung up.

"I don't know and don't care," he snapped. "I'm not her bank. If she don't call Tony or Niki, then I know it's a lie."

"She might call them; she may really need it."

"Yeah, but with Niki, it's going to be more money and the crying. Tony is going to question her to death, and he's going to want the bills or something in writing He's not going to give her cash."

"If you wasn't mad at her, what would you have done? I'm curious."

"I probably would have wired her the money, without any questions asked."

"Oh really?"

"Yeah, but that shit ain't happening anymore. I can't do that because my wife won't let me, and I don't want to."

"Um, and I'm laying here with you," Karla said, smiling, "and you didn't tell me you were married. What's her name? What she look like, in case I run across her in the streets?"

"She looks a bit like you, and her name is Karla Tyler."

He rolled on top of her, threw her arms behind her head, and start caressing her body and kissing her.

"You do know it's more to come?" he asked. "Are you ready for the ride?"

Yeah, let's ride it out, Ranger Rick," she said. "Let's do it."

CHAPTER 10
JUDGE
WEDNESDAY, AUGUST 12, 2009

Damn, he thought as the swearing-in ceremony dragged on and on, *it's 90 degrees already, and it's just ten o'clock in the morning. No air is blowing from no angles; now I know how a damn turkey feels in the oven at 400 degrees.*

He wiped his forehead, smiling, trying to look like he was really interested.

This ceremony is going to be all morning, at least until late noon; we still got to hear all of these influential speakers, but it's worth the journey to something bigger and new. If this man don't hurry the hell up, Imma pass out from a heat stroke, sitting up here in all this shit, a robe and a suit. I swear, I can't do the heat thing anymore, and his ass dragging on about what? I should throw the good book at his ass, or I should stand up and cut his ass off. We got it already; just give us our damn gavels and let us go. Got damn, it's hot.

"I guess I better wrap this ceremony up," the speaker said. "I see a few people getting a little agitated from the heat and with me. I know I can go on and on, so I'm going to end this with congratulations to each and every one of you."

"About time," Rick said. "Damn."

"Son, that was a good ceremony," Derickie said. "I'm proud of you."

"Thanks, Pops, but is this coming from the same man who asked was he my father? The same one who said he should have left me at the hospital?"

"Yeah, and I'll say it again, but for real, from deep down in my heart, I am proud to take the oath of being your father. I guess I am glad I didn't leave your ass at the hospital. I wouldn't have anyone to pick with other than Tony, and I got to lay off him from time to time. Niki don't live here; he thinks he's too good. I guess he don't love his pop; he's in his own world, doing whatever he does, that loud crazy music the young folks listen to."

He threw his hands up in the air and walked off toward his truck.

"Pops, why do you always say that?" Niki asked. "I just live a good distance from you, that's all. I'm still not good enough, huh?"

"Niki, hold up, man," Rick called out. "I need to talk with you."

"Rick, not now, man. I need a moment to myself, before I punch him in his head; he gets on my nerves, keep saying that shit."

"How you going to have a moment to yourself, if Nicole is walking with you?"

"Rick, not now; leave me alone."

"No, man I'm not. I need to talk to you about something, man. Niki, stop, damn it."

"What, man?"

"Look, that slick remark from Pop, he knows that wasn't cool," Rick said. "He always got some old-ass negative shit to say about me. I'm tired of that shit; that still bothers me to this day. You'd think I would know how to handle his ass by now, but it still gets on my nerves. He acts like I'm doing some illegal shit. I feel like I'm still waiting on his approval for what I do."

"Man, go catch up with your wife," Niki said. "We can talk later."

"Nah, I'll call her," he said. "She can take Nicole; let's talk about it now. I'll get Tony."

"Man, ride with your wife."

"Babe, Nicole needs to ride with you," he said. "Me and Tony riding with Niki; I'll see you at the restaurant."

"Marisa, go ahead," Tony said. "I need to ride with my brothers."

Just then, Derickie walked over to the brothers.

"What the hell is he walking over here for?" Niki asked. "I thought only you and Tony; why is he coming? I don't want to hear no more of his shit; he fuck around, I might throw Daddy from the train. I'm so serious."

"Niki, let the man ride; shit. I'm hungry and thirsty as hell from sitting in that damn heat half the morning. I got him; he'll be all right."

"I wonder what's wrong," Cheryl said. "What happened? Nicholas doesn't look to happy at all."

"Ma, who knows?" Cerise said. "When they all get together, you never know with them."

"No, Nicholas is pissed; something is wrong, I know it. I know all of you; Niki made a comment so freely, but there's more to it."

"Ma, try not to worry yourself too hard. I'm sure everything is okay; they're probably just having a misunderstanding."

"Grandma, why my uncle Niki look so sad?" William asked. "He look like he was crying."

"Crying? You saw uncle Niki crying? Cerise, I told you something was wrong!"

"Ma, he said 'look like'; why you always get so excited when it comes to them grown men of yours? Do you act like that with us girls? Probably not."

"Yes, I do, Ms. Cerise; yes, I do."

"Are we at the food place? William asked. "I'm hungry; can we eat? I want a hamburger and French fries."

"William, you are not getting no hamburger or fries; they don't sell any of that here."

"Grandma, then why we come here, if they don't have hamburgers and French fries; that's all I want."

"I don't know, William; ask your Nana."

"But you're my grandma," he said. "What's a Nana? Why she not my grandma? I don't know what's going on; I'm lost; do I have two grandmas or what?"

"William, you got two grandmas, okay? Now unbuckle yourself and let's go eat."

"How you doing, Ms. Cheryl?" asked Eugene, Renee's husband.

"Hi, Eugene; I'm fine. I see you are gracing us today with your presence."

"Yeah," he said. "I took time out of my busy schedule to attend this event. I wouldn't miss this for nothing in the world."

"Um, I know you wouldn't."

"Eugene, sit down here beside William."

"Renee, don't get cute; you try to tell me what to do. I sit where I want to. I may not want to sit beside his little ass; he asks too many questions."

"Uh, Eugene, don't use that tone toward my grandson. I know you don't want him to tell his father, and I asked you before not to do it."

He waved his hand in the air at Cerise.

"Yeah, whatever; as much as your father and husband curse, please girl, y'all be killing me."

"So Eugene, how come you and Renee didn't make it to the ceremony today?" Tilley asked. "We missed you."

"Tilley, leave it alone," said Sandy.

"Oh, did I say something wrong? I was just asking. Okay, I see how this is going; let me get the waitress's attention. I need a drink."

"So, Aunt Karla, that was a long ceremony, wasn't it? Now that Uncle Rick is a judge, there's going to be interesting stuff to hear from the courtroom, now huh?"

"Nicole honey, don't hold your breath to hear it; he's not going to tell you nothing."

"For real? He doesn't share his stories with you?"

"Nope, and that's fine with me. I don't want to hear it. I doubt if he brings his work home, at least not all of it."

"Dang, you're married to a judge; go ahead with your bad self. So how's everything coming along? Any babies yet?"

"Girl, you're a nosey young lady; everything is coming along just fine, and no, there's no baby coming. We got grown children; we're not starting over."

"So you're not going to give Uncle Rick no babies? You know, he might want another child."

"Nicole, we're going inside to sit down, motormouth; leave that subject alone."

"Karla, where is Alicia, Kareem, and Ric?" Sandy asked.

"They rode together," she said. "They were behind me; I guess they'll be here soon."

"And I'm sure they will with no money, at least your two, anyway."

"Renee, you just keep on, don't you?"

"I was just saying, Ma. I'm not starting anything."

"Yeah, okay, I'm just saying too."

"Waiter, could you please bring me a bottle of white wine and fill it to the rim?" Karla said. "I see how this is going to go."

"I wish I could, ma'am, but I can't bring the bottle."

"Okay, that's fine; just bring me a glass."

"Excuse me, but whose tab is that going on?" Renee asked. "Not mine; I'm only paying for my own. Or will you be paying for you and Eugene?" said Nicole,

"Nicole!"

"Okay, Nana."

"Don't do it, please; don't add no more to her foolishness."

"Ma, you better get your granddaughter; she needs to stay in her lane. Where is your money, missy?"

"I got money; thank you for the offer, though."

"Probably not enough. I'm sure your daddy is going to pay for it, like he does everything else for you."

"And if he does, why does it bother you so much, Aunt Renee? You need a life; stop being so mean and mad for no reason at all."

"Oh, here comes part of your family now, Karla: Tim and Monique Brown, Joe-Joe, Nettie and Big Tim, and following behind are your children: Alicia, Kareem, and Rick's son Ric."

"You know what, Renee, you need to get some real business and stay out of ours."

"Karla, call Rick," Cheryl said. "See where they are. They should be here by now; what are they doing?"

"I did; he's not answering."

"Oh, my God, did something happen?"

"Ma, ain't nothing happened," Cerise said. "They may have stopped off somewhere. They'll be here shortly; let's just snack until then."

"Niki, what's wrong with you, man?" Tony asked.

"Man, just feeling a little messed up right now."

"What happened? You were fine a minute ago; what happened that fast?"

"Tony, just drop it; don't worry about it. It's okay. Rick, congratulations on your new job, man."

"Yeah, thanks, man, but let's talk about them new artists you got coming out soon; what they sounding like?"

"I hope it's isn't none of that rap stuff," Derickie said, "or whatever they call it today."

"Pops, you know I don't do no rap music; you can't never say nothing nice. Damn."

"So Niki, what's up?" Tony asked. "What's going on with you? And don't start talking about something else, trying to throw me off track."

"Tony, who the hell you talking to like that?"

"I think he's talking to you, Nicholas."

"Rick, if I wasn't driving, I would punch you in your damn face, for calling my name like that!"

"Well, you better keep driving then, nigga; start talking. Anthony is waiting on his answer."

Niki didn't respond; he was thinking of how he was going to blast his father out.

"Pops, you know you just keep disrespecting my feelings, my work, and my life; why is that?"

"What did I say?"

"Oh, now you can't remember? Then let me just throw this at you: For some reason, you always make me feel like I still need your approval. When you say shit, I feel like I'm sitting on edge, waiting to see if you approve, as if you don't love me. You do it even more when other people come around; you have been doing that shit for years, and then you talk about me as if I ain't shit. Why is that? You never tell me that you're proud of me, like you do with Tony and Rick. You always make it seem as if you're ashamed of me; my life is just as good as theirs. For once in your life, can you just say one good positive thing about me? You never tell me you love me in front of everyone. Nope, and I'm the one who don't love you; shit, it appears to me you don't love me."

"What you talking about?" Derickie replied. "I never do that. I treat y'all all the same way. Niki, you don't call me; you don't talk to me like Rick and Tony. You always so damn private."

"Pops, you haven't called me, either. Ma calls me, Rick, Tony, and everybody else, except you and Renee, and she only calls when she wants something. You don't even pick up the damn phone when I call, and I call there all the time. Ma always answer the phone; caller ID still exists, doesn't it? So what I'm gathering is that you never see me calling, right?"

"Man, watch that damn car; shit, slow it down. How about you just stop, got damn it. I'll drive if you that damn mad."

He slammed on the brakes; the car behind them almost ran into them.

"Niki, do you want me to drive?" Rick asked.

"No man, you just sit back there; you dragged him along, so you keep him company."

He hit the accelerator hard, driving faster down 395 South.

"Niki, come on, man; Pops can't take fast driving no more."

"Really? Because I couldn't take the hard blows to my heart, either, but he still does it. He can dish out the hard pain that he shows me, even after all these years, so we're even. You would think I had learned how to deal with it, but I haven't. It still hurts to know your father never showed you any love, even as a grown-ass man. I'm still searching for his love, to gain his approval."

"Niki, lay off the man," Tony said.

"Hell no; you asked me what's wrong, now I'm telling you. Why do I look so damn unhappy? I told you to let it go, but no, so I'm not finished. I send him things for his birthday, Father's Day, or just anytime. He never picks up the phone to say nothing; not a 'Thank you, son'; nothing. Why not, Pops? If you didn't want it, why keep it? You should have had Ma to send it back to me; what did I do to you, Pops, besides being your first-born son, but that was Ma's choice, right?"

"Niki, lay off him," Tony said. "You're hurting his feelings."

"Really? Now he knows how it feels, don't he?"

"Niki, I'm so sorry if I ever hurt your feelings, son."

Rick looked over at his father and saw his pain. He knew their father did all of what Niki said, but he never knew why; whenever he asked if he talked with his oldest brother, he wouldn't say anything.

"Pops, why you never spoke so much of Niki like you do us?" Tony asked. "Why you never called Niki to thank him or just call him?"

"Why y'all fighting me?"

"We not fighting you; we just want to know why?"

"Nicholas, I'm sorry that there was always distance between you and me."

"Why? I'm your son, right?"

"Yeah, you're my son; you want to get a blood test? I'm the father of all y'all. I guess 'cause when you were a baby, you always clinged to your mother, and I was jealous; for a long time, I felt like you were taking her attention away from me."

"Pops, are you serious? Come up with something better than that; it sounds so damn stupid."

"Yeah, I am serious; your mother was not just my wife; she was, and is, the protector of my soul and heart. Then we had you, and I felt like she pushed me away. I felt like a lost child again, when my mother left us. She never cuddled us, like your mother did; my mother left us alone and showed us no attention or affection. But your mother gave me all of that. I didn't know how to accept sharing that when you came along. You were our baby, and I was supposed to love you. As you got older, I tried, but you were so spoiled by your mother that I resented you. Then you became a teenager, and then you had Nicole. I made you work hard to be a good father, but I also wanted you to feel my pain. Instead, I watched you love that girl hard, and I learned how to love through you.

"You're a damn good man and father," he continued. "I guess that's why I love her a little more than the others. That love should have been given to you in the beginning. I lost your love, so I made it up double in her, one for you and one for her."

He was crying so hard, his breathing was getting shorter; he started choking, gasping for air.

"I'm so sorry for that. I love you so much, but I didn't know any better. I didn't know how to love a baby. I'm so sorry; please forgive me."

"Niki, roll the window down," Rick said. "He can't breathe!"

"I'm so sorry; you're my first born. I love you all the same; please forgive me, Niki. Please forgive me, boys."

Niki pulled over, threw the car in park, jumped out, and snatched open the back door. He yanked Derickie out and hugged him tight.

"Breathe, damn it," he said. "I forgive you. I love you too, man. I always did, but you never let me in."

Derickie was crying on Niki's shoulder for the first time ever.

"Let's come in together, son. I want you in my heart; come to me, son."

"What the hell?" said Rick.

"Rick, let it go," Tony said. "This is never to be spoken of again to nobody."

Rick's cellphone rang.

"Babe, where are you?" Karla said. "We're here waiting; is everything okay?"

Rick sighed and said, "Yeah, I guess so. We're on our way."

"Yeah? Okay, from the sound of that."

"We'll be there in a few minutes."

Not long after, Derickie, Niki, Tony, and Rick all walked through the door, looking like they had been through a war. Derickie tried to stand tall, but he was still shaken up from his episode. Niki looked like he had been crying, and Tony and Rick looked like they had just been slapped by a ghost.

"Derrick, what's wrong?" Cheryl asked. "What happened that took you all so long?"

"Nothing babe, let's eat. I'm hungry."

"Yeah, okay, Derickie. I'll wait until we get home. I know something happened."

Tony sat down beside his wife, and Niki sat next to his father. Rick sat down beside Karla; he whispered in her ear, "Dang, babe, how many drinks did you have already?"

"Why? Just one; this my second glass. I'm good now, but I can hardly finish it. I feel sick from the heat. What took y'all so long? Your mother was worried; what did you do?"

"It wasn't me this time; let's just say it was informative; we'll talk about it later."

"Granddad, me and Natalie want hamburgers and French fries; we don't want that other stuff."

"William, I already told you they don't have it here," said Cerise.

"You two come sit with your granddaddy; let's try something new together. No burgers and fries, okay?"

"Derickie, them kids are big enough to sit at the table; they're three."

"They are going to sit with me," he said. "It's all right. I got them and the rest of my grandbabies too; whatever they want, I got them."

Rick and everybody started snatching menus off the table and scanned through it, hoping nothing started up again. They all placed their orders, ready to eat.

Oh, boy, Rick thought as Eugene came over, *not now.*"

"So Rick, man, are you planning on having a party for your big celebration? I know it's going to be the bomb; let me know when and where. I know it's going to be a lot of honeys there."

"No party, Eugene, and no honeys."

Eugene twisted his face up at Rick and took a long sip of his drink.

Karla whispered in her husband's ear, "Babe, aren't you having a celebration party?"

"Yeah, but I ain't telling his ass; he's not coming. You heard the dumb shit he just said."

"Granddaddy," Nicole said, "did you see the gift my dad brought you?"

Tony and Rick looked up at Derickie.

"No, I didn't."

"Nicole, this is not the time or place, okay? Let it go."

"Dad, go ahead give it to him; he'll like it. Granddad, my dad bought this for your birthday."

Derickie opened the box; to his surprise, it was an 18 karat gold cut diamond herringbone bracelet, engraved D. Tyler; the inside of the bracelet said "Nicholas." Derickie leaned over and kissed Niki on the head and hugged him.

"Thank you, son. I love you, man."

Everybody was shocked; nobody said nothing. They just smiled. They all continued to talk and laugh and even shared a few tears and memorable stories of each other. After everyone finished eating, Rick got the waiter's attention; he came running over with the check already in his hand.

"I need to leave, so Imma pay this now."

"Wait," Tony said. "How much is it?"

"Wow, damn," Rick said. "What did you hungry folks get? Y'all should've listened to William, got burgers and fries; it's over two grand."

"Are you serious?"

"Nah, Tilley, I'm making it up," Rick replied.

Tilley dropped three hundred on the table, and Rick dropped a twelve hundred on the table.

"That covers my family and half the bill."

"Wait, son; you're not paying the bulk of this bill. It's your day; we got this."

"Dad, we know he's not paying that by himself," Cerise said. "I don't know why he dropped money on the table; we got this. Calm yourself down."

"Pops, it's okay," Rick said. "I got my family."

"Since you said you got your family, does that include your grown children?" Renee asked.

"Yeah, it does Renee; they're my family. Anytime they with me, I got them, no matter how old they are. They're mine, not yours; you don't ever have to worry about covering my family."

"And I got Nicole, Ma, and Pops," said Niki.

"And I got my family and Cerise and her family," said Tony.

Everybody else stated their claim and dropped money or cards on the table, except Renee and Eugene. Niki snatched the twelve hundred off the table, slapping it back in Rick's hand.

"Little brother, take your money, he said. "We got this."

Niki and Tony waited to see if Renee or her husband were going to pull out some money, but neither one reached for their wallets.

"Babe, don't do it to yourself," Karla said. "Let's go."

"I'm not," he said. "I don't know about Tony or Niki, but I told you I was done with Renee long time ago; we ain't paying their debts. Hell, no."

"Nigga, I didn't ask you to pay our bill," Eugene said. "I got money."

He threw a hundred and twenty-five on the table, as if he was a big spender. Karla was holding Rick by his arm; he calmly pushed back from the table.

"So you telling me you two ate $62 apiece," Rick said. "I know for a fact you two had market price meals, with several drinks and desert, and you giving up a hundred and twenty-five dollars."

He laughed so hard, hitting the arm of the chair; nobody knew what to think of him laughing like that.

"And I bet you thought all y'all asses was going to eat on my got damn dime, today. You two niggas are on your own, so Renee, I suggest you pull out some more money, honey."

"Rick, don't try to get cute cause you're a damn judge now. I got money."

"Renee, I was cute before I was a damn judge; now put your got damn money up."

"Rick, I'll pay it," Nettie said. "This going back and forth is not necessary; just let it go."

"Wait, I got a question," said Tony. "Why every time, when they do shit like this, we always have to pay their portion, and we have to drop it? I'm not dropping shit; I'm sick of this shit."

"Renee, I love you, sis, but this fool, you need to let his ass go. He's worthless as hell. But today, Booty-luscious and Hamster, you need to shake, shake, shake out some more dollars."

Eugene got up from the table and headed for the door. Niki jumped up behind him and caught Renee by her arm.

"Wait, sista," he said. "You still owe some money."

"Get off me, Niki," she snapped. "We gave you what we had; he invited us, so he should pay."

"Baby girl, I doubt that he did, and if so, I'm sure he didn't say he was paying, now did he?"

She snatched her arm away from Niki's grip.

"You know what? Never mind, Renee; you and your broke-ass, no good husband can go. We got this, but remember: You can't get shit from me ever again, and I mean it. Nothing. Since you married this fool, let him take care of you, and stop calling us. You just like him: worthless."

Eugene stepped back in Niki's face.

"Man, don't put your hands on my wife again," he said, "and don't be talking to her like that; that's my wife."

"Man, shut the fuck up," he said. "I ain't talking to you. I'm talking to my sister, about you and her."

As Renee ran for the door, Eugene swung on Niki, hitting him on his chin. Niki was shocked from the punch and took off behind him, like a raging tiger. Derickie was like Flash Gordon; he leaped directly toward Niki, grabbing him with both arms. Eugene tried to sneak another punch in; Tony stepped around Derickie and knocked Eugene clean through the door, nearly on the back of Renee's heels.

At that point, the manager came running to the door.

"Sir, please stop, or I'll have to call the police."

"Nicholas and Anthony, don't hit him again," Derickie said. "I'll deal with him later; let's just pay and go home. I'll take of him myself."

Renee was helping Eugene get up off of the floor, brushing the dirt and broken pieces of glass off of him.

"You ain't going to do nothing to me, old man, or your punk ass sons. We're out of here anyway, and y'all still going to pay the bill."

Derickie smiled and said, with his deep Jamaican accent, "See, boy, what you don't understand, these sons of mine got something to lose. I don't; trust me, I will get you."

"Grandma, what about the money on the table?" Nicole asked. "You already paid with your card."

"Leave it on the table for their troubles," she replied. "I'm sure they'll need it to pay for the broken glass door. Let's get out of here. I'm so embarrassed; all that was just uncalled for."

The whole party walked out the door, whispering about what just happened.

Rick grabbed Karla's hand and whispered in her ear, "Babe, let's go home and get in the pool, so I can mess up your hair."

"We ain't going home to get in no pool," she snapped. "Didn't you see your mother's face? You know you started that bullshit, but don't you say shit until we get to the car; nothing, damn it."

Marisa was fussing Tony out; as they were walking out the door, he kept trying to explain his side.

"Shut the hell up, Anthony. That shit was embarrassing as hell, acting like some damn fools, over some stupid shit. You know how they are."

Tony looked over at his brothers and his dad; they all smirked at each other as they quietly walked out to their vehicles.

"Before any of my sons take their black tails home," Cheryl said, "meet me at my house; not after you finish doing whatever, I mean now. And matter of fact, that goes for all of my children. Spouses, you can come and make yourselves comfortable in the basement or on the porch, I don't care, but not in my upstairs. I got some words for these Tyler children of mine."

As soon as she got in their car, Cheryl said, "Derrick Tyler, I should slap your darn face right now."

"For what? What did I do? All I did was stop Niki from kicking his ass in there."

"Yeah, right, but you let Anthony hit him and knock him clean through the glass door; you acted just as crazy as them."

Derickie rolled his window down and lit his cigar, puffing and trying to explain himself.

"I didn't do anything wrong; he's a grown man. I can't stop him; you see how big that boy is?"

"Who the hell are you hollering at, Derrick Tyler? You are just as guilty as they are. And what's going on that all of you took your time getting to the restaurant, and then you kissed Niki on his head; you saved Eugene from getting his butt kicked by Niki. What the heck is going on? Any other time, you would have stopped it before it got this far; now all of sudden, you didn't."

He flicked his cigar out the window with a smirk on his face.

"I see you over there with that stupid look on your face, Derrick; just hurry up home, so I can put a fire under their butts. You all embarrassed me in public; they know better. They are adults and acting like wild children; oh, hell, no."

He didn't say anything all the way home; he kept puffing on his cigar and making faces and cutting his eyes over at her.

"Ouch," Rick yelled. "Damn, babe, did you have to pinch me that hard?"

"Oh, who's laughing now?" Karla asked. "Y'all done pissed her off."

"I know, and she almost cussed too, but she held off on her words."

Everybody arrived around the same time; they nearly ran into the house, all except Rick, who was taking his time. Tony jumped out of the car so quickly, he didn't even open the door for Marisa. He and Niki hit the steps at the same time, with their two sisters and their husbands behind them.

"You better hurry up, Rick," Karla said. "You think she's playing with you?"

"Babe, I'm coming," he replied. "Damn. I'm taking my jacket off."

He stopped and chatted with his parents' neighbors, thanking them for coming to his ceremony. Karla left him standing outside and went inside the house, going down to the basement. Cheryl and Derickie came in the back door; she threw her purse on the chair and roll-called them. When they were all together, she began:

"First of all, I am so damn embarrassed that you all acted the way you did; you're grown adults. You didn't act this crazy as little children. Nicholas and Anthony, I'm so damn mad. I swear, I could slap the shit out of you two now, and where is the got damn judge? Somebody better get that nigga in here now, before he needs a judge."

He finally walked through the family room door, acting all nonchalant. She slapped him hard across his arm and back. He jumped from the sting.

"At this point," she continued, "I agree with your father; maybe I should have given your smart mouths away. I should have given all your uncouth asses away. And Rick, why in the hell did you start that foolishness? It was going to get paid; all of that was so uncalled for. Why would you …"

"Ma, I didn't …"

"Rick, sit your tail down before I beat you down, damn it. Don't you interrupt me."

"All I was going to say is why Renee not here?"

"Rick, shut up," Cheryl replied. "And Cerise, if you ever tell your me to calm down again from worrying about one of you, I'm going to punch your lights out. Y'all are my children, and if I want to worry about you, then I can. I love all of you the same; you all are my favorites."

"Ma, we don't all get treated the same," Niki said.

"Niki, shut up. And put your hand down; all that bull comment you just made, throw it out the window. You were just as guilty as your father. I know all about that; I've been fighting your father for years on his behavior toward you. But you take some guilt too. And Rick, you started that whole thing; you know that she's working with a no-good husband. Trust me, son, I wasn't feeling him being there either. But he was, and I knew I was going to cover their end. As soon as you walked in and saw him sitting there, I knew it. But I didn't think it was going to go this far. The only ones acted like they had some sense were Sandy and Tilley; maybe the rest of you need to follow their lead."

Tilley was hitting Karla on her knee, laughing; they were all downstairs listening to Cheryl lay into the men.

"Yeah, we act better than you and Mr. Smart Ass."

"Shut up, Tilley."

"So Marisa, what are you going to do to Tony?"

"Girl, I don't know, but it was kind of funny though."

"Funny ain't the word," said Tilley. "That shit was hilarious, but I dare not fall out laughing. I thought I was going to die when that bamma threw his money on the table like he really left something; after he and Renee drank the best top shelf liquor and had a market price meal. I know their bill had to be at least $250."

"Marisa, stop laughing." said Karla.

"Tilley and I were floored," Marisa said, "when Tony stepped around Derickie and punched him so hard he fell through the door, right on Renee's heels; the way she looked back and skipped out the way, all I could do was hold my head down and snicker. I was almost crying. I know Cheryl is up there reading their asses; it was embarrassing, though."

"Karla, it was, but he really deserved more than that," Marisa replied.

"All right, ladies, y'all need to calm your husbands down; they're out of control."

Tilley fell out laughing again. Cheryl laid each one of them out, one by one, including Derickie.

"You all can leave now," she said. "I need to lay down because I can't believe what happened today. It was just too much, but I know one thing for sure: This better not ever happen again in my lifetime. So go get your spouse and children and get out of my house."

"Ma," Cerise said, "you have to laugh; it was kind of funny, the whole thing; okay, granted, licks were passed that shouldn't have been, but it was funny."

"Cerise, those were punches, and it wasn't funny. I'm going upstairs, and I don't want to see any of you for a few days, so get out."

Rick jumped up and grabbed his mother from the front and held her tight; she couldn't get away from him. Niki hugged her from behind, and Tony just jumped in and kissed her all over her face and head; they all started apologizing.

"Ma, I'm sorry," Tony said, laughing. "It was Niki's fault."

"Get off of me," she snapped. "I don't want no hugs and kisses from y'all; get out! Derickie, I'm going up; bring me some tea with ice."

"Why I got to bring you some tea?" he asked. "You walking through the kitchen; why can't you get it yourself?"

"I know one thing: It better be up here by the time I change my clothes."

"Dad, you're already in the hot seat," Sandy said. "You may want to get that before it gets much hotter."

Tony ran downstairs; Marisa was on the floor, crying from laughing. Tilley was holding onto the bar, laughing, and Karla was stretched out in the chair, laughing and crying too.

"Aw, you think that shit was funny?" Tony asked.

"Hell, yeah," said Tilley.

"I do too," said Marisa.

"That damn Rick started that shit," Tilley said, "but you finished it. Thank goodness Alexandria police didn't come; could you picture that: Rick's ass being locked up on the day he was sworn in. The headline would read, 'Judge and his two brothers and father locked up.' Damn, Karla, I guess you would have had to bail them all out."

"I guess so."

"Well, here comes the judge, finally; late as hell. We glad we ain't in the courtroom, waiting to solve our issues," Tony said. "Your ass is late."

"Whatever," he said. "I had to suck up to Ma."

"What about Karla? How are you going to suck up to her?"

"I'll suck up to her later," he said. "I got a plan, and probably the same way your ass is going to suck up to Marisa, but for now, let's toast."

Tony opened a bottle of Champaign and passed out glasses to everybody in the basement; for the rest of the evening, they all stood around giving toasts, laughing, and talking.

CHAPTER 11

NEW BEGINNING
FOUR MONTHS LATER
SATURDAY, DECEMBER 5, 2009

"All right, babe; we relaxed enough," Rick said. "Now we got things to do. Fun time is over, let's make this happen today."

"Okay, like make what happen?"

"I'll tell you later; get up and get ready."

"You get on my nerves when you say that," Karla replied. "You know I don't like that; why can't you tell me now?"

"Because I don't want to tell you now; damn. Why you always ask why? Just come on."

"All right, on one condition, though," she said.

"What's that?"

"Come back; let's make love again."

"You're too funny, but since I'm a sucker for you, I'm going to oblige your request. After this, though, you're getting up."

He flipped himself over the couch on top of her; her legs were already open, waiting for him to jump in, but instead of making slow love to her, he gave her a quick fuck. She screamed out laughing.

"Okay, okay, I heard you," he said. "Since you want to be so smart, I'll fix your ass."

He fucked her so hard, he kept flipping her over and over; all she could do was holla.

"Okay, okay," she said. "Stop. I got it; damn. I know your ass called yourself breaking me off a hard one, but that didn't work, did it?"

"Hell, yeah, Mrs. Tyler; it did, for you and me."

"Yeah, I thought you'd see it my way."

He slapped her on her ass and pulled her up off the couch.

"Go ahead get in the shower," he said. "Damn, I feel like I'm coming down with something, like I need to vomit."

"Yuck, babe; do you think it's something you ate?"

"No, the only thing I had was that curry food; maybe something was spoiled in it, or it could be a virus."

"Well, I'll drive if you still want to go out; you think you will be okay?"

"Hell, no," he said. "I'll drive. I'm okay now; I'm good. I'm not fooling with you or your driving. We'll be there in no time flat. I'm already feeling nauseous; I don't feel like being swung around."

"Not today, we're not in a rush."

"But get out of here soon, I'll be okay."

They got dressed and went down to the truck. He rolled the windows halfway, inhaled a deep breath, and sighed, and then he pulled off.

"Okay, Karla," he said, "what are you going do about your house? Do you want to sell it, rent it, or let Alicia and Kareem stay in it?"

"I never thought about it," she replied. "Why, do we need the money?"

"No, I just need to know; if you're going to keep it and let them stay in it, then let's pay it off. If you're going to rent it, then I won't pay it off; let the renters pay it off."

"I'm really not sure; what do you think is the best thing to do?"

"It's your decision, babe; I'm waiting on your response. It's your call. I was just asking, since you don't live there anymore."

"Well, let me think about it; when do you want an answer?"

"Well, soon, I hope. Maybe this week, but if you need longer, hopefully before the year is out and not five years from now."

"I'll talk to them and see what their plans are."

"Okay, but you know they'll want to stay; it's convenient for them.

Keep in mind, you have two choices on that one: If they stay, you need to charge them rent. Even if I pay it off, still charge them rent, even if it's three hundred dollars apiece a month."

"Yeah, you're right, babe."

"You can take the money and put it in an account for them. I know they are not little children, but let them have it; it will keep them out of our pockets."

"What about repairs?"

"What repairs? I'm going to have a few of my men come over and check everything out; anything that needs to be done will be taken care off, so there shouldn't be any repairs."

"Okay, Mr. Tyler, the decision shouldn't be too hard. I'll talk with them before the week is out."

"Okay, cool. I'll be waiting on you."

He hit the auto dial on the dashboard and called Tim Brown.

"Tim, what's up, man?"

"Nothing much; sitting here watching a Disney movie with the kiddies."

"Okay, cool; we're taking a ride out. I thought we'd stop by on our way back from Annapolis."

"That's cool; we'll be here. See y'all later then; peace."

After he hung up, another call came in.

"Hold on, babe. I need to take this call."

"Hi Mr. Tyler; this is Beth from WEN Moving Company, calling to see if you were ready to set your moving date."

"Beth, thanks for calling me back, but no, I haven't confirmed my date as of yet. I'm waiting on my wife; she's the hold-up."

He looked over at her, showing his brightest smile.

"No, seriously, she's not the holdup, ma'am," he said. "I just said that because she's looking at me like I'm crazy. Actually, whatever date is available in the second or third week of this month is good."

"Are you sure, Mr. Tyler?"

"So far, yes, Beth; if you could, please send me a confirmation email."

"Yes, sir, I can do that. Now if there's a change, please give us a call back; goodbye."

"You heard that," he said, "so you don't have time to be playing around."

"Well, since you already made the date for the moving company, I guess I need to pack up like yesterday."

"Okay, since you put it like that, then yeah, but I don't know what the hell you're packing, besides your clothes and all that other stuff you got. You don't need furniture; you still got jewelry in the house and fur coats. You may not want them to touch that, if it's not insured, but the other stuff, yeah."

"And just where the hell am I supposed to put my things? You barely have enough room for your things."

"I know, but it will all work out; trust me." He looked over at her and smiled.

"Don't get quiet on me now."

"I'm not," he said. "Just wondering if you're going to be a good wife."

She smiled back at him. "Yes, I am; it's whatever you want, babe. Heck, the question should be, are you going to be a good husband?"

"It's not about what I want," he said. "What I wanted, I got, and it's you. And that you always need me and love me like I love you unconditionally, and that you make love to my heart and my mind, not just my body."

"I do and will, but babe, we know there'll be days it's not going to be sweet."

"I know; nothing is perfect."

"I guess that's why we are married," Karla replied. "I promise I'll be there for you, no matter what. And I'll definitely make love to your heart, soul, and mind, just as much as I enjoy making love to you physically."

"I'm honoring my vows," he said, "and when I said whatever you want, it's just like I said, meaning anything I got, you got. I couldn't ask for a better person than you to take as my wife. And for the record, the movers will move your things, not you. If it seems like I'm running everything and making plans without you, I just want to get it done and not procrastinate; you know I don't play that. If I say I'm going to do something, I make it happen. I know you know that."

"Yes, babe. Damn, I know you're not a procrastinator, and yes, it does seem that way, that you make the plans and decision without me, but that's you; go ahead."

He grabbed her hand and kissed it.

"I apologize; it won't happen again."

They pulled into a driveway; it was the house he brought her to before.

"Wow," she said, "that landscape is beautiful; this the same house we came to before?"

"Yeah, when you were acting all crazy? This would be the place."

"And why are we back here?" she asked. "You haven't settled on this yet? Is the client still buying the house?"

"Girl, just come on in."

"How long are we going to be here?"

"Why are you in a rush to get somewhere? What you got to do later on?"

"Nothing, but I'm getting hungry; you didn't feed me, remember?"

"Girl, come on. I'll feed you as soon as we're finished here; it won't be too long."

He unlocked the door.

"Wow," she said. "Nice house."

"You want to look around?" he asked. "The potential buyers are not here yet?"

"Not really," she said. "I don't like to look around in somebody else's house; I wouldn't want anybody looking around my house before me."

"Come on, babe they won't know. We'll make it quick."

"All right, but hurry up; when they come, I want to be done and waiting outside."

"Why, you scared? Ain't no time to be scared or nervous now; we're not trespassing. You're with me."

"Shit, who the hell are you, besides a damn judge? This is not our house."

He grabbed her by the hand and pulled her up the spiral steps. All the floors had custom-made wood flooring. The walls and ceilings were freshly painted bronze; it was so smooth it that looked like wallpaper. When they hit the top of the stairs, all you could see was the sun shining through the skylight that stretched from one end of the hall to the other. He opened the first set of double doors to the master bedroom door.

"Watch your step down, babe; you looking up in the sky."

"Wow, this is a nice bedroom," she said. "Plush cream-colored carpet; this room is huge. Oh, my gosh, it even has a separate sitting room in here; that's huge a bay window. Wow, that's a pretty waterfall down there."

He snickered at what she said and shook his head; he took her by the hand again and dragged her through the rest of the bedroom, down a small foyer to the master bathroom, with a built-in tub, a separate spa-size shower, and separate toilet; there were granite countertops around the wall of the bathroom, with a double sink and mirrors around the walls.

"Come on, babe, get out the mirror," Rick said. "You have to see the rest of the house."

"Okay, but let's hurry up. I don't want these people to come here and see us roaming through their house."

"They won't if you hurry up."

He led her to the end of the hall, showing her the three other bedrooms, which were just as nice but smaller. All of them had the same plush carpet, with a large adjoining bathroom to each room. They went down the back steps into the huge kitchen; off to the side was a huge dining room. The family room sat off from the kitchen, with a corner fireplace built into the wall.

"This is a nice house," she said. "Lovely so far of what I've seen; now let's go back and wait until they come."

"Do you want to see more, babe?"

"Not really, but since you keep dragging me, I might as well."

He took her all through the rest of downstairs and then to the basement, which was set up as a lounge with a pool table, a bar, and another fireplace in the wall, with a closet enclosing the big-screen TV.

"Wow," Karla said. "Damn, the first thing the owner had delivered was a pool table and not a bed; um, that's so sad."

The doorbell rang, and Karla practically ran back upstairs, leaving him behind.

"Come on, babe, they're here. I told you I wanted to be sitting on the steps when they got here."

He chuckled as he walked behind her.

There was a tall, skinny woman at the door who looked like Jane Hathaway from *The Beverly Hillbillies.*

"Mrs. Neely, good evening."

"Good evening to you; how do you like the house so far?"

"Uh, it's nice, but can I talk with you in the other room? Babe, keep looking around; we'll be right back."

"Oh, no, I'm good; I'll just sit here on these steps."

"Thanks for coming out today," Rick said softly. "I appreciate you bringing the documents with you, but my wife doesn't have a clue that this is our new house. She thinks someone else is buying this house and I'm out here to meet with them. This is a surprise to her, so I need to break the news to her first."

"Oh, how sweet of you, Mr. Tyler. I think that's a wonderful thing to do; do you mind if I watch?"

"No, but don't be surprised about what you hear."

"Mr. Tyler, if I was being surprised like this, I don't know what I might say, either."

"Okay, here we go; let me spring it on her. So babe, what you think about the house? How do you like it?"

She was sitting on the steps, snapping her fingers, humming, and tapping her feet as she looked around.

"It's a nice house, but when are they coming? I'm getting hungry and sleepy again."

"Soon, babe, soon. First, I need you to take hold of these keys; they go to our new house."

She jumped up off the step.

"What?" she yelled. "Hold the keys to our house? What the hell? Are you serious?"

"Yes, babe; we're that client. I couldn't tell you this morning. I wanted to surprise you, so surprise!"

"Mrs. Tyler, this is such a beautiful home," Ms. Neely said. "If my husband surprised me like your husband just did, I probably would have passed out."

"Ms. Neely, my heart is beating some kind of fast. I was so nervous about being in someone else's house, and to find out it's our home is more comforting now. Babe, is this why you kept asking me about the other house?"

"Yes and no, but we'll talk about that in the car."

"Mr. and Mrs. Tyler, let's sign these documents so I can leave you two to enjoy your new home."

Karla yanked Rick back by his jacket.

"Wait," she said. We have to sign? I don't make your money to carry this house if something happens; why is my name going on the deed?"

"Babe, this doesn't have anything to do with money, and if something happens to me, you and this house are taken care of. This is our house, and whatever my name goes on your name goes on. Come on, don't act like that; you'd carry this house if you had to; we're in this together, and about this money thing: We'll talk about that in the car too. Let's sign these documents so I can get you something to eat."

They followed Mrs. Neely to the kitchen to use the countertop to sign the documents.

"Mr. Tyler, I'll make copies of all of these documents and overnight them to you; your deed will come within thirty days in the mail."

"Okay, thanks," he said. "That's good. I know you're hungry," he said to Karla. "So am I. let's go eat."

"Yeah, we need to go, since you already told Tim we we're coming through."

"All right, we'll stop for a few minutes and then go to dinner."

"Yeah, right; I know how this is going to play out; more like hours."

"No, we got some unfinished business to attend to later on. Now get in the truck, girl."

"Okay, I just got to ask: Why such a big home?"

"Because one, I always wanted a big house, since I've always had condos and it was just me, or shall I say me and Maria, and I want a house with you and our babies."

"Babies? We got three grown-ass children; why would we want to start over?"

"They are grown, and I want our babies, me and you."

"Uh, babe, I'm not sure if I want to be pregnant again. That means I got to start all over again, and that was a struggle."

"Karla, you're not by yourself," he said. "That was then, and this is now; you made that choice back then to struggle."

"But who said you can't leave at any time? Marriage doesn't mean shit."

He glanced over at her, frowning.

"Now, do you really think I'm going anywhere? After all I went through to get you back in my life, I'm just going to leave you? No. I want to see my children grow up and be in their lives. I never got that."

Karla rolled her eyes and stared out the window.

Oh my God, she thought, *this is the longest ride ever to those black iron gates down there; they can't open fast enough. I wish he would change the subject. I don't want to talk about having babies. There's his phone; good, Maria called just in time. Let him talk with her.*

"I'll call her back in a few hours," he said. "We'll see how she's doing and see if she wants to relocate again, for the last time."

"Shit," she said, then added, "Oh, sorry; how's she doing?"

"She's fine, last I talked with her, a few weeks ago."

"Babe, maybe her plans are to relax; you drove her crazy. She's getting older, and I'm sure she had enough of you from the last twenty years or so."

"No, she hasn't; she'll come, plus she won't be working for me. She will be working for us."

"Working for us, doing what? I can clean and cook."

He burst out laughing. "Really? When the hell do you cook? I do all the cooking. You do clean up, but for the most part, I've done that too."

"So what are you saying, Rick Tyler?"

"Nothing, babe. I love you. I actually enjoy cooking and cleaning for you; it's not a problem, but I know with our work schedules, we won't have time to cook and to do all of that, and once you're pregnant, I know you can't do all of that, and you'll need help with the baby."

She looked at him with her face twisted, frowning as if she wanted to slap him. The more he talked about babies, the more he got excited. They finally made it to US50, heading south to Bowie to Tim and Monique's house. He was still talking about babies and Maria; she tried to tune him out on the whole conversation: more of the pregnancy thing.

Shit, she thought, *I'm forty-five, he's forty-six. Why now? Ugh, he can't be serious. I can't do that again.*

"Babe, what you thinking about? You're too quiet, which is unusual for you."

"Uh, nothing; just relaxing my brain from today's excitement, that's all."

He pulled the truck into their driveway.

"Well, well, well, I see Derickie is here too," he said.

"Look, I'm not fooling with you," Karla said. "I'm hungry, I got to go to the bathroom, and I'm starting to get a headache, so make this stay quick."

"All right, go ahead inside. I'm behind you."

Karla was ringing the doorbell, dancing around.

"Come on, open the door," she said. "I got to go."

"Hey, Aunt Karla," Tim said when he opened up.

"Move out my way," she said. "I don't have time to play."

"So Rick, how did the house thing go with her?" Tim asked. "Was she surprised?"

"Yeah, man. I thought she was going to explode, but she did good. I showed her around before Mrs. Neely got there; she worried me to death about leaving, 'cause it's not our house; you know how she does."

He followed Tim to the kitchen and took a seat at the counter.

"Damn, we just in time; you cooked? Can my wife have some food before she passes out?"

"Man, you better feed that fussy woman of yours."

"Damn, look at that," Derickie said. "Rick Tyler is fixing his woman a plate."

"Shut the hell up, man, and yes, I am, and the problem is?"

"I see Karla got your ass hooked again; what else, do you do the cleaning too?"

"I do it all," he said. "She's giving good loving and taking my mouth; why not?"

"Hey, crazy Derickie and the fellas," Karla said when she returned form the bathroom. "What's up?"

"Babe, come on and eat; leave Derickie alone. Don't start with him today."

"Damn, he must do that on a regular basis, and you didn't give him any lip?"

"Yes, he does; is that a problem for you?"

"Hell, no. Maybe one day, I'll have a wife I can do that for."

"But the only problem is, Derickie can't keep up with who he serving," Rick said. "If he does one, that means he has to do them all, and shit, somebody may get called somebody else's name, and since he can't keep up with them all, he does none."

Derickie fell out laughing.

"Cousin, you got a point there."

"Man, where you been? I was lucky to catch you today," said Tim.

"I been working late shifts," Derickie said. "You know I'm one of DC's finest detectives, so I got to give them their time too.

"These streets getting crazy, damn bad ass kids out here doing all kinds of shit, parents on drugs or just don't give a damn. The fathers run with their sons, teaching them the ropes of this bullshit street life. The mothers go to the clubs, with everything hanging out, from their titties to their asses, which got an invisible sign on it, saying 'Free Pussy,' and the young girls following their game. This shit is crazy; all this fuckin' shooting is out if control. They killing each other off out here; after a week of that, man, it can drain you, but I keep knocking them down."

"Oh, so you don't mind the women showing their body parts in public?" Karla asked.

"Hell, no. I'm a man, but I don't want to see no man body parts."

"So if she shows you her body parts in public, do you think it's good enough for you to touch her?"

"Let me explain something to you, Karla; don't get me confused. I'm not that bad; I talk a lot of shit, but I do have respect for women. I got enough crazy-ass women in my circle now. I'm not bringing no extras. I have experienced some shit in the past, and for the record, that was not my baby. Everything that looks good is not good for me. I'm a little older now, and I do have some scruples. I got eight children; my oldest is twenty-nine, and my youngest is five. I got four baby mamas, but I'm done.

"I'm a grandfather, so I can't be playing this nonsense freestyle game no more, but now if you got any available girlfriends or friends looking for some fun, call me."

Karla laughed.

"No man, I don't know nobody that wants your bullshit."

He hugged her around her shoulder and fell out laughing, kissing the top of her head.

"So Rick, where you all coming from?" Derickie asked.

"Coming from Annapolis, man. We just signed the deed to our new house."

"Congratulations; is this the house you secretly designed?"

"Yeah, man."

"Wow, man, you don't play around, do you?" said Derickie.

"So Karla, now that you're moving into the big house, what you going do with your house?" Tim asked.

She sucked her teeth, as she was putting their plates in the sink.

"I don't know at this point," she said. "I don't want to talk to y'all anymore; I'm going upstairs with Monique."

"Okay, I see how that works," Joe-Joe said. "You fix her plate, and she removes them after you all finish. Okay, I got it."

"Joe-Joe and Derickie, take notes," Karla said. "When your day comes, I'm going to make sure my ass is sitting near to run all this back to you."

"I'll come get you when I'm ready," Rick said. "We won't be long."

Karla knocked, pushed, and walked through the door at the same time.

"Monique, I thought you were asleep, girl."

She flopped down on the side of her bed.

"No, I heard you down there, being entertained with Derickie's foolishness; who can sleep when he's in the house? His voice carries."

"Girl, I just got a surprise that blew me away."

"What's the surprise, are you pregnant?"

"No, Rick took me out to our new house."

"Oh, my God, I'm so happy for you, but I really thought you were going to tell me you're pregnant; now that would have been a big surprise."

"No, but we both signed the deed; I feel a little eerie about that."

"Why? What's the problem? How in the heck do you feel eerie about signing a deed with your husband? What's so eerie? What the hell is wrong now? I swear, this man has gone out of his way to make you happy, but you keep finding stupid stuff to fault him on. You got the man; it's been what, a year now, or almost. He's been good to you; what do you want, a knock upside your head? Damn, are you happy?"

"Yeah, I am, but more shocked than anything; it's so damn big. It's too big."

"You don't sound so happy; what's wrong with the size? You sound so unsure of everything. Damn. Why you acting so weird? What is wrong with you?"

"I don't know. I guess I'm used to just me, doing what I want, when and how, without a mate."

"Wait a minute; do you love him, or you just playing with him?"

"Yeah, I do, but I'm scared."

"Of what? Tell me when the hell have you ever been scared of anything? As much stuff as you have done and places you been that you probably shouldn't have been; girl, get outta here."

"One, of being hurt," she said. "Two, I'm not on his financial level, or educational level; what can I bring to his table? All I have is me."

"What the fuck is that, Karla? You sure you don't smoke anymore, cause you sounding really weird; that has nothing to do with it."

Monique sat up on the side of the bed, shaking her head, looking at her in confusion.

"He married you for who you are and how you make him feel," she said. "It has nothing to do with money or education levels. Girl, you tripping; you can't convince me you don't smoke drugs. Please help me understand what you so scared of; make me understand. I swear I'm not getting it."

"You don't understand," Karla said. "I've been by myself for so long, and to marry someone with this kind of stature is frightening. You never know what he may decide to do; he's in control of everything, and I'm just a little old federal employee with my yearly salary; it's not even half of what he makes."

"Is that what this is: money? Hold up, Karla; what the hell? You come from a family that is loaded and is the got damn Mafia, and you're telling me you're scared; girl, I should hit you in the head my damn self."

"Yeah, that's true, but they're not my biological family."

"It doesn't matter; now all of sudden, they aren't your biological family. You were raised by Georgie and Theresia, who would have given you the world, but you chose not to have it. Didn't you separate yourself from him? Now this man comes back in your life and gives you his world and some more, and you are afraid of money; girl, you are really on some shit. You need to go get checked out. I ain't never seen you act like this before; you need to seek some help. You sure you don't smoke drugs?"

"I know, it's like I can't get control of my feelings all of a sudden."

Tim walked through the bedroom door; Karla was sitting on the floor, looking like she wanted to cry.

"Good," Monique said, "you're in here; you need to talk to your aunt."

"About what?" Tim asked.

"She said she wasn't financially or educationally on Rick's level, and she feels eerie about the house."

"Damn, Monique, do you tell him everything?"

"Not everything, only what he needs to know."

"Really, Karla? What, you think he's going to hurt you? This man has jumped over boundaries for you. I know him just like I know you. I know things about him like I know about you; nobody's perfect, but he wanted you, and you wanted him. He knows you're not on his financial level or education level; that has never been an issue to him. The crazy thing is that he said the same thing about you, that you wouldn't want him because of that. He know y'all lived two different lifestyles, but Karla, let's be for real here. This has nothing to do with money, does it? Because you already knew he had money. So what the fuck is the real problem?"

She burst out crying, saying, "He wants to have a baby, and I don't want to. What if things don't work out, and then I'm stuck with a baby to raise by myself. I'm not doing that again."

"Are you fucking kidding me, Karla? So all of this is about a got damn baby. Girl, get the hell out of here. Rick's downstairs waiting on you; get out!"

He shook his head.

"Your husband is ready to go; you might want to get that look off your face before you go downstairs."

Tim and Monique followed her down the stairs. Rick, Derickie, and Joe-Joe were standing right at the entrance door.

"Babe, what's wrong with you? Monique, what you do to my wife?"

"I didn't do anything to your wife. Just let us know when y'all move in and get settled; we'll come visit."

"Yeah, what do you need me to help you do, cousin?"

"At this point nothing, but when you come out, you just don't fuck with the women in my neighborhood; please, not so close to our home."

"I know, right? That may not be a good idea anyway, but since I can't mess with your neighbors, can I take the Aston for a ride?"

"Derickie, I don't think so; you are not getting me in any more of your trouble. I'm good with who I got."

He took her hand and led her to the truck. "Come on, babe, let's go; you sure you're okay?"

"Yes," Karla said. "Why do you ask?"

"'Cause you look like something is puzzling you, face all frowned up, or is it something I said? What, you don't want the house?"

"No and no."

"No, you don't want the house?"

"Yeah, I do want the house; I just got a headache. I don't feel like talking."

"All right; no problem. We're on our way home. I won't bother you then."

Karla lay her head back, staring out the window, revisiting her conversation with Monique. They rode in silence.

"Damn."

"You all right over there? You been quiet all the way home. He drove a little faster."

She snapped on him.

"Yeah, and stop asking me that."

"Oh, I won't ask you again; not a problem. You keep acting ugly, Imma throw your ass back in the sea; keep it up. I'm parking as fast as I can."

He jumped out of the truck and ran around to open her door, not saying a word.

"Please, madam, let me help you; I'm here to serve you."

She shook her head and gave off a half-smile. He walked behind her as if he was a servant, carrying her bag.

"Oh, wait, my queen; let me get the door. I must do my job so that I can continue to pay for my wants and needs."

He continued on his role all the way upstairs; she kept walking and left him standing in the living room, still carrying on. He hit her butt as she walked passed him, then he sat on the couch, thinking.

"Good, take your grumpy ass to sleep; I'll talk to you later. I know one thing: While you back there laying down, you better be gathering your thoughts together on that house. She playing too much. I need to move money and make some more money; this condo is going on the market tomorrow. Already sold the condo in LA, got a damn good buy on that; this one here, I might have to take a hit. People here on the East Coast don't like spending no money; everybody want a deal. Everybody want the goods for cheap and want you to throw in the extras, but if I have to rent it in the meantime, I'll let this one ride. Um, but that's cool if she decides not to sell; at least we have a place to stay in the city if we wanted to, but I really think she's going to keep it so Alicia and Kareem can have a place to stay, which is cool too; whatever she want."

He jumped up off the couch.

"Time to get back to my grind, put out some more bids on these building contracts, review some resumes and get these lawyers in place to work, so I can be up and running within six months or so."

My head is killing me, she thought, *from his talk about having a baby; that won't be happening. I'm making a doctor's appointment first thing Monday morning. I'm getting some pills, before my luck runs out. Ugh, I wish he would have said something before now; I wouldn't have married him, and yeah it's petty. Okay, stop tripping, Karla, just get the pills. Oh, too many thoughts going on my head: make the decision on my house soon, do I pay it off for them three grown folks, or do I want to rent; well, at least we'll have a place to stay in the city.*

Hum, nah, I rather for them to be there and not with us, she thought; *they're old enough to take care of themselves. They'll be okay. I know he's going to bring his ass back again, as soon as my headache goes away, with some more of his foolishness. God knows I don't have the heart to tell him that I don't want to have any more children. That's going to crush him, and then he may be subject to go out and have children with other women. Like Derickie said; okay, self, you going crazy over this. Just go to sleep.*

He busted through the door and flicked the light on.

"I thought you were asleep."

"No, just laying here, getting ready to take a shower; maybe that will help. Why?"

Dang, I should have invited him in, so he knows I'm not ignoring him.

"Um, I just asked. I don't want anything." *Shit*, he thought, *I'll let her be, 'cause if I get in that shower with her, it might not be good for either one of us. I'll go in the other bathroom.*

By the time she got out of the shower, he was in the bed with the TV on. She climbed in the bed and slid up against him. He pushed her off and moved over to the end of the bed. She leaned up on her elbows, touched his face, and then kissed him. He tried not to kiss her back, but that didn't work.

"I'm sorry, babe, but I do have a headache, and I'm sorry for neglecting you."

"Yeah, okay," Rick said.

"Okay, I take that, but I decided to keep the house."

"So should I pay it off or what?" Rick asked.

"If you want to, I can keep paying the mortgage on it," Karla replied.

"Look here, it's not if I want to, do you want me to? I know you don't ask for help or say what you need or want, but you need to say it to me. I'm not going to bite you, at least not from you asking me for help or to pay something off for you. Now I'm going to ask you this again, do you want me to pay it off?"

"Yes, babe," she replied. "Why are you making me say all of that?"

"Because I'm your husband, like I told you before I got you on whatever it is; damn, all you have to do is say it. What you crying for now?"

"Because I feel afraid. I know it sounds crazy, but I'm used to being by myself. Now I'm married, and I don't know what to do."

"Wait a minute. You gave yourself a got damn headache over being afraid of being married. A whole got damn year later, and you're afraid, girl? Yeah, go to sleep, fast; you are tripping."

"I know, right? I do sound crazy, but my mind went all over the place after we left the house."

"What? 'Cause this shit sounds crazy to me too. You haven't started talking to much of nothing at this point that makes sense."

"My mind took me to another place; one of you having an affair and having babies with someone else."

"What the hell? Where you going with this stupid shit, Karla? Are you serious?"

"I know, but you said you want babies, and my heart damn near fell out of my body."

"So what? You don't want my baby?"

No; yeah. Uh, that's not what I'm saying."

"Then what are you saying? Your answer wasn't clear."

"I'm not prepared to have any more children. I didn't think you wanted more, since our children are grown."

"So let me understand this: You don't want to have my baby, correct, and you worried about me having a baby with another woman. Um, okay, all right, if that's how you feel, then there's nothing I can do about that, so we don't need to talk about this anymore. No worries. I don't ever want to put you in a position of doing something you don't want to do.

"And to the second statement, me having a baby with someone else: That won't be happening. I'll tell you this, so it won't be no misunderstanding: So you won't get pregnant, I'll make sure we use condoms or you can use the birth control pill; it's your call. That topic is closed. I'm not entertaining that shit anymore."

"Wait, let me think about it, babe."

"Karla, you don't need to think about it; you already said it, so on that note, I'm going to sleep. Tomorrow, get the papers together so you can contact the mortgage company to pay off the house."

He rolled over on his side and went to sleep. She laid there with the TV still on, flicking the channels, until she fell off to sleep.

Damn, he thought when he woke up, *I wish it was Monday, but it's Sunday. Look at her ass all in my back; I should roll over and kiss her, or maybe I should push her ass on the floor. Nah, fuck it; let it go. If it doesn't happen, it's not like I'm going to love her any less, but that crazy conversation fucked me up.*

He nudged her off of him with his butt, got out of the bed, and walked off as if he hadn't done anything.

"Where you going," Karla said. "Look, I'm sorry."

"I'm not going anywhere, why?"

"I was dreaming you were leaving me and you divorced me. I'm so sorry; please don't leave me."

"Babe, don't start that shit again. Look, you made your own personal decision, so I got to live with that. I still love you; nothing has changed. I'm not leaving you, but yes, you blew me away with that decision. I'll get over it, okay, and where I'm going is to the bathroom, then to the kitchen, if you don't mind. Do you want some breakfast?"

"No, I want to make love to you."

"Um, sorry, babe; emotionally, I'm not there at this point, and we need condoms, and you need some pills, so once you get that, then we can revisit this making love thing."

He walked out the room to the kitchen, leaving her sitting in the middle of the bed, with her mouth wide open in shock at him rejecting her.

"Is she serious?" he said to himself. "She wants to make love, and we're not using no protection, but she don't want no babies. I ain't got no damn condoms in here nowhere; what the fuck? Let me get something to eat, because she's fucking my head up with all that bullshit; damn if she is going to make me lose my mind."

He thought he was mumbling, but instead it came out loud and clear.

"Bring your ass in here so we can eat," Karla said to him.

"Oh, okay; I see you're fully dressed. Where you going?"

"In the city to get the paperwork for the house."

"Okay," Rick replied. "But why you all frowned up?"

Karla said, "Didn't realize I was."

"You jumped up like a crazed woman," he said, "asking me where I was going, but now you're dressed and going out. So what vehicle you taking since you're going in the city?"

"I'm driving my own car, I'm not taking yours, since you said it like that."

"Naw, that's not a problem. I don't care if you take the Aston; just be careful. Who knows, one of these young dudes see you by yourself and might try something, that's all I'm saying."

"Try something like what?"

"You know exactly what I mean; they see you in that type of car, shit happens."

"Well, what's the difference if you were driving it? The same thing could happen to you."

"Yeah, that's true, babe, but I don't feel comfortable about you being by yourself in that car, not just yet."

"Um, whatever. Don't worry, I'm not touching your car. Like I said, I'm driving my own car. I had no plans on taking your car anyway."

"That's not what I'm saying, babe; you can drive my car anytime; we're always together in that car. Take the damn car, just don't drive through the neighborhood with the most shit going on, and you know what I'm talking about too."

"Um, whatever, Rick. I'm good; let me go. I'll be back."

"When?" Rick asked.

"I don't know; it won't be too late."

"Damn, how long is it going to take you to gather some papers up?"

"Not long, Rick. Why? You made plans for us to do something today?"

"No, I was just asking."

She snatched her keys and purse off the table and walked out the door, slamming it behind her. He threw the plates of food in the sink.

"Okay, she really is tripping." His phone rang. "What the fuck is it now? Hello?"

"Rick, what's up, man?" Tim said. "Where Karla?"

"She just left out the door, tripping."

"Still?"

"What you mean still?" Rick asked. "What make you say that?"

"Listen, man, I don't want no part of your business; she's my aunt, and I'm concerned. Did y'all talk?"

"She talked, and I listened about some bullshit about being afraid and not wanting to have my baby, so since you called and you're so concerned, you're a part of our business now. Tell me what you know, so I can know too, damn it."

"Man, the shit sounds stupid to me too, but hey, that's how she feels; you don't know, but she vowed she'd never have any more kids, because she didn't want to be a single parent again."

"What the fuck is that? I don't know how many times I've told her; she's not and will not be by herself."

"Wait, man; calm down and put yourself in her shoes. Think about it, man; you didn't have any other children, 'cause you wanted both parents to be in the same household, right?"

"No, I didn't, and yeah, true, but come on, man, she knows me better than that."

"She also feels that she's not on your level."

"And what level is that?"

"Come on, Rick; you know what I mean by that. We had this conversation before; you're probably what every woman wants. You got the money, the fame, you're a well-off man, and you got style and charisma, and you're educated as hell. If the average black woman could marry a rich, well-educated, and intelligent man, they would be in glory."

"Tim, man, that's not true. Monique married you; you got the same, so what?"

"Yeah, but I don't have half the money you got."

"Man, the money, the fame, and education; those were my choices. I'm not tripping off her level of education or her damn salary; she makes decent money for herself. She could have had anything she ever wanted, even if I wasn't in her life, from Georgie. Money and fame have nothing to do with it; it's about her having a baby."

"Look, I told her to let her feelings go, just let them flow; she was going to be all right." Tim replied.

"Yeah, right; man, when she told me that last night, I felt like a horse kicked me straight through my back and stomped me to the ground."

"Y'all really need to talk about that; you come too far for something as small as that, but big at the same time, but let me ask you this before I hang up: Did y'all ever discuss it?"

"I don't think we did. I guess I just assumed."

"Well, stop assuming and talk with her. Y'all talk about everything else but failed on that important part. Man, you know Karla is touchy on some shit."

"You're right; this some crazy shit. I'll talk with you later."

"Damn, Karla, are you serious?" Rick said to himself.

"I don't think I can do this. I can't do him as my forever." *Damn*, Karla thought as she drove to the house in DC, *maybe I shouldn't have told him I didn't want another baby, at least not so harsh. Shit, this is about him accomplishing his desires to have children, not mine; he got one out of two: He's married. I'm not doing it; if he wants a divorce, then I'll grant him that. Not a problem; I can go back to my life. Shoot, I tried to apologize last night and this morning; he didn't accept my apology, and the bamma had a nerve not to want to touch me. I dare him, after he worried me all those others times, not that I didn't want to too, and now he said no. That's okay; I'm not playing his game. This is not a football game to see who can tackle the other and hurt the opponent. Ugh. All right, I'll make this quick, get back home before he has a hissy fit. Let me go in here and get these damn papers, talk with the young folks, let them know they will be paying rent immediately, like next month. They can do it, even though they're in school; they have jobs too. But knowing my Rick Tyler, they probably won't pay rent. Oh well, I'll just throw out an amount to see if they bite; they need to pay something.*

"Hey, who's here?"

"We both are, Ma," said Alicia.

"Good, come on downstairs. I need to talk to you two."

"Why? What's going on?" Kareem asked. "Is everything okay? Rick just called to see if you made it yet; he sounded pissed. I told him you weren't here; he said he was on his way up here."

Just then, Rick appeared; he came through the back door, gave Alicia a kiss on the cheek, and gave Kareem a brotherly hug and some dap.

"Rick, what's going on?" Kareem asked. "Why you both here?"

"Got damn, you were on my heels," Karla said. "You got here fast; what, you didn't believe me?"

"Girl, please, I drove like you drive: crazy. I came to apologize to my wife, first of all."

"For what?" Kareem asked. "What happened?"

"Nothing. I'm talking to your mother."

"Really? Nothing, when you just said you came to apologize to your wife?"

"You know what, Kareem, you remind me so much of myself when I was your age; let me give you a lil' story: One day, my parents got into it, and I was fired up, ready to fight my father. I stepped up to him, and he told me, 'Boy, you better sit your ass down somewhere; this is between your mother and me. I'm never going to do anything to hurt her or disrespect your mother; this is a love quarrel between me and her, so mind your business.' I told him, 'She is my business.' The next thing I knew, my mother was jumping sides with him, and they kissed and made up, and my ass was punished. So the point that I'm making is, just be quiet."

"Ma, what's wrong?" Alicia asked. "What you want to talk to us about?"

"Yeah, tell her what's wrong, babe. Tell her."

"Nothing is wrong."

"After all this, babe, you got nothing?" Rick asked.

"Ma, you want to slap Rick? You always said you wanted to anyway," said Kareem.

"Yeah, well, she probably wants to, so I'll tell you: Your mother is upset because I want to have a baby with her, and she's afraid that I am going to leave her one day, and the second thing is she supposed to be asking you if you want to stay here and pay rent or what?"

"What?" Alicia asked. "Is that all, Ma? Go ahead, give him a baby; that way, you won't be here worrying us. You need somebody else to worry besides us, and we cool staying here by ourselves. We'll pay the rent, and by the way, you're afraid of what? As much trash as you talk, you're afraid?"

They all laughed, except Karla; she rolled her eyes and walked upstairs. Kareem was laughing so hard he was almost crying.

"Rick, man, I'm sorry, but please keep her safe with you; we had our time with her. She's all yours."

"Kareem, leave your mother alone; let me get some water and go talk to her. Y'all are crazy."

"No, you and my mother are crazy," said Alicia.

"Hey, babe, we don't have to act this way," he said after following her upstairs. "All of this is crazy. I apologize for my attitude this morning and about my car. I'm sorry; please forgive me. Let's not do this; I love you. Do you forgive me?"

"I guess so," Karla replied, still shuffling through her papers in her file cabinet.

"The answer is not I guess so, babe; either you do or you don't. Which one?"

"Whichever one you pick. I'm looking for those papers; leave me alone."

"Wait a minute," he said, pulling her back by the back of her pants. "Don't walk away; give me a clear answer. Look here, missy, don't ignore me like you did last night."

"Rick, let go of my pants please."

"No."

"Will you stop? I gave you an answer," Karla replied.

"That answer doesn't sound too good, does it, babe?"

"Okay, no it doesn't. Damn, I accept your apology, now let go."

He let go off her pants, spun her around, and thrust his tongue down her throat. She couldn't resist if she wanted to; he wrapped his arms tight around her. She couldn't get away from him.

"Now are you still afraid?"

"Yeah, that one kiss didn't change anything," Karla replied.

"Then don't roll up under me tonight, since you're so afraid; let whatever it is get you, and don't call me. Find them papers and let's go. I got things to do, and watch the game this evening."

"On Sunday? Um, I'm so glad I don't work for you; I wouldn't answer your calls."

He laughed.

"You wouldn't have to work for me; you would be sleeping with the boss, but you'd be answering the phone."

"You're such a creep, just like I said."

"So are you, creepette."

"I found the papers," Karla said. "What else do you need, or are you still paying the house off?"

"Just give me the damn statement; I said I was paying the house off. Why would I change now? Now if you decided you wanted to walk today, I'd still pay it off for you. I said I would. Oh, there's one other thing I need."

She smacked her teeth and rolled her eyes up in head. "What now, Rick?"

"You. And there's really no need to be afraid; I'm not leaving or cheating on you or any of that crazy shit you got going on in your head. I understand your feelings, so I'm not saying any more about it. It's closed; just bring your ass home with me."

"You act like my father and you can tell me what to do," Karla replied.

"I'm not your father. And it appears he couldn't tell you what to do at some point, either."

"Get out of my room."

"Here we go again; the last time we were in this room, we had a crazy-ass discussion, and you tried to put me out then, but this time, you can't put me out."

"Why not?" Karla replied.

"Because we're legal now, and you don't live here, so come on, let's go."

"Lord, this is going be a long haul," she said. "Please help me; did I do the right thing?"

"I hear you talking to the Lord, babe; he's not answering you, and yes, you did the right thing, so come on. Alicia and Kareem, we're leaving."

"You have enough food in here?" Karla asked. "Somebody better cook."

"Babe, stop it. If they don't have food, then that's on them, and if they don't cook, then they'll be hungry. They got that. They are living on their own; handle it."

"Rick, please take her home with you," said Kareem.

"If something goes wrong, they know how to reach us; we're out, and we're leaving that car here."

"We don't need three vehicles."

"What am I supposed to drive? You act so stinky with your car."

"Babe, you can always drive the car, that's not what I meant; this morning, you took it to another level, not me, and you know it."

"Let's talk about this in the truck; we out. Love you."

They walked out the back door and got in the truck, headed back home to Virginia.

"You been so disobedient to massa in the last twenty-four hours," he said. You got out of control, tripping over some nonsense; you will need to do some sucking up real fast to me, and I'm hungry."

"Like what? 'Cause I'm hungry too."

"What's for dinner? That's one thing you can do is cook."

"What, me cook? And what else?"

"Don't worry about the 'what else'; you can handle that when I get to it."

"Oh, then we should've stopped and picked something up," Karla said. "I'm not up for cooking today."

"No? You're going to when we get in the house; you're going to pull something out that freezer, stand over it until it thaws out, and start cooking, then come over and rub my feet in between commercials, and after all that is done and I eat, you'll clean the kitchen, run my bathwater, wash me, and come make love to me."

"Yeah, okay, massa, but can I at least eat so I can have some strength to do all that, 'cause massa, you wear me out. I need to keep up so you don't beat me no more."

"Naw, I don't want you to eat. I like it when you weak. I Tarzan, not man."

They both fell out laughing.

"Seriously, babe, are you hungry?" Rick asked. "I did take something out for dinner; we got time. I'll cook it in between commercials."

"All right, but listen to me very closely, Mr. Tyler: You told me not to be afraid anymore. I'll work on that, but it doesn't happen overnight. Second thing, I am your wife, we go side by side. I am your queen, not your servant, but please do continue to be concerned for my well-being, as I will for you, and for the record, you know what scares me the most? I beat myself up wondering will I be able to meet your standards of being your wife. You've dated women more on your level of education, but that's not me I'm just an average woman that works every day. I plan out my finances, and yes, that was my choice. I'm trying to put all of that out of my head and move with my heart; yes, I do know most of your ways but not all of them, because we never lived together. But now, we'll learn more of each other's ways in time; some will be pleasurable, and some not, but full of much grace for us both. And third, you had me at hello when you first came back in town a long time ago. I'm finished; did you get all of that? I hope so because I'm not repeating it again."

"Whatever, babe; if I wanted them, I could have had anyone of them long time ago, but I wanted you, so listen up, Mrs. Tyler: If you come home with some more nonsense shit like that again, your ass will be checked damn good."

"Or what?" Karla replied.

"Mrs. Tyler, there's no 'or what,' okay? Just don't come with that talk to me; all of sudden you can't talk to me? We talked about every damn thing else before, even when it wasn't my business. Now all of a sudden, you can't open your damn mouth."

"Look here," she said. "If we're going to make it and grow strong as one, let's try to stay on the same page, keep the communication open, okay? I promise I'll do the same."

"I want the Karla that's feisty, sassy, and talkative," he said, "not that crying and scared one. Imma let this go. I ain't messing with you, and now I'm going to finish cooking for your rotten ass."

He pinched her breast and kissed her on the forehead and walked out the room back to the living room; just then, he heard the fax machine ringing.

"Wow; hey, babe, a fax just came in; we got a buyer that actually wants to buy it for more than the asking price! This is good. I better hurry up before they change their mind. I'll use some of that money to pay your house off."

He walked into the kitchen and leaned on the counter.

"What?" Karla asked; she had not heard him.

"I said, we got a buyer and I'm paying your house off, and with the rest, you can open your shop. How did you not hear that, nosey?"

"Babe, I don't have to open a shop now. I got time. I can do it after we get settled and you get your law firm running."

"Karla, why wait? Do it now; you can resign at any time. I don't know why you still go to work anyway; why not focus on what you want to do? You said this is want you want, so let's make it happen. I'll take you by the hand on the legal aspects of things, so don't worry. You'll be okay; you do your part, and I got the rest."

"Okay, but I'm still not sure of the location," Karla replied.

"We'll shop on that together; location and safety for you is a must. We're not just picking anywhere; how many people will be working for you? Whatever you do, don't hire any family or friends, and you don't need a business partner either, you got me. I'll finance you until you say stop."

"Okay, dang; you don't have to be so hard about it. I wasn't having any family work for me, maybe Alicia to come help me out or Sandy, depending on the amount of clientele coming in and out, then I can add more to the roster."

"Okay, but you can't be in there by yourself; maybe I can come in there to work with you."

"Uh, never mind, I'll find another person. I'd never get anything done. But the one good thing is your creepy friends like to spend money, so that's good for my business."

She cracked up laughing. He snickered and shook his head.

"She's back," he said aloud. "Always got jokes."

"See, babe: I can be a good slave girl for massa."

"Now you know what massa told you, but you didn't obey him, so you need to be beat."

She dropped to her knees and wrapped her hands around his ankles.

"Okay, well, beat me, as long as it's not ruff and hard, 'cause you a mighty fine buck, and I need to try you out to decide if I want to keep continuing to be your slave girl."

She stood straight up, taking her clothes off and walking around him in circles.

"Ma'am, can I at least take a bath in your pond?"

He smiled at her, watching her every move into the kitchen.

"Nope."

He grabbed her around her waist on her last turn, wrapped his arms around her breasts, and rubbed his hand down the front of her body, touching and pulling on her nipples, kissing and licking her down the side of her neck, stroking her pussy with the other hand from the inside and out with his finger. Listening to her moan, he entered her from the back, pulling her nipples at the same time, still kissing the side of her neck.

"Oh, babe," Rick said.

He moaned, and she moaned with his every touch of her body. He got harder and harder as he pressed into her more and more; he stroked her slowly, grinding his hips deeper into her.

"Do you want me to stop?" he panted. "I don't have a condom on."

"I think it's a little too late now," she said. "I'm sure of that."

"We ain't eating that; we'll get them in the morning," said Rick.

They left everything just like it was; he led her down the hall to the bedroom. She had control of him and his body. She kissed him so passionately; he was getting harder and harder, the more she sucked and licked his lips and his chest down to his stomach.

"Aw, babe," said Rick. "I'm the dominate one tonight, so enjoy the ride."

The next morning, they woke side by side.

"Good morning," Karla said.

He rolled her over toward him and pecked her on her lips.

"Good morning to you, babe. I'm not fooling with you this morning, so don't be looking at me with those beautiful eyes, trying to lure me into your web again. I was wondering if you would please give me back my dick; I think you took it last night. I don't see it, and I got to get out of here in a few hours."

She poked her head from under the covers.

"Oh sure," she said. "I got it right here; let me put it back on you."

She threw the covers back on him, got out of bed, and stood in the middle of the floor, naked, smiling, and slapping him on his butt.

"Not a problem," she said. "I got to leave you too; thanks for last night. You were great. I'll call you."

"Did you just treat me like a trick?" he asked.

"Yeah, how did that feel?" she replied.

"Cheap," Rick replied. "Wait, little pimp; before you go, is everything ready for the movers next week?"

"Yeah, I'm trying to get a doctor's appointment today, so you may want to ride into the city by yourself. I need to stop by my mother's house today, so I'll see you later this evening."

"Okay, babe; that's cool. I know I'll be at the courthouse for a while anyway. Just call me when you're on your way home."

Karla jumped in the shower first; he ran behind her and bumped her to the back of the shower. Rick hurried out and got dressed; she finally dragged out without making conversation. She stripped the bed with a towel wrapped around her and straightened the room and then got dressed, while Rick cleaned the kitchen. She grabbed her big purse and keys, and Rick grabbed his briefcase and keys, and they both walked out together. Karla took the truck, and he drove the car, and they both headed into the city.

"Man, I sure hope this doctor can give me some pills today," she said. "We can't keep doing it like this."

She hit 395 North, driving like a wild woman through rush hour traffic.

"I know parking downtown is going to cost my whole damn body for a thirty-minute appointment. Charging people by thirty minutes' increment; it's a got damn rip off."

"Good morning, Mrs. Tyler," the receptionist said. "How can I help you? I don't see you on the schedule for today."

"I'm hoping Dr. Hoze can squeeze me in today.

"Well, you're in luck. I have a cancellation for 10:30."

"Good, that'll be fine."

"Mrs. Tyler, you know the routine: your last cycle, please."

"Uh, I didn't capture it this time. I know that sounds crazy but I've been stressed. All I want is some pills."

"You know Dr. Hoze is not going to just give you any prescription without checking you out, and since you're not taking anything now, you need to take a pregnancy test first."

"All right, let me make this quick. I know I'm not, but I guess I got to go through the process before I can get these pills."

Karla sat patiently in the waiting room, reading magazines, waiting her turn.

"Mrs. Tyler, Dr. Hoze wants you to drink thirty-two ounce of water before he sees you."

"Why? All that for some pills? Is he serious?"

"He didn't really say; you know him. He'll call for you shortly."

She sat in the waiting room, pacing the floor, drinking water, and flipping pages in the magazines for another forty-five minutes.

"Karla, come on back. Go in room 4; the nurse is back there, waiting for you with more instructions."

"Well, what brings Mrs. Tyler in here?" the doctor asked. "I haven't seen you since what, last year? This will be a little cold, but here we go. Let's see why you are having these cramps you say."

The doctor examined her for several minutes with saying anything.

"Dr. Hoze, would you please stop saying um and say something?"

"When I'm finished, Ms. Karla; don't rush me. I've been your doctor for years, so you just wait. I know what I'm doing; that's why you're in my office."

"Dr. Hoze, you know I'm going to take that one, 'cause you're right: If I knew what the problem was and how to make my own pills, I would have had my own remedy and not be in here talking trash with you."

"Well, you know what, missy? You're right, because you know what? You won't be needing any pills. The only cramps you're having, as you say, is that you're pregnant."

Karla's mouth flew wide open, and her eyes lit up like a 100-watt bulb.

"I can't be."

"I tell you what: These sonograms don't lie. Why are you so surprised? You don't take any birth control or use any other protection, and you said your husband is very sexual."

"Okay, yeah, but I figured it wouldn't happen; it's been years."

"Well, your luck ran out twelve weeks ago; in fact, you're pregnant with triplets."

"What the hell. Oh, my God, are you serious, Dr. Hoze?"

"Yeah, let's look at this together. I'll count them for you, since you think I'm pulling your leg; apparently his sperm is much stronger than what you thought. One, two, and three; you can push back and get dressed, and then come see me in my office."

"Oh, my goodness, I did have to pee, but not anymore. I'm too blown away; this just took my breath away. Not one, but three; oh, my goodness. I feel like I'm going to faint."

"Well, go ahead, but come see me when you get up and get dressed, because it's still three babies," said Dr. Hoze.

She jumped up off the table, ran in the restroom, and then got dressed. Dr. Hoze looked up and over his glasses when she went into his office.

"Come in, Karla; take a seat. I know you said you didn't want any more children, but you haven't been taking anything. I don't know what you thought was going to happen. I personally don't think it's really a good idea to think about having an abortion; you could be at risk. You're now over forty; you'll be monitored closely by me, but you're strong. You're going to be okay, and so will those babies. Now how and when are you going to tell your husband, because I need you back in here soon, for a follow-up and to do another sonogram to determine their sex. I want you to bring him with you. Also, if you don't want any more after this, then what's your next step for you and him? What type of protection are you two willing to take?"

"Well, it's a little too late now, wouldn't you say?" Karla asked.

He smiled, pushed his glasses up on his face, nodded his head yes, and start writing in her chart.

"Uh-huh, well, make an appointment to see me in three weeks."

"So soon, Doc?" Karla replied.

"Three weeks, Mrs. Tyler; don't look at me like I said something wrong; I don't care what time. I'll be here, and bring your husband."

Karla walked out of the office as if she were in a dream; she rode the elevator down to the lobby, walked out, and went down two blocks to the garage where she parked. Before driving off, she called Rick.

"Hey, babe; when you get a break, call me back. Love you. Bye."

Well, she thought, *half my day is gone. It's two o'clock now. I still need to go by mama's, then I'll head home.*

She walked through the door of her grandmother's house, straight to the kitchen.

"Mama, it's me, babe."

Her grandmother stood in between the kitchen and dining room door, staring at her.

"Chile, those clothes a little snug on you," she said. "They don't fit you like they used to; has your husband noticed that?"

"Mama, what are you talking about? My clothes are not snug. Why? If he did, he didn't say anything."

"Um, so how many weeks are you?" Mama asked. "I know you're pregnant."

"How do you know?"

"Child, I'm old. I know these things; you ain't never had that much breast and weight on you. I know he ain't cooking like that, is he? You're just a little thicker than your normal; so when my great-grandbaby due here?"

Mama kept turning her around, looking at her; Karla sucked her teeth and blew.

"I'm twelve weeks; I figure in the spring, April, and it's not one baby but three."

"Child, what did you say? Three? Lord! What's the sex of them?"

"I don't know yet. I have to go back and take Rick with me."

"Have you told him yet?"

"No, Mama. I just found out myself today, this morning. I left him a message to call me back. I'm going home. I need to ride while it's no traffic."

"Babe, before you leave, I have a question."

Karla stood in the doorway with her hand on her hip, rolling her eyes up in her head.

"Yes, Mama?"

"How long are you going to work and carry those babies? 'Cause I'm standing here looking at you, and girl, there's no way you can do it."

"How do you know?"

"Karla, you can hide this for a while, and I mean a while, like maybe one more month; after that, your tail is blowing up. Them going to be some big babies."

"Mama, you're on punishment until I return; you have gotten out of control. This is secret for now, hear? I'll let you know when you can spread the word, okay?"

"Okay, babe; you call me after you tell that husband; now drive safely."

"I will, Mama. I love you so much."

"I love you too, Babe, and call your mother."

Karla, Rick thought after checking his voicemail, *what did you do to leave me a message like that?* He called and left her a message: "I love you too, babe. I'll be leaving here shortly. It's 7:30; I should be home soon."

Just as he reached his car, his phone rang.

"Hey, Chocolate Man, what's up?"

He laughed and said, "On my way home. What's up, Whitey?"

"Man, this shit is crazy; this woman was brutally murdered. We can't even identify her because she was badly beaten; we're waiting on dental records to come back."

"Damn, she was that bad?" Rick asked.

"Yeah, man. It's was ugly."

"Have you talked with Sabrina? Maybe it was the woman she told me about."

"I talked with her, but she doesn't know what she looks like. She's waiting on her friend to send pictures. Rick, I haven't seen nothing like this in a long time; we don't have no kind of leads. I've been working with my man over at LAPD, but we got nothing. As soon as Sabrina gets back with me, hopefully something can be done with that picture, put out on the news bulletin, missing person."

"Okay, man, keep me posted; send it my way, and I'll let my cousin know about it,"

"Man, you are funny; that Derickie still holding it down over there, huh? Tell Karla I said hello. I'll see her when I come into town."

"Yeah, man, you know my cousin: doing his thang. I'm out, heading home; hit me up when you get something."

The traffic was light; he cruised down 395 South with no music on and not thinking about his conversation with Whitey, all the way home. All he could think about was Karla.

She was going by her mother's house, he thought. *I figured she'd be there later than me; some crazy shit must've happened. Let me find out what happened, make sure she didn't hit nobody upside their head and it turned into a brawl.*

He walked in on her and heard her, as she was standing in front of the mirror. "What you doing that you have to count while rubbing lotion on yourself?" he asked. "That must be some good-ass lotion."

"Nothing and no, it's the same lotion I've been using; have you eaten yet?"

"No, but I can snack on something," Rick replied. "Why, you cooking?"

"I can; what you want? I'll fix it."

He stood on the side of the bed, undressing, and burst out laughing.

"Hold up," he said. "What's wrong, babe? What did you do? First the sweet phone call, and now this; what's up?"

"Okay, I'm sweet," she protested. "What's wrong with that? I called you."

"Babe, yes, you are sweet, but it's the way you left that call and like now, you offering to cook; what the hell did you do?"

"Uh, babe. I got something to tell you."

"I knew it was something; what you do? None of this was feeling right. Come on with."

"I didn't do anything, okay? Maybe and maybe not, but the question should be directed to you: What did you do?"

"What did I do? I wasn't with you; this sounds like some of your shit."

She finished unbuttoning his shirt and unfastened his pants and belt; she slowly pulled his shirt off for him and then said casually, "I'm pregnant."

"Stop! You're what?"

He fell out laughing even harder.

"Oh, wow; really? How many months?

"I'm twelve weeks."

"Oh wait; before I get too excited, what's the deal? What do you want to do?"

"Rick, it's done; I'm twelve weeks pregnant with triplets."

"What the fuck? Damn, are you serious?"

She flung herself backward across the bed.

"Yeah, well, I guess we're having triplets in the spring. I think they may be identical, 'cause they're all in the same birth sack."

"Hot damn," he said, "I'm so happy, babe: one, two, and three. I must have got some powerful shit, huh?"

She muscled up a smile and shrugged her shoulders.

"Yeah, babe; you do."

CHAPTER 12
FIVE MONTHS IN THE NEW HOUSE

Rick and his purebred bullmastiffs were sitting on the floor in the family room; he was rubbing Moon and looking over at Karla, who was trying to get comfortable on the couch.

"It's hot," she complained.

He smirked and shook his head.

Damn, he thought, *she's cranky as hell; the more I look at her, I swear she's getting bigger by the day, stripping her damn clothes off everywhere in the house and at everybody else's house. I can't help but laugh at her sometimes; poor thing is so miserable, been going through this since she was five months, and it's still a roller coaster. Nothing I can do but wait and help my babe and babies.*

He jumped up and grabbed his camera off the shelf.

"You can't move that fast anymore," he said. "Let me get this picture of you, girl! Looking like another earth, fat as shit."

"Rick, don't you take another got damn picture of me. I'm sick of you and that damn camera. Don't bring your ass over here. I know what I look like."

"Come on, get up," he said. "Bring your ass on; we are going for a walk to tire yourself out, so you and I can get some sleep."

"No, leave me alone," she replied. "I'm all right."

"Come on, babe. I still love you, fat and all. I did it to you; all for my babies. I can take that heat of you being mean. I would say I'm sorry, but I'm not, so get up and let's go, grumpy lady."

They walked slowly around their neighborhood with the dogs; he just kept snapping pictures of her waddling from side to side.

Lord knows, he thought, *you're so beautiful pregnant, but driving me insane. I'll be so glad when we have these babies, cause every night tossing and turning or she walking the floors scaring the shit out me. I don't know whether to sleep or what; she's up walking, looking crazy.*

"All right, babe," he said. "We can go in now; hopefully you're good and tired so we can sleep tonight."

"Stop touching me," she snapped. "Tell me who the hell is 'we,' 'cause you seem to be doing very well when I look over at you, sleeping hard; ain't shit funny?"

"But I ain't always sleep," he said, "so how about I run us a tub of water when we get back? I'll rub you down to relax you; you look a little stressed out over there."

He took her by the hand and walked her one more time around the block, until she couldn't do it anymore and headed for home.

"All right, babe," he said, "waddle up these steps straight to the tub, so we can both sleep good tonight. I know you're tired, cause I'm tired from walking in circles around this damn community."

He ran the water and lit some candles, making it cozy and relaxing for her; he turned on some soft music and dimmed the light. He helped her into the tub. He adjusted the water flow and massaged her neck and her stomach, until her feet looked wrinkled.

"All right, babe. I think you should be good and sleepy now; hopefully, you and I can sleep all night."

"Babe, I can't sleep," she said.

"Why am I not surprised?" he asked. "Let me talk to them; they need to go to sleep."

He rubbed her stomach and kissed it over and over.

"Rick Tyler babies, pleeeease stop moving so your mommy and I can go to sleep. Daddy has to get up in the morning. I need to make a little more money before y'all come here."

Good, he thought, *they stopped, and she's sleep; it's two in the morning. Maybe I can get in at least four hours of sleep.*

"Babe, what's wrong now?" he asked a little while later, after she shook him awake. "I just dozed off."

"I'm having labor pains," she said, "and they are coming really fast. Oh! My water just broke."

He jumped straight up out the bed, soaking wet, searching for some sweat pants and a shirt.

"What you are doing?" he asked as she headed for the bathroom. "Why are you going to the shower? Girl, you ain't taking no damn shower; if they coming that fast, we're going, babe."

"Okay, wait; help me. I need to push."

"Karla, don't you push in here. Stop."

"I can't stop it; one is coming now."

She was squatting down to the floor. "Ooh, it's coming!"

"Babe, stop. I don't know what to do; damn."

She screamed at him at the top of her lungs, "Come here and help me up now! I need to push down on something; oh, God. Please, Rick; help me, damn it."

"Where's the house phone, so I can call the hospital?"

"Damn the phone," she yelled. "I got to go now; ow, they coming fast, Rick. Hurry up."

"Fuck it, come on, babe: one step at a time. Blow in and out, keep breathing, but don't push yet; let's get downstairs."

They made it to the bottom steps, walking down the hallway that leads to the kitchen. She grabbed hold of the wall and squatted again to the floor.

"I feel its head coming out; ow, shit. It's coming; do something."

He snatched the phone off the counter and dialed 911; while talking to the operator, he heard something hit the floor and then heard a loud cry.

"Oh, shit; my wife just had the baby on the floor. It's a boy; we got two more to go. Hurry up," he said, "the garage door will be open. Hurry; she's still pushing."

"Uh-huh, I got to push again," she cried. "Shit, oh, my God; it's coming."

Blood and bodily fluids were all over the hallway floor; he ran back over to her, slipping and sliding in the blood.

"Hold on, babe. I got to lay him on something, not this cold floor."

"Rick, just lay him down on the floor; he'll be okay. I can't breathe!"

"Babe, I'm here. The paramedics are at the door; hold on, breathe slowly. Calm down; we can do this."

"Who the hell is 'we'? Why you keep saying 'we?' It's me. I'm doing this by myself."

"Karla, I'm not laughing with you; this is serious. I'm not laughing or playing; don't ever worry me no more about no more babies. You got one here and two more en route; this it."

"Okay, babe, we'll talk about that later."

As the paramedics came through the door, out came the second one.

"Ma'am, we got your baby boys," the paramedic said. "We're lifting you up. Do not push. We're putting you on the stretcher and are ready to take you to the hospital."

"I can't promise you that," she panted. "I got to push again, and I can't wait."

Just as they got her on the stretcher, she pushed again and out popped the last baby, screaming at the top of her lungs.

"It's a girl," said Rick. "Thank you, babe; they're here: Chad, Najee, and Mia Tyler. Welcome to the world; your daddy is right here."

CHAPTER 13
STALKING
THURSDAY, NOVEMBER 25, 2010

Look at this creep, Karla thought, *trying to act surprised that this woman just showed up after two years.*

"So what," she said. "You're having an affair with her again now?"

She slapped him so hard across his face, his head snapped.

"You son of a bitch," she growled. "I gave my life to you and gave you babies, and you do this to me? I hate you! It hasn't even been a got damn year after having these babies, and here you come with the same old shit."

"What the hell you slap me like that for?" Rick asked angrily. "What the hell you talking about? I don't know nothing about her being here."

"Really, Rick? She just shows up today at your parents' house, on Thanksgiving, and you don't know why she's here? Really? Okay, you know what? I'm going home, and you can do whatever you want. I'm out of here, so you get home the best way you can. Oh, tell me now: What else are you doing out here that I need to know before I get another surprise? Or shall I say who else are you hiding?"

"I'm not hiding anything," he snapped. "What the hell is wrong with you? I'm just as surprised as you."

"I'm taking my kids and going home; you handle that. I'm not fucking with you; we done. Apparently, you had some communication in order for her to just show up."

"Karla, what's wrong? Sandy asked. "Where you going?"

"I'm going home," she said. "Ask your brother about his bitch. I'm out."

She packed all three babies, Mia, Najee, and Chad, and walked out the door, fussing and crying to herself all the way to the truck. On the way home, the more she cursed and fussed, the more they cried; all the way up Route 50 to the Davidsonville exit. She finally pulled over at a gas station, threw the car in park, unsnapped her seat belt, and reached across the seat to calm them down.

"What's wrong with you little people? Mommy sorry for carrying on like that; it's your daddy's fault, his cheating, lying ass. I'm sorry; Mommy loves you. We're almost home; as soon as we get home, you'll get a bath and your bottles for the night. You can sleep with me tonight; take his spot. He's not getting in the bed with us."

As she was calming the babies down, a woman approached her car.

"Ma'am, are you okay?" she asked.

"Yes, I'm fine," Karla replied.

"Oh, okay. I saw you pull over in a hurry, like something was wrong; you sure you don't need any help?"

"No, I'm fine, just my babies are really crying; thank you."

"Okay, just checking; you never know these days. Anything could be wrong; there's been a lot of accidents out here on these interstates. Well, take care and watch yourself; you never know who's out there."

"Um, that was mighty nice of her to be so concerned," she said aloud. "Never had that before. I guess I better slow down. I must be really driving crazy; I got these kids. I'm going to handle him when he gets home."

Her phone rang.

"Hello?"

"Babe?" Rick replied.

"What the hell you want, Erick."

"Oh, I'm Erick now?"

"That's your fuckin name' or is it something else?"

"Ha ha, Karla; where the hell are you going and why?"

"I'm on my way home," she snapped. "Where the hell do you think I'm going? You think I'm sitting here, and your girlfriend is there, and you act like you don't know what's wrong? You got to be crazy. I should have left your ass alone; just leave me the hell alone."

"You tripping over nothing," he said. "She's not my lover or girlfriend, and I did not know she was in town. I haven't done anything wrong."

She started crying, trying to wipe her eyes and keep focused on the highway.

"Your old lover or whatever she is just shows up, smiling at your black ass, and I'm supposed to just sit there and indulge in your bullshit? Fuck you. Why didn't you just leave me where I was? I was okay, just fine without you."

"Look, Karla, what the fuck you talking about? Leave you alone? I'm on my way home; you have gone off the deep end for nothing."

She hit the End button on the truck panel while he was still talking. She felt herself picking up speed; the more she cried, the faster she drove. She finally reached the house and pulled into the garage; she sat there for a few minutes, breathing hard and still crying, trying to get herself together. She got out of the truck, took the babies, and went into the kitchen.

"Your cheating daddy said he's on his way home," she said, "but his lover is in town, so he can't leave her just yet. Um, maybe he decided I'm not good enough for him after all; since I had these babies, I've gained weight. Maybe he's just not attracted to me anymore."

There was a noise outside.

"What the hell is that loud banging? Who is it?" she asked.

She opened the door and someone struck her in the face; a set of hands grabbed her neck and choked her, while she still had the babies still in her arms.

"What the fuck?" she yelled. "Get off me; who are you? What the hell do you want?"

"Bitch, you know what I want," a voice said. "I want what he owes to me. You bitch, if I couldn't have him, neither will you; after I kill you, I am going kill your fuckin' babies."

She wiggled free from the hands and took off running through the kitchen.

"What the hell? Shit! Oh, my God; hold on, babies."

"I got you now, Mrs. Tyler; you can't hide, and you won't get away."

"Who the fuck are you?" Karla asked angrily.

"We don't have to answer your questions; all you need to know is somebody ain't coming out of here alive tonight."

"Really? I know who is, if not me, at least my babies. I promise you that, whoever you are."

She was running through the kitchen, down that long hallway, heading toward the front of the house for the upstairs. The strange woman ran behind her, slowed up, and grabbed a sword off the wall; she swung it toward Karla's feet as she was running.

Karla reached the top of the steps, ran into their bedroom, and went to the huge master closet with the babies; without knowing where they would land, she placed them on the closet floor. In her mind, they were safe.

Yvette, the crazy woman, caught her coming out the closet. She was standing in a low, defensive stance, ready.

Yvette came flying across the floor like she was Wonder Woman, swinging the sword through the air. Karla flipped across the bed and pulled another sword from under the bed. She karate-kicked Yvette back across the floor, stood straight up, and started swinging from left to right, up and down, slicing into Yvette's body.

Robin, another intruder, came rushing through the bedroom door and jumped on Karla's back, bringing her down to her knees. Karla scuffled with the heavier woman and managed to flip her off her and started punching her repeatedly. She stunned her and took off running out of the room.

Yvette stumbled and got up, going back for more; she followed Karla, with blood dripping from her wounds, shouting at her. She caught Karla in the hallway, this time by her ankles.

"You bitch!" Yvette yelled.

Karla and Yvette tumbled onto the floor, blows going into each other's body. Karla finally got her on the rail and beat her like she was a punching bag; she broke her nose and blackened her eyes. Finally, she threw her over the rail onto the glass coffee table; after a brief silence, she began screaming:

"You bitch, he cheated on me with your ass. He's my baby father; this supposed to be my house, not yours. Get the hell out; you whore, you won't be here long. I'll make sure of that when I get up."

"So this about my husband," Karla growled, "and you're telling me he's your baby daddy?"

"That's right, bitch; your husband, Rick Tyler, is my kid's father. He owes me!"

"Well, you know what, bitch? It seems to me that your ass is a little sliced up; you won't be getting up no time soon."

Karla finally ran back down the stairs, out of breath, to the kitchen. *Where hell is the damn phone?* "Uh, hey, you need to get your ass here," she said after he answered her call. "Your other baby mama and her friends are here, said they was going to kill me and your babies."

"What?" he yelled. "Who?"

"How the fuck would I know?"

He heard another woman's voice hollering in the background, announcing herself. Karla turned around with a look of surprise on her face, threw the phone on the countertop, and started scrambling for gun they kept in the drawer. It wasn't there.

"Shit!"

"Well, well, well, Ms. Karla, I'm Alondra," this woman said. "I'm glad to know you; that is one down; now it's me and you. May the best woman win, and I'm sure it will be only me left standing."

"Well, whatever your damn name is, let's do it. Good luck to you, and why are you here?"

"You must be the dumbest bitch I've ever seen; why do you think I'm here? To take my husband back."

"I'm sorry, and who is your husband, crazy woman? That one laying on the floor said Rick was her kid's father. And the other one never said what he was to her."

"Bitch, don't play with me."

Robin finally came around and ran down the back stairs to the kitchen, hollering at the top of her lungs, "I'm going to kill you."

Karla took off running again, toward the front part of the house. Robin caught her in the middle of the hallway, jumping on her again like she was the Flying Nun, with a heavy piñata stick in her hand. She cracked Karla across the back several times and the back of her head; blood exploded from everywhere.

Karla was dazed, stumbling, and trying to stand; sliding against the wall, she heard a voice inside her head: *You better not fall; get up. Keep fighting.*

She stood up and snapped back with what she had left in her.

"Okay, bitches, she yelled. "Let's go!"

Robin pulled a knife from her boot, plunged it into Karla's chest, and dragged it down the front of her body, twisting it over and over into her stomach. Not realizing she was seriously injured, Karla charged Robin so fast, she dropped the piñata stick. Karla kick-boxed and punched so fast, she nearly beat her to death; blood was flying everywhere. You couldn't tell who it was coming from.

She grabbed the piñata stick and hit Robin's face so hard, she broke the stick into pieces. The blood from her mouth flew across the floor and splattered on the wall.

Alondra was standing a few feet from them, pointing a gun directly at Karla.

"Wait," she said, laughing. "What is your name, honey? Something like Mrs. Tyler?"

"Don't you know?" Karla snapped. "You broke into my damn house; you should know your victim's name."

"I'm Alondra and I always get what I want. We're going to play a little game; you know what it's called. Now let's see, if one of these pretty little things doesn't hit you, then you'll live. You do know how many come on a clip, right? So you may want to start counting as you run, or you can just stand there. Your choice, okay? You're going out of here dead tonight."

Karla slowly backed her way into the kitchen, feeling weak and light-headed.

"Look lady, Alondra, or whatever you name is, I don't know what you want; just get out of my house."

"You know what I want: my husband back."

"Lady, your husband? Since when was he your husband? And why you not going after him? Why the hell you coming after me?"

"Because I know if I kill you, then he'll come back to me; he owes me and he don't love you. He still loves me. You see, those two other broads came for the same thing; he owed all of us, but I knew one or both of them would have to die, which is fine by me. I can pay the survivor out, but once you're gone, he's mine. See, all of this was supposed to be mine."

"Look, lady, just leave my home, okay?"

"Bitch, this is not your home; your ass will be carried out of here in a bag tonight. I want what's mine."

"You're crazy; this don't have to go this way. It's not worth it, Alondra, if that's your real name."

The woman was so angry, she fired her .357 magnum at Karla's head. She ducked just as her cellphone rung; she managed to snatch it off the counter and hit Talk. Rick heard Alondra screaming in the background.

"You bitch!"

"Derickie, hit them damn sirens," Rick said after the phone went dead. "You got to move, man. I need to get home; it's a crazy lady at my house, trying to kill my family."

"What the hell is going on, and who the fuck is Alondra?" Derickie said. "This not my jurisdiction; we have to call in to Anne Arundel County Police."

"Man, I don't give a fuck who you call it into; just drive, and I'll tell you later."

Karla managed to limp out of the kitchen.

What kind of women did this fool have, she thought. *He must have really did some shit to them, got damn it. Now I'm caught up in his shit, fighting for my damn life.*

She crawled back up to their bedroom, trying to get her babies and the gun in the nightstand drawer, but Alondra was on her heels.

"I know it's one in here, I saw it!"

Alondra stood over top of Karla and fired again at her head.

"Now, Ms. Karla, let's see who's the last woman standing."

Karla kicked Alondra's feet from under her, just as she fired another round into the ceiling; her gun flew out of her hands and landed across the room. Alondra caught herself and jumped on top of Karla; they began fighting for their lives. Alondra was giving her a good fight; as they struggled for the gun, more shots rang out, one after another. Alondra's body fell, pulling Karla down with her.

As the sirens died out, Rick, Derickie, and the Anne Arundel County Policemen finally rushed through the door, all at the same time. Rick stood there with his mouth wide open, with one hand on his waist and the other hand stroking his head.

"What the fuck? What brought you to my house, and for what?"

Yvette was lying in the pile of broken glass. Rick didn't know if she was dead or alive. He ran up the steps, three at a time. He reached their bedroom and saw Karla on the floor, with Alondra's body on top of her.

"Oh, my God! No, babe; oh, my God. Karla, can you hear me? Stay with me, babe."

Derickie ran upstairs with the police and paramedics and was shaken by what he saw: his cousin's wife laying in a pool of blood, unconscious.

"Mr. Tyler, please step back," a paramedic said. "We need to see if we can get a pulse."

"What hospital are you taking her to?"

"Anne Arundel Medical Center," he said .

"I'll escort you to the hospital," one of the officers said.

"Not yet; where are my babies? Shit, where are my babies? I don't see them."

He ran from room to room; nobody. He stood in the hallway, still looking and listening.

"Derickie, do you see any trace of them? They're not in their cribs;

that bitch better not have harmed my kids. Chad, Najee, Mia: cry so I can hear you. Oh, my God, where are you?"

He heard faint cries, so he ran back into the bedroom. He stood on the other side of the bed and looked under; there was Najee, not moving.

"Aw, shit, he's needs to go the hospital now; he's not moving."

He searched the bedroom, the bathroom, and both closets; there was Mia, balled up in a knot, just looking around, and Chaddie was push up against the wall, asleep. Both were unharmed.

"Mr. Tyler, we have a pulse; we need to go now. She lost a lot of blood; she's slipping in and out of consciousness."

"Okay, my son Najee is not moving, either. We don't have time to wait for another ambulance; take them both."

"I'll ride behind you and call your parents," Derickie said.

"I'm taking Mia and Chaddie with me," Rick said. "Make sure you get Georgie or Theresia directly on the phone; don't just leave a message."

"All right, man; the hospital was notified, and emergency doctors and nurses are standing by," Derickie explained.

They pulled Karla out of the ambulance and immediately started working on her, running through the doors, straight to the shock trauma unit. Rick went over to the nurse's station.

"Excuse me, ma'am, they just brought my wife in, she was with my baby. Can you tell me where they are?"

"Sir, you need to complete these papers," the receptionist said. "You can't go back there. The doctors will take her from here, so fill these out until someone comes out for you."

"Girl, what the hell is wrong with you?" Derickie snapped. "Are you that damn stupid? The man just said his wife was brought in, and they taking her to shock trauma, and so was his baby. If you don't pick up that got damn phone and get somebody out here for this baby, it going be some serious shit going down here tonight; he don't have time to fill out some damn papers. Get somebody out here now."

"Who the hell you think you talking to?" she said. "You got me all mixed up; don't think 'cause I'm white, you're going to punk me.

I'm just doing my job, and like I said, he needs to fill out the papers. Those are the rules."

Derickie snatched the white girl up by her uniform top and shook her.

"Look here, little girl: I'm his cousin, a DC detective. Now I'm telling you one more got damn time: You better pick that phone up now and get somebody out here for this baby. He ain't filling out no got damn papers now; can't you see the man is disoriented?"

"Get your hands off me," she snapped. "I'm just doing my job, you dumb-ass DC cop, think you know everything."

"Trust me, babe, I do. You got five seconds to make that call."

Rick walked off, leaving them to fuss; he found a doctor to take Mia and Chaddie through emergency, just to check them out. After a while, another doctor came and found him.

"Mr. Tyler, I'm Dr. Lipinski; we're going to do everything we can to save your wife. She is in a life-threatening condition, in bad shape. I'll come out once the operation is finished. I just wanted to let you know we are working on her, and it's going to be awhile. You can take a seat; the other doctors are checking on your babies. So far, they seem to be doing okay, just a little shaken up."

Tim and Monique arrived at the hospital first; they met up with Derickie in the waiting room.

"Man, what the hell happened?" Tim asked.

"I'm just as lost as you are," Derickie said. "I'm not sure, but it don't look good this shit is serious."

Rick's parents and his and Karla's sisters and brothers all trickled in, one by one.

"Aw, shit," Tim whispered. "Here comes Georgie and Theresia; they must have been nearby. I know this is going to be ugly; you know how he is when it comes to his girls, and it's Karla. It's going hit the fan now; let me step off. I need to go the restroom. I don't want to hear this fool cut up."

"Wait a minute, Tim," Betty said. "Don't leave, I might have to slap the shit out of this damn Italian man. Look here, Georgie," she said. "Don't come in with your bullshit; we all know how you feel, and we feel the same way. We don't know any more than what was told, and that's nothing yet, so don't go trying to throw your power around and intimidate people. Don't nobody care about you; you let Theresia ask the questions. You just be silent."

"Ms. Betty, what happen?" said Theresia.

"I'm not sure what happened."

"Tim, what happened?" Georgie asked. "I know you know; tell me. If that motherfucka had something to do with it, he's going to pay."

"I don't know, Georgie; I'm sure he knew nothing of this; once he gets himself together, we'll find out what happened. Stop blaming that man; it could have been a robbery."

"That's my heart. I protect my girls, and she's my babe," said Georgie.

He knelt down, pulled out his beads, and started praying in Italian. Tim looked around to make sure it was only them two standing off to the side; this couldn't be Georgie, the demon of all demons. He was so surprised he didn't know what to do or say; he just stood there and let him finish. Rick came from the back with Mia, Chaddie, and Najee in his arms, squeezing them tight. He sat in the corner by himself, slowly rocking them back and forth. Just then, the doctor came out again.

"Mr. Tyler, may I speak with you in private?" he asked. "We saved your wife, but there were some serious complications."

"Like what?"

"Your wife had several blows to the head, and there's swelling on her brain; she slipped into a coma, and we're unsure how long she'll be in that stage. It could be days or maybe a month; we don't know."

Rick was speechless; he couldn't say anything. He just broke down and cried.

"Oh, one more thing, Mr. Tyler; your wife was six weeks pregnant. She won't be able to have any more children; the wounds were pretty deep. Her stab wounds were from her chest down; the knife was grinded all the way down into the fetus. It was dead on the spot, cut into pieces; her right shoulder was cut up really badly, and her hand and feet are bruised up, but that'll heal over time."

He cried even harder; he just fell down in the chair with the babies still in his arms, crying uncontrollably.

"Mr. Tyler, would you like me to tell the rest of the family or will you?"

He waved his hand, given him the okay to tell them. The doctor went out to the waiting room.

"Hello, everyone. I'm Dr. Lipinski; can I have your attention, please? First, let me say that Mrs. Tyler's surgery was a success; her husband will give you more details later."

He saw their questioning facial expressions, so he hurried back through the swinging doors so he didn't have to answer. Rick put the babies in Monique's lap and walked behind the doctor, back to her bedside. Everybody was in total shock; no one knew what to say. They just looked at each other, trying to understand what happened; Nettie caught him at the door to comfort him.

"Rick, I'm so sorry; it's going to be all right. I promise you, she'll make it through. I'll stay back here with you for a while until my mother is ready to come in, okay?"

She wrapped her arms around his shoulder, hugging him as they walked to her bedside.

"Tim, I'm going back there now," Georgia said.

"Georgie, calm down; I'm not sure who they are letting back there yet, but if anybody gets to go back there, it's my grandmother, his mother, and Theresia."

"Guess you got a point there, since she's not my biological child; better not overstep that boundary with Ms. Betty, she'll raise hell. First thing out her mouth: 'You not her father, just her godfather.' I hate that woman.

"Okay, Tim, let's go. I need to speak with him, like now."

"Uh, look, Georgie, this not a good time to try to speak with him; he's not in his right mind or in any condition to go through your iterations. Why you don't give him at least a day or so?"

"I want some answers today."

"And so does everybody else, but you're not getting them, so let the man be."

"Only for you, for today, but I'm talking to him before I leave here, which is no time soon. I want you to know I feel like walking up to him now and beating the hell out of him."

"Ms. Betty, you ready to go to the back now?" said Cheryl.

"No, not really," she said. "I don't want to see my daughter like that, but I guess I have to. Y'all can go with me."

"Who would do this to you, babe?" Theresia asked as she stroked her hair and kissed her forehead.

"She was pregnant," said Rick.

"Again?" Theresia and Betty both asked.

"Yeah, six weeks pregnant; the fetus was cut into pieces when she was stabbed. She won't be able to have any more babies."

"Uh, Rick, you don't need no more babies," Betty said. "Don't you think three is enough at your age? Why would you want her to have more babies anyway? That's just ridiculous."

"Ms. Betty, that's enough," Cheryl said. "He doesn't need to hear that. Son, what else did the doctor say?"

He stood beside Karla's bed, telling them everything the doctor told him.

"I'll be here until she comes around; it's all my fault."

"Son, it wasn't your fault; you didn't know. You can't stay here every day; we'll take turns caring for her. Your babies need you too."

"I know, Ma, but she needs me at this point; if you could look after the triplets for a couple of days, I'd really appreciate it."

"I'll help with the babies too," Theresia said. "I'll be here for as long as you need me."

"Well, I'm not watching no babies," Betty said. "They cry too much and they too little for me to handle. I got things to do."

"That's fine, Ms. Betty; we got them. We know you don't have time for them," said Theresia. "Let's all go home and get some rest; at this point, it's nothing we can do but wait. Rick is staying, and I'm taking my grandbabies home with me."

"Well, I'm staying at your house to help you out," Theresia said. "Let's get them and get out of here; let him sit with her. It's nothing we can do."

"Cheryl, what happened? What were they looking for?"

"I don't know, Derrick. I have no idea. I guess we'll find out later; let's just go home."

Derickie kept looking back at the babies and then out the window. "Something ain't right about this; it just don't sound right," he said. "Who were they after? Were they actually after her, or was this one of Tina's stunts? I can bet my last she has something to do with this; I'm telling you, Cheryl, she's crazy. I can't stand her ass anyway. I'd put my life on the line it was her, damn criminal-minded broad, and she supposed to be a criminal lawyer. Picture that one: a criminal mind as a criminal lawyer."

"Derrick, you don't know that. Said Cheryl, Just wait until Rick talk to us; he don't know anything. He was at the house when it happened; all he can do is wait for the police and the crime scene people to give him some information."

CHAPTER 14
TWO WEEKS LATER
SATURDAY, DECEMBER 11, 2010

"I'm not leaving here until I know my daughter is alive," Georgie said. "I will not lose my daughter again over him, and especially not like this. Imma kill his ass if she dies, and I mean it. He won't be the first I killed and damn sure won't be the last. Afternoon, ma'am, I need to see my daughter, Karla Tyler; what's her room number?"

Georgie walked in the room and saw Rick sitting in the chair on the side of the bed, looking out the window in a daze.

"Rick Tyler, if anything happens to my daughter, I'm holding you responsible."

"Man, get the fuck out of here. I am not up for your shit now."

"I don't give a fuck what you not up now; that's my daughter laying in that bed, and she damn sure is not having a baby. She's fighting for her life. And I know you had something to do with this; I feel it. If she dies, your ass is mine."

"You know what, Georgie? Fuck you, and if she dies? What kind of shit is that to say? You pick a fine time to come pick some shit; if you got a problem with me, then you should have come months before, but not now."

Rick swung his feet around off the window seat and stood up.

"You come in here with your fuckin' bitch-ass threat; you need take that shit back to wherever you got it from. I'm not the one, today or any other day."

"Oh no, this is not no bitch-ass threat, Mr. Big Shot; it's a promise.

I know you had something to do with it; tell me why she's in a damn coma."

A nurse came into the room and said, "Gentleman, I can hear you two down at the nurse's station. You cannot do this here; you need to leave, sir. And you are?"

"I'm her father."

"Okay, well, Father, you cannot come in here having that discussion, and that means you too, Mr. Tyler. We don't allow that behavior in our patient's room; if you need to talk or fight, please take it completely off our premises, or I'm calling security."

"I'm not going anywhere yet," said Georgie.

"Nurse, you can call security and have Mr. Lombardo removed, or there will be a fight in here."

"You don't have to call nobody to remove me," Georgie said. "Ain't a motherfuckin' soul going to remove me. I leave when I want to, and I want to see my daughter."

"Mr. Lombardo, please! If you stay, you must lower your voice; don't do this to your daughter and the others in here that are trying to recover. Have some respect and compassion for the injured."

"Imma stay a few more minutes then I'll leave, 'cause I see another injury is going to happen soon. Erick Tyler, this not over; we will talk real soon."

"That's Judge Erick Tyler to you, and I'll be around you; know how to find me. I got nowhere to go."

"That nigga is good as dead," Georgie said after he left the room. "He lucky the only good thing out of that is she had my new grandbabies. I'm going to see all of my babies, then get somewhere and get me some sleep, before I do something without thinking about it." He called his other daughter. "Hello, princess, you got room for your dad? I need to lay down before I kill him."

"Daddy, stop it," Sherri said. "You can't do that."

"Why not, princess? Yes, I can. I'm so damn angry now, I swear I was getting ready to shoot him right there in that room."

"Daddy, I'm sure you are; come over here before you get yourself in some trouble."

"Not yet. I'm going to see my new grandbabies first and check on Alicia and Kareem, then I'll be out there."

"Daddy, don't you go up there and start no trouble. I mean it; don't you do it."

"Princess, I won't. I'll be over soon."

"Hurry up, your brother's en route, and I don't want no mess out of any of you; we do not need no family feud going on, and you don't know the whole story."

"Sherri, you're not my mother; you're my princess, okay? So don't be giving me no orders. I do what I want."

"Okay, Daddy, I don't have to be your mother; you just hurry up and bring yourself over here and get you some sleep."

"Imma get to the bottom of this. Babe, I'll be back; Rick calling me. I'm going up to the hospital."

"Hey, son; how are you? Sorry, I know that's a crazy question to ask."

"You all right, Pops; you're good. I'm a little better than the last few nights; she still breathing, so that's a plus. What's up?"

"Good to hear; I'm on my way up there. I told you mother you called me, in case she asks."

"Yeah, I know; got it, Pops, but where you really heading to?"

"Up there."

Okay, well, I'll be here, but for what? I'm okay; how's my babies? I'll be down today anyway."

"Nothing; your uncle and I coming up so we see you soon; I'll bring you some change of clothes. I'll stop by your house; what you want me to get you?"

"Pops, nothing. I'm good; don't go by there; the investigators are there. I can't even go there yet myself."

"Like I said, I'm coming by the house after I stop by Karla's house to check on the dogs and get the babies some more stuff, then I got to go to the store, pick them up some more food and Pampers. All right, Rick? So we'll see you soon."

"Hey brotha," Derickie said. "Be there in five minutes; ride with me up to the hospital and to Rick's house, before it gets too late; this story ain't right."

"Derickie, you can't just go to that house; it's still considered a crime scene."

"Yeah, I know, but Ricky, this shit isn't right. I'll be by there in a few so be ready. I need to talk this out; he's lying."

"All right, come on, 'cause you ain't going to stop. He might not be lying; he just ain't telling the whole damn story, but your nosey ass got to know. That's always been your problem; you just can't leave it alone. I swear, man; hurry up."

"Now he got my darn wife questioning me about where I'm going; damn. Honey, I'll be back; going with Derickie to make a run."

"Hit it, man; hurry up before she gets out the door," said Ricky. "Got damn, this woman calling me already. I just got in the truck; I told her I'll be back."

"Hey old man," Derickie said, "I know you and Uncle Derickie on your way out to Rick's house. I just called your house; don't do it. Just wait for me. I can give you a little bit of what happen."

"What you know, boy?" said Ricky.

"Dad, if you just wait."

"All right, you want us to meet you somewhere? Derickie flying like a bat out of hell; he knows we can't get in the house, and I don't know what the hell he's looking for. I swear, my brotha is nosey as hell; he thinks he can save everything and everybody."

"Yeah, true that. He is, and he does, but stop where you are; I'm en route. Meet me at the K-Mart in Crofton. I'll be there shortly; don't move."

"Hey old men, or shall I say Inspector Gadgets, y'all some nosey old men."

"Okay, Derickie, what do you know?"

"Man, tell me something; this don't sound right; why her? What were they after?"

"Uncle Derickie, I'm not sure; he called me. I was already heading toward your house; he asked me to take him home. He was hysterical as hell; I don't know why he didn't ask Tony or Niki, since they were already there. By the time I got in front of the house, he was running out the door, shouting to hurry up, something was going on at his house. He called her back; we heard screaming in the background; by the time we got there, it was a bloody mess. I called Anne Arundel County; just so happened a friend of mine got the call. He and some other officers responded. I ran in behind him and there was some woman laying through the table. I called the ambulance while he was going through the house; by the time me and the other officer got upstairs, Rick had Karla in his arms, rocking her and crying."

"Where was my grandbabies?"

"Najee was under the bed, balled up, and Mia and Chaddie were in the closet; I must say, Uncle Derickie and Dad: She went down fighting; she kicked some ass up in there."

"Well, she learned from the best, got damn black-ass Italian Mafia."

"Did she have her gun? 'Cause I know if she did how that was going down."

"Derickie, how you know they really Mafia?"

"Come on, man; we all know they are. They try to hide their shit; them dudes been ruthless all their lives, from the father on down. Rick and your boy know them oh so well; they run with them ones around their age and some of the cousins and nephews."

"I tell you what, you go up the East Coast or in these streets and drop that last name, see what you get."

"I'm curious," Ricky said. "How did she get in their family?".

"That's a whole other story; tell you that at a later date."

"All right; beside all that, you got an idea of what happened, and for the last time, Inspector Gadget, don't go to his house."

"I am going in this K-Mart, get him something he can slip into."

"Like what, Derickie? You know your damn son; he ain't wearing nothing from no K-Mart."

"Well, I got to get the man something to wear; I'll just get him a pair of sweatpants, tee-shirt, and a pair of flip flops and some personals, but I should just go to his house anyway and see if they let me in."

"Hey son, I brought you some things."

"Thanks Pops, but I'm going by the house in DC. I got clothes there."

"So I spent my money for nothing," Derickie replied.

"No, I'll take the bag, but I can't put them on here. I need to shower."

He leaned into Karla, stroking and kissing her forehead.

"Babe, stay with me," he said. "I'll be back; hold on, please! I'm begging you."

He walked out behind his father and uncle, mumbling to himself.

"Lord I know I had some mess with me, but I pray to you please restore my wife's life, all of her; if it's anything that I did, then make me suffer, not her, not my family. Is this why you let me have happiness and love to take it away from me? Then why did you give it to me? Nurse, I'll be back in a few hours; you'll call me if anything changes? If she makes a sound or blinks, you will call me, right?"

"Yes, Mr. Tyler, we will call you if there is any change, just go. I'll call you."

"Okay, thank you, but can I ask one more thing?"

"What's that?"

"Is there any way you can track who comes to visit her?"

"No, Mr. Tyler, we don't do that; is there something we need to know, since you asked that question?"

"No, I'll be back in a few hours. I was just asking."

He leaned against the wall, waiting for the elevator, replaying in his mind what he saw and why.

Alondra, Robin, and Yvette, he thought; *seriously, how long ago was our relationship over? Many, many years ago; damn, I was in my thirties. Maybe with Robin, I was thirty-eight; I wasn't even fuckin' with crazy-ass Tina. And another weird shit is all of sudden, after almost two years, I started getting emails from Tina; she even sent cards to our house. I'm surprised never mentioned anything about it, she just left them on the counter until I tore them up and threw them away. And now, just out of nowhere, she showed up at my parents' house; how did she get my home address? It's undisclosed to the public.*

He walked through the hospital garage, still wondering why.

"Hey Ma, I'll be by there shortly," he said. "I'm stopping at Karla's house, get me some clothes and shower. I'll bring the babies some more clothes and food; what else do they need?"

"Son, they're all right, but your oldest called; he's en route home. He's really upset; it took me a long time to get him to calm down on the phone. I finally got Alicia and Kareem under control; they want to see their mother too."

"Yeah, I'm sure they do."

"Rick, don't let them see their mother like that, at least not now, maybe in another week or so."

"Ma, I can't stop them from wanting to see their mother; I'll try to talk them out of it, at least until she heals some. I'll be there shortly. I'll be quick."

"Georgie, come on in," Cheryl said. "How are you?"

"Hanging in there; I come to see my grandbabies, to give me some relief."

"Okay, well, all of them are here in the house somewhere."

"Where is my oldest grandson, Ric?"

"Oh, I didn't know you were talking about him."

"Why wouldn't I? I don't have nothing against him, never did; whatever issue I have is with his father. That doesn't mean I don't care and love him. That boy has been a part of my daughter's life for so long, I couldn't help but love him. I treat him just like my other grands, and he can tell you that. I never did him wrong."

"Georgie, I never said you mistreated him. I just didn't think you considered him as your grandson; he should be here shortly."

Georgie strolled to the back, looking mean and mad as hell and almost red as a crayon; before he could even get through the door and sit down, Theresia let him have it.

"Georgie, I'm telling you now: Rick on his way here. It's getting late, so don't you start no mess, and I mean it, Georgie Lombardo. If you do, your ass is going to be so sorry."

"Um, as long as he doesn't say nothing to me, it won't be no mess. I come to see my grandbabies. I ain't messing with him."

"Hi Georgie's babies; Papa haven't seen you in a while. Oh, there's my grand princess, Alicia."

Rick and his son came through the door at the same time, talking. Kareem heard them and came downstairs and joined in on the conversation. Rick hugged Kareem, and they walked into the family room.

"Shit," Rick said when he saw Georgia, "not this motherfucka again."

"Rick, watch your mouth."

"Ma, excuse me; let me just get my kids and go somewhere with them."

"I'm playing with them," said Georgie.

"Man, if you don't let go of my kids, I'll kick you in your motherfuckin' head, without a thought."

"Papa, let them go; he's serious. Please give them to him; don't do this."

"I'm playing with them, princess; he can wait until I finish."

Rick punched Georgie right upside the head and kicked the shit of out of him, and then he snatched his kids out his arms.

"You nigga!" he yelled, swinging.

"Dad, Rick, don't kick him again," said Alicia.

"Imma kick that motherfucka out the door; get the fuck off my kids."

Georgie flew backwards onto the couch; he got up, charging.

"Georgie," said Theresia.

"What the hell you screaming at me for? This nigga just hit and kick me."

All you could hear was a trigger clicking, click, click, and the babies screaming and crying. Alicia shouted at Rick, and Cheryl and Theresia looked scared to death.

"Georgie, put that gun away," Theresia said. "These babies are in here in as well as other damn people; why didn't you just give him his kids?"

"The next time, you better shoot it and make it worth your time; the next time, you won't get that opportunity to pull it out again."

"I listen to your shit long enough and your fuckin' threats; you ain't going to do shit to me," said Rick.

"The next time I will, Rick Tyler, and no one will save your ass."

"Stop it, Georgie," said Theresia. "This is not the time or place for all of this; you are not going to do anything to that man. He is our daughter's husband, and these kids' father."

"Ain't nobody save me this time," Rick replied.

"Georgie, if you got something to say to my son, you talk with him in private," Cheryl said, "but keep in mind, he is not a young boy anymore, so whatever he says back to you, he's a grown man. His wife is fighting for her life; we don't need this, so why don't you just leave now?"

Georgie stormed out the door, slamming it behind him.

"I ain't never give a damn about him anyway," he said as he drove away. "This shit ain't over; got my daughter fighting for her life. I should have shot him in the head; she don't need him. I can help her take care of them babies; when she comes out of this, she's divorcing him, and I mean it."

"I'm so sorry for all this, Rick."

"Theresia, no need to apologize for him; you know Georgie, the ass he can be. I still love you. I'm going to lay down; they all upset. We going to take a nap for a few hours, then I'm going back to the hospital, but let me check on her first before I lay down, just to make sure."

"Rick, if there's any change," Theresia said, "I'm sure someone will call you; just go take you a nap. If someone calls, we'll wake you up."

"Yeah, well, Imma call them first, then I'll go lay down."

He dialed the hospital.

"Good evening, this is Rick Tyler."

"Mr. Tyler, this is Nurse Jefferson; I told you not to worry. I would call you if there was any change, and there was none. Take care of what you need to do. I will call you even if she blinks, okay?"

"Okay, but I needed to know before I closed my eyes. I'll be back in a few hours."

He hung up and took the kids upstairs and lay across the bed, kissing all their little bodies and tickling them until they all fell asleep; they slept through the night, until the next morning.

"Dang, were you in a wrestling match?" Cerise asked when she saw him after he came downstairs.

"I feel like it," Rick said. "They were all over the bed, all night, pulling and moving; they wear you out while you sleeping."

They all fell out laughing.

"Well, brotha, I must say you did a good job on fixing that little girl's hair, and you got them dressed and now fixing them some breakfast. Wow, let's see how this works."

"Yeah, I know, but my babe taught me well, and note to y'all to let her know I did it. The hair thing, baths, and dressed them, but that hair thing still gives us trouble."

"Rick, I'm so glad to see you have a little laughter left," said Theresia.

"Yeah, they keep my spirits up; those the other part of my heart."

He was going in circles, from highchair to highchair. Mia ate like a little princess, eating all slow, and Najee was eating as if he hadn't eaten in days, trying to force the spoon in his mouth and grabbing at his food; poor Chaddie couldn't keep anything down. He would stretch out in his highchair, then fall out, crying and crying until Rick picked him up and sat him on his lap, still reaching for his bottle, so he paced the floor, trying to soothe him from crying, walking from the front of the house to the back, back and forth.

"Um, I need to take some leave at least a month, and I need Maria here to help me; they want their bed and Mommy, and I do too, but first things first: I need my damn house cleaned up."

His phone rang just as he walked outside with Chaddie in his arms.

"Hey, Lil' Brother, where you at?" said Niki.

"I'm at Ma's house; why? What's up with you?"

"I'm driving down. I should be there in a few hours; you need some company? We need to talk."

"Yeah, okay, about what?"

"You, man, just in case."

"Hold up, just in case? What the fuck you talking about?"

"Man, you know what the fuck I'm saying; you need to be preparing for the worst. If she comes out of this, you don't know if she's going to need a lot of caretaking; this serious. Let's think this thing out; stop being in denial. I know you don't what to hear this, but I'm serious. Let's be realistic about this. I understand you going downhill fast, full speed. You probably don't see it; those kids going to need you, for better or worse."

"Man, why would you call me with that? I'm not ready to hear that part, damn it. Nik, man, I see you when you get here. I'm on my way to my house to check on my dogs."

After he got to the house, he went over to the dogs.

"Hey, pups, Daddy been gone too long; sorry about that. I know if only you could talk, I'd get an earful. I'm sure I would."

"Who was it, Sun; do you know, Moon? How about you, Star and Cloud; who was is it? Tell Daddy."

The dogs cried and rubbed against him.

"Come on, let's go inside. I know you need to eat; you been deprived for a couple of days. So sorry for that." "Damn, and she probably never got a chance to bring you in."

He was walking along the side of the fence and noticed wires hanging from under the porch; he stopped in his tracks and ran in the house, hunting for a flashlight in the kitchen drawers. He found it under the sink and ran back outside, scanning along the fence and under the porch.

"Damn," he said. "The got damn security line's been cut; this had to be somebody who knows these lines are under the porch; this space is kind of tight. Somebody had to check this out before to know; well, at least I know it's a woman, and I see she lost her earring; this a start. In the meantime, I need to call my tech, get him here, check this out, and replace it real soon. We need to come back home. I don't want to stay at nobody else's house. Come on, pups; let's roll out. I been in here long enough. I got a couple more errands to run, then back to the house in DC. No need to hit the alarm; the damage is done. Let's see who else is coming tonight; the tape is still rolling."

"Oh, I see Nicholas made it here in Niki time, out front on the phone already; motherfucka must've been closer than he tried to make me believe, saying he was a few hours away. Shit, I know better."

"Aw, I see we got extra house guests," Kareem said when he saw the dogs.

"Yup, we sure do, and they're going to be here as long as we're here; problem with that, son?"

Kareem laughed and started wrestling with the pups; their big feet were slamming against the floor, sounding like bricks being thrown, jumping up and down and running around in circles; Cloud, the bodyguard, followed Rick on his every move in house.

"I see my babies knocked out; who brought them home, you, Niki?"

"Yeah, I stopped by Ma's house. Alicia wanted to bring them home with her, so we did."

"Did Chaddie eat? He wouldn't eat this morning."

"He ate what I cooked; they been eating since we got here, or shall I say fatty Chaddie has. Every time I put something in my mouth, he cries for it too. Damn, that boy can eat; shit, I got tired sharing my food with him. It's time for bed, and he's still eating."

"Niki, leave my big baby boy alone; he can't help it if he likes to eat. He got it honestly."

"Alicia, Kareem, and Ric, I need to talk with you. I know you don't want to hear this, and I don't want to say it, but we got to talk about this now, just in case."

"What you mean, just in case?" Kareem asked. "You act like you want her to die."

"Just in case she doesn't make it, just in case she becomes paralyzed, or just in case she stays in a coma. That's what that means, Kareem."

"Alicia, stop! You're right, but when she comes out of her coma, she'll need help, and I know you will pitch in to help when we call on you. We really need to pull together and make a plan. Now, Alicia and Kareem may have to come live in the house for a while, and Ric, you need to go back to camp; at this point, it's nothing we can do but wait. It's nothing none of us can do at this point; me or your sister or brother will keep you posted of your mother's status. In the meantime, go back to practice. I know it's hard to do, but we got to be strong for your mother, and I need to stay strong for these lil' people."

Alicia ran up the steps and burst out crying. They all were sitting with tears in their eyes. Rick was holding back as much as he could, but his tears were streaming down his face too.

"I'll be back," he said. "My daughter, who's been the strongest throughout this whole thing, needs the most comforting right about now. It's okay, Alicia babe, cry all night. Just cry, I'll be right here with you."

"All right, Rick," Niki said when he came back down, "now tell me why those women were at your house; was it for you or for Karla? I think that was meant for you."

"Niki, I don't know why they were there; if it was for me, why not come after me? They had all the time in the world before now; this some strange shit. I haven't seen them in years; how did they even know where I live?"

"Well, apparently they did."

"I haven't had any contact with them in years. I was shocked to see them laying on my floor; all of this is a mystery to me. You know what? I wonder if that fuckin' bitch Tina had anything to do with this; it's funny she showed up all of a sudden at Ma's house."

"Yeah, I think everybody was shocked about that," Niki said. "Just out the blue, and Cheryl Tyler was not happy about that at all."

"Yeah, I know she wasn't, and I'm surprised Pops didn't go off this time." He sat very quietly. "But look hear, Nik. I went back to the house and found a note in the house and an earring under the deck; one of them cut the wires to the alarm under the porch."

"A note?" Niki echoed. "Why didn't you tell the police?"

"I just found the damn thing; it was from Tina."

"How you know? Did she sign the note? One of your other women could have done that."

"From the statement on it, I know it's her; now what the other three got to do with her is really a got damn mystery."

"This is too much to take in when you sleepy," Niki said. "I got to go to bed. I need to sleep; all this shit here is way too fuckin' much."

"Shit, then why didn't you go? You started talking to me; I came in here with my own thoughts. Take your ass to sleep. I'll see you in the morning, Nicholas. I might as well go to bed too; tomorrow is going to be better, with good news."

Najee woke up crying like he was the lead rooster; the whole neighborhood could have heard him crying at the top of his lungs. Chaddie was laying at the bottom of the bed, like an overstuffed turkey.

"Uh Rick, what you doing?" Alicia asked.

"I'm getting their bottles, so I can get them ready for a bath; getting them ready is an adventure."

"Yeah, you right, but they don't want no bottles; they want food. At least fat Chaddie do; it may hold them for a minute. I'll help you out; while you giving them a bath, I'll cook them some breakfast. How about that?"

"Alicia, babe, that's sweet of you, but it's not your responsibility to take care of them. I appreciate all that you do as their big sister; I got it. I'm good; go back to sleep. I'll come get you if I need help."

"Okay, Rick Tyler babies, y'all going to take these bottles first while I get you ready and dressed, one by one. Ms. Mia, you're easy, but tackling that hair, I'll leave that for your sista. All right, Najee, don't give me no troubles, lil' man. Let's do this nice and slow; good job, but I know I'm not getting lucky with your big brother; look at him down there, spread out like Ted the wino, sucking up his bottle. Okay, Chad Tyler, let's play some ball; I see how this is going.

Rick was struggling with Chaddie, twisting and turning all over the bed, trying to get away from getting bathed and dressed.

"All right, done with you little ones; y'all going in the crib while I take a shower. I'll come back, get dressed, and then get some breakfast before you have a screaming attack."

"Hey Rick," Alicia asked, "why that car sitting over there, looking over here?"

"Alicia, why you hanging out the window so early? I thought you were still upstairs."

"Look, it's a burgundy Ford Taurus with Florida tags."

"Nosey, can you tell if it's a man or woman?"

"I don't know. I can't make that out; I saw the car from my bedroom window last night, and it's still here. The person never got out; you think they're dead?"

"I don't know; maybe you should go see. What you think?"

"Uh uh, Rick, I'm not going over there; why don't you or Niki go?"

"Hey, Niki, come upstairs in the kitchen; check out this car out across the street. Alicia said it's been out front all night."

"Yeah, I saw it too," Niki said. "I thought that was strange; the person never got out the car. You know who that is?"

"Man, I don't know who the fuck that is or what they're looking for; shit, it could be some drug stakeout, and they just happened to be sitting in front of our house. I got to go to the courthouse today for a few hours, then go by Ma's house, and then we going up to the hospital."

"Well, go ahead and handle that," Niki said. "I'll be here with them; if he looks like he wants to bring his ass over here, and nobody knows him, he's short. I'm strapped. I don't leave home without it. I'll fire that ass up, and you know it. By the way, for the record, you need to start strapping up again, especially now, considering your circumstances."

"Yeah, I know, but I got to keep it clean for now. I can't be moving with a weapon on me like that. I'll take my chance with my fist, first."

"Rick, this no time for keeping it clean; this not making any sense of what happened just out the blue. Don't you have your license and approval to carry your shit?"

"Yeah."

"Then put it on you, at least until this is solved; you're going to need that while you are moving back and forth in the streets."

"I'll keep that in mind, but I got my kids with me from time to time, so I'm not really trying to carry it. I'm good for now. Look, I'm out; keep me posted on that car; if you can get the tag number, see if you can reach Derickie. Get to him to run it."

"Man, shut up. I know what to do; you handle your business at the courthouse and hit me back later."

"Oh, well, I didn't meet the early bird special," he said after he drove to the courthouse. "That's cool. I'll park in the garage down the street. I need some air and exercise anyway; I can walk."

"Good morning, Judge Tyler," the court clerk said. "I slipped a note in your mailbox from Judge Lenare; she wants to meet with you today as soon as possible."

"Okay, thank you. I'll give her a call shortly."

Um, he thought, *this woman speaks to me every day, but I have no idea what her name is. I need to find out, I hate talking with someone and can't address them by their name; that's some foul shit, when they know your name and you don't know theirs. I'll find it out today before I leave. Let's see what's on the agenda for today, get my thoughts together since the morning is quiet and calm, so far, with no interruptions.*"

"Good morning, Judge Lenare."

"Good morning, Judge Tyler; how's your wife doing?"

"Not so good; she's still in a coma."

"I'm sorry to hear that; come to my office and let's finish this conversation. Have a seat. No worries; you're not being fired under any circumstances. I called you in for this brief meeting because

I've reassigned your cases for you. I spoke with JB, and he explained what's going on. I don't need you here, not being able to focus, so you go home, be with your family, and take all the time you need to help your family get back together."

"Judge Lenare, thank you so much. I don't know what to say."

"Erick, there is nothing to say; just lock your office and give me your keys, in case I need to get in there for your files."

"Judge Lenare, if you have questions or need answers, please give me a call."

"Erick, we won't be calling you about any cases. I said for you to go home and take care of your wife and those babies; they need you. We will be okay. Now please go before I do fire you, at least for a couple of days. Now get out of here. We're all praying for your family; keep me updated on her status, and Rick, if there is anything I can do, please don't hesitate to call me. I don't mean about your cases; I mean helping you and your family."

"Yes, ma'am, I will, and thank you. I'll give you a status report before I leave and bring my keys."

I got a lot done this morning, he thought. *All is wrapped up and its almost noon, I got to get out of here soon.*

"So do we finish this conversation now or later?"

Rick chuckled and lifted his head up slowly. Georgie was standing in his office doorway.

"Georgie, I was finished with you at the hospital, but if you want more, let's do this, so you can get the hell out my face, at least for a while."

He got up and closed his door, and Georgie took a seat on the other side of his desk.

"Nice office," he said. "And lovely pictures of the family."

"Yeah, okay, stop the small talk; what the hell do you want now?"

"I'm here to find out why my daughter is laying up in the damn hospital bed. I told you before, if anything happens to my daughter, I was holding you responsible. I know whatever the reason is, you're behind this."

He pulled out his gun and twisted the silencer onto it, laying it on his desk and pointing it directly at Rick. "Your mother is not here to save your ass this time, so start talking, boy"

"Georgie, my mother didn't save me the last time, so if you're going to shoot me in my chambers, then go for it, but do know you only get one shot, so make it good. Now let me reiterate this again to you: I'm not afraid of you, never was and never will be; all that threatening shit may work with somebody else, but not for me, so if you got another way, then let's do it."

Georgie tried to interrupt.

"Oh no," Rick said. "This my chambers, so I'll be doing the talking in here."

"Oh because this is your office, I got to listen to you?"

"That is correct; you walked into my space, Mr. Lombardo, I didn't walk in yours, so you're going to listen to me. If you don't want to hear, then there's the door, father-in-law, that same one you invited yourself in."

"This is why I made her get that damn abortion a long time ago; you're such an ass. That's why I didn't want her with you. I knew you were going to hurt her."

"Oh, so you made her do it? It wasn't her decision?"

"When I finish with your ass, Rick Tyler …"

"I told you before, that's Judge Tyler to you."

"Whatever! You're a piece of shit, Rick Tyler; just know your ass will be stepping down soon. One of DC's finest judges, and you'll never practice law nowhere or be a damn judge; if anything, you will be judged. So you need to get your resumé together to find you a damn decent paying job, because you're going to need it. What other skills you got besides being a damn lawyer and a judge?"

"Georgie, you're not even funny," Rick said. "I got plenty of skills, and can't nobody make me step down, other than my wife. I will be a judge until the day I choose to step down. You can't take shit from me, and just in case you forgot, you fuckin' half-breed black Italian, we got three older children, three babies, and for the record, she was pregnant again with a fourth one of my baby. So you didn't stop nothing. You came to me with your bullshit to blame me. I didn't come to you for shit. Let's talk about your bullshit that you got going on with your business. I can have your ass behind bars. Your money issues and those illegal documents and the other shit you got going on; yeah, I know all about that."

"You don't know shit about me or my business."

"Really? I know more than you think, about shit I don't even care to know about. I know about you filing your business taxes and those illegal documents; those cargo ships that're moving across the waters: What's in them? That was created to cover up your years of bullshit corruption. I even know about some of those mysterious murders that somehow keep coming back to you and Gray. Now if Theresia ever knew about that, she would be hurt, and so would your daughters.

"Now you want to talk about putting people's lives at stake?" Rick continued. "There are a lot of lives that you hold in your hands with your shit, Georgie, so don't come at me, telling me that I caused my wife to be in this situation. You don't know anything about me; we don't connect in any way. You're not even my father-in-law. "And remember, I was a lawyer first, I've been on the scene for a long time. I didn't just play football; I'm from the streets too, so I get both sides. So to answer your questions of what other skills I have, I have several careers. I can get a job as an architect or engineer, and I also have a construction company; if you feel you got power like that to bring me down from a judge and destroy my credentials, go ahead. I still will be standi, and I still can take care of my family, no matter what you try do."

"You can't take care of my daughter or grandbabies."

"Oh, no? Why not? you think you're the only one that can do that? Oh, that's right; you got it all. You rule everybody; everybody jumps when you say jump. Man, I don't give a damn about you being the Mafia. And I don't do well with threats. I don't give them too often, but when you come after me and mine, I make good on my promises."

"Rick Tyler, I know you got something to do with this. You ain't nothing but a punk."

"Georgie, at this point, this has nothing to do with Karla. This is about me and you; this just happened to be a good time for you, but bad time for me. The way I see it, you taking the sucker way out; if you felt like this before, you should've come before it involved my wife's life."

"You're a smart-mouth nigga."

"Okay, so what else is new? I've known that for years. And if I'm a nigga, then what the hell are you? Nigga and Italian; get the fuck out of here."

"What, you think you got power because you were a big-time lawyer over in LA, and now you're a sorry-ass judge."

"For the record, Georgie, I'm still a big-time lawyer, and yes, I am now a judge."

"You ain't nothing but a fucking asshole, Judge Tyler."

"Okay, I been told that too, so what else you got? At least I'm a good asshole, and you're not; oh, and shall I mention your other women and the secret child that you think nobody knows about?"

"How in the hell do you know about that?"

"I told you, this East Coast street talk from New Jersey on down DC streets; I know your bullshit."

If looks could kill, Georgie would have killed him on the spot and had his ass thrown in the Potomac, never to be found.

"So Georgie, how many is it: one, two, or three? Shall I stop?"

Georgie jumped out the chair and swung on him.

"Oh, am I hitting a nerve? The truth hurts, don't it? Remember, you came into my space; you can leave at any time. I'm not asking you to stay. I got work to do anyway; you wouldn't want me to tell Theresia or your princesses now, would you?"

"Are you threatening me?" Georgie growled.

"Nope. I told you, when I give a threat, I make good on it. I'm just letting your ass know that I know all about you. But for real, I guess I am making a threat."

"So what, you're trying to extort money from me?"

"Georgie, all the money you got ain't enough. I don't want shit from you, except for you to get the fuck out of my face. I'm done with you."

"You don't scare me, and I don't scare you."

"My wife's life is on the line, and despite how you feel about me then and now, I love Karla. I always did and still do; there's nothing in this world I wouldn't do for her. Most of the time, she takes what she wants from me; she's the only woman I allow to take from me. I don't have any secrets with her, and if you only knew the damn drama I had to go through to get her back in my life, any other man would have left her alone and chalked it up as a loss. No, not my crazy ass. I'm a glutton for her punishment; I'm not letting her go. This wasn't an easy ride to get her. You think I'm giving that up for some cheap one night of pussy? Hell, no. I've had enough of that lifestyle. She's mine, my wife, my babe, not yours anymore."

"Well, I'm sure you're not making it any better," said Georgie.

"You right on that; I can't tell her no."

"Look here, Rick, I guess I never gave you a chance. I didn't know how much you really loved her."

"You think I married her for playtime? This is for real; this is for keeps, for a lifetime, for better and worse. Right now, we're at our worst, and Georgie, your fight is not on my agenda."

"So how long have you two been seeing each other." said Georgie.

"What does it matter? It's been for a long time, even when she was in other relationships; what difference does it make now?"

"So you were you in a relationship too?"

"Yes, I was," Rick replied, "and the problem is?"

"So you want me to believe you will never cheat on my daughter, while you were with someone else; if you cheated on them, then you damn sure will cheat on my daughter."

"Your daughter was with someone else too, so what did that make her? She wasn't no angel."

"She never said one word to nobody that she was still seeing you."

"Well, if she hadn't talked with you in a while, then you wouldn't know, but what concern was that to you? It's her life, not yours."

"I knew this day was coming," Georgie said. "I just didn't know when; I knew that you would ruin my daughter's life, and to this day, she still don't say too much to me because of you. Maybe I was wrong; I shouldn't force my control over her decision, but she's my daughter."

"Man, just because she's your daughter didn't give you the right to control her like she was an animal; you probably never asked her of her choice."

"You're right. I know that now. I was cutting her out of my life all long; she complied with my bullshit until she came of age and cut me out her life, a long time ago. That's why she didn't come up state for a long time, and when she did, the only person she saw was her grandfather. All because I made her get the ..."

"Please don't say that word again," Rick snapped. "I got it, Georgie, go on."

"I saw her future heading for hell; you were a good-looking young man, and you had a lot going for you, and if she would have had that baby, you would have cheated on her."

"What made you so sure of that? How you know she wouldn't have cheated on me?"

"Come on, man, you and I both know; you were you in school on the road to the NFL, with women throwing themselves at you. You would have eventually slept with one of them, 'cause that the shit some men do. One is never good enough."

"Well, Georgie, we'll never know, but I guess things happen for the best. But still, it wasn't your call; it was her decision."

"I didn't want her to be hurt. I was her protector."

"Georgie, there's a lot of people that'll be hurt behind the stuff you've done."

"Well, that's my secret family, and no one will find out, or it'll be ugly."

"Um, don't throw stones, man, when your shit is raggedy. Look, man, I could help you clean up your illegal documents; let me know, and I'll provide you legal advice, but if you want to keep being shady, then seek someone who plays that game; leave my name out of it. If you bring my name into any of your mess, then that means you are trying to pull me down. I won't let you destroy my family. I ain't having it."

"I got you," he said. "I'll get back with you if I decide to seek your business."

"All right, so now we talked, get out of my chambers and don't come back with no more of your bullshit and threats."

Damn, he thought after Georgie left, *I got some shit with me too, but got damn: He got extended families, bad business, and shit going on in the streets, along with the gambling and more. His whole family be affected by that shit.*

He walked over and closed his office door. He went back to his desk, sat down, and swirled around in his chair.

Just then, someone came through his door.

"Hi, babe." It was Tina.

"What the hell you doing in here?"

"I came to see you," she said. "I let myself in the door; it was open."

"Excuse me? Well, let yourself out and leave my office."

"Why? I'm in town for a hearing, so I was stopping by to see if your wife was okay and to see if there's anything I can do to help."

"Now why in the hell would I want you to do anything for her?"

"But there is something you can do for me."

She walked around his desk and stood seductively in front of him.

"Anything come to mind?"

"Leave," he snapped.

"Damn, is that how you feel?"

She unbuttoned her blouse, leaned into him, and rubbing her leg against his dick.

"You know you want to touch me, don't you? Go ahead; it's all right."

"Tina, get the hell off me," he said. "What you trying to pull? I'm married and love my wife."

"I'm not trying to pull nothing, but I do know a lot about you since you left me for her."

"I didn't leave you for her, I left you for me."

"Well, it sure is funny that by time you got here, you got married and had children in no time; was that your plan? 'Cause that's how it seems to me, Mr. Tyler."

He pushed her away from his desk.

"Okay, Tina, you stopped by, you saw me; yes, I'm happily married with children. Now get the hell out of my chambers, before I call security to have you removed, and that won't look good for you as a lawyer, being removed from a judge's chambers."

"Okay, but what shall I tell our son, that his daddy don't want to see him?"

"What son?"

"Our three-year old son."

"Really? Then show me some proof; you might have a kid but it ain't mine."

"I got to show you proof of our son, for real?"

"Yes."

"Now how's that going to look when you tell your wife about your son by your old fiancée?"

"First of all, you were never my fiancée or girlfriend or woman; you were just like I said before: a fuck partner. If you can provide me with some proof of a child, then we can go from there, but until then, bye."

"Don't you want to know his name?"

"No!"

"It's Ian."

"Okay, good, now get the hell out. Wait, before you leave, let me see a picture of this Ian."

"I don't have any pictures of him with me now, but I can mail them to you."

"What? Really? Come on, Tina, no pictures, not even on your phone? None? That's hard to believe. You come back to the East Coast, just so happen to have some business here, and you find me to ask me how my wife doing and to tell me I got a son with you, but you don't have one got damn picture? Girl, get the fuck out of here."

"Do you have pictures of your babies on your phone?" Tina asked.

"Yup, all on my phones, and you see them all on my desk."

"Yeah, I see you with your pretty little wife; what a great family picture. I'm leaving now, Judge Tyler, but I'm sure we'll meet again."

"That will be business only, Tina; business only."

This bastard thinks he got off this easy, she thought after leaving his office. Not! Now that I know where his ass is, I'm good. Let me get the hell out of here just in case that bastard calls security. I really don't have no business at this court; my business is with Judge Rick Tyler. I can't believe this bastard left me for her and gave her children; he played me. I told him I was going to be Mrs. Tyler; he thinks I'm playing with him. In the meantime, I need to find a picture of a three-year-old; I know who got one: Genette got some baby boy picture that he has never seen before."

She got down to the lobby and went over to the information booth.

"Hi, ma'am, could you please tell me where Judge Erick Tyler chambers is located? Is he on the third floor?"

"I'm sorry, ma'am. I can't give out that information."

"Okay, fine, whatever; then what time does he usually leave?"

"I think he leaves about six o'clock. I'm not really sure."

Tina rolled her eyes and walked off.

Ugly bitch, she thought. *Like it's going to kill her to say yes or no, but you can tell me what time he leaves. I tell you, got damn, you put a welfare-ass bitch behind a desk and on a phone, they'll tell you where Jesus is. I should report her dumb ass, but not just yet. I may need some real information from her again. I'll just hang around for a while.*

I wonder what he's driving these days, she thought as she went into the parking garage. *Is he still driving that Aston Martin? If he is, Imma key the shit out of it. Let's start on P2; he's likely to park there, on the back row. It's now about 3:45, so I got about two hours or so to scan for his shit.*

"Ma'am, can I help you?" a security guard asked. "You look like you lost your car."

"Yes, I am, but I think it's on this level."

"I saw you on the camera," he replied. "I said I better come out and help this pretty woman with those sexy high heels on. I know they got to be murder on your feet. I sure would like to rub them down later; what you think?"

"No, I'm okay. I'll find it, but thank you. I might just take you up on that offer."

"Okay, just wave if you can't find it. I'll come running, with your pretty self."

"I will, thank you."

I might just take him up on his offer, she thought, *if I have to come back tomorrow; my time is running out soon, but first things first.*

She left the garage, pissed off, swinging her hair in the wind; car horns were honking at her as her dress was flying up in the air with the wind, as she sashayed down the street. She yelling out as if she knew who she was talking to.

"If I had time, fellas, I would stop for a while, but I'm on a mission. I'll catch the next one later. I got some planning to do this evening. Aw, another garage; maybe it's in here."

She walked down the ramp to the second level and went straight to the back, scanning.

"Oh, my good pussy, did I luck up today or what? I know this his truck. Well, well. And it is the same one I saw him driving the other day, with three lil' car seats."

She forced the lock on the passenger side, slid in, and popped the glove compartment, looking for his registration.

"Bingo, this is it," she said. "Damn, and he even got pictures of them all over the damn place. Who carry that many pictures of their family, and he got baby toys in here too. My, my. Aw, isn't that cute; he got a gift in here for her. Oooh, sexy white baby doll set with matching thongs; he knows just what to buy. He never bought me nothing like this. Oh well, she won't need this; where she going it's not required, anyway. White horsey, where are you? I know you in my pocket somewhere; come to mama. Let's take a quick ride so I can do my business. You won't die, love; you'll just be a little fucked up, and then I got you. Finished just in time, but my damn car is parked here. Fuck it. I'll just walk around here for a while, then I'll come back and get it."

"This shit has got to be a bad dream," Rick said. First Georgie with his shit, then Tina and her bullshit; please, let me wake the hell up; what can possibly happen next?"

He approached his truck and noticed the passenger door open.

"What the fuck? Fuck it! I hope they found what they were looking for. I'm going home, then to the hospital. I'll fix this later; get the hell out of here."

As soon as he turned the key in the ignition, the hood of the truck exploded right before his eyes; the explosion was so strong, it cracked his window and locked up the electric system. The security guard jumped behind the wall, ducking and peeking around, looking. Rick was scrambling around, climbing over the babies' car seats, kicking the back window.

"What the fuck?"

The parking attended ran toward Rick, screaming, "Call 911; call 911."

"Motherfucka, you call 911; you see I'm trying to get out the damn truck. The shit is on fire."

While the truck was quickly going up in flames, the security guard finally called the fire department. Rick ran across the street, all shook up; he paced along the sidewalk, cursing and watching his truck go up in flames, and so was Tina, standing in the background, watching and smiling to herself.

"Who's truck is this?" said the policeman.

"It's my truck. I'm Judge Erick Tyler."

"Okay, Judge, then we need to talk."

"Man, about what? My damn truck on fire. I could have been killed, and you drill me with all these damn questions. I don't know why the damn truck blew up, and I don't have no answer for all your other questions. But you can have my information that is needed to take this report, so I can get a police report to get another vehicle; that's it, that's all I got."

"Judge Tyler, you're lucky," said a fireman. "It looks like a homemade bomb was planted under the hood, and from the looks of things, I would say this truck is done."

“What? This shit is getting crazier by the minute; who the fuck is doing all of this, and what the hell do they want? Damn. You got my attention; is all of this necessary?”

“So you do know who did this?” the policeman asked.

“Hell, no! I was just saying … Shit. You just finish the damn report, so I can get my shit towed.”

He took out his cellphone and called his brother.

“Got damn, Tony, call me right back,” he said. “You’re not going believe what just happened. I need a ride home.”

Then he called his cousin.

“Derickie, damn it! Call me back; you’ve been ducking me for the longest time. I need your black ass to call me; it’s urgent. My damn truck just blew up from a got damn home-made bomb; call me back.”

“Rick, I saw you called,” Tony said after calling him back. What’s up?”

“You at the courthouse today?” Rick asked.

“Yeah.”

“Can you come get me? I’m at the garage down the street.”

“Why? Where’s your truck?” Tony replied.

“Man, if you listened to my got damn message, then you would know where my truck is: up in flames!”

“Well, I didn’t hear the whole thing,” he replied. “I gather your ass is okay, since you talking shit.”

“Can you leave now and give me a ride home?”

“Man, I’m on my way,” Tony said. “I’m wrapping up anyway for now; I’ll be there in ten minutes.”

“Man, get the hell in the car,” Tony said after picking his brother up. “What the hell is going on?”

“Well, first thing this morning, Alicia tells me a car been sitting in front of the house all night. Then Georgie bring his ass down here with some bullshit, threatening me with his gun, and then Tina’s ass shows up with her bullshit, talking about we got a baby and I'm the father, and now this shit here."

"Damn," Tony said. "You got a kid with her?"

"I doubt it; if she was pregnant, I would've known about that long time ago. I hardly ever fucked her without a condom."

"Man, you need to step back, do some thinking; you got so much going on, you slipping. Normally, you be on top of things. I know Karla is most important to you, but right now, she's not going anywhere. Get this solved and get on point. Everybody is chipping in to help you out with the kids and Karla, but if you keep letting these people play this cat-and-mouse shit, you're going be laid up beside her, or dead."

"Tony, I'm almost sure it's Tina. I found a note at the house from her; I just need to catch her ass and prove it." Just then his phone rang. "Wait, wow, he finally calls. Well, got damn, Derickie, where you been, man? I've trying to reach you for the longest. You ducking me?"

"No, I been working on some shit for you under the got damn table; where are you?"

"I'm in the car with Tony; he dropping me off at home."

"Rick, tell Derickie meet us at Karla's house if he can," said Tony.

"I can't," Derickie said. "How about later on, around ten tonight?"

"That's cool. I'm going up to the hospital **for** a couple hours. I'll call you on my way back."

He went into the house to tell Niki and the others he was heading up to the hospital.

"Wait, what about us?" Kareem asked.

"I know you want to go," Rick said, "but I need to leave now; we all can go tomorrow. Y'all need to stay put for today; it's some strange stuff that's happening. Just stay put for now, son, okay? I don't want anything to happen to nobody else."

"All right," Kareem replied, "since you looking all crazy and sounding all disturbed. I'll lay low today, but tomorrow, I'm going, with or without you."

"Come on," Niki said, "you can't control them like this; they want to see their mother. Kareem is having a hard time with this; it's killing him inside. At least take him."

"I know, but right now, I can't take that chance. I don't know if they are waiting to get us all; at least let me keep moving. Let me be the target for now. Where's my babies?"

"Sandy came around earlier and took them off Alicia's hands for tonight," said Niki.

"No, they are to stay here," he said. "I appreciate that, but hell no. Where is she?"

"I think she went back around Ma and Pops' house," Niki replied.

He flew out the door, jumped in the other truck, and hauled ass around to his parents' house. Tina was there.

"Sandy!" he called when he got there.

"Oh, she's gone," Tina said.

"Why are you still here?" he snapped. "I'm not talking to you; I am talking to my sister. Renee, where's Sandy?

"She just left."

"How long ago?"

"I don't know, maybe thirty minutes or so, why?"

"Oh, Rick," Tina said, "how's your wife? Is there anything I can do?"

"Yes, Tina, there is something you can do: get the fuck out my face and leave, like I said earlier. It ain't shit you can do for me or my family; you've done enough."

"I didn't do anything," she replied. "I'm really concerned."

"Tina, I don't want you to do nothing for me, nor do I appreciate your help or concern. Stay the fuck away from me."

Now why the hell she in there with Renee and nobody else is here? he thought as he drove off. *I'll deal with Renee ass later. I got to catch Sandy, to get my kids.*

He called his sister. "Sandy, where are you?"

"Why?" she asked. "I'm on North Capital Street. What's wrong?"

"I don't want you to take my kids. I appreciate you giving Alicia a break for a while, but I need them home tonight. I'll bring them back to Ma's house in the morning; stop where you are."

"Okay, but it's getting late," she said. "You can't keep taking them in and out from place to place. They are just little babies."

"Yeah I know, but they my babies, and I need them close to me tonight. I'm heading toward North Capital now, so don't move."

"All right, hurry up; you know I don't like pulling over like this."

"All right; you by yourself?"

"No, Tilley with me."

"Okay, you safe, then; I'm en route. Hold on."

Now why in the hell of all nights, people driving like turtles? he thought as he got stuck in traffic. *In any other time, I can be down this stretch in no time flat. Oh well, damn, was that my life that flashed or the flash from a ticket camera? That's just how crazy it's going at this point.*

He found his sister's car and walked over to knock on the window.

"Damn, did you have to knock that hard?" she asked.

"Sorry, you shouldn't be sitting on the dark side of the street with your lights off; are you crazy? Tilley must be sleepy; he didn't even notice. Man, be alert; what's wrong with you?"

"Sorry, man, long day."

"Um, tell me about it; love you guys, and thank you again for stopping. I got them; we out.

"Back home, Rick Tyler babies; no sleepovers tonight."

"Hey Tony, I'm home. Never made it to the hospital; come around if you want."

Before he could hang up and sit down, Tony was walking through the door.

"All right," Tony said. "I've been thinking about this; have you made any plans of how to handle your wife's situation?"

"What kind of plans, Tony? You and Niki keep saying the same thing. I don't want to talk about that now."

"Look here, man, don't take this the wrong way. I want to see

Karla recover too and come home, but what if she doesn't make it? She may need a lot of physical help; you don't know if she'll be able to walk on her own or how her memory is. This is going to be a long road to recovery; you need to get a plan, like now. Start looking around for some recovery institutes that can help her. Stop acting like she's going to jump up and go home; let's be realistic about this. It's not going to happen that way."

"I don't want to think about that, but I know I have to. I know I won't be able to help her now."

"It's not that you can't help her," Tony said. "What she may need, you may not able to help her on that. Think about this real soon, bro."

Just then, Derickie drove up.

"Damn, look who's here," Tony joked. "This a shocker; what happened? World's record for you: on time. Oh, no; let me change that: early. This needs to be recorded in a book somewhere: Derrick Tyler was early."

"Niki, was that car still there after I left this morning?" Rick asked.

"Yeah, stringy-haired white boy, looked kind of thin from what I can tell; he just sat there smoking cigarettes one after another. He just left not long ago. I got the tag number."

"What car?" Derickie asked.

"It was a burgundy Ford Taurus with Florida tags; he watched the house all night and all today; shit, I walked up on him earlier, he must've been sleep. I should've snatched his ass out the car."

"All right, let's check this white boy out. I'm going to run these tags in right quick to one of my ladies on duty."

Derickie got on his phone and spoke for several minutes.

"All right, that's what I'm talking about: quick turnaround. It's definitely a rental; a Janice Lee rented the car from Dulles Airport. Rick, they checking for prints on what's left of your truck."

"Hey let me ask you this: Do you have a picture of Tina?"

"Hell, no; for what?"

"One of the officers I know said a parking lot attendant said he saw a lady poking around in the garage, and I need to show it to him;

maybe he can tell us what car she came in. So since you don't, you might have meet up with her and get a picture, and then we can move from there."

"Hold the hell up," Tony said. "Oh shit; you think Renee may have told her something? 'Cause they mighty close all of sudden; she might have a picture of her."

"You know what, Tony? She just may have, since she was at the house with her this evening and nobody else was home; she still mad at me from the wedding and cutting her completely off," Rick said.

"If Renee was talking to Tina, I bet you she knows where she's staying too; call her," Tony said.

Rick called his sister.

"Hey, Renee," he said when she picked up.

"What?" she snapped. "What the hell you calling me for, 'cause I'm not watching your got damn kids."

"I know you not, and I don't want you to watch my got damn kids, either."

"Put her on the speaker," said Tony.

"Where the hell is Tina staying?" Rick asked. Since y'all was at the house talking so buddy-buddy, I know you know."

"Why you want to know? You got a wife; oh, what, now you want Tina, since your wife is dying?"

"If I was near you," he replied, "I would kick your motherfuckin' ass, and I don't give a damn about you being my sister. Now tell me where she staying."

"I'm not telling you nothing," she said. "You figure it out yourself; call her."

"Renee, look here, girl, Niki said. "Give up the got damn information now, or I'm coming over and choke your damn neck."

"Niki, you shut up, you don't scare me, and you don't tell me what to do."

The Jamaican accent he suppressed for a long time came from the bottom of his stomach; he was pissed.

"Renee, if you don't give us that got damn information, girl, you will be sorrier than what you already are."

She hung up, but Niki called her right back.

"Renee, you ain't finish, girl," he said. "Don't fuckin' play with me. I'll come over there and kick that door in that I paid for, and you know I will, so give it up or have a place with no door."

She told him where Tina was staying and gave him her new cell number and then hung up again.

"All right, since Niki threatened my cousin, you got to go tonight," Derickie said. "Let's go get the picture, or an ID, something."

"Tonight?" Rick repeated. "Man, I'm tired; shit."

"Tired my ass; you going tonight. I'm putting my job on the got damn line for your black ass. This ain't even my area for real. I'm helping your ass, so let's go, nigga. I'll take you myself and wait; that way you can't stay around for nothing, and you know what I mean by nothing. Let's hit it, Mr. Tyler."

"All right, I don't want nothing from her, and I ain't calling her; how about I just show up at the hotel?"

"I don't give a damn how you do it," Derickie replied. "Let's just go; my damn adrenaline is pumping hard."

They hit 395 South, flying across the bridge to Virginia out to the Embassy Suite hotel in Crystal City. Derickie parked the car on the corner across the street from the hotel, with the car still running.

"Hurry, man, just get a picture and let's go; don't be in there looking at her ass."

"Naw, that ain't happening; that shit is over. Fuck her ass and everything on her; that shit don't excite me no more."

He walked straight to the elevators and went up to her room on the fifth floor; he knocked on the door, playing it cool.

"Hey, babe," she said when she opened the door. "I thought you would never come."

This bitch is really crazy, he thought when he saw her wearing the lingerie he had bought for Karla. *How else would she have gotten that?*

"I came here to see this picture of Ian," he said. "I want more information on him, like when was he born? Let me see a birth certificate too, anything you got that say he's my son."

"Oh, so what, you don't believe me?"

"Uh, hell, no, I don't fuckin' believe you."

"Sit down and stay awhile; I'll get the picture and birth certificate."

"Nope, I need to get home."

"So what the hell did you come over here for, if you had to get home?" Tina snapped. "Why aren't you there? Instead, you're here in my face."

"Tina, the only reason I'm here is because I want to know more about this baby; if he's my son, then I want him."

"You ain't getting him unless you pay me and pay me damn good. Remember, I was supposed to be your wife. But since I'm not, then I guess I have to keep you along for the ride forever. So now that you're here, I know you want to make love to me. I know you; I know how you like it. So I'm going to the bathroom; you want to come with me? I know how much you like it in the shower. I know you want this; I know you miss it, considering the circumstance of your wife. I know you need some pussy now.

Do I kick this chick now or throw her out that got damn window? he thought as she closed the bathroom door. *Um, stay calm, Rick; don't explode.* "Naw you go ahead. I'll be in here waiting for you."

"Come on, babe; let's play awhile in the water. Come on."

"Naw, I'm good." As he spoke, he was going through her pocketbook.

"Jackpot," he whispered. "Okay, she got a LA driver license, and her Social Security card; these two will do. Fuck her, I came for what I want."

He threw the wallet back in her purse and walked out the door.

"Derickie, let's get the fuck out of here," he said when he got back. "This bitch is the one that put that homemade bomb in my truck."

"How you know?"

"She got on the got damn lingerie set I bought for Karla."

"What?"

"Yeah. Man, get this shit and run it as soon as possible. See if you that parking lot attendant recognizes her from this ID. It took all I had from slapping and beating the shit out of her. I should've went in that damn bathroom and choked her ass."

"Good thing you didn't," Derickie said. "We already crossed the line. I'm way out of my jurisdiction, and you're a fucking judge; stealing information, now what kind of shit is that? How in the hell could we explain that to these Virginia commonwealth cops?"

"You know what, Derickie? At this point, I don't give a damn; fuck it. I'll step down if I have to, but that's my wife, and that's my family. As long as I'm still alive, ain't nobody fuckin' with them. She should have come directly for me, not her or them."

"I truly understand," Derickie said. "Fuck it. I would do the same. I got your back, cousin. I'll run these past the night shift and have them run this driver license, see what we come up with. In the meantime, cousin, get you some rest. Karla is going to pull through, I'm sure of that. Hell damn sure don't want her; the devil got enough shit going on down there, and heaven don't like her mouth, so trust me, cousin: She'll be back to you. She ain't finish with you yet. But just know: When she gets well, your ass is grass."

"Yeah, that crazy-ass woman caused me so much pain and damn drama," Rick said. "See what fuckin' lust gets you? Love and hate will bring you to your knees, to the one you love and the one you hate."

Thank you all for reading my first book. I hope you enjoyed it. Stay tuned to find out what happens in my next book, *Unconditional Love*. Go to my website and email me your conversation; let's chat: www.lyricnolan.com, or reach out to me on Facebook at Lyric Nolan, the authoress.

Peace and much love

Printed in the United States
By Bookmasters